BLOOD MOON

–BOOK ONE–

A.D. RYAN

Blood Moon

Ryan, A.D.
Blood Moon / A.D. Ryan

(Blood Moon Trilogy ; 01)

ISBN 978-1496045720

Text and Cover design by Angela Schmuhl
Cover Image: Shutterstock, © Serov

Dedicated to all who believed.

CONTENTS

ACKΠOWLEDGΠΕΠTS

Here is where I try to thank those who offered me nothing but their full support throughout this entire journey.

First, and foremost, I'd like to thank my incredible husband for bearing with me through all of this. You've never once complained about what started as a hobby, and as I decided to publish, you've continued to cheer me on. You're my rock, and I couldn't have asked for a more incredible man to share my life with. I love you with all my heart.

My children, who've always made reading fun, I want this to encourage you and be proof that you can achieve your dreams, no matter how unattainable they may seem at times. Aim higher and reach for those stars.

To my mom for always encouraging me in anything I've ever done throughout my life. You've been such a source of inspiration—the pinnacle of strength that every young woman needs in her life. The sacrifices you've made have not gone unnoticed, nor has your unyielding faith in your children.

Having shown me that losing yourself in a well-written book can be one of the best things a person can do, I thank my dad. With a book almost always in his hand, his love of reading became my own favorite pastime.

Tiffany and Lynda, two of the most helpful and supportive women I've had the pleasure of meeting—even if not yet face-to-face. I don't know if I'd ever be able to truly convey through words just how incredibly grateful I am to have you both accompany me on this journey. Believe me when I tell you just how much I appreciate all of your help over the years and how much I appreciate your willingness to point out each and every one of my grammatical flaws. Your constant critique has only strengthened my writing, and for that I will be eternally grateful. From the bottom of my heart, I thank you.

Always willing to read my new story ideas, my baby sister has always been my biggest fan, always chomping at the bit for more—even when it isn't quite ready to be read. The support she has offered me has been above and beyond, always pushing me to go bigger and better than before, and always taking that extra minute in her day to talk me down off the ledge of plot-twist suicide.

My little-big brother, who's played his role in all of this, also deserves a shout-out. Without my family behind me through this process, none of this would have been possible.

And, finally, to my beta readers and the fans of my earlier work. Jennifer, whose first read-through offered me so much constructive critique with which to work off and improve the flow of the story. You helped me strengthen and fine-tune these characters before I offered them up to the rest of the world, and I thank you for it. Felicia, Nicole, Sandy, Tracy, and Becky, your love of this world I created has pushed me to complete the second in the series far sooner than I'd originally intended. The excitement you all had is what pushed me to put this out there even more than my own desires, and for that I thank you.

You all made this happen. I won't ever forget that.

Cheers,

Angela

Blood Moon

PROLOGUE | ORIGIN

A young man, newly twenty-one, sat in a crowded bar. His eyes searched the room as he drank from his bottle of beer when, suddenly, he felt a pair of piercing eyes on him. As he looked directly to his right, he spotted the most beautiful woman he had ever seen. He couldn't take his eyes off of her, afraid that if he did he might lose her in the crowd.

Somewhere in his periphery, his sister was off dancing with her boyfriend, and while his father had given him express orders to keep a close eye on her, he knew she was in good hands. He knew she would be safe from the evil that had been plaguing their city for weeks.

The entire city was on high alert due to the rising numbers of grisly murders, and while the police were doing everything they could, they had yet to break the case. The lack of evidence made finding a suspect difficult, but they refused to give up. With the promise to find the person responsible, the city worried a little less, and life went on as usual.

The man locked eyes with the stunning blonde creature, and he found himself most taken by her. Captivated, even. He admired the way the short black dress hugged her glorious curves, and how the strapless neckline showed off her well-sculpted shoulders. As he openly gawked, he thought about how he had never seen such a beauty before... Except, he *had* seen her before. At that frat party he was just telling his sister about.

The mysterious blonde exuded confidence with every step she took toward him, her ice blue eyes staring into his and a coy smile slowly spreading across her face. He watched, entranced, as she licked her ruby-red lips and made her way through the crowd toward him. Her long blonde hair swayed behind her as she walked forward with purpose, and he imagined wrapping it around his hand to pull her head back for a kiss. Suddenly nervous, he swallowed thickly as she approached. He recalled feeling this way when he first met her, too.

"So, we meet again." Her melodic voice floated on the air between them, and her cool breath washed over his skin, tempting him to act on his fantasy from only a moment ago. "Where did your friends go?" she asked, looking around, causing her luxurious blonde hair to sway in the breeze of her movement.

It didn't escape his notice that the way she held herself was almost regal, her posture perfect, and he could only assume she was a dancer by trade given her natural grace.

"Oh, they went to go dance," he informed her, glancing back toward his sister and waving when the smaller red-haired girl looked his way at the same time. With curious eyes, she regarded her brother's unknown companion before turning her attention back to her boyfriend.

Smiling, the blonde woman arched an eyebrow. "And you don't dance?" she queried.

The man laughed, knowing just how uncoordinated he was. "I try to refrain from anything that could make me look foolish in front of members of the opposite sex," he told her honestly.

His eyes wandered over her porcelain features, and he watched her lick her lips again. It surprised him just how taken he was by her. She was a stranger to him, yet he felt so comfortable in her presence, like there might be something more between them. Was it preposterous to think this way about a woman he just met? In most cases, yes, but something about her just felt right, and he needed to know more about her.

"So, what made you decide to come out tonight?" the stranger inquired. "When I invited you and your friend over there" — she gave a nod toward the dance floor — "you said you weren't so sure."

He found his voice and shrugged as he answered, "It's my birthday."

"Really?" she purred, the vibration travelling beneath his skin and settling in his groin. "Well isn't that just...lovely." She gave him a small smile as her fingers played with the large tear-shaped pendant that hung near the swell of her breasts. The color of it reminded him of blood.

Realizing where his eyes were focused, he quickly snapped his attention back to her exquisite eyes and not how she delicately fidgeted with her necklace or how her fingers skimmed her skin, causing her flesh to pebble in their wake. Embarrassed, he swallowed thickly, causing her to laugh softly, like she found his ogling endearing. "Can I buy you a drink?"

The smile that graced her lovely face was wide and showcased a set of perfect white teeth. "Well, I am quite thirsty." She leaned in to whisper in his ear, her breath tickling his neck and sending a chill down his spine. "But I was thinking we could maybe get out of here. Go somewhere a little more private."

He was shocked — there was absolutely no doubt

about it. Normally, he wasn't the kind to be so impulsive, but when he looked into her dazzling blue eyes, he was no longer in control of his own body. Without a moment's pause, he took her outstretched hand and let her lead him from the club.

Outside, the temperature had gone from dry and arid to crisp and cool. She pulled him down the alley beside the club and pressed his body against the brick wall. Barely any light from the street lamps along the sidewalk reached them, but he had enough to see the excitement on her face. Her hands traveled wildly over his chest, and the speed of her breathing seemed to increase with her zeal.

Something about her made his inhibitions disappear completely, and soon his hands came up and gripped her biceps firmly. His earlier desire came rushing back, and he wrapped her hair around his hand and tilted her head back, bringing his face down to kiss her neck. Her skin tasted like vanilla and sex as he moved down over her collarbone and toward her ample breasts. It intoxicated him, making his entire body hum with anticipation.

Feeling energized and unlike himself, he turned and pressed her body against the hard brick wall, ready to hitch her leg around his hip and grind himself against her, but the woman wasn't impressed by the loss of dominance. In an effort to reassert her control, she fisted his hair in one of her hands and lifted his head away from her, rolling them along the wall until he was, once again, pinned.

Nervous, his eyes danced between hers. "I've never done this before," he said before realizing how inexperienced this confession made him sound. He gave his head a quick shake as if to clear the fog that confused him and tried again. "I mean, I've done *that* before. I've just never been so…impulsive before."

The woman continued to smile at him. "Well, I promise to take it easy on you, then." She leaned her head in slowly and pressed her lips to the hollow of his throat, her tongue darting out and tasting him. He expected the heat of her mouth against his flesh, but was instead met with the chill of what he could only assume was the biting wind of the approaching season change.

As she licked and kissed his throat, he groaned softly, trying desperately to pull her body into his. "I don't even know your name," he panted, clutching her hips tightly, his growing arousal firm against her belly.

He could feel her lips curl up against his throat before she lifted her gaze back to his. "Gianna," she replied, a dangerous edge to her voice that didn't register right away.

The softness of her lips returning to his neck made his eyes roll back, and he reveled in the current that shot up and down his arms, making his fingers and toes curl. Then there was a sharp, piercing pain in his neck. It only lasted a second before adrenaline surged through him, causing mass amounts of pleasure to overwhelm him. His head felt light, like he was high, and then his knees gave out beneath him without warning, and everything went black.

CHAPTER 1 | CELEBRATE

October twenty-sixth.

It was a day I'd rather not remember, but, just the same, it came and went every single year. This year would be no different than the previous seven, because I would be forced to endure it, all while holding my head high and pretending as though everything was all right. The worst part of it all was the expectation for me to celebrate it. Every. Damn. Year.

I guess my biggest problem was that everything was far from all right—it hadn't been "all right" for quite some time, actually—and the last thing I wanted to do was celebrate anything. What I wanted to do was stay hidden from the world and remain under my blankets until the clock beside me, flashing its bright red numbers, struck midnight and signaled the end of this day for another year.

As the early morning sunshine started to stream into the room from the window above my bed, lighting everything with its shiny, happy glow, I pulled the blanket up over my head in an effort to stay in the dark for just a little bit longer. I didn't want to see the colorful artwork that adorned my walls, the dark ebony dresser and vanity that sat along the far wall, or the deep purple bench that was at the foot of my bed. It was all too bright and cheery, and I just wasn't interested in feeling anything but glum.

Escaping from the world was a futile attempt, though, as the phone rang, the shrill sound echoing through my house. "Ugh! Leave me alone!" I shouted, my voice muffled slightly by the blanket that still covered my face.

When the phone went silent, I momentarily assumed that the caller might have actually sensed my ire at their early morning disruption. It wasn't until I heard a soft and familiar voice in my kitchen that I knew the true reason the noise had ceased.

"Hello?" my mother's voice said into the phone, or at least that was what I assumed. It was possible that she was calling out for me as well. There was really only one way to be certain, and I wasn't sure if I was ready to meet the day head-on just yet. Unfortunately, I knew I didn't have very long before they both came looking for me. Being that this was his baby girl's "big day," it was safe to assume that my dad was with her as well.

Of course they're here, I thought to myself as I threw my blanket to the end of my bed. Turning onto my left side, I used my arms to sit up, giving myself a moment before I placed my bare feet on the cold hardwood floor of my bedroom.

"Brooke, honey?" my father's smooth, deep voice called out through my small house, echoing off the walls of my narrow hallway.

Staring at my manicured toes, I sighed deeply before responding. "I'm just getting up. I'll be right out." The pads of my feet met the chilled floorboards as I stood and stretched my body tall—well, as tall as someone who was five foot five could stretch.

I struggled to find the will to begin my day even more now that I was actually out of bed. Especially since my rising truly meant that I would have to face the fact that it really was my birthday. Most people welcomed their birthdays, but, to me, it was the worst possible day of every year, and not something I wished to remember, let alone celebrate.

As I made my way for the bedroom door, I could already hear the banging of pots and pans in my kitchen, thus signaling that Mom was preparing my breakfast. Breakfast with my parents wasn't always a birthday tradition. Only in the last couple of years had they started coming over first thing in the morning so we could eat a large breakfast together. To "keep my strength up," as my father would say.

I laughed darkly to myself. How I wished that bacon and eggs could give me the strength I truly needed to deal with today…

Not ready to face my parents, I walked the short distance from my room to the washroom. "I'm just going to have a quick shower," I announced monotonously as I walked in and closed the door behind me.

Leaning into the shower stall, I turned on the water before flipping the switch for the showerhead. Once satisfied with the water temperature, I stood upright and pulled the glass door closed before moving to the porcelain sink to brush my teeth. The room started to fill with a blanket of fog, which seemed only fitting given my somber mood.

My soft facial features seemed a little worse for wear, the bags under my deep green eyes the visual reminder of the late night celebration with my co-workers the night before. The pounding in my head, the physical. I pulled the elastic band out of my long red hair and allowed it to cascade loosely down my back as I ran my brush through it a few times to get rid of any knots that had accumulated from tossing and turning in my sleep. Again.

After removing my T-shirt and shorts, I tossed them into the hamper next to the door and stepped beneath the near-scalding spray of water. I pushed my face beneath the water in an attempt to wash away the final remnants of sleep and the nightmare that plagued me year after year.

Flashes of the sky that night, the stars dull behind the blanket of smog that hovered over the city, and the red-hued moon filled my head. Even though it had been seven years, I could still remember every smell and sound that surrounded us while we waited to be let inside that exclusive nightclub.

When my lungs started to burn from a lack of oxygen, I opened my mouth to allow myself to breathe while I continued to push the memories aside. Water trickled in, so I expelled it and clenched my eyes shut. Sadly, the memory of that night continued to assault me more forcefully, and my heart raced with panic as I relived it all again.

Losing sight of him. Finding a way outside through a side exit when I was unable to get through the sea of people at the front doors. Searching frantically, only to find…

I fought the urge to wretch, coughing and sputtering on the water I inhaled accidentally. I took several deep breaths, letting the water course down my entire body, the heat permeating every cell and cleansing me inside and out as I leaned forward. Letting it soothe me, I rested my head against the light brown ceramic tile wall. I remained like this for a minute, allowing the hot water and the cool tile to send conflicting sensations through me.

I was pulled out of my misery when my mom knocked on the door and told me breakfast was ready. With a sigh, I stood up and washed my hair and every last inch of my skin—twice—still not wanting the solidarity of my shower to end.

When the water finally started to run cold, I shut

it off with a pout and grabbed my towel off the silver rack beside the shower stall. I draped the fluffy pink fabric around my body, fastening it around my chest, and squeezed the excess water out of my hair before stepping out to finish my morning routine.

I quickly ran my brush through my hair once more and then opened the bathroom door. The frigid air attacked any and all of my exposed, damp flesh, causing goosebumps to prickle over my arms and legs. The smell of coffee was heavy in the air as I padded back to my bedroom to get dressed for the day ahead of me.

I rifled through my top dresser drawer before letting my towel fall to the floor around my ankles so I could pull my underwear on, and then I made my way to the closet. I caught a brief glimpse of my slender reflection in the mirror before grabbing a pair of dark denim jeans and a purple long-sleeved shirt. While I wasn't particularly vain, I did take pride in my looks, and I worked hard to stay in shape, both for work and for myself.

As I pulled my clothes on, I felt more and more like a wolf in sheep's clothing, once again going out to fake my way through the day in hopes of fooling everyone around me. In spite of that feeling, though, there was one person I could be myself around today, and I looked forward to my visit with him. It was the highlight of my birthday every year.

As soon as I was ready, I walked toward my bedroom door and reached for the knob. My hand gripped the cold metal firmly and waited at the ready to turn it. Clenching my eyes shut, I placed my forehead against the solid wood door as I took one final cleansing breath. Pulling a smile from the very depths of my soul, I stood up straight, swung the door open, and walked out to face the day.

The lively walk I sported was one I had worked hard at perfecting over the last seven years. Was I proud of my deceit? Not particularly, but it beat the constant stares of worry I received from my parents, my peers, and even strangers on the street who knew nothing about me and my...situation.

I walked into my cozy little kitchen, a smile on my face, to find my parents laughing softly at something I missed. They were both seated around the small table in my modest dining nook that connected my kitchen and living room. The sunlight filtered in through the smaller bay window next to the table, warming the natural color of the wood. Smelling too delicious to ignore any longer, I filled the cup that'd been left out on the counter for me with coffee. Steam spiraled from the surface of the black liquid as I added a splash of cream and several heaping teaspoons of sugar before settling at the table between my parents.

"There's our birthday girl," my mom cheered, leaning over to kiss my cheek as I brought my cup to my lips and took a tiny sip.

"Mmmm," I hummed with a nod as the hot beverage coated the inside of my mouth and slid smoothly down my throat. "Thanks for the coffee. It's just what I needed."

It wasn't an accident or an oversight that I didn't acknowledge her comment, and it was evident by her jubilant expression that she never expected me to either. She understood how hard the day was for me...for all of us.

Sitting at the light-colored table, sipping at my morning coffee and trying to keep the wall I've worked hard to build from faltering, I looked between my parents as they easily fell back into their conversation. They knew me well enough not to pressure me into opening up before I was ready. That only brought more pain for everyone when I was like this. They knew to give me time.

Catching part of my mom's story about her lunch with her friends yesterday, I smiled—even laughed a little—but didn't say anything. She noticed my response, though, and reached out to grasp my forearm lightly in reassurance. She knew. There weren't a lot of people who didn't. I held her gaze, hoping to draw in some of the strength I so desperately craved.

Laura Leighton was a stunning, well-put-together woman of fifty, and considering what she had been forced to deal with in her life, it didn't seem to tear at her the way it did me. Which was a relief, because I hated feeling the way I did. It was too much most days, and I would hate to see anyone else have to go through it as well.

As my mother leaned back in her chair, her soft blue eyes never left me, and my forced smile slowly morphed into one that was genuine as I watched her turn to tell my father more of her story.

A momentary feeling of contentment flooded me, bringing me out of my misery long enough to be grateful for this one shining moment.

The sun's rays peeked in through the blinds above my kitchen table, bouncing off of her immaculately styled blonde hair, and when she laughed, I saw the subtlest hint of the laugh lines around her sparkling eyes.

I was constantly told that I looked like her, but with my coppery-red hair and bright green eyes, it was hard to see the similarities. We were the same height and build, though. That much I could see, but where I was usually confident and outgoing, Mom was a little more soft-spoken and easy-going.

This didn't mean she was a pushover, though. Far from it. She'd let you know if you had gone too far. Believe me.

But the fact remained that she was a gentle soul.

My father's boisterous laugh caused my attention to shift to him as I took another pull of the coffee from my mug.

Normally, when somebody met Captain Keith Leighton for the first time, they considered him a particularly intimidating man. At fifty-six years old and standing six feet tall, he'd been with the Scottsdale Police Department for the past thirty-six years — Captain for the last sixteen.

His green eyes were the mirror image of my own — in color anyway. I was aware of just how jaded I had become in the last seven years, and how it showed in my eyes the most. My dad, though? He had two different looks, and I knew both of them equally well.

As we sat together around my little four-person table, drinking our coffee, his eyes exuded nothing short of pure happiness. However, when we were on the job, his eyes grew hard and determined. He never let anyone in. Not anymore.

His dark brown hair was always kept short, and flecks of silver streaked through it from his years of late nights, both working and child-rearing. Yes, Captain Keith Leighton was an intimidating man, and not a man you messed with. But to me, he was nothing more than a big teddy bear — my daddy.

As they continued to banter on about my mom's latest interior design disaster, I realized that I was quite content to sit there and listen to the two of them talk for the better part of my day. It would be a welcome change to what I knew was coming tonight. My eyes suddenly drifted to the empty chair across from me, and my stomach rolled uneasily.

My mother must have seen something deeper in

my expression, because her eyes showed her concern. "Brooke, are you feeling okay?" she asked.

Running my fingers through my long, wet hair, I smiled slightly. "Uh, yeah. I didn't sleep very well last night. The guys at work wanted to take me out to properly celebrate my promotion to detective," I partially lied, not wanting her to know that I'd been plagued with the same nightmare that had been haunting me annually.

My father shook his head disapprovingly. "Samuels, of all people, should know to take better care of his partner."

With a sly smirk, I cocked an eyebrow in my dad's direction. "It wasn't just him. You have the entire department to blame."

I watched as my father's warm smile reached across the planes of his face, his sparkling eyes meeting mine. "What are you up to this afternoon, kiddo?" he asked.

"Well, I've got the party at your place tonight," I said, trying to sound genuinely excited about it. It fell flat, though. "But this afternoon, I was thinking I would go and visit Bobby for a bit." My posture suddenly slumped as my mood shifted right back into my previous state of depression.

My mother's hand reached back across the table and found its way onto mine. "That sounds lovely, dear. Maybe we'll join you." She turned to look at my father. "Wouldn't that be nice, Keith?"

I bit the inside of my cheek and squinted my eyes. Hurting their feelings wasn't something I intentionally set out to do, but this was something I did alone every year. "Look, I don't want to sound unappreciative or anything, but this is sort of something that Bobby and I do alone."

Sad, my mother pulled her hand back slowly, the

smile fading from her face at my sudden refusal of her idea. "It's not that you shouldn't go see him. You should. It's just...well, we've always spent the morning together. Just the two of us, you know?"

"No, it's fine. Of course I understand, Brooke. We'll stop by later then, okay?" Trying to hide her face as she stood up, I caught the slightest glimpse of her glistening eyes. Guilt consumed me, and I looked toward my father for some kind of answer as to what I should do.

He placed his hand on my cheek and smiled softly. "It's fine," he whispered so low my mother wouldn't hear him. "Well, we should get going. Make sure you're at the house by seven. Wouldn't want to miss your own surprise party, now would you?" He flashed his bright smile and winked at me as he stood.

"Definitely not," I replied, rolling my eyes. I stood from the table, my half-empty coffee cup still in my hand, and walked with my parents through the kitchen and to the front door, where I gripped my mom in a tight, one-armed hug. "I'm sorry," I whispered.

When she pulled out of the embrace, she was smiling again. Though it seemed a little more distant and sad. "No, sweetie, it's all right. You should have your morning. Happy birthday." She kissed my cheek and walked through my door, followed shortly by my dad.

Once they were gone, I tidied up my kitchen before grabbing the keys to my white Mustang and heading for the door. As was part of the tradition, I stopped at the flower shop before I hit the highway. It seemed odd that a woman would be buying flowers for a man in most cases. However, my case was *not* most cases.

The drive down E Roosevelt was quiet. I was alone with my thoughts, and I felt bad that it had been so long since I'd gone out to see Bobby. I used to make this trip more often, but with my promotion, it was difficult. I crossed the bridge and turned south on N Hayden Road until I saw the parking lot. As I pulled the car to a stop, I admired the flowers that spread far across the wide-open area. The over-whelming variety of different species in a rainbow of color against the grass that covered the ground was beautiful.

It was warmer today than it had been, the rainy season over now that we were moving into fall, but I could feel that slight nip to the air, despite the sun being out and free of the clouds. The grass was start-ing to lose a little of its green luster, the drier weeks having taken their toll on the vegetation, but this was home. I couldn't imagine living anywhere else. I loved the desert.

My nerves grew, and my palms began to sweat as I made my way down the familiar paths, taking a series of rights and lefts that had become second na-ture to me. As I walked, I inhaled deeply, appreciat-ing the trees, both the ones that were native to Arizo-na and the ones that weren't. When I found our spot, I slipped off my low-heeled shoes to feel the plush green grass beneath my bare feet and sat down.

With a smile brighter than any other one I'd sported all day, I sat in my usual spot and leaned against the cold stone. The bouquet of wildflowers I had picked up on my way here sat at my side, and the warm sun was beating down on me, keeping me warm. "Happy birthday, big brother," I whispered into the soft breeze as it blew a tendril of hair across my face. "We're twenty-eight today. I suppose that's something to celebrate." I turned my head to the gray headstone I was leaning against and sighed. "Unfortunately, I can't seem to get into the spirit, considering the one person I want to celebrate it with most isn't here."

Turning my body to face the solid stone completely, I stared at the beautiful script that held his name.

Robert Alexander Leighton
Beloved Son & Brother
October 26, 1986 – October 26, 2007

The irony of the dates engraved below his name taunted me. The day of his birth—of our birth—was also the day of his death.

Pulling my knees to my chest, I wrapped my arms around my legs and rested my chin on my knees. "Mom and Dad said they were going to stop by before the party. They actually offered to come with me this morning, but I needed it to be about us, you know?" I laughed softly, reaching down and uprooting a blade of grass from beside my foot. "Mom didn't understand at first, of course. Not until I explained that it was something you and I have been doing for as long as I can remember."

It never even occurred to me that I'd begun crying until I felt a warm tear trail its way down my cheek. "I miss you, Bobby. More than anyone can even imagine. Not a day goes by that I don't feel your absence in everything I do." With a sniffle, I wiped my tears on my denim-clad knee. "I made detective yesterday, and the first person I thought to call was you. I knew you'd have been so happy for me."

My wall of strength crumbled, and I began to cry into my knees. The muscles in my back strained against the sobs that wracked my entire body. Eventually, it seemed like too much work to try to hold back my cries of anguish, so I wrapped my arms tighter around my body in an effort to quell the pain that was ripping a giant hole through my heart. It didn't matter how much time had passed; it never got any easier.

"I'm sorry," I sobbed through labored breaths. "I'm trying to be strong…to move on, but it's just…" I sniffled. "It's still so hard."

Moving onto my knees, I pulled my fingers through my hair, my eyes focused on the grass beneath me. "Especially today, when everyone expects me to want to celebrate. It's all I can do to *not* think about how you should be by my side during it all."

A warm breeze picked up and wrapped itself around me, almost as though Bobby was here with me. I closed my eyes and allowed the feeling to overtake me, a few fallen leaves swirling around my feet. Even though I knew it was silly to believe it was him — or even a spiritual piece of him — there was a small part of my subconscious that clung to that tiny particle of hope I had left as though it was my lifeline.

The air around me felt comforting and safe, and I figured that it was probably the best note to leave our visit on. Still sniffling, I wiped the tears from my eyes as I stood and smiled down at the headstone. "I should probably go. It's a long drive back home, and I have a party to get ready for." I grimaced at the thought, and I pictured Bobby laughing at me as I did. "I'll come by again soon," I promised before turning away and heading back to the parking lot.

Back in my car, I sat for a minute and tried to get a hold of myself so I could drive home. I didn't want people to be concerned about me today or any other day, so I knew I would have to pull it together. One look at the clock told me I had less than six hours to make that happen, so I put the key in the ignition and left the parking lot of the Green Acres Cemetery.

When I finally arrived back home, my neighborhood alive with color from the various trees and cacti, I couldn't help but smile as I approached the door to my 1,100 square-foot South Scottsdale bungalow. I'd bought the house about a year ago and fell in love with it. It was perfect for me, especially the low-maintenance, grassless yard that was filled with tiny stones and several different forms of desert plants that needed little to no care at all. Most people wanted a large, plush yard, imagining their kids running around in it, but that wasn't who I was.

I parked in the driveway and walked up the path to my front door, and there, beneath the eaves of my little light brown house, I found a vase full of white stargazer lilies waiting for me. I knelt down and picked them up by the exquisite crystal vase, pulled the huge blooms to my nose, and inhaled their sweet smell. For the first time since waking up, I found my happiness starting to shine through.

I unlocked my door and set my flowers on the kitchen table before I removed the small card from the center of the bouquet. I already suspected whom they were from, but the written proof only lifted my mood a little more.

Happy Birthday, B
Love, David

I sighed contentedly. *Maybe the party won't be so bad after all,* I thought to myself. Okay, so it wasn't so much the party that had me excited — it was getting to see David. His general empathy and compassion made him one of the easiest people to be around. He cared for me as deeply as I did him — quite possibly even more since he wasn't guarded like I was. He accepted me for who I was, though, and that was huge, given my past.

While the thought of spending the evening with David brought a smile to my face, that didn't mean the party itself wasn't still going to be tough. In fact, getting ready for my party was going to take a lot of preparation. Not just physical, but emotional as well. It was no secret to my family and friends that I didn't handle parties very well, so to be expected to behave like a normal person celebrating their birthday today was actually asking a lot.

I would try, though.

I mean, it had to get better eventually, right.

Chapter 2 | Ghosts

When I arrived at my parents' beautiful home on Carolina Drive, most of the lights were out, which was par for the course when it came to surprise parties. However, knowing about the party did little to assuage my apprehensions, and my heart continued to thunder in my chest. It wasn't typical for us to ruin a surprise party for others, but my parents felt it necessary after what happened five years ago when my friends attempted the same thing. To say I had a meltdown would have been an understatement. It had been two years since Bobby's death, and I still hadn't fully processed everything, which meant that I was still in a major state of depression. It wasn't good; an ambulance ride and sedation were both required in order to subdue me. I sought grief counseling after that, at the behest of my parents.

Needless to say, two weeks ago, when my father learned that the guys at work had decided to throw me a party upon finding out my birthday was looming, he felt it only right to forewarn me. He even offered to order them to forget it, but I couldn't let them down like that, and as much as I wanted to, I couldn't keep running away from it. It was upon my telling him it was fine that he volunteered their house in

North Scottsdale.

The house that was now dark. Hiding the decorations for a celebration I wasn't sure I was ready for. My hands shook, and my apprehension skyrocketed. Breathing became difficult, and I had to force myself to take a moment as I tried to calm down.

My usual confidence gave way to the panic, and I gripped the wheel so tightly that my knuckles turned white, and my heart continued to pound against my ribs like it was trying its damndest to break free. Nervous as hell, I sat there for the better part of ten minutes before the pounding of blood in my ears finally subsided and my hands loosened their death grip on the wheel, my fingers numb and starting to tingle. I inhaled a deep, shaky breath and climbed out of my car, being sure to lock the doors before making my way up the long path.

Even though the temperature had dipped, the cool air making me shiver, I stopped for a moment and stood in the dim porch light, taking a few more deep, cleansing breaths before walking in to meet my fate. I counted to ten, pushing my hair back over my exposed shoulders…then twenty, smoothing the satiny fabric over my figure all the way down to my knees, adjusting the strapless top and making sure I wasn't going to be the victim of an unfortunate wardrobe malfunction — wouldn't that just be the cherry on top of an already craptastic day? And then thirty, before reaching the front door.

As the door swung open, the light in the front room turned on, and I was accosted. "Surprise!" they all shouted. One look around the room, and I noticed that everyone I worked with was mingled amongst the crowd of my friends and family. It was an oddly comforting feeling to have them all here…and comforting wasn't a feeling I was all too familiar with as of late.

Having already known about this for a while, I was forced to feign shock and bewilderment as I took in the rest of the room before me. It was heavily decorated with streamers and balloons, the guests all standing in the living room around the beautiful white couches my mom had reupholstered last month. There were several empty glasses on the dark cherry-colored coffee table that stood in the middle of the room, signaling that people had probably been here for a while, waiting for me to arrive. There were also two long tables, dressed in white linens, with all kinds of food and alcohol set out, and a fire burned in the corner fireplace, warming the room. What was usually a very modern and classy family room had been transformed into a celebration I never asked for...

"Oh my god! I can't believe you guys did all of this," I cried out, forcing my smile impossibly wider and truly hoping that no one would see through my façade. Chances were that almost everyone would buy it, but there were a select few who wouldn't.

Toward the back of the crowd, my gaze fell upon a familiar pair of blue eyes, and I offered him a warm smile before turning to the people who were currently crowding around me. Eager to get to him, I made my way through the group of people, thanking each person who wished me a happy birthday, until I reached the beverage table against the back wall just outside the elaborate dining room.

The more I heard the words "Happy Birthday," the more my anxiety increased and I felt the need for more alcohol than the human body could possibly handle.

With trembling hands, I grabbed one of the goblets and poured myself a glass of red wine, filling it more than the standard halfway point. As I brought the glass to my lips, I felt a familiar, and fleeting, touch on my lower back, and when I turned my head, I found myself looking into that same pair of baby blues that I spotted earlier.

There was something about him that always made me feel at ease. I think it had to do with him being pretty easy-going and someone you felt comfortable opening up to. Plus, his strength and protective nature made me feel safe. It was that feeling that drew me to him in the beginning, and I basked in the slight reprieve his presence offered me now.

"So, how long have you known about the party?" David's smooth voice asked as he walked around to stand in front of me. I eyed him up and down appreciatively and couldn't help but admire how extremely sexy he looked semi-dressed up in a pair of dark jeans, white dress shirt, and dark suit jacket. The top couple of buttons of his shirt were undone, exposing the tiniest hint of his muscular neck, and the jacket was cut to emphasize the strong, athletic build of his six-foot frame. The dark brown hair atop his head wasn't combed neatly, but it wasn't a tousled mess either. Having been privy to his morning routines, I knew that it took more work to make it look that way than he wanted the world to know.

My laugh was soft, but sincere, as I answered his question. "A couple of weeks, actually."

His smooth brow furrowed, his lips pursed in disappointment, and he cocked an eyebrow at me. "Well, where's the fun in that?" he asked, eyeing me through his periphery as he poured himself a glass of cognac. I admired the strong cut of his jaw as I thought about how to answer.

"David, I think the fun is in me *not* being hospitalized and sedated for another nervous breakdown."

He wasn't amused...even though I really did mean it as a joke. Winking, I scrunched my nose, hoping he'd see the playful nature of my words. "I'm just sayin'," I countered before taking another pull from my glass. The warm, sweet liquid filled my mouth and throat as I swallowed it slowly, savoring it, willing it to give me the buzz I craved so badly, hoping it would quell the shaking in my hands.

Looking concerned, his eyes met mine. "How *are* you doing?" He knew about my past and what this day really meant to me, so it didn't come as a surprise when his eyes reflected his concern.

"Fine."

"Brooke..." he said softly, setting his short glass down and moving for me.

Before he could finish, I inhaled a steady breath and smiled. I knew he could see in my eyes that I was far from "fine" — that I was barely holding it together — but I couldn't afford to lose my composure in a room full of people we both knew and worked with. He understood this and didn't push, which made me appreciate what we had even more.

"Did you get my present?" David asked, changing the topic. The way his eyes locked on mine was...intense, but it was an intensity I welcomed and held onto like it was my only tie to this mortal plane.

With a coy smile, I nodded softly. "They're beautiful. Thank you."

"You look fantastic," he told me with a Cheshire cat grin as his eyes roamed my body almost hungrily. I had the strongest desire to do a little spin for him — tease him a little more, because it was what we did — but I knew it would draw too much attention from those we had worked so hard to keep everything from. Instead, I got caught up in his scorching eyes and bit the inside of my cheek gently as I imagined what he could possibly be thinking. I knew from past experience that it couldn't be innocent.

Suddenly, I had the undeniable feeling in the pit of my stomach that we were being watched, so I nonchalantly turned my head while sipping at my wine to find my father eyeing the two of us. I smiled and raised my glass to him, only to have him raise his drink in return. I wasn't naïve enough to think I'd be able to keep our relationship hidden forever, and I knew it was inevitable that he would find out about my relationship with David sooner or later. I just hoped to be able to tell him on my own terms just how serious we'd gotten.

"You know, my father is going to suspect something is up if we keep meeting like this," I teased, returning my attention back to David.

He laughed softly as he disregarded my statement. "Brooke, we're partners. As far as he knows, we're discussing work."

"That," I said with a flick of my head back in my father's direction before continuing, "is not the look of a father who thinks that this is simply a working relationship."

I knew the instant that David's eyes met Dad's when he lifted his drink and nodded his head. I giggled softly into my glass when his eyes took on a look of fear and he gulped back the last ounce of his drink.

"Would it really be so bad if he knew?" David's eyes begged me to finally admit the truth, however, I just wasn't ready for the world to know. Everyone in this room already knew far too much about my personal life, and I just wanted to keep one tiny piece for myself.

Was that so bad?

This discussion was always a source of discord between us. He wanted to shout from the rooftop that we were together, and I just wanted to keep my private life...well, private. It wouldn't be the end of the world if people found out; I just wasn't ready. Why was that so hard to understand?

Instead of angering David tonight, I decided to try and keep the subject light. I cocked my right eyebrow at him and smirked. "You've seen him in the gallery, right? The man doesn't miss," I joked.

David's eyes burned into mine with the intensity of the sun, and I shivered beneath the force of his stare. "I'm being serious, Brooke. We've been together for almost two years now. Isn't it time to tell him?"

With a despondent sigh, I turned my head away. I couldn't bear to see the hurt on his face as I denied him what he so desperately wanted from me. "It's complicated...*I'm* complicated." I paused for a moment, waiting for him to tell me he understood, but he didn't. "Look, we can't talk about this here. Let's just enjoy the party, okay? Are you still coming over tonight?"

"Samuels." My father's voice was right behind me, but I felt fairly certain he hadn't heard our conversation since David still seemed relatively calm. Though, his calm demeanor could have very well been an act, or it could have just been him not giving a damn anymore. The ball was in anyone's court at this point.

"Captain," David says, formally tipping his head.

My father moved to stand beside me as he continued to look at David. "You're monopolizing the guest of honor here." Dad wrapped his arm around my shoulder, giving me a gentle squeeze. I briefly wondered if he could sense the tension between us, and that was what drew him here.

"Dad, be nice. David was just wishing me a happy birthday, weren't you?" I smiled up at David as his eyes moved between my father and me.

He ignored the question, his eyes telling me that this conversation was far from over. It was obvious that he had grown tired of the pretense, and I suddenly feared that he was done trying. Period. I didn't want that, so I desperately hoped I could fix this. "Well, Brooke, I should go mingle." He tossed a glance back toward a group of our coworkers and chuckled softly. I couldn't tell if it was one of amusement or distrust. "O'Malley looks like he's about to attempt a move on our new officer. I should probably go and intervene. Maybe remind him why that's not a good idea." Stepping around me, he flashed me a look. "Happy birthday. I'll talk with you in a bit, all right?"

I pushed aside my feelings of unease and offered him a smile in return. "I'll be around."

"He's a good kid," my dad said, causing my focus to shift from David's retreating form back to him. "You could do worse."

Unsure what to say, I took a sip from my almost-empty glass and smiled at him as I swallowed my wine. "Yeah. He's a great partner." While I already suspected he knew about my little tryst with David, I wasn't quite ready to confirm it just yet.

My dad looked at me knowingly; I was foolish to think we'd gotten away with it this long. "Brookie," he began, using the nickname he'd given me when I was three. "I just want you to be happy."

"I am happy," I assured him shakily. "Really." It wasn't a complete lie; most days I was — with the exception of today, of course, because when *this day* rolled around, I found it hard to take a breath, let alone function at all. Usually, I was able to get up, shower, dress, and carry about my day just like everyone else. I laughed when something was funny, made jokes, and hung out with David without having him constantly worried that I was going to go into some kind of catatonic state.

Yes, most days I was as close to happy as I guessed I ever would be.

"So, are you enjoying yourself?" Dad asked tentatively.

And, just like that, my distraction from what today really meant disappeared, thrusting me right back into reality with one loaded question.

I took another sip of my wine and shrugged. "You and Mom did a great job decorating. The wine is good. And the food smells delicious," I replied, sidestepping his original question.

I knew if I lied he'd see right through it, and then this conversation would take another turn entirely.

Too late.

My father's eyes narrowed, and he scoffed lightly at my response. I dropped my eyes from his knowing stare, admiring the dark polish on my toes as they peeked out from the tiny holes in my shoes, and fingered the stem of my wine glass nervously. "You know how hard this is for me," I reminded him softly, feeling the prickle of tears stinging my eyes. Had this party been thrown on any other day and not my actual birthday, I may have been a little more mentally sound.

May have been.

When I raised my head, his eyes saddened as he acknowledged his own empty glass. "It's hard for all of us, Brooke."

I nodded in agreement. It wasn't that I meant to be selfish, thinking that I had been the only one affected by the loss of Bobby. I wasn't. My parents lost him, too. I knew this. The thing was, though, that Bobby and I were close. Closer than most siblings.

Maybe it was a "twin thing" or maybe it was just a "sibling thing." No one could be certain — all I knew was that when I lost Bobby that night, I lost the other half of myself, and I couldn't be sure if I'd ever find it again.

The rest of the room was abuzz with laughter, talking, and music, but a heavy silence hung between my father and me, numbing me to everything else. When he cleared his throat, I looked back up at him to find the worry he had for me clearly etched on his face.

He opened his mouth to speak, but I wasn't sure I would be able to handle it in my current state of mind. The last thing I wanted to do was become hysterical in front of everyone. Choking back a quiet sob and blinking away my tears, I stood on my toes and placed a soft kiss on his cheek. "I'm going to go out onto the patio for a breath of air. I'm fine, Daddy. I promise."

I set my empty wine glass down on the kitchen table as I quickly passed through the abandoned kitchen and slid the patio door open before stepping out into the brisk night air. Being the tail-end of October, the night was always a bit more frigid in the desert, and it was only going to get colder. In an effort to keep warm, I wrapped my arms around myself and roughly rubbed my hands over them, hoping the friction would help a little.

The night sky was clear of clouds as I made my way toward the pool, and I could see the stars and the waxing crescent moon with perfect clarity. An unseasonal warm breeze, similar to the one I felt in the cemetery, picked up, and I felt that same overwhelming sense of peace fall over me as I stood alone outside. The coolness of autumn seemed to soften just enough that I was comfortable, and I finally felt at ease being cloaked in the darkness, away from all the prying eyes inside the house. It was as though I could breathe again without being under everyone's watchful eyes. Inside was so bright, and I was the main focus of everyone's attention. Part of me wondered if that was only because they were secretly waiting for me to completely melt down, or if it really was because it was my "special day."

Probably the first, Brooke, I told myself with a sad sigh. Though I knew I deserved to be treated like I was made of porcelain today, it became a little unbearable after so long, and I had to wonder how much longer it would go on for. Surely after seven years it should have passed, right? The only reason I could think of that it kept me from moving on — that kept us all from moving on — was that we never were able to figure out what happened in the alley that night. Bobby's murderer was never found, and his case remained unsolved and locked away in a cabinet of cold cases.

We lacked the closure that solving his case should have brought, and I was reminded of it most on this day: the anniversary of his death.

"Happy birthday, beautiful." The sound of a very familiar voice from my past pulled me out of my silent torment. My body stiffened as a multitude of memories flooded my mind. These weren't memories I openly welcomed, however; they were painful and just another reason that I was who I was.

I didn't have to turn around to know exactly who had found me. Nick Evans. My ex. I whispered his name, and my voice shook before being carried off into the night. He must have sensed my unease, because he stopped walking toward me, based on the lack of his footsteps.

Very slowly, I turned to him, fear gripping at

every part of me as I struggled to meet his eyes. Though, as soon as I did, I was lost in the warm, blue-green color. He looked…

Damn it, he looked good.

Dressed in dark jeans and a fitted gray sweater, the sleeves pushed up to his elbows and showing off his thick forearms, he took another step forward. His sandy-blond hair was longer than I remembered, but intentionally so and not like he'd simply forgotten to go to the hairdresser. I found my fingers itching to run through it to see if it was as soft as I remembered. He looked nervous, his face tight, back rigid.

Entranced as I was, I couldn't ignore how anxious Nick's sudden reappearance in my life made me. Maybe it was because he was there the night that Bobby died, or it could have been because not too long after that horrible night, he broke off our engagement and left me. There was no real explanation given, either. What was worse was that I never even saw it coming.

Nick was the sweetest boyfriend. Even though he was a total jock in high school and college, he had a soft side…maybe it was just for me. I liked to think so, anyway. He was always going above and beyond to please me. Always sending me flowers, taking me out to fancy dinners or dancing. It was rare that we didn't spend our free time together…

But in the weeks following Bobby's death, everything had changed. Nick had grown more distant from me, always claiming to be busy, until suddenly he packed up his things and left, breaking my heart even more than it already was. It didn't matter how much I begged him to stay, he simply claimed he needed "space," that he was going through some "changes," and how he hoped I would "understand."

I understood, all right. I understood that I was—

still am — beyond damaged after finding my brother dead in an alley. Who the hell would want a piece of that?

"What the hell are you doing here?" I didn't mean for my question to come across as rude as it sounded — or did I? Regardless, it was too late to take it back.

His smile widened, his shoulders relaxing slightly, probably thinking I wasn't as angry at him as he feared. Wrong. As he worked on closing the gap between us again, his easy gait reminded me of how he used to be so carefree. I thought I could still see that cocky glimmer I used to love in his eyes, but it disappeared, suddenly replaced with a seriousness that could only come with age and tragedy. I would know.

"Well, I was in town, visiting my folks, when I ran into your mom at the supermarket this morning."

"She invited you?" I demanded, suddenly angry that my mother would even consider something like that.

Nick shook his head. "No. It just came up in conversation. She has no idea I'm here."

"Trespassing," I interjected callously, glancing down at the clear water in the pool. "Typical."

"I missed you," he confessed, coming to a stop right in front of me, his head dipping lower and causing his unruly hair to fall over his forehead. I'd forgotten how tall he was at just over six feet, having to tilt my head back to meet his gaze. My eyes remained trained on him, and his lips came perilously close to mine.

And then I slapped him, the sound travelling across the backyard. My hand stung, but Nick's face hardly moved beneath the force of my blow. An angry red welt started to form on his cheek, but he didn't look angry. His face remained unreadable, his chiseled jaw clenching while the rest of his prominent features softened. He looked like he understood why I had done it, and that only made me angrier. "I haven't heard a word from you in almost seven years." The venom in my tone didn't deter him, and he reached for my hands — probably to stop me from lashing out again.

"I'm seeing someone," I managed to choke out, taking a couple steps away from him.

Confusion reflected back at me in his mesmerizing eyes. "Oh? Your mother never mentioned…"

"Because it's *none* of your business. It stopped being your business the day you walked away."

"Brooke?" David's voice caused me to jump, and I turned toward the patio door. He looked between the two of us, confused at first, and then annoyed. He was the one good thing I had going for me right now, and I cared for him more than I could even imagine. So, to have him find me out here with my ex worried me. Especially after what happened inside. Would he think something was going on? Surely he knew how I felt about him — even if I didn't want to share our relationship with the rest of the world?

What if he doesn't? It was that question that made me realize I couldn't lose him. I couldn't lose someone else I loved.

I averted my eyes from his as he crossed over to me, staring at everything from the silver moon above to the millions of tiny stars surrounding it, and then down to the recently manicured toes peek-a-booing through the tips of my shoes again. When I felt his hand lay flat against my back, I could sense that he wasn't angry with me. What I did pick up on, however, was a certain level of possessiveness, and while this wasn't a characteristic I normally found too appealing, the fact that he was silently challenging Nick was somewhat thrilling.

A smile played at the corners of my mouth, and I looked over at him, even though he never took his narrowing eyes off of his apparent rival. His angular jaw clenched, and it was probably a good thing he had one hand on the small of my back and the other wrapped around the stem of one of my mother's crystal glasses. On second thought, maybe the glass wasn't such a good thing; we had been sent out on enough domestic abuse cases to know that anything could be used as a weapon.

"Aren't you going to introduce us, Brooke?" Nick suggested, his tone of voice changing ever so slightly into one I no longer recognized. It was no longer soft and compelling, but lower and almost territorial. Not that he deserved to feel like he had any say over what I did and who I did it with.

"Oh, um, right." I uncrossed my arms and wrapped one around David, mirroring his hold on me, hoping to stop the quiver that continued to move through me. "David, this is Nick. He's an old friend."

"Friend?" Nick inquired, his voice shifting back to its previous, much lighter sound. "Surely, we were much more than that, Brooke."

My eyes narrowed, shooting daggers at Nick, and David's hand pressed harder against my back. I could sense his restraint, and I hated that Nick was trying to get a rise out of David like this. What was worse was that it seemed to be working. While I'm sure it wasn't Nick's intention to piss me off further, he'd failed. I squeezed my right hand, testing it to make sure it felt okay enough to slap him again. It did.

I looked at David, and his rising irritation concerned me on a number of levels. Mainly because he was usually so calm and collected — it didn't seem to matter what was happening, he just was. The only time I'd ever seen him get this upset was when we were out on a call last year and a perp slugged me. David may have used a little more force than was entirely necessary to subdue the son of a bitch.

I rubbed David's back soothingly and rested my other hand on his chest, feeling his heart pound violently beneath my touch. Knowing I needed to calm him down, I glared at Nick and spoke with a seething hatred that still burned through my veins from his total abandonment. "That was a long time ago, Nick." He glanced down at me briefly before retraining his steely gaze on David. "You should probably just do what you do best and go."

Nick's eyes sparkled with the knowledge that he was getting under David's skin. "You're right. Maybe I should have called first."

I flinched as his words struck an exposed nerve that I thought had been severed long ago. By the time I found my voice again, he was already hopping the fence into the neighbor's yard, probably afraid to announce his party-crashing ways to my parents.

A very large part of me didn't want to let him get away with just showing up here, but I made it all of two steps before David's hand gripped my wrist and pulled me back to him. He lead me into the cover of darkness and pressed my back to the side of the house as his lips met mine in a kiss that was filled with so much need it made my knees shake.

Nick was forgotten as David's arms snaked around my waist, his hands moving down to cup my ass as I wrapped mine around his neck. Goosebumps rippled over my body as I stepped up onto my toes to bring myself closer to his height. I held him as close to me as possible, moaning into the kiss and pushing my body against his, feeling his growing arousal against my thigh.

I knew that he needed me to assure him that I was his completely — that nothing on this Earth would take me away from him. I yearned for the same thing. Tears of regret mixed with those from being emotionally overwhelmed started burning behind my closed eyes as David and I passionately embraced on the dark patio. Since David made no secret about the way he felt about me, I knew that I had to take the next step in our relationship. For him. For both of us. He'd given me so much already, and I had done nothing but take.

Even though I really didn't want to, I found a reserve of strength and broke our kiss. Feeling a little light-headed, I had to take a minute to catch my breath as David gripped my hips, his thumbs delightfully pressing into the soft flesh above my hipbones. This sent tiny shockwaves through my lower body that settled between my thighs, and I found it hard to focus.

Licking my lips, I opened my eyes and looked up at him through my thick, dark lashes. His blue eyes appeared dark with lust as they danced between mine and my tingling mouth, and it filled me with joy on a day that usually brought me such despair. It was another welcome relief. I loved him so much. This was the perfect moment to prove it.

"I can't lose you," I confessed softly. "You're far too important to me."

Anger flared in David's eyes. "What that Neanderthal did — leaving you? — I would *never* do that." I nodded my understanding, but still held my doubts. "I love you, Brooke."

I knew he meant it; it was obvious in the way he acted around me daily. The fight to keep my tears at bay was lost the moment I closed my eyes, and I was angry that I let Nick's unexpected visit affect me like this. They rolled down my cheeks as I turned my face into his hand and kissed the palm of it. "I...love you, too," I confessed honestly into the warmth of his touch before turning and meeting his blazing stare. "And I want to tell everyone."

David's eyes widened with surprise, his happiness pouring off of him. "Really?" I nodded, and he wrapped his arms around me, picking me up off the ground and spinning us around.

I laughed loudly and, in that moment, forgot the horrible memories that today brought with it. This was huge for me. When David set me back on my feet, he kissed me so hard, I got a little weak in the knees and had to clutch the front of his jacket to help keep my balance.

"Take me home?" I pleaded when he pulled away, wanting desperately for the two of us to be alone and pick up where we left off.

David chuckled, leaning down to kiss the tip of my nose. "Sweetheart, the night is still young, and your parents kind of have a whole evening planned."

It didn't take me long to realize that we hadn't really been here that long — regardless of the fact that time seemed to be dragging — and I laughed lightly at myself. "I guess it just feels like today's already gone on long enough."

David pulled me toward the house, and I stopped before reaching the door. "You ready?"

"Are you?" he replied back. "If you'd prefer to wait..."

I shook my head hard. "No. I want to do this. Like you said, it's been two years. Besides, I figure my parents would love for this day to hold happy memories. Let's go make that happen."

With a smile that could light up a starless night,

David pulled me against his side and pressed his lips to mine once more. "As you wish, sweetheart."

CHAPTER 3 | TRUTH

Even with the unexpected and joyous turn that last night took, Nick showing up at my party and rea-wakening that period of my life cut deeply. How did he not realize the possibility of that happening? As if it wasn't hard enough to deal with the night I found Bobby, but for Nick to come back seven years *to the day* and act as though nothing had happened? How did he expect me to react? He left me. *He* left *me* when things got just a little too hairy for him; it didn't seem to matter what I was going through.

I loved him — needed him — and he just left. Over the years, I thought I'd made peace with how things ended between us, but seeing him again... Well, it brought back memories of every tender moment we'd shared, and they almost eclipsed the resentment I harbored for him.

Almost.

My eyes burned, bloodshot and beyond exhausted, as I stared at the white wall ahead of me. I was still lying in bed after a long, sleepless night obsessing over Nick's return to town and feeling guilty that my thoughts were about him and not the man sleeping next to me in my bed. With every minute that ticked by on my bedside clock, I had hoped sleep would find and hold me, but it was sparse and never lasted more than fifteen minutes at any given time. David had done what he could to help take my mind off everything, and I'd given in, momentarily forgetting my troubles in exchange for the way he made me feel whenever I was in his arms. But he fell asleep, and I couldn't shut my mind off long enough to follow him.

I heard a soft groan behind me, and the mattress dipped beneath David's weight as he rolled over. Suddenly, his heavy arm draped over my waist and hung there for a minute before his fingers started to dance over my exposed abdomen. "Good morning," he greeted gruffly, his warm breath wafting over my neck and making me shrug against the ticklish sensation. "How did you sleep?"

"Um, fine?" I really have to work on speaking with ironclad conviction, because he didn't buy it.

His fingers stopped moving, and he pushed himself up. With a sigh, I rolled onto my back and looked up at him. His hair was a disaster, making me grin like an idiot, but his eyes instantly sobered me. "Brooke—"

"David...don't."

"No." He shook his head. "Jesus, Brooke, you can't keep doing this."

Perplexed, I pushed myself up onto my elbows, the collar of my T-shirt feeling tight against my neck. "Doing what?"

"Pretending like everything is...'*fine*.'" Frustrated, he threw himself off the bed and yanked his jeans on over his boxers.

"I-I don't know what you want me to say," I whispered, pushing up until I sat cross-legged on the bed, fidgeting with a loose string on the hem of my shirt.

"Sweetheart, it's not about what I *want* you to

say…" David sighed and planted himself back on the bed in front of me, taking my hands in his and bringing them to his lips. "You can't keep this shit bottled up inside."

A sad nod from me. "I know." My eyes met his, and I gave him a half-smile. "It's not that I mean to keep you at a distance… It kills me that you even feel that's what I'm doing…" Then I heaved a heavy sigh. "Seeing Nick last night just opened an old wound — more than usual." David's eyes grew sad, like maybe he thought it brought back more than just the despair I felt when Nick left after Bobby died, so I tried to explain. "I don't love him. N-not anymore. But" — the first of several tears fell down my cheek — "on my *birthday*? When he knows what that day means to my family?" I hated crying; it made me feel weak, and it was something I usually kept others from seeing, but these past twenty-four hours had been a little more emotional than years past.

David reached over and took my hand in his, bringing it to his lips and placing feather-light kisses over my knuckles. I was grateful to him for being here for me and listening without judgment, and it was a relief that I could explain this to him without fear of him misreading how I felt about Nick. To show him just how much I appreciated his support, I raised my face and kissed him, closing my eyes and sighing as his lips molded to mine.

The desire to lose myself in him like I did last night — to forget about everything — overwhelmed me, and warmth bloomed throughout my body, starting in my belly and emanating outward until my skin tingled. In a flash, my hands moved up to David's neck, my fingers twisted into his hair and tugged lightly. He responded in kind by tangling his own hands into my long, pillow-mussed hair, and I shifted above him, straddling his strong thighs with the need to be closer when he pulled his lips from mine.

"Brooke...*wait*," he rasped. "We can't."

My breath shuddered as I drew it in, my hips moving against him and relishing the feel of how aroused he was. "Mmm," I hummed teasingly, shifting my hips slightly to see if I could persuade him. "I think your body's suggesting otherwise."

David laughed, but I could see that he was seriously reconsidering his decision. Sadly, he stuck to his guns, but not without a little torture of his own. He leaned in close, his lips brushing the shell of my ear, and whispered, "As much as I'd really love to throw you down on this bed and do"—his hands moved down under the hem of my shirt and grabbed my ass firmly—"*ungodly* things to your beautiful body..." I closed my eyes in rapture when I felt the warm, hard truth of his words pressing against me. Then he got serious, sighing heavily. "The simple fact remains that if I stay wrapped up in your arms all morning—which, again, I would love more than anything—then we're going to be late for work."

I pushed my bottom lip out in a mock-pout. "Oh, boo." David nibbled at my protruding lip gently, making me giggle.

"Come on." Using both hands, he playfully tossed me onto the bed before standing up. "Get dressed. I'll go start on breakfast."

David grabbed a T-shirt from his drawer before leaving me alone, and I took a minute before getting out of bed, looking out the window at the blue sky of a new day. I could already feel the arid heat seeping into the air in my room, and I sensed that it would be a little warmer than yesterday.

But something still felt off.

Even though everything seemed just a little bit

brighter thanks to David's positivity, I still felt acutely aware of my troubled past. Usually, the day after my birthday found me feeling a little less distressed about everything. But not this year. It could have been Nick's surprise visit to the city, but it somehow felt like more than that. I really wished I could put my finger on it.

Taking a deep breath, I headed to the bathroom for a quick shower before David finished preparing breakfast. After showering and dressing in jeans and a T-shirt, I dried my hair and applied a little makeup to hide the signs of my sleepless night. Then I headed out to the kitchen to find David setting two plates of bacon and eggs on the table.

"Smells delicious," I told him, kissing his cheek and preparing to take my seat.

Before I could sit, though, David wrapped his arm around me and pulled me to him, burying his nose in the crook of my neck and inhaling. "So do you," he whispered, making me giggle at how overly corny he could be from time to time.

"You're so hokey," I teased, pushing him back and shaking my head.

"Don't deny it." He stepped back and let me sit down. "It's why you love me."

A smile tugged at my lips. "Perhaps that's part of it."

Looking intrigued, David sat next to me and inquired, "And the rest of it?"

"Isn't really appropriate talk for the breakfast table," I confessed, my voice dropping to a lower, much sexier, tone.

Smirking, David took a bite of his eggs. An unexpected silence fell between us as we ate, and when I looked at him again, he seemed lost in thought. When I finally asked what was on his mind, he set his fork down and met my gaze. The look in his eyes was star-tlingly afraid. "Why did we wait until now to come out with our relationship?"

"You know why," I replied quietly, pushing my eggs around my plate.

"I think I do," he said. "But it feels like there's more to it than that. Is it..." A pause. "Is it because of *him*?"

"Nick?" I questioned, even though I knew that was exactly who he meant. "A little, yeah." I shrugged despondently. "It's been hard for me to open myself up to anyone else after he left...maybe because I was afraid of anyone else seeing me the way he did." David looked at me, his eyes a combination of curiosity and sympathy, and I took a deep breath before I concluded. "Broken."

Sighing, I dropped my eyes to my now-fidgeting hands and continued. "After Bobby died, I never real-ly got over it—how could I? The police couldn't find anything that would lead us to who killed him, and his case was eventually filed away, unsolved." While David already knew most of this, he'd never really gotten the full story on Nick and me or how serious our relationship really was. "I withdrew emotionally from everything. Bobby was my brother, and one mi-nute he was there with Nick and me at the club, and the next he was just gone.

"Nick obviously couldn't handle having a girl-friend who was in a near-constant state of catatonia. My moods had become...unpredictable, and I guess he just couldn't deal." Because I'd already cried for the loss of my first love, I was able to tell David all of this with little to no inflection in my voice, even though talking about it was slowly reopening the hole that Nick left in my heart. "He stopped coming around as much, and when I was lucid enough to ask him what was going on, he just told me that he was going through some changes. It was pretty obvious that he didn't want to be with me, really."

"I'm sorry," David said softly, reaching across the table and taking my hand. "I knew he hurt you, but I never realized just how badly."

I purposely left out the part where Nick and I were engaged. Not because I thought it would hurt him, but because I didn't think it was really relevant to the story. It wasn't like we were actually married and I had a divorce under my belt. We were young and impulsive, and then he broke it off. What's to tell?

I laughed dryly because David's apology seemed a little out of place. "It's not your fault."

"It's not yours either. He should have been sympathetic to what you were going through, and he wasn't. He was thinking only of himself." David's words resonated deep within me, and I felt a little bit better having gotten all of this off my chest. He was right; Nick was being entirely selfish when he decided to leave.

"Well, his loss was your gain," I told David, standing up with my plate and taking it to the sink. "And I, for one, couldn't be happier about that."

Flashing me that Colgate smile, David pushed his chair from the table and crossed the room, pulling me into his arms. "Me either," he declared. He looked at the clock on the stove and sighed. "I suppose I should go hop in the shower so we can hit the road, huh?"

I groaned when David released me, but agreed to do the dishes while he got ready. It was only fair, after all. I was just putting the last plate away in the cupboard when David's arms circled my waist and his chin rested upon my shoulder.

"I'll meet you at the precinct?" he said, kissing my shoulder softly.

Smiling, I turned in his arms and looked him in the eye. "Why? That seems like a waste of gas." He looked confused, which made me strangely giddy. "How about we take my car today?"

David looked...well, he looked absolutely shocked and delighted, and I promised to make him look like that as often as possible for as long as possible. "Really?" I nodded once. "And if people start asking questions?"

Bringing my hands up and resting them on his shoulders, I stepped up on my toes and kissed him once. "Then we tell them." I arched an eyebrow. "Besides, maybe this will get Keaton to stop asking me out."

"I don't know," David said with a laugh. "I don't think Keaton is so easily dissuaded." He leaned in and his lips brushed mine, sending a welcome shiver straight down my spine. "A little PDA might be in order." Then his lips captured mine tenderly, almost as though he was thanking me, and my fingers curled into the fabric of his dress shirt, tugging him closer.

"Come on," I whispered after pulling my head back. "We should go before we're late. Now that he knows, we can't let my dad think the reason we're running behind is anything more than car trouble."

Nodding, David released me, and I headed to the bathroom to pull my hair up before grabbing my jacket, keys, gun, and badge. "Ready?" he asked, holding the front door open for me, and I walked through, my stomach flipping with excited butterflies.

"Let's do this."

CHAPTER 4 | ATTACKED

When we arrived at the District 1 precinct, there were several officers outside who instantly noticed us. They watched as we walked from the lot toward the precinct side by side, but they didn't say anything other than a quick "good morning" to us both before snuffing out their cigarettes and following us inside.

The minute we stepped off the elevator and made our way for our desks, Dad noticed too. "Leighton, can I see you in my office, please?"

I glanced warily at David across our desks before addressing our captain. "Yes, sir. Right away."

Once inside his office, Dad sat at his desk, and I closed his door behind me. "Have a seat," he offered, and I obeyed, sitting directly across from him with perfect posture brought on by a bout of sudden nervousness.

Now that we were alone, though, he went back to being my dad, and offered me a smile. "How are you today?" he asked, concern lacing his even tone.

For a brief moment, I considered omitting some of the truth, but he'd always been able to see through me—which was why I shouldn't have been so surprised to find out that he knew about David and me prior to last night. I took a deep breath and shrugged.

"Better, but still a little rattled."

"I suspected as much," he said empathetically, folding his hands atop his desk. "Samuels told me that Nick showed up and confronted you."

"I wouldn't say *confronted* me…" Wait. Why was I defending him? "Honestly, I don't know why he was there. Causing trouble… You know, Nick stuff."

"What did he say?"

I allowed the memory of Nick finding me outside of the house last night play through my mind on loop, and I couldn't believe the balls he had to just approach me as if nothing was wrong between us. What was he thinking? And while I was sure David didn't enjoy finding me with my ex, I was certainly glad he showed up when he did.

Dad stared at me, still waiting for a response, so I exhaled a dry, humorless laugh. "Not a whole hell of a lot. Like I said, I think he was just there to stir up trouble."

My dad's eyes moved past me and out the window that connected his office to the main one. I turned to see what caught his attention and found David rifling through some case files, occasionally glancing our way. "How did Samuels react?"

"Like a saint," I answered, "even though he should have been pissed when he found us both alone on the patio."

"And the two of you…?" His question trailed off, and I assumed it was because, even though he knew, I still had yet to vocally address my relationship status with David.

Having promised David that I'd no longer skirt the issue, I smiled. "We're fine. Together and happy."

"Good to hear. Thank you for finally feeling like you could tell your mother and me, by the way."

My eyebrows lifted with concern that he'd misread *why* I'd kept my relationship from him all this time. "Dad, it's not that I felt I couldn't come to you or Mom," I started to tell him. "I just liked having control over this one part of my life, and I was scared that things would start to sour if I let anyone else in. I couldn't lose more than I already had...and I wouldn't put you and Mom through that again, either."

"Your mother and I are a tad more resilient than you give us credit for, kiddo." Laughing, I rolled my eyes, and the smile on my dad's face faded slightly as he nodded his head toward the door. "All right, well, I suppose I shouldn't keep you from work."

"Okay," I responded, standing up and heading for the door. "Thanks for the pep-talk, old man."

"It's what I'm here for." I pulled the door open when he stopped me again. "And, Brooke?" I turned to him, and he was all business again. "Be sure you go to HR and inform them of your relationship."

"Yes, sir. Thank you."

When I returned to my desk, I found David absorbed in one of the case files. He was so transfixed on what he was reading that I had to clear my throat as I perched myself on the edge of his desk to draw his attention.

"Hey." He closed the file in his lap and smiled warmly up at me. "How was your talk?"

"Good." I dropped my voice and leaned in close so no one else could hear me. "I didn't know you told him about Nick showing up."

David shrugged, the tips of his ears turning a light shade of pink. "I wanted him to know that someone was trespassing."

I smirked, disbelieving, and crossed my arms. I knew jealousy when I saw it. "Mmm hmm," I challenged. "That's all it was?"

It was never hard to coerce a confession out of David. I prided myself on it. "Okay, *maybe* it was a little more than that," he said with a wink, tapping the side of my thigh with the file.

We'd always had a good work rapport, but I had to admit that it was nice being able to banter back and forth like this without worrying that someone would start a vicious — albeit true — rumor about our involvement. Even though we weren't hanging off of each other or showing massive amounts of PDA, it was also a relief not having to tiptoe around the office. All this time, I thought that everybody knowing would only serve to complicate things for the two of us, but that was quickly proving not to be the case, and it was such a relief.

David and I went about our day filing the final paperwork for a few recently closed cases I'd assisted with before my promotion. This was the best part of the job, because we were able to help the families of victims find the closure they needed to take the first steps toward healing — something I longed for, but knew I would never obtain after all this time. It was fine, though; I'd come to accept this, and helping others gave me purpose and made the job worth it.

I remembered with perfect clarity how difficult it was to wait for answers, and how absolutely horrible it was to hear that no arrests had been made. These were just some of the reasons that I made it my mission to try and bring closure to each case. No family should ever have to live in fear that the criminal who hurt or took a loved one from them was still free.

Unfortunately, not every case was so open and

shut, and it was these ones that forced me to lose sleep and relive my past.

"You ready to go?" David asked, pulling me out of my silent musings.

One look out the window behind David's desk, and I could see the sun had already started to set. It painted the sky in warm hues of pink and orange, and it darkened with every passing minute. My view of the sky was interrupted when David stood and pushed his chair in, signaling the end of our shift.

When our eyes locked, I smiled and nodded. "Yeah." I replied, shutting my computer down and grabbing my things. As we walked, David took my hand — the first physical sign of our relationship to the public — and we made our way to the car.

The moon was already high in the sky, and it was a little colder than the night before. It made me yearn to curl up under a blanket with David and a glass of wine while we watched television back at my place. Where that led to...well, it had yet to be determined, but I was hoping we'd pick up where we left off this morning.

We made our way through the lot, passing a few of the others who were just starting their shifts and told them to have a good night. When we reached the parking lot, David pulled me into his arms, sandwiching my body between him and the hard metal frame of my car, and I shivered for an entirely different reason than the dipping temperature.

He kissed me softly, his soft blue eyes locked on mine before speaking in a low voice that traveled through my body with a gentle hum. "Even though we haven't acted any differently when in the presence of our coworkers, it was nice to know we're not actually hiding anymore."

"It was, wasn't it?" I agreed, resting my hands on

his hips and pulling him forward by the belt loops on his jeans.

He hummed, his nose brushing mine as he pushed his pelvis against me. "Not hiding our relationship was extremely liberating. Perhaps we should have done this months ago and saved ourselves the stress." The heat of his body affected my ability to speak, and he chuckled, brushing his stubbled jaw against my smooth skin. It scratched and tickled at the same time, which sent a tingle through my body that made my toes curl. "Now, why don't you let me take you home so we can pick up where we left off before breakfast? No distractions."

David opened the passenger side door just as I was just about to answer with a resounding "Yes!" when, behind me, static blared over the police scanner before the dispatch officer's voice filled the air. "All available units to Chaparral Park for a reported one-eight-seven."

Turning abruptly, I looked at David before he ran around to the driver's side and slid behind the wheel. After turning the car on, he flipped the siren, alerted dispatch that we were on our way, and the red and blue lights flashed in my rear window as we peeled out of the parking lot and raced up N Hayden Road for Chaparral.

When we arrived, there were several other cars already there. We saw O'Malley off near the edge of the park with two young women whose eyes were wide and terrified as they looked at him with their arms wrapped tightly around themselves. It wasn't hard to see they were in shock, and it was probably pretty safe to assume that they were the ones who reported the homicide.

David's hand on the small of my back refocused me as he guided me to where the medical examiner and several of our colleagues hovered over a body that lay approximately fifteen feet off the cement path. As we approached, I noticed the victim was a woman in her mid-to-late twenties. Her skin was pale, and her body seemed twisted disproportionately, almost as if she'd been dumped here by her attacker in a hurry.

"What do we have here?" David asked the medical examiner.

"Twenty-three-year-old female named Samantha Turner, according to her license. Nothing seems to be missing from her purse — cash, credit cards — it's all here," Detective Keaton announced, handing the woman's wallet to David. "CSU is walking the grid, but so far they've found nothing worth reporting."

"Cause of death?" I asked, crouching down next to the body, being careful not to interfere with Dr. Hobbes, the medical examiner.

Her black hair was pulled back into a tight ponytail as she continued to take notes, and when she looked up at me from behind her thick-rimmed glasses, she shrugged her shoulders. Her hazel eyes met mine, and her unease was palpable, affecting me as well. "I won't know for sure until I examine her further, but she's been dead at least an hour based on her liver temp."

I examined this poor woman from a distance, noticing her designer clothes — from her cashmere sweater, right down to her expensive jeans and the leather shoes that had mostly slipped off except for where the straps held them around her ankles. Upon closer observation, I noticed something that really popped out to me: a spot on her neck mostly covered by her long brown hair.

Curious — for a reason that niggled at me in the back of my mind, but I couldn't quite pinpoint — I turned to David and held out my hand. "David, can I have a pen?"

Without question, he reached into his jacket and retrieved a pen to give to me. I took it, keeping the cap on, and slipped it under her hair to lift it. Unfortunately, before I could get a good look at it, I heard something to the right of us rustling in the sparse brush there. Something about this entire situation felt a little...off, and I stood up, my eyes focused on the trees across the park.

"What is it?" David asked, gently placing his hand on my arm.

I narrowed my eyes, trying to decipher if the movement I saw was from the wind or a possible suspect. The foliage was thin, but it was dark outside now, making it hard to see.

"I'm not sure..." I said hesitantly, taking a careful step forward. "I thought I heard something."

Through my periphery, I noticed David train his eyes on the trees ahead, but nothing happened. No sound. No movement. Nothing.

"I'm going to check it out," I informed him. "If someone's out there, we have to stop them."

David nodded in agreement, drawing his gun and switching the safety off as I did the same, and we started toward the disturbance together slowly. Once there, he silently suggested we split up and walk around the perimeter to see if we can find anything. He mouthed the words *"be careful,"* which I reciprocated just as quietly before we began to circle.

I hadn't made it halfway around before I heard another rustle of leaves, and my body tensed, my index finger slipping onto the trigger and preparing to fire. "Come out with your hands up!" I ordered firmly, taking aim. I waited a minute for a response of some kind, but there was nothing at first. "I said, come out with your hands up!"

The leaves rustled again, the sound getting closer, but instead of heavy footfalls, I heard the ground being disturbed beneath the sound of a low, threatening growl that chilled me to the bone. I took a step back, horrified that what I'd stumbled on wasn't our human perpetrator, but some kind of wild animal out looking for its next meal. My concern was confirmed the minute the animal's glowing yellow eyes locked on me, and I swallowed the lump of fear that formed in my throat.

"Hey, doggie," I said soothingly once it came completely into view, removing my finger from the trigger and backing away slowly. The tiny hairs all over my body prickled, and my muscles tensed as I broke out in a cold sweat. "Good dog. Look, I didn't mean to scare you."

The large dog stalked toward me slowly, looking around us and then back at me, and once the silver light of the moon shone down on its thick brown coat, I could see that it wasn't *just* a dog, but a wolf that had me in its sights. I tried to pass this off as an impossibility because wolves were extremely rare in Arizona as a whole, let alone Scottsdale. There were maybe fifty endangered Mexican gray wolves in the state, and they never *ever* came this close to civilization.

The more I looked at this animal, though, the more I realized it *was* indeed a wolf. However, this wasn't like any other wolf I'd ever seen, either, looking to be about twice the size, which frightened me a little. Gray wolves didn't grow this big, that much I knew. There wasn't a doubt in my mind that it had to weigh well over one hundred eighty pounds, which meant it would most likely be able to take me down with ease.

Its long, sharp canines glistened before it brought its eyes back to me, its lips curled back into a snarl, and it took another stalking step toward me. It was obvious that this animal wasn't going to back down, and I didn't relish killing it, but it was becoming obvious that I wouldn't have much choice. My life was at stake now, not to mention that I couldn't let a wild animal remain out here in a public park. While my instincts told me it was unlikely, this could be what killed that woman.

I raised the gun again, steadying my arms, and took aim. "I don't want to do this," I told it, my voice trembling, and just as I was about to pull the trigger, it sprang forward. Almost two hundred pounds of solid muscle and bone tackled me to the ground, forcing all of the air from my lungs. My gun went flying when my back slammed into the ground, and my head throbbed from the impact. As I struggled to free myself, the hot, somewhat putrid breath of the wolf nearly suffocated me when it leaned in with a warning growl. Its huge paws were on my chest, holding me down and robbing me of the ability to breathe. It continued to growl and snarl, its eyes scanning the darkness — probably for anyone who might try to help me. Before it could bite me, I brought my hands up and grabbed hold of the looser skin around the animal's neck, pulling upward in an effort to hold its face far from mine.

The wolf was ridiculously strong, and I started to think I wouldn't win as the muscles in my arms trembled with fatigue. It barked again, just as my left arm gave out, and its teeth sank deep into my shoulder, tearing right through my leather jacket and shirt. Teeth scraped bone, and I screamed in pain when a burning sensation shot through my arm. The adrenaline that coursed through my body gave me a sudden burst of strength, allowing me to bring my right leg up between us until my foot was pressed against the animal's chest, and I heaved it off of me.

The wolf yelped as it hit the ground several feet away from me, his eyes wide and panicked, and then several shots were fired to my right. I heard another yelp from the wolf, and a spray of red misted the air above its right flank.

This didn't slow it down, however, so David fired another shot, but missed when it darted quickly back into the cover of trees, howling.

"Brooke!" David cried, tearing up the grass as he fells to his knees next to me. "Jesus, Brooke. Are you all right?"

"Damn it." I inhaled sharply through my teeth, almost hissing, and pushed myself up with my good arm, trying to keep my left shoulder from jostling too much. "Yeah. I think so."

Without warning, David pulled me into his arms and held me, disregarding my injured shoulder in lieu of his relief that I was okay. I hissed painfully, and he released me before helping me to my feet and peeling the shredded jacket from my shoulder once I was steady. "I-it bit me," I told him while he ripped the collar and sleeve of my shirt open so he could get a better view of my bloodied shoulder. "God, that thing was strong."

"Sweetheart, this doesn't look good." I craned my neck to look at my shoulder as David pulled out his flashlight and inspected the damage. It looked horrible: the skin broken and torn where the wolf's teeth sank in, and blood flowing from several deep and jagged lacerations. "Maybe we should go to the emergency room," he suggested, looking at me worriedly and cradling my face. "It looks like you'll probably need stitches...and a rabies shot might not be a bad idea while we're there."

Going to the doctor was the last thing on my mind, knowing that we had a homicide to investigate, and the only reason I followed David back to the car was because I knew I wouldn't be any good to anyone if an infection set in or I started foaming at the mouth.

On our way, some of our coworkers asked what happened, and David quickly filled them in before telling O'Malley to call Animal Control to have the park combed thoroughly for the wolf that bit me.

"What the hell happened back there?" David asked as we pulled out onto a main street. "Did you see anyone?"

I shook my head and looked down at my shredded shoulder again, wincing when the car flew over a pothole and my arm bumped the seat roughly. "Nope. Just that damn wolf." Lifting my head, I caught David's concerned gaze. "H-how about you? Anything?"

He shook his head, frustrated. "Nothing." There was a brief pause as David changed lanes and turned right. "Did you get a good look at the body?" he asked, changing the subject. It was pretty obvious that he was trying to keep my mind on something besides my injury.

"Can't say that I did." I thought back to the few minutes I had with the victim before I went off and got attacked by a wild animal, suddenly remembering something. "There was a mark on her neck and shoulder — trauma of some sort — but I got distracted before I could really look at it."

"I'm sure the coroner will record it, and we can look over the report tomorrow morning."

By the time we pulled up to the emergency room doors of Osborn Medical Centre, the pain had gone from a dull throb to feeling like a hot poker was being dragged down each and every tear slowly. Flames shot through my veins like lava, and it took everything in me to not give in to the pain and pass out.

After throwing the car into park, David rushed around, opened my door, and helped me out of my seat, wrapping a protective arm around my waist to guide me through the entrance.

The waiting room was full, which wasn't surprising, nor was it a good sign that I'd be fortunate enough to be seen right away. We walked toward the admissions desk, and David filled the woman in on why we were there. She gave us some paperwork to fill out and asked us to have a seat in the waiting room — as if that was going to somehow make me more comfortable as the flames of hell lapped at my shoulder and traveled down my arm. After easing me into a seat, David sat next to me and offered to fill everything out.

Once my information had been documented, David took it back to the front and rejoined me, taking my hand in his and lacing our fingers before raising them to kiss my knuckles softly. "How are you doing?"

"It feels like my shoulder is on fire," I whispered honestly. "It's not constant, though, so I guess that has to count for something."

"We'll be in soon," he tried to assure me.

As the minutes ticked by, I watched as several of the other people were called in. We'd been waiting just under an hour before my name was called, and David insisted on coming with me. I didn't try to dispute it, because the truth of the matter was that the idea of getting stitches made me more than a little nauseous.

Once inside the bright, sterile room, David and the nurse helped me out of my jacket, and I fought back several curse words when the nurse took to peeling the fabric of my ruined shirt from my skin. The doctor joined us a few minutes later and inspected the area thoroughly.

Dr. Calvin was an older gentleman with graying hair and kind brown eyes hidden behind stylish glasses. Upon first impressions, he seemed like someone I could feel at ease with. "So what happened here?" he asked, touching my shoulder gently.

"I was attacked by a wolf in Chaparral Park," I replied through clenched teeth as he cleaned the area with antiseptic. It stung like a bitch, but I knew it had to be done, so all I could do was squeeze the ever-living hell out of David's poor hand until it was over.

The doctor worked quickly, and before I knew it, I was being released with a shot of morphine, twenty-three stitches, a rabies shot, and a prescription for both an antibiotic and a mild painkiller. After thanking the doctor, David and I headed over to the pharmacy to fill my prescriptions. Even though my mind was still pretty foggy from the morphine, I wanted to stay ahead of the pain, so I opened the painkillers the minute we were in the car and took one.

By the time we reached my house, the pill had kicked in. I had always had a pretty low tolerance for drugs and alcohol, so it wasn't surprising when everything started to feel a little hazy, and David had to help me up the front steps and down the hall to my room. Always wanting to take care of me, he settled me onto the bed before heading for my dresser, and I groggily watched him go through my drawers for a fresh shirt to sleep in. When he found a tank top and some flannel shorts, he helped me into them and kissed my forehead softly.

"Can I get you anything?" he asked quietly. "Are you hungry?"

"Mmm mmm," I hummed, shaking my head. "I'm a li'l sleepy."

Chuckling, David pulled the comforter back and ushered me beneath it. "Okay, you lie back, and I'll go grab you a glass of water in case you get thirsty."

I wasn't sure if it was because of the attack, or because my state of mind had been altered from the painkillers, but a sense of panic rose from my belly and clenched in my chest. I didn't know what brought it on; all I knew was that I didn't want to be alone. Before he could leave the room, I reached out and snatched him by the wrist. "Wait." He turned around, his eyes moving from mine to my bandaged shoulder. "You'll stay with me, right?"

Smiling, David cradled my jaw in his free hand. "Sweetheart, I'm not going anywhere. I'm just going to the kitchen, and then I'm going to phone your parents to let them know you're okay." He paused to press his lips to mine lightly. "I'll be right back. I swear."

I nodded slowly and lowered myself into bed, pulling the warm comforter up beneath my chin. Closing my eyes, I allowed the fog in my head to take over until I found myself on the precipice of sleep, and the last thing I remembered was the bed dipping behind me and David pulling me into his warm embrace.

CHAPTER 5 | AWAKE

Her cold, dead eyes stared up at me, pleading with me to help her as I circled her body slowly, looking down on her broken form with intrigue. The pallor of her skin was whiter than white, and her long brown hair moved in the gentle breeze, small wisps flowing across her face and neck...

Her neck.

Something in the back of my mind flickered, but before it had a chance to ignite, the crisp wind picked up, bringing with it the refreshing scent of a rare rainstorm on the horizon, and I inhaled deeply.

Along with the elemental smells of water and earth, I picked up something entirely different... something not unlike that of death and decay. I tried to tell myself that it was just the body, but that didn't seem plausible since I could tell from just looking at her that she was nowhere near the decomp phase. The smell intensified even as the rain began to fall, and every hair on my body prickled, my instincts telling me to run. Without questioning the urge, my feet moved until I was running for cover in the woods.

The dirt was cold and wet against the pads of my feet, and I could smell the leaves on the trees and the cactus blooms as I darted past, around, and under.

Faster and faster, my legs moved, propelling me deeper and deeper into the forest. Trees whipped by at an alarming rate as I raced along the rugged path left by hikers and animals, and the wind blew through my hair.

Everything seemed a little sharper to look at, and I could hear absolutely everything around me — the birds in the trees, the worms in the earth — but it was the low growl ahead of me that forced me to stop in my tracks. The deep, rumbling sound grew louder until everything else cancelled out entirely, and a pair of glowing yellow eyes appeared in the shadow of the brush before me.

The urge to run disappeared as the brown wolf stalked toward me and the lingering smell of death dissipated. Uncertain, I remained in place and assessed the situation. I didn't *feel* threatened by the animal, but I was definitely intrigued by it, looking over his thick coat as it gleamed in the moonlight and admiring the grace in his gait. He was beautiful, and I felt a kindred connection between the two of us that I couldn't quite explain.

Smiling, I held out a hand and crouched down to the wolf's level, my instincts telling me that I wasn't in any danger. The animal stopped walking, eyeing my hand curiously, but when his beautiful yellow eyes locked on mine and narrowed, his ears flattening against his head, I inhaled sharply, realizing my error.

And then it leapt for me, its jaws open wide, and its long, sharp teeth gleaming in the moonlight.

I jolted awake, sweat on my brow and the images of my dream already beginning to fade as the burn in my shoulder grew hotter. Not everything from my dream was forgotten, though; I still remembered the wolf lunging for me, and it stirred up memories of the night before. Some of the events were hazy, at best—which was probably thanks, in large part, to the pain medication I had taken—but I remembered David and me arriving at Chaparral Park, the woman, the wolf...

Pain pulsed in my shoulder again, spreading the fire further down my arm as I recalled the strong jaws of the wild animal sinking into my flesh, burying so deep they grazed the bone before I kicked it off of me and shots were fired. The trip to the ER and everything after that was a little fuzzy, but I could recall bits and pieces of it.

When the pain was too much to ignore, I carefully pushed myself up on the bed, being sure to move slowly so I didn't pull any stitches or disturb David, who still slept soundly behind me. Walking on my tiptoes, I walked down the hall to my bathroom so I could attempt to look at my shoulder to rule out an infection. The medical tape was difficult to peel back without tugging a little on my wound, but I managed to release the top strip and pull the bandage down to inspect it. The reddened area around the stitches was slightly swollen, and even the gentlest touch sent white-hot pain shooting down my arm and torso.

"That looks awful," David said from the doorway, startling me.

I had been so focused on my shoulder that I didn't see him appear in the reflection of the mirror. He stepped into the bathroom in nothing more than his flannel pants, but before he could get a closer look, I quickly pulled the bandage back up and turned to face him. "It's fine." He arched a brow, silently calling my bluff, and I rolled my eyes while pulling the bandage away again. "Okay, it'll *be* fine," I amended.

His fingers were cold against my feverish skin, and I tried not to recoil from his touch when another stab of pain moved down my arm quickly, making my fingers tingle and seize. "We should try to clean it, but if it doesn't look any better by the end of the day, I want to take you back to the hospital."

While I understood his concern, I really thought he was worrying over nothing. "David, I was attacked by a wild dog less than thirteen hours ago," I reminded him with a smile I hoped wasn't coming across as forced as it felt. "We have to give it time to heal."

"But—"

Shaking my head, I refused to let him finish. "Look, if it's still bothering me or looks *worse* than this, then I'll go to the hospital without a fight." This appeased him for the moment, so I continued. "But other than a little pain, I'm fine. I promise." He nodded but still didn't seem convinced. "Look, it probably just needs to be cleaned. Why don't you go put a pot of coffee on, and I'll be out in a minute."

"Do you need a hand with the back of your shoulder?"

I considered his offer for a second before deciding I couldn't risk letting him know it hurt more than I was letting on. "I don't think so, but if I change my mind, I'll come get you, okay?"

Seeming somewhat uncertain if he should take me at my word, David remained in the bathroom for a moment before conceding and heading to the kitchen. After closing the bathroom door, I removed both bandages entirely and set to work cleaning my shoulder. Turning the faucet on, I waited until the water ran warm, and then I soaked a washcloth and gently cleaned the area around my stitches. The pain in some areas was almost blinding, and I had to bite my bottom lip to keep from whimpering too loudly and alarming David.

With my wound clean, I applied a new bandage to the front of my shoulder, but had trouble with the back, so I opened the door and called for David. In a flash, he was at my side, a fresh cup of coffee in his hand for me.

"What's up?"

I took a small sip of the rich brew, smiling when I tasted the copious amounts of sugar he'd added, and then set the cup down on the vanity. "I can't get the bandage on the back. Would you mind giving me a hand?"

Smiling, he slowly turned me around and reached for the pre-taped patch of gauze. "Not at all, sweetheart." Once the bandage was in place, he leaned forward and pressed a soft kiss to the un-marred skin of my neck, sending a shiver of desire through me. "There you go."

With my shoulder all patched up, I finished getting ready for work. Once my hair and teeth were brushed, I picked up my coffee and headed to my bedroom to find something to wear.

The minute I pulled on a button-up blouse, the constricting fabric rubbed against my bandages and exacerbated the throb in my shoulder. I took the blouse off, trading it for a sage green ribbed tank top that wouldn't tug on my bandages; it wasn't the most professional attire for a detective, but I was pretty sure the captain wouldn't mind under the circumstances.

"What are you doing?" David asked from the door of my closet as I fastened my belt.

Turning around, I arched an eyebrow. "Um, getting ready for work?"

"Brooke, you were attacked last night and wound up in the ER." He paused, stepping closer to me and looking a little nervous. "Don't you think you should stay home and rest?"

Shaking my head, I pulled on a pair of jeans and buttoned them up. "Can't," I replied. "Not with this new case." My shoulder throbbed again, and something in the back of my mind nagged at me. I wasn't entirely sure what it was, but I knew it had to do with this case, and I *craved* answers. David looked like he was about to call my father so they could devise a way to keep me from the office, so I decided to just be honest about why I couldn't stay home. "It's just…there's something about this case that's not right, and I don't think I'll be able to think about anything else, anyway."

Thankfully, David empathized with this, knowing that he would have reacted the same way if something didn't sit right with him, and he nodded. "Then I guess I'll go start breakfast while you finish up in here," he said, kissing me softly and exiting the room.

As soon as I was dressed, I grabbed my gun and badge from atop my dresser and affixed them to my belt before slipping on the silver crucifix that Bobby gave me on our eighteenth birthday. The pendant rested against my sternum, and a warm and tingly sensation spread beneath my skin, but I passed it off as nothing more than some kind of transference from my shoulder.

Breakfast smelled amazing as I made my way toward the kitchen, and I found David standing in front of the stove, cooking French toast—my favorite. Sliding my hand down the muscular length of his back, I pressed a kiss to his bare shoulder and wound my good arm around his waist. "Smells yummy."

Chuckling softly, he turned his head and kissed

my temple while I scratched an itch on my chest. "Thanks. You mind watching it while I go get ready?"

"Not at all," I agreed, taking the spatula from him.

David wasn't gone long, returning with the glass of water from my nightstand and my two prescriptions. He dumped the water and refilled the glass before handing it and the pill bottles to me. "Here, you should take these before we go."

"Thanks." I took the bottles and collected one of each pill in my palm, swallowing them both with a gulp of cold water from the glass. When I set the glass back on the counter, I caught David staring at me quizzically, his eyes on my chest. I was about to chastise him for being a pervert when his eyebrows pulled together and he lifted my pendant.

Cool air hit my skin, offering me instant relief from that incessant itch, and when I looked down, I saw the source of David's concern: a three- to four-inch red and splotchy rash surrounding a dark red cross shape on my chest.

"Huh," I said, touching my hand to the rash gently. It tingled and was warm to the touch. "I've never had this happen with this necklace before. Must be an allergy." I removed the necklace, taking it back to my room. My palm tickled as I held it, and I put it back in my jewelry box before heading back to the kitchen to find breakfast already on the table.

As expected, breakfast was delicious, and I ate quickly—almost ravenously. It was unlike me, but I was absolutely famished. So hungry, in fact, that I inhaled four pieces, shocking even David.

Somewhat embarrassed by this, I offered David an apologetic smile. "I guess skipping dinner last night was a bad idea," I joked.

He laughed, and I was instantly relieved. "Clearly." Eyeing my empty plate, he nodded toward the stove. "Do you want me to make more? We have a bit of time."

Feeling sated for the moment, my belly full and content, I shook my head. "No thanks. I think I'll be okay until lunch."

Working together, we cleaned the kitchen, and then David grabbed the keys to my car and helped me into my other leather jacket. It felt off to me, but only because I didn't wear it as often as I did the other, so it wasn't as worn in and soft. Since the other was shredded, though, this one would have to do.

When we walked into the precinct, all eyes were on us, and it was clear they'd all heard about what happened in Chaparral last night. I assured everyone that I was fine as we made our way to our desks, and I slipped my jacket off and hung it on the back of my chair to give my shoulder a little more air and mobility. The painkillers had kicked in, so it felt a lot better, which would make it much easier to concentrate on our case.

"So, you guys have finally come out of the closet, huh?" O'Malley's voice carried as he flopped down in David's chair and slapped a folder down on the desk across from me. "It's about damn time."

My eyes scanned the office to see several others were watching and smiling, their expressions proof enough that David and I had done a horrible job hiding our relationship all this time. "How long has everybody known?"

"Please," O'Malley scoffed. "You work with a bunch of detectives…investigating is what we *do*."

"No," I said with a laugh, circling around my desk toward O'Malley. "Investigating is what *we* do." I pointed at everyone in the room *but* him, teasing. "I still haven't quite figured out what it is *you* do, Patrick."

Howling with laughter, O'Malley stood. "Good to see your little injury hasn't affected your natural charm, Brooke," he teased, patting my good arm firmly before heading back to his own desk.

David picked up the file O'Malley left and leafed through it. I naturally assumed it had the coroner's report for last night's victim, and just as I rounded the desk to take a look, a loud voice cut through the room.

"What are you doing here?" my dad demanded. He stopped next to my desk, concern etched into every line in his forehead and around his eyes. "You should be at home." He turned to David. "She should be at home."

"I'm fine, sir," I assured him.

He looked around the office again, and everyone who had dropped what they were doing to watch us quickly returned to work. "You have a habit of saying that...even when it's not entirely true."

He wasn't wrong, and I could plainly see that his worry was that of a parent whose only living child was hurt while working a case. While I was alive, and would probably have several sizable scars to show for it, I knew this could have turned out so much worse.

Before David could tell him that his own attempt to keep me home was futile, I spoke, keeping my tone soft and apologetic. "I know, but I couldn't stay home. I would have driven myself crazy thinking about this case. If I start to feel off, I'll go home, okay?"

Nodding, Dad agreed to my terms. "Fine." Turning to David, he pointed a finger at him, his eyes narrowing sternly. "Samuels, I'm trusting you to keep a close eye on her."

"Of course, sir. I'll make sure she's not overdoing

it."

After Dad retreated into his office, I perched my-self on the edge of David's desk and looked down at the file in his lap, arching an eyebrow inquiringly. "Whatcha got there?"

David looked down at the manila folder and ex-haled loudly, raking his fingers through his short hair. "The coroner's report for our vic," he informed me, holding the file out.

"Cause of death?" I asked, opening the folder and quickly reviewing the crime scene photos and what little information the coroner's office reported. I read through the report and found the answer to my question before David could reply.

Either he missed the distress on my face as I read the word over and over again, or he said it in hopes of pulling me out of my stupor. "Exsanguination." His tone was solemn, and even though I already knew this, my stomach churned when I heard it out loud.

Slowly, my eyes rose from the file, meeting his. It wasn't hard to see how worried he was about how I might handle this, and he had every right to be; I'd only ever heard of a few other cases like this, and they were so long ago that only a few select cops would even remember them this vividly...them and my fam-ily, anyway. "Th-they're sure?"

David nodded once, his eyes full of remorse. "The lack of blood leads them to believe so, yes."

I was slipping fast, my head spinning with this new revelation. Taking a deep breath, I composed myself and dropped my voice to just above a whisper as I leaned in to address him privately. "Has my fa-ther seen this?"

"I'm honestly not sure," he told me. "The file just got dropped off, so if he has, he hasn't connected the dots yet."

"Then he hasn't." I stood up and took the file to the captain's office, David hot on my trail, and knocked rapidly.

"Come in," he bellowed through the door, and I pushed it open. "What can I help you with, Detectives?"

"Have you seen this?" I dropped the open file on his desk, startling him and forcing his gaze away from his computer screen.

"Only briefly," he replied, picking it up and looking at it a little more closely.

"Briefly?" I was on the verge of losing my composure again. "You get a case where the cause of death is exsanguination, and you only glance at it?" That got his attention. I really tried to remain professional, but that line was blurred the minute this case mirrored my brother's and a rash of murders just like it from almost a decade ago. "Tell me I'm seeing things. Tell me this isn't happening again," I pleaded, my voice shaking slightly.

"I-I didn't realize..." He read the report, and I Recognized the minute he came to the same stark realization as both David and I had. His eyes widened and his jaw dropped slightly. "I'll...uh..." He struggled to form a sentence as his eyes remained glued on the file. "I'll put somebody else on this. Immediately."

"No." Firm in my conviction, I leaned on the front of his desk and pressed my index finger onto the file. "I want this one. *I'm* going to solve it. If this is the same sick freak that took Bobby, you better believe I want to take him down. Personally."

"Brooke," David whispered from the doorway behind me, and I turned around sharply. "Maybe he's right. I think you'd be too emotionally involved in the case if it turns out to be the same guy."

"I'm not emotionally involved," I corrected him.

"I'm *invested*."

"Regardless, I don't think it's a good idea," David said, his tone a little more firm. "You were just promoted. Is this really the case you want to start your career with?"

I looked at him point-blank. "Yes."

David and my dad exchanged a look. I could tell that David really wanted it assigned to someone else, but with a resigned sigh, Dad gave the final order to keep us on it. "Fine. But the minute I see that this case is becoming too much for you, you're off it, do you understand me? I won't have you fall back to where you were seven years ago, Brooke."

Before he could take it back, I nodded, snatching the file from him. "I understand. Thank you." As I turned to walk away, a photo slipped from inside and fluttered to the floor. Kneeling, I picked up the picture, but when my eyes focused on the close-up image of the victim's neck, I inhaled sharply, my entire body freezing as it triggered a long-forgotten memory. There, at the apex of this woman's neck and shoulder, was a strange laceration, and the longer I stared at it, the more I realized it wasn't the first time I'd seen something like this.

Bobby.

"Brooke?" David asked. His voice sounded distant as I was thrust back to the night I found Bobby in that alley seven years ago. I felt his weak pulse against my palm again, his blood pumping from a wound on his neck—a wound very similar to the one in the photograph—as his heartbeat slowed and eventually stopped.

Lost in the memory of that night, my lungs burned hot with every breath I took, and it was growing more and more difficult to breathe the longer I stared at this picture. The room felt like it was getting smaller, the panic in my chest tightened as my vision started to darken around the edges, and my ears rang. When my knees trembled and threatened to buckle, I reached out, dropping the folder and all its contents, and grabbed the front of David's jacket to hold me upright. His reflexes were quick, and he grabbed me around the waist.

"Whoa! Easy," he soothed, steadying me.

"I don't..." My tongue was numb, and my skin prickled with an icy sweat as I clung to him, my shoulder throbbing harder and burning hotter than before. "I don't feel so good."

"Okay," he whispered, picking me up in his arms and carrying me quickly through the office and outside. "I'm taking you to the hospital."

My vision faded in and out, and I fought the urge to pass out. David tried to talk to me, telling me to stay with him. I tried — I did — but I went limp in his arms, my limbs heavy, like they were filled with lead. David carried me with ease from the precinct and toward the car despite this, making me feel somewhat weightless, too.

The last thing I remembered before I lost consciousness was David shouting my name.

CHAPTER 6 | OBSERVATION

The entire world slipped away whenever I was in his arms. I always felt so safe and secure with him around, and he'd proven himself to be there for me on more than one occasion. I foresaw a long, happy future together, even if we were both still so young. He was all I could see when I looked into the future...which was why I'd accepted his marriage proposal three days ago. He was the love of my life, and he had proven time and time again that I was his.

Of course, I never expected this feeling to dissipate as quickly as it did at the first sign of tragedy.

"Hey, where did your brother go?"

I searched the darkness for a glimpse of Bobby's bronze-colored hair or even the sweater he changed into before we left the dorm, but couldn't find him. I didn't understand. He was *right there* a second ago...talking to some blonde chick. I'd only looked away for a minute — if that. Panic rose in my chest, bile churning in my stomach as I feared the worst...no, not just *feared* the worst; I could sense that something was wrong.

"I...I don't know." Detached from everything but the feeling that something was terribly wrong, I pulled out of Nick's arms and walked toward the table. My hands shook as I pushed through the crowd and headed back to the last place I saw my brother, but he wasn't there. His beer hadn't even been touched, and there was no sign of him here at all. Not his jacket, not his keys, nothing.

The tremble in my hands spread to my entire body, and my heart raced. Something wasn't right; I knew this. I took one more look around the club, hoping that maybe I'd spot—or even sense—him, but I came up empty once more.

"Babe?" Nick was as concerned as I was, and I grew more and more frantic by the second. My chin quivered, my hands gripping the hair at my temples tightly, and tears burned my eyes. "Maybe he stepped outside," Nick said behind me, trying to calm me down, but I shook the thought off before letting it sink in.

"No," I disagreed. "He would have said something. He'd have come to tell us if that's what he was doing."

"He's twenty-one, Brooke," Nick argued, but I was already headed for the door when something unseen and unexplainable drew me in that direction. "Brooke?"

The crowd was too thick, and I struggled to get through; it was like they were unwilling to let me pass—trying to keep me inside. Eventually, I gave up and scanned the bar for an alternate exit. When I found an emergency door, I rushed toward it, not stopping for anyone who tried to get in my way. I threw the door open, stepping into the back alley so quickly that when I stopped abruptly, Nick almost bowled me over. The tingle that still covered my entire body intensified until all the tiny hairs on my body stood on end. I was close. I knew it—*felt* it.

Trusting my gut, I turned and ran in the direction

I thought I sensed him, skidding to a stop at the mouth of the alley when the feeling faded. I looked out into the street, desperate for even a glimpse of him — anything to indicate he was okay. There were too many cars, though, and so many people that I found it hard to make out anyone's face.

Then I felt it: that sharp tingle shooting up my spine until I turned back toward the alley.

He's there.

I turned slowly, my eyes falling to the darkened alley floor where a slumped shape was hidden in the shadows a few feet in. A passing car's headlights illuminated the still figure, and I gasped, recognizing the shirt and his hair in an instant. Everything else left my mind, my thoughts only on Bobby, as I bolted down the alley, falling to my bare knees at his side.

The pain from the cuts and scrapes of sliding over the pavement was nothing compared to the fear I experienced when pulling Bobby's limp body into my arms. His green eyes were wide — terrified — and completely void of life. And his skin — *oh, god* — his skin was so cold and pale...almost as though his life had been drained from him.

"Help! Somebody, help me! Please!" I screamed, the tears I'd been able to hold back now flowing freely down my cheeks. I sobbed, my lungs burning as I tried to gulp in a breath of air, and loud footsteps approached hard and fast behind me.

"Oh, dear god," Nick gasped, and while he stood right next to me, I couldn't stop looking at Bobby as I attempted to shake him awake.

I screamed again, crying out his name as I shook him harder, causing his head to roll lifelessly to the right. There, illuminated by the light of the full moon, were two perfectly round puncture wounds with a thin trickle of blood seeping from each of them.

Bright white light blinded me as I forced my eyes open. I tried to bring my right arm up to shield my eyes, but an uncomfortable tug in the top of my hand stopped me. It pinched and it stung. Groaning, I opened my eyes a little more to let them adjust to my surroundings. I was in a room I didn't recognize, and a high-pitched beeping drew my attention to the monitors next to the bed I occupied. As my vision cleared, I followed the leads hooked into the machines down to my arm and realized the tugging was from an IV catheter that violated the back of my hand. It itched again, and I wanted it out.

"Hey, you're awake," a rough voice said to my left, and when I looked toward it, I found a worse-for-wear David lifting his head from my bed. His left hand was wrapped firmly around mine while the other reached for the call button. He pushed it several times. There was a commotion in the hall before two nurses bustled in and started fussing over me.

"Wh-what happened?" My voice sounded hoarse — even to me — and I tried clearing my throat. It didn't help; it only hurt more.

David's brow furrowed, and he ran his free hand down over his weary and unshaven face; I had never seen him look this frazzled…this worried. "You don't remember?"

One of the nurses lifted the hand with the IV in it and checked my pulse — regardless of the fact that I was hooked up to one of those heart monitors. It was weird and I admit, I questioned the reason behind it. My head throbbed, and I let my eyes wander around the room, taking in the institutional white of the walls and the generic artwork that adorned them. I was in a private room—swanky—and one look out the window indicated that I was back at Osborn. The nurses finished checking my vitals before assuring both David and me that the doctor would be in momentarily, and then they left us alone.

Slowly, bits and pieces fell into place as I remembered the events that led me here. "We were at work—looking over that case, and then I passed out." There was more...*I think*...but it was really vague, and I couldn't be sure it wasn't part of a dream while I was out. "I remember feeling like I was floating through the air, and then the smell of leather before a high-pitched wailing filled my head..." *Sirens...they were sirens*, I realized. As the memory played out, I remembered that my eyes opened briefly to see David behind the wheel of my car and racing through the streets. His voice was soft and soothing, but there was also a note of panic that laced it; even my muddled brain picked up on that.

"That's the gist of it." Hearing his voice so low and full of worry caused my stomach to clench; I hated that I put him through this.

My eyebrows pulled together in shame, and I glanced at him as he looked down at our hands, his thumb moving back and forth over my skin.

"You picked up a picture that fell out of our case file, and then you went blank. You stared at it for a few minutes and whispered your brother's name... Do you remember that?" As he told me this, I definitely recalled it happening, and the horrific image of the woman's neck came crashing back to me.

"You've been out for two days," he concluded before I could say anything about the picture, my focus snapping back to him like a rubber band.

"W-what?"

He nodded sadly. "You scared the hell out of me, Brooke."

"I don't understand," I rasped, trying to wrap my head around why I would remain unconscious for so long with no real trauma. Realization slammed down on me, weighing heavy and causing my stomach to churn, and I squeezed David's hand. "The bite... Was it some kind of infection?"

David's expression transformed to one of relief and bewilderment. "No, actually. When I mentioned your attack to the doctor, that's the first thing she checked out. She seemed to think you could have contracted something, but when she took your bandages off, the wounds were already healing. She was shocked when I told her you were only stitched up the night before and how inflamed it was the next morning."

It wasn't that I didn't believe him, but I needed to see this for myself. I tore the left shoulder of my hideous hospital gown down and looked at the bright pink and healing skin that was so inflamed and angry-looking the last time I saw it. There was still some healing to go, but the jagged slashes from the wolf's teeth had closed and the stitches were removed.

I delicately traced my fingers over it, noticing that even the suture marks had faded significantly. "How...?"

I didn't have to look at him to know he was smiling; I heard it in his voice. "I have no idea. I guess it wasn't nearly as bad as we thought it was," David offered, bringing my hand to his lips. "God, Brooke, I'm so glad you're okay." He peppered kisses up the length of my arm, standing up and cradling my face in his hands. His eyes were red from sleep deprivation, and they held my gaze as he rested his forehead against mine. "I was so worried."

I tried to nod; it was difficult given his hand placement, but I was able to tilt my face upward and press my lips to his gently. "I know," I murmured against them, "and I'm sorry."

A throat cleared from the doorway, forcing David to take a step back, dropping his hands to mine again. For a brief moment, I panicked when I saw my father in the doorway. Still getting used to the idea of others knowing about our relationship, it took a second to register the stolen moment of intimacy we shared as *okay*.

I shifted in my bed, sitting upright. "Hey, Dad," I greeted sheepishly, and he exhaled a sigh of relief. Nodding, I tried my hand at a bit of humor. "Yeah, I'm getting that a lot."

It was weak, but he laughed and stepped into the room, setting the flowers he brought with him on the little table beside my bed. "It's not funny."

"Then why are you laughing?" I said, jabbing him in the shoulder lightly with my free hand; David had yet to relinquish his hold on the other — not that I could blame him, really.

"I'm just glad to see you're awake," Dad told me. "Your mother will be thrilled to hear it."

"Is she here?" I asked, anxiously looking around him and expecting to see her in the doorway.

Dad craned his neck, following my gaze. "She just went to grab coffee. We didn't think you'd be awake."

My eyebrows knit together apologetically as I took in his haggard appearance. "Not sleeping well, huh?" The inflection in my voice made it sound like a question, but it was obvious from the dark circles under his bloodshot eyes that this was exactly the case.

"Yeah, those waiting room chairs aren't exactly the most comfortable things to sleep on."

Beside me, David laughed. "Don't worry, sir, I didn't fare much better in here."

Hearing David allude to having stayed by my side these past two days shocked me, and my eyes snapped to his. "You were here the entire time?"

"Where else would I be?" he asked with a smile, bringing a hand up to gently cup my face. "I couldn't go home and leave you here to wake up alone."

Tears burned my eyes; I blamed the drugs being pumped into my system for the lack of control over my emotions as they trailed down my cheeks. I brushed them away, but they only worsened the minute my mother walked into the room and rushed to my side, thrusting two cups of hospital coffee into my father's waiting hands.

"Oh, Brooke," she wailed into my shoulder, her hold almost constricting. "When you're father told me what happened, I was so worried."

I pulled my hand from David's and wrapped both arms around her, holding her as firmly as possible in hopes to assure her that I was going to be fine. "I'm sorry. I didn't mean to scare you. Honestly, I don't even know what happened."

An unfamiliar female voice jarred me from the tender moment shared with my mom, and my eyes were pulled to a woman in a long white coat who stood by the door. "Usually during a traumatic event—like your animal attack the other night—our bodies run on a surge of adrenaline until we know we're safe," the woman—my doctor, presumably—explained as she stepped into the room and grabbed the chart from the foot of my bed. "Now, following the impulse to survive, there's a natural instinct to discharge any additional adrenaline from our systems...in the case of wild animals escaping a predator, their bodies will tremble or jump around until the residual adrenaline has been expelled from the body. In your case, your brain overrode the instinct to discharge this extra energy in order for you to think clearly enough to get to the hospital. From there, you were medicated, essentially interrupting the natural order of things and locking the adrenaline in your body.

"Everybody expels the energy a little differently once the body and mind have relaxed following the initial incident, but in your case, you blacked out. It's quite common."

Looking up from the chart, the doctor smiled. "I'm Doctor Channing. It's good to see you're awake, Miss Leighton."

"Brooke," I corrected her, trying to process everything she just told me. "Does this mean I'm fine, then?" Looking around the room, I saw that both David and my parents were watching Doctor Channing hopefully.

"You will be," she replied with a curt nod before looking back down at the chart, her eyebrows furrowing with concentration. "Based on your vitals, I'd like to keep you at least one more night. Your temperature is a little high still, and I'd like to rule out any infections that might be causing it."

I decided not to argue with the medical professional, so I nodded. "Okay. Yeah."

The room fell silent, and then I heard David chuckle. "Wow, I think that's the first time I've heard you agree so willingly to someone telling you what to do."

I shrugged, unable to think of anything else to say; while I didn't particularly *want* to stay in the hospital, I wasn't about to go against the recommendations of my doctor — not to her face, anyway.

"Well, I'll leave you to rest," Doctor Channing

announced, flipping the chart closed and returning it to the foot of my bed. "Be sure to call for the nurses if you need anything, and I'll be back to check on you a little later."

"Perfect," I responded. "Thanks so much, Doctor."

The minute the doctor vacated the room, Mom pressed her hand to my forehead, and her own creased with worry. "She's right. You're burning up."

"Am I?" I asked, bringing my fingers to my cheek. "I actually feel fine." Skeptical eyes met mine, and I laughed lightly. "No, really. I feel pretty good...all things considered."

While I understood my parents' and David's uncertainty, I really did feel fine—other than a slight headache, that is. It was possible that I was just being pumped full of painkillers, and that was the reason for my lack of symptoms, but I felt pretty confident I'd be experiencing some kind of residual haze if that were the case. And, truthfully, I'd never felt more clear-headed as the foggy details of the other day started to unfurl again.

"Brooke," my dad interjected, almost as though he could read my mind. "If this is about work—"

"What?" I asked, trying to appear incredulous. Naturally, he didn't buy it—not entirely, anyway.

Instead of reprimanding me, Dad smiled. "Listen, Brookie." I rolled my eyes at the use of my nickname in front of David—who didn't try very hard to suppress an amused chuckle. "I want you to take the next few days off. Samuels can handle your caseload until you're well enough to come back."

Feeling the need to assure him once again that I would be fine, I opened my mouth to protest, but David stopped me. "He's right. A lot has happened in the last few days, and you're clearly overwhelmed."

Deep down, I knew they were right, but I couldn't stop thinking about the similarities to the slew of unsolved investigations from 2007. The last thing I wanted to do was put them through anything like this again, so I decided that now was not the time to discuss anything regarding the case. "You're right. I'm sorry."

Dad shook his head. "Don't be. I love that you're so dedicated — it's why you got promoted, but, speaking as your father and not your captain, I need you to take care of yourself."

"Got it," I affirmed with a nod. "No work. Can I make one small request, though?" The look that Dad and David gave me was almost identical, and I smiled innocently. "I'm starving. Any chance I can get someone to run out and grab me a burger or something?"

With a nod, David smiled. "Of course. I'll go."

Dad stood up and clamped a hand down on David's shoulder. "I'll join you, Samuels. I think we should give the ladies a chance to talk in private."

"A double, please!" I called out before they disappeared.

Dad and David had barely left the room before my mom ran her fingers down the length of my hair, smoothing it, and smiled. It should have been obvious when Dad offered to go with David what it was my mom wanted to talk about; the look in her eyes spoke volumes. I fidgeted nervously with my bedsheet, waiting for her to begin her interrogation.

"So, we haven't really talked much since the night of your party." A pause from her. A nod from me. "You and David, huh?"

She launched into her questions, and I did my best to answer them, but low voices in the hall distracted me. It was a conversation I probably wasn't meant to hear, which was why they waited to leave the room before having it.

"You know she's going to find out eventually, don't you?" David said, sounding so clear it was like he was still in the room. I heard the elevator doors open, which blew my mind, because it was all the way down the hall.

How is that possible?

Dad sighed. "I know, but if we tell her now, she won't rest and she'll demand to come back to work as soon as she's released, and I don't think she's well enough."

"And how do you expect her to keep from reading about it in the paper...or flipping through the TV channels and finding one of the many news reports?" A brief moment of silence fell between them, and then the doors closed, muffling their voices slightly, but not completely. "It's not going to be easy to keep three more murders from her."

And then their voices disappeared from my head, leaving me stunned.

Three more murders in the two days I'd been unconscious. This wasn't good.

CHAPTER 7 | RAVENOUS

I was forced to stay in the hospital for another day and a half. It wasn't so bad, really—except for the feeling like a caged animal part. They let me walk the halls, and David was able to bring me some actual clothes so I didn't feel like a patient under constant monitoring, even though that's exactly what I was.

I understood it—I did—but that didn't mean I liked it.

The nurses and my doctor were concerned that my temperature was still too high, but it had apparently leveled out just above 101 F. I assured them that I was feeling fine—great, even—and would just prefer to go home. They were reluctant to agree at first, but as soon as I was able to convince David that I'd be more comfortable at home, he charmed them into helping me break the hell out of there. They discharged me shortly after noon, armed with instructions to pick up some ibuprofen and to drink plenty of water to help bring my temperature back down should it spike up over 104 again.

"I'll be staying at your place," David informed me, opening the passenger side door of his black Challenger. He must have expected me to protest, because he was quick to cite his reasoning. "In case you need anything."

With a laugh, I looked up at him somewhat coyly. "You don't need to make excuses. I would love it if you stayed…even if it is *just* to take care of me."

Smirking, David bent over and placed his hand on my jaw, his thumb moving softly over my cheek. "Maybe my motives are partially selfish, as well," he whispered, leaning forward and pressing his lips to mine.

I was certain the kiss was meant to be a quick and innocent peck on the lips, but desire quickly burned within me. My hands found their way into David's hair, pulling him closer and deepening the kiss. David's body was warm — even against my own rising temperature. Slowly, my hand moved down his neck, trailing along his carotid and feeling the pulse beneath the pads of my fingers. I took my time following it, every beat of his heart sending more blood through the artery. Why? I wasn't sure, exactly, but feeling the rhythmic beat of his blood moving through his body — sustaining his life — thrilled me in a way I couldn't describe. My entire body sparked to life, crackling and humming like a fallen live wire snapping against the cold, wet pavement. It awakened something inside me — something…ravenous — and I pulled him closer, using more strength than I thought possible. His pulse was so strong beneath my fingertips that I swore I could hear the steady thump of his blood moving through his veins, and warmth radiated through my entire body, my arms and legs tingling as I curled my fingers into his shirt and tugged.

I needed him closer.

Before I could get too carried away, David wrapped his hands around my upper arms and parted us. He struggled slightly against my reluctance to let him go, and his mouth curled up into a goofy grin against my lips.

I finally stepped back until I hit the car behind me, my mind whirling, and my skin still buzzing with excitement and need. "Sorry. I don't know what came over me."

David snickered, leaning into my body and pressing his forehead to mine. "Do you hear me complaining?" He paused, and I felt his forehead wrinkle against mine before he pulled back and placed the back of his hand to my cheek. "Shit. You're burning up again."

"Am I?" I felt both of my cheeks and then my forehead. I couldn't tell the difference, and I didn't *feel* feverish. Hot and bothered? Check.

"Maybe we should get you home to rest a bit more. Get some ibuprofen into you to help bring your temperature back down." David ushered me into the car and then ran around to his side and hopped behind the wheel.

Traffic on N Scottsdale Rd was backed up, which wasn't unusual at this time of day, so while we waited at an intersection for our light to change, I glanced over at David. "Have you been into the precinct at all? I mean, when you haven't been visiting me."

He nodded, easing into the intersection when the light turned green. "I went in yesterday and then again this morning before I came to pick you up. Why?"

It would be a lie if I said I hadn't thought about the investigation every day since I woke up in the hospital. The truth was I'd been dreaming about it, too, and it wasn't *just* the case; I dreamt about the night of Bobby's death a lot more than normal, too.

David was still unaware that I knew about the other three murders, but that didn't mean I hadn't been reading the paper or going online with my phone to find whatever information I could in the meantime. There didn't seem to be a particular victimology that the killer was following. The only similarity was the M.O. and that the victims were aged between twenty and twenty-five.

Timothy Dent was victim number two, murdered the day after Samantha Turner. His body had been reported well after I'd been admitted to the hospital. He was a twenty-one-year-old student at Scottsdale Community College with blond hair and brown eyes. He had good grades, stayed out of trouble, volunteered.

Why him?

Then, there was Sarah O'Dell, a twenty-five year-old dental assistant. Her blonde hair and blue eyes didn't lend anything to a possible pattern, so there was no way for her to avoid being chosen by this freak.

Lastly, Jason Smith fell victim to this monster. A brown-haired, blue-eyed tourist visiting from Houston, he had no connection to any of the previous victims, so his death couldn't have been prevented. His girlfriend reported him missing when he didn't come back to their hotel the day I woke up. Apparently she wasn't feeling well. Turned out she was about ten weeks pregnant—awesome—and he'd gone out to find her something to help with the nausea. But he never returned.

The only similarity they shared was the peculiar neck wound, but no one could tell what type of weapon was used or if it was the work of the same person.

But *I* knew. I could feel it. I'd never been so sure of anything in my entire life. I couldn't explain how I knew; it was just a feeling I got deep in my gut.

Another question I asked myself was: why now? Why disappear seven years ago and come back now? Was it some kind of ritual killing spree? Return to the scene of a past crime every so often and relive it by killing someone new to get your rocks off? I couldn't make sense of it...but, of course, I wasn't a psychopath.

"O'Malley's working the case," David informed me, almost as though he knew exactly what was on my mind.

"Oh?" I replied, feigning innocence. David laughed, seeing right through me, so I cut the act. "Any leads?"

David inhaled a deep breath and shook his head. "Nothing. He's found absolutely nothing." He was frustrated, and to be completely honest, so was I. Four murders and not one clue? It was unheard of.

Almost, anyway.

"How is that possible?" I asked. "Did they check the neck wound? They had to have found something in there. Traces of DNA? Something that could tell us what the murder weapon was? What about the other—"

I cut myself off, but it was too late; he knew I knew.

He sighed again, keeping his eyes trained on the road ahead of us. "I knew you'd find out. Your dad didn't want to alarm you."

"Fat load of good that did," I quipped.

"The answer is no. We haven't found any useful evidence on any of the bodies. Any time they think they've found something, they come up empty."

I dropped my eyes to my lap and laughed dryly. "Just like Bobby and the others."

My frustration mounted, and, as a result, a mild tremor traveled through my body. I couldn't understand how this was happening again after all this time, and I was scared that this was only going to unearth everything my family had done to move on with our lives. It wasn't easy, but we managed to get through most days.

"Brooke, we can't be certain that this is the same guy who killed your brother," David said softly, reaching over and taking my hand in his while he turned onto my street.

"Are you kidding?" I demanded. "They were drained of blood—they all were, right?—there's no way to tell what killed them... And what about that mark on their necks, David? They're the exact same as the one I found on Bobby's neck. That can't be a coincidence, can it? Tell me you don't believe that."

David was silent for a minute, and I waited for him to say something. I wanted to tell him to forget about going home and to take me to the precinct instead so I could look over the files. There were two problems with that idea though: one, David was driving and would never do it, and two, even if he did, my father would kibosh the whole thing before I took more than three steps toward my desk. No, I would have to be patient and wait another couple of days to return to work like my doctor said.

Of course, that's not to say that I couldn't have David bring me the files to look over; it wouldn't be the first time we brought our work home when we were so close to closing a case.

"We'll figure it out," David finally said, giving my hand a reassuring squeeze. "We always do."

"Not always," I mumbled, reminding him of the grim reality of our job. Thinking back on all of the cases that had gone unsolved over the years, an uneasy feeling stirred within my belly. Unable to handle this one getting away from me, especially when I was almost certain that the similarities to Bobby's murder weren't just a coincidence, I turned to David. "I know you want to believe that this isn't related to my brother's investigation, but can you at least try to entertain the idea? I mean, what if it is? What if you overlook it and it turns out I was right, and this guy gets away? Again."

Eyebrows furrowing in contemplation, David nodded slowly. "Okay," he conceded willingly. "We'll cross check the past and present files and chart the similarities, but you have to promise me that you won't let this case get to you if it turns out you were right." He turned to me, his eyes holding mine briefly before flitting back to the road. "Promise me that you'll stay professional and won't go off half-cocked if we narrow down a list of suspects. I get that you want to catch the guy responsible for your brother's death, but if we don't go by the book on this, Brooke, then we'll jeopardize the entire investigation."

A vision of me taking down a man twice my size raced through my mind several times. Each time was different. In some instances, I shot him; in others, I took him out with my bare hands, beating him until he was bloody and unrecognizable.

For some reason, I took pleasure in these...fantasies, and the corners of my lips quirked up. It wasn't until I caught a glimpse of myself in the passenger side mirror that I noticed the wicked gleam in my eyes, and I was instantly horrified about the morbid turn in my thoughts.

"What is it?" David asked, parking the car in my driveway and turning to me. "You got awfully quiet just now."

Sighing, I let my head fall back against the seat. "It's nothing," I lied. "I just don't know what to make of all this." There was so much going on in my head — everything from the last few days bouncing off of each other — that it was hard to focus on one thing specifically. My head was crowded and somewhat congested, like a headache was starting to make itself known.

Sensing my current state of discomfort, David opened his door and nodded toward the house. "Come on. Let's get you inside."

Agreeing, I opened my door and stepped out, meeting David around the front of the car. Once inside, David ushered me to the living room and sat me down, pulling the blanket off the back of the sofa and covering me with it. I wasn't cold, but the gesture was sweet, so I didn't say anything. He was just trying to take care of me after everything that happened.

"You hungry?" he asked, placing a tender kiss on top of my head.

Food wasn't really on the top of my priority list, but the second David mentioned it, my mouth watered. "Actually, yeah, now that you mention it."

"What are you in the mood for? I wasn't able to make it to the grocery store before you got released, so we don't have much."

I tried to pinpoint what it was I craved, but I couldn't; I was way too damn hungry. "Um, I don't know."

David headed to the kitchen, and I heard the fridge open. "Well," he bellowed, "we have apples, some leftover something-or-other that's probably no longer safe for human consumption, bread, bacon, eggs…"

My mouth watered again, and my hands trembled. "Bacon," I replied quickly, licking my lips. "I want bacon."

"Okay. And what else?" he inquired, poking his head around the corner. "I could make you a BLT?"

It didn't sound nearly as appealing as a plate full of bacon, but I knew I should have a somewhat balanced meal. "Sure." From my spot on the couch, I heard him set the frying pan on the stove, and I swore I smelled the raw bacon as he opened the package. It was ridiculous, and I figured it must have been my voracious appetite toying with me.

"Can I have extra bacon on it?" I asked loudly, and David chuckled.

"Of course."

I licked my lips again at the thought of all of that bacon. "Seriously, though...I want *extra* bacon."

His laugh grew louder, but he assured me he'd make the sandwich to my liking.

With David in the kitchen cooking, I leaned forward and snatched the TV remote off the coffee table and flipped the power on.

Nothing held my interest for long as the smell of the bacon infused the air, making me kind of impatient. I stopped flipping through the channels, focusing more on the sound of David cooking. It didn't make any sense to be so hung up on this, but it was all I could think about. The fact that I wasn't drooling surprised me, to be quite honest.

The click of the stove being switched off excited me. I sat up quickly, criss-crossing my legs in front of me on the couch in anticipation of my meal. David rounded the corner from the kitchen, and my mouth watered more, my stomach growling.

I picked up one of the triangular halves of the toasted sandwich, appreciating the sight of so much bacon folded between the lettuce, tomato, and bread, and took my first big bite. The taste of the bacon was the first thing to bathe my tongue, and I moaned in satisfaction as I chewed...then, something rancid infiltrated my mouth, ruining my meal. After I managed to choke the bite down, I lifted the top piece of bread, looking to see if maybe the lettuce or tomato had gone bad.

"Something wrong, Brooke?" David asked, sitting down next to me.

Shaking my head, I lifted the tomato and gave it a tentative sniff, recoiling as the sweet smell permeated my nostrils. It didn't smell *bad*, but it also didn't smell appealing to me. Dropping the tomato to the plate, I picked up a piece of bacon and popped it in my mouth while I determined if the lettuce was the problem. Turning it over, it looked fine, but, again, the smell wasn't enticing—not that lettuce had ever really held that sort of allure before now.

"Sorry," I said, pulling the lettuce and tomato off of the other half of my sandwich. "I guess I'm just not in the mood for rabbit food."

David chuckled, relaxing back onto the couch and throwing an arm behind me as I continued to pick off one piece of bacon at a time. "No worries. I'm just happy you're eating. Gotta keep your strength up."

While I ate, David changed the channel, settling on ESPN, but I was too into my lunch to really pay attention to what he was watching. When I finished, I kicked the blanket off so I could take my plate to the sink prompting David to quickly hop up.

"Here, let me take that. You just relax," he said, reaching for my dish. Before he could take it, though, he froze, looking at the food left on my plate and arching an eyebrow questioningly.

I shrugged, glancing at the scattered bread slices, tomatoes, and lettuce. "I guess I wasn't really feeling the sandwich. Sorry."

"Don't be." He took the plate. "You ate, that's all that matters."

After discarding my trash and washing my dish, David returned to the couch and pulled me into his arms. I draped the blanket over the both of us and snuggled into his side while we watched television. Now that I'd eaten, my thoughts seemed a little less muddled, but they were still far from the here and now; I was thinking about work again.

"So, I know I'm supposed to be taking it easy," I spoke up softly, "but, honestly, I feel great — better than great, actually — and I was — "

"Wondering when you could go back to work," David finished for me.

I nodded once. "Well, yeah. It just doesn't make sense for me to stay home, feeling useless, when we should be out there figuring out who killed these people. I've already missed more than enough time thanks to my extended stay in the hospital."

"Brooke — " he argued, but I quickly interrupted.

Sitting up and shifting onto my knees, I looked right at him. "Look, before you tell me no, let me assure you that I promise to take it easy. I'll let you know if I feel like I need to slow down. But I can't just sit at home while this psychopath gets away with it."

I was more than ready to continue pleading my case when David smiled and placed his hand on my knee. "I believe you, and I'm just as desperate to solve this thing. Let me talk to your dad, okay? I'll let him know that you're feeling better and that you'll be coming in with me tomorrow."

Even though it wasn't a "yes," I was relieved by the possibility of returning to work as soon as tomorrow. Honestly, I couldn't wait to sink my teeth into this case; while I trusted O'Malley as a fellow detective, I sensed there was something he might be missing — something he didn't see that I might.

Chapter 8 | Rush

The sun wasn't even out by the time I woke the next morning. I looked at the alarm clock and saw it was barely after four a.m. Realizing that I still had two hours before the alarm was set to go off, I rolled over, intent on trying to go back to sleep. But I was wide awake already, feeling my excitement about returning to work growing by the second. I was sure it had something to do with why I was up so damn early, and why my heart raced with what could only be anticipation.

True to his word, David called Dad last night and told him I wanted to return to work. My father was less than willing to agree to this, but once David promised him that he'd watch me for signs that I might be overworking myself and take me home immediately, he conceded. Knowing that within the next few hours, I'd be at my desk and looking over our latest case made me happy. I'd never really been the housewife-type, so the thought of staying home wasn't exactly the most appealing thing in the world. No, I'd rather go to work and try to solve these murders. Be productive.

David remained locked in a deep sleep next to me, snoring lightly, and I smiled at how adorably innocent he looked when completely unaware that I was watching him. I took in how smooth his forehead was when not etched with the lines of worry that had plagued him over the last few days, the brown stubble that was lightly scattered along his square jaw, and the way his pulse jumped through his carotid. I still didn't know why, but I was more than a little fascinated by the sight of it, feeling almost hypnotized by its steady rhythm.

An hour passed, and I was still no closer to falling asleep. In fact, I was even more restless than before, like I needed to be up and moving. It was no longer excitement, but anxiety that crept into me, making my arms and legs tense, my chest a little tight, and my skin tingly. Concerned, I considered waking David up, but figured it would be rude since he had admitted to not sleeping well while I was in the hospital. I crawled gently out of bed, pulled on some shorts and a tank top, and tiptoed down the hall to the spare room where I kept my treadmill, thinking I might just need to burn a little energy.

I started off slow, attempting a proper warm-up, but soon tired of the sluggish pace. Something inside of me *needed* to go faster. I bumped the speed up to my regular pace, but even that wasn't sufficient after the first few minutes, and my feet grew uncomfortable in my shoes. I paused my workout, kicked off my shoes, and then resumed, turning up the speed once more. Soon, I was running twice as fast as I normally would, and I felt great—exhilarated. Breathing deeply, my lungs expanding with the fresh pull of oxygen, I closed my eyes and ran faster. The fan from my treadmill pushed cool air over my face and chest, and I imagined myself running outside, my bare feet sinking into the cool dirt before kicking it up behind me. The sky above me darkened, the silver light of the moon shined down on me, and I felt more at peace than ever before. The scene I painted for myself surprised me at first, but something about it just *felt* right. Like it was where I belonged.

"You're up early," a deep voice called from the doorway, startling me slightly.

"Oh, hey," I greeted with a bright smile. It shocked me a little how steady my voice sounded considering I'd been running for thirty-three minutes straight. Still feeling pretty fired up, I continued to run as I talked to David. "Yeah, I woke up around four and couldn't fall back asleep."

David looked stunned, and also a little concerned. "You've been in here since *four*?"

Laughing, I shook my head, finally feeling the first signs of fatigue when my lungs burned slightly. "No. I've only been in here for just over a half hour. I was feeling pretty restless, and you looked so peaceful. I didn't want to disturb you." I slowed the treadmill to a brisk walk, feeling pretty good as the first wave of endorphins flooded my body. "How'd you sleep?"

"Like a rock," he assured me, stepping into the room and standing next to the treadmill.

"Good." I leaned over, kissing him lightly before continuing my cool down. "You want to run for a bit? I'm going to go hop in the shower and then start breakfast. What do you feel like having?"

"I'll cook," he offered. "What do *you* want?"

"No way!" I exclaimed, hopping off the treadmill with a fresh surge of energy. "You took care of me the last few days." I wrapped my arms around his neck. He responded in kind by draping his arms around my waist and pulling me closer. My body tingled when his hand moved down over my backside and then teased the waist of my shorts. "Let me cook for you." I looked up at him through my lashes. "I want to."

Chuckling, David conceded. "All right then. Surprise me. Let me go change, and I'll get a quick run in."

Kissing David on the cheek, I passed by him and headed into the bathroom to have a quick shower. Down the hall, I heard the sound of David running, and I stripped down, discarding my slightly sweaty clothes in the small hamper. Reaching into the stall, I grabbed the faucet handle and turned it. Much to my surprise, the metal groaned and snapped off in my hand. I stared at it for a moment, trying to figure out what the hell just happened before I tried to reconnect it. It was no use. I tossed the broken handle into the trash basket, wrapped my towel around myself, and ventured back down the hall.

Seeing the expression on my face, David slowed his jog to a walk. "What's wrong?" he asked, slightly breathless after just a few minutes.

"The shower handle broke." He moved his hand to turn the treadmill off, but I stopped him. "No, it's fine. I just need to know of a temporary fix so we can shower until I can grab a new one tonight."

"How bad is it?" David asked.

"The actual mechanics of the faucet still look fine. I think it's just the handle that broke."

He contemplated this for a minute before saying, "Try the adjustable, open-ended wrench that's under your kitchen sink."

I located it without much trouble and headed back to the bathroom to figure out how to use it to get my shower started. My entire shower was spent trying to figure out how I managed to snap it off in the first place. It wasn't as though the house was that old. Was the faucet just a cheap shortcut that they used to save a couple bucks? I'd have to be sure to not repeat that mistake when I replaced it, that's for sure.

After my shower, I brushed my hair and teeth, and then headed back to my room to get dressed. On my way, I passed David in the hall as he headed to the bathroom to shower, and he gave me a playful swat on my towel-covered ass. I giggled like a silly schoolgirl, but before I could retaliate, he closed the bathroom door behind him. My spirits were high, probably thanks to the endorphins from my longer-than-usual run and the fact that I was returning to work after almost a week away. I quickly dressed, choosing jeans and a green fitted, long-sleeved shirt before heading out to the kitchen.

Rifling through the fridge, I decided on bacon, eggs, and breakfast sausage. I debated a fruit salad, but my stomach wasn't receptive to that idea, churning with displeasure. I did cut a grapefruit in half for David, though, just in case he was in the mood to balance his meal. While the food cooked, I opened the fridge to grab the glass carafe of orange juice. I barely grabbed the slender neck of the bottle, and it shattered in my hand. Pain shot through my index finger and up my arm as dark red blood seeped from a long slice in the pad of my finger. What the hell was going on? It was like I'd been exposed to Gamma radiation or something equally comic-book-like, because everything I touched was falling apart.

Using my good hand, I formed a cup and held it under my bleeding finger as I ran for the sink and turned the cold water on. I thrust my sliced finger beneath the cool stream, using my good hand to help wipe away the blood so I could get a good look at how deep the cut was. The first pass over the pad of my finger opened the wound more, causing more blood to escape and be washed away, and I deduced that I might need a couple stitches if the bleeding didn't stop soon. Every pass over the cut stung a little, but the pain ebbed as the frigid temperature numbed my finger. The water washed away the latest stream of crimson, and my eyes widened in disbelief; the blood stopped flowing so freely, and what I thought was a deep laceration was actually no more than something the size of a paper cut. Had I imagined the severity of the cut? No. I was fairly certain I knew what I saw. It was a deep cut. It *had* to be to bleed that badly.

"What the hell happened out here?" David demanded, stepping over the spilled juice and shattered glass still on the kitchen floor as he rushed to my side. Freshly showered and dressed in jeans and a blue button-up shirt, his forehead was creased with worry. Because of me. Again.

Still not entirely sure what happened, myself, I tried to explain. "The juice carafe broke when I grabbed it. The fridge must have been too cold, and the glass was a little more fragile when I grabbed it." It was a plausible explanation, backed up by science.

David took my hand, pulling it from the cold water and inspecting my finger. "You cut yourself."

"I did," I replied softly. "But it's not very deep. Just a scratch, really."

He lifted my damp hand to his lips and pressed a kiss to my fingertip. The pain was almost completely gone, only the slight sting that accompanied something like a minutes-old paper cut remaining. "You've really got to stop scaring me like this," he teased, winking at me before turning to pick up the glass.

I was so lost in the playful glint of his eyes that I almost forgot our breakfast was still on the stove and on the brink of burning. Gasping, I rushed over and saved it before I ruined something else today. I was lucky this time, and stayed focused on breakfast while David offered to clean the spilled orange juice and carefully discard the shards of glass.

When we sat at the table, David eyed my protein-rich meal and quirked an eyebrow. I shrugged in response as I scooped some scrambled eggs onto my fork. "I had a craving."

"A craving," he repeated, the word sounding a little more uneasy coming from him than I'd originally intended.

Understanding, I smiled at him reassuringly. "Sorry. Not that kind of craving." I picked up a piece of bacon and took a bite, savoring the way it tasted. "It must have something to do with my accident. Low iron, maybe? I don't really know."

"Sounds like that's a possibility," David agreed, taking a bite of his own breakfast. "It just struck me as odd, is all. You're usually a French toast and fruit kind of girl."

My lip curled in distaste at the mere mention of fruit, and even I thought it was a bit weird. It was probably just a post-accident phase, one I'd overcome in a few more days as my system righted itself and my body healed fully. Whatever it was, I was surprisingly okay with it, because as I finished my breakfast, my energy levels were renewed once more and my appetite sated.

David drove us to the precinct in his car, and I willingly agreed to it, still not sure if I trusted myself not to have a repeat incident of the other day. I wasn't completely blind to the fact that my increasing energy levels could very well be residual adrenaline from everything that happened. If I blacked out the last time it wore off, there was a very real possibility that it could happen again.

When we walked into the office, everyone welcomed me back, and as I approached my desk, I saw a few bouquets of flowers waiting for me. It was a sweet — and totally unnecessary — gesture, but I appreciated it nonetheless.

"Thanks, guys," I said with a genuine smile. Before I could tell them that I just wanted to go about work as though none of this ever happened, O'Malley approached me and told me that the captain asked to see me the minute I got in.

David nodded me toward Dad's office. "Go on. I'll get everyone gathered for a briefing to get you caught up."

Taking a deep breath, I headed for the captain's office. He still wasn't completely on board with my return to work so soon after being released from the hospital, but I hoped that he would see how good I was feeling. Maybe then he'd be a little more accepting.

His door was slightly ajar, but I still knocked before pushing it open. "O'Malley said you wanted to see me, sir?"

I heard the rustling of paper, and when I stepped into the room, he frantically closed a file on his desk. "Brooke," he greeted, his eyes finding mine and softening with relief as he folded his hands on his desk. "How are you feeling?"

I closed the door and sat in the chair opposite him. "I feel good. I got in a good run this morning, had a hearty breakfast. I feel better than good, actually." My eyes fell to the file under his folded hands. "What do you have there?"

Dad looked nervous, his eyes falling to his desk and then flitting to his blank computer monitor. "It's, um…" He scrambled for an answer — one that I guessed might not be entirely truthful — so I leaned forward, reaching out for it. Dread stirred inside me, and I was almost certain I knew what was in the file.

"Dad," I whispered, and one look into my eyes was all it took before he surrendered the file to me. I took it, and my stomach rolled slightly when I saw that the file had been marked as a cold case. Then I read the side of it: *Robert Leighton – Homicide – October 2007*

"Wh-why do you have this?" I managed to choke out, unable to bring myself to open it and view the contents. For the hundredth time.

Dad sighed heavily, leaning back in his chair. "When you passed out in here the other day after going on about the similarities between these murders and your brother's, I picked up the picture you dropped and saw what you saw."

"Is that why you called me in here? To tell me you think this is the same guy?"

He nodded solemnly. "That, and to see with my own eyes that you're on the mend." Pausing, he shrugged. "I think there's a good possibility that you're right, and I've been authorized to re-open these cases so we can see if we can find a pattern." He picked up the other unsolved files from seven years ago and handed them to me.

Hearing this stunned me into silence, and I just stared at the files in my hands. "I'll find this son of a bitch," I said softly, though I wasn't sure if I was reassuring Dad or myself...or maybe I was making a promise to Bobby and the other victims.

"I know you will, Brooke." Dad tilted his head toward the door and smiled. "Now get to work."

After leaving Dad's office, I met up with David, Keaton, O'Malley, and several other officers on our case in the briefing room. Upon first glance, I saw the whiteboard had been filled crime scene photos of the latest four victims as well as any leads O'Malley thought he found in my absence. I looked it over, but there really wasn't much there other than how they assumed these victims were found in a secondary crime scene. They figured there were primary scenes still out there with blood evidence that may or may not tell us who did this.

But I wasn't so sure. Something deep in my gut told me there was more to this than everyone else was seeing. I still couldn't explain why I felt this way—I just did.

Before David started the briefing, I opened Bobby's cold case file and rifled through the pictures until I located the one that haunted my every thought since I wound up in the hospital. All eyes were on me as I walked to the front of the room and stuck it on the board, directly beneath the blown up image of the wound on the victim number one's neck. Upon first glance, they appeared to be an exact match, but only an in depth analysis would tell us for sure.

"This photo was taken at a crime scene seven years ago," I said, pointing at the picture of Bobby's neck. I glanced once at David, who knew this wasn't easy for me, and he offered me a sympathetic smile before I continued. "And these"—I pointed at each of the most recent victims' photos—"were taken just last week in Chaparral Park. I don't know if these cases are related, but I don't think we can afford to dismiss the similarities at this point. We don't have any solid leads *yet*, but I'm confident we can change that. We'll exhaust every avenue searching for this guy, but we *will* find him."

When I finished, David allowed O'Malley to take over since he'd been heading up the case over the last few days, and then we doled out individual tasks for everyone to carry out. O'Malley had already spoken to the victims' next of kin, but I mentioned how I would feel better if I could talk to them as well. Maybe see if they'd let me take a look around to see if I could find something. David agreed with this plan of action, and we prepared to head out. Before we left, I stopped by the break room for some coffee while David headed out to grab the car. By the time I stepped outside, David still wasn't back with the car, so I waited on the sidewalk and went over any questions I wanted to ask the families.

Lost in thought, I stopped paying attention to my surroundings, jumping when a familiar and unexpected voice came from behind me.

"Hey, Brooke."

I turned around quickly, startled and staring up into the nervous blue-green eyes of Nick. Dressed in faded jeans and a white T-shirt that hugged his muscular torso, he walked toward me, and my breath faltered slightly. His longer, disheveled hair and stubble-riddled jawline still came as a bit of a shock when compared to the usual clean-cut look I was used to seeing on him. Seven years ago.

My stomach flipped like it used to back then, and I took an involuntary step toward him before my brain registered what my feet were doing and forced me to stop. We continued to stare at each other, and the gloomy look in his eyes unnerved me.

He took a hesitant step forward, possibly afraid I was going to toss my coffee to the ground and pummel him again, and his eyes shifted to the ground between us, then back up to mine. "Do you have a minute? I think we need to talk."

CHAPTER 9 | INQUIRY

I didn't say anything—what was I supposed to say? He wanted me to spare a minute to talk? After leaving me without so much as an explanation seven years ago? It wasn't a good idea, and I really didn't owe him anything. He was probably just having an attack of conscience and wanted me to absolve him of all his wrongdoings. Too little, too late, if you asked me.

"Please," he pleaded, clearly seeing the uncertainty on my face.

"I'm working, Nick," I replied, looking around for David's car. "I don't have time for this." I turned to walk away from him, but he refused to give up easily.

"How's your shoulder?" he called out, forcing me to stop walking and turn back around. I opened my mouth to ask how he even knew about it, but he cut me off. "My…uh…my mom heard from yours that you were in the hospital following some kind of wild animal attack. Are you okay?"

"I'm fine. Thank you for your concern." We stood there, staring at each other for several seconds, letting the awkward silence thicken the air between us. It was hard for me to look into his eyes and not see the man I thought I'd share the rest of my life with, and, slowly, my resentment toward him wilted. My carefully constructed walls crumbled, and Nick smiled slightly, sensing the beginning of a thaw between us.

Then, the stark realization that he left me when I was at my worst ripped through me like a knife, reopening a wound I'd worked long and hard to mend. "What are you doing here, Nick? Why did you come back? Why now?"

His smile disappeared, and his posture deflated as he shoved his hands in his pockets. He looked like a lost little boy — a broad, six-foot-tall, lost little boy. "That's why I wanted to talk to you, Brooke. Please. I know you don't owe me anything, but—" His words registered with me, hitting me so hard in the gut that I was winded, and they reminded me that he was exactly right: I *didn't* owe him a goddamned thing.

He must have seen the fire in my eyes, because he rushed forward, his expression no longer full of apprehension but instead flooding with regret...remorse. "I'm so sorry," he said softly, his eyes never once straying from mine as one of his hands cupped my face.

Without thinking, my eyes closed, and I pressed my face into his palm, welcoming the warmth, and his fingers tangled into the hair at the nape of my neck. I inhaled deeply, taking in his natural, woodsy smell, and he whispered sadly, "I never meant to hurt you. I was scared. I didn't know what else to do. I panicked."

His words reached me, and I immediately snapped out of my dazed state, taking several steps back and watching his arm fall back to his side. "*You* were scared?" I demanded, my rage bubbling below the surface. "My brother died. *Died*, Nick. In a filthy alley outside a nightclub, and instead of being there for me—for my *family*—you just packed up your shit and bailed."

Something flashed in his eyes—surprise, maybe?—but it disappeared just as quickly as it had arrived. I couldn't quite pinpoint it or what brought it about in the first place. I didn't get a chance to question him about it either, because he was quick to contribute to the conversation. "I know what I did back then was a shitty thing to do, but you don't understand, Brooke—"

"Because you never gave me a chance to!"

Something behind me caught Nick's attention, and his face twisted in annoyance before he looked back down at me. "I didn't come here to fight with you. I came to apologize for what happened the other night, and to try and explain myself."

I rolled my eyes and waited, but he shook his head with a nervous laugh. "It's a...long story." Reaching into his back pocket, Nick pulled out a piece of paper and held it out for me. "Here's my number and the address to my place."

"Y-your *place*? You're staying in the city, then?" I asked, my voice cracking slightly as I looked at the scrap of paper in his hands; the address was less than ten blocks from mine. Since my hands were full, I couldn't take it, so Nick took it upon himself to slip the piece of paper into the pocket of my jeans. His fingers brushed my hipbone, and a forgotten—and all too familiar—sensation passed through me. I hated that he still had this affect on me after all this time.

Nick nodded in answer to my question. "I've got some business to take care of, and I can't be sure how long it'll take. I'd stay with my mother, but I don't want to disrupt her life when I'm coming and going at all hours of the day, so I'm staying at a house one of my buddies owns."

My head bobbed in understanding, but I didn't know what to do or say; I was honestly still trying to wrap my head around his more permanent return to town.

I heard footsteps behind me, and when I turned around, I saw David rushing up the sidewalk. And he didn't look happy. Behind me, I swore I heard a low growl coming from Nick, but when I looked back at him, he was watching me expectantly. "You should—"

Nick nodded. "I'm leaving," he interjected. "Just...*please* call me or stop by. We need to talk. And soon. There's something I need to tell you. Before the next full moon, preferably."

Before I could question his odd request—or even give him a response—he turned and took off down the sidewalk, limping slightly as if favoring his right leg. It was likely he didn't wait for an answer because he didn't want to run the risk of me telling him where to shove his small piece of paper—which was exactly what I should have done—but a part of me was curious to see what he had to say. Now, while I wasn't sure if I was going to call him or not, I didn't want to upset David by telling him that my ex just slipped me his number and was staying in the city for a little more than just a few days.

"What did he want?" David asked, taking his coffee from me.

"He, uh, wanted to talk," I told him honestly, turning around and leading the way to where David left the car.

"About?"

I shrugged. "I don't know. He never got the chance to say." Before David could question me further, I continued. "You ready to go?"

Mrs. Turner was a little nervous to talk to David and me when we showed up on her doorstep. Thankfully, David convinced her that this was just a routine follow-up, and that we only wanted to look around and double check a few details. After giving her consent, she invited us into her home and offered us both some tea while we asked our questions.

Mrs. Turner's home was full of pictures and memories of a happy childhood, and while her daughter didn't live here anymore, it was obvious that she had a good upbringing. David sat on the sofa across from Mrs. Turner while I walked around, examining pictures for...something. I knew that the chances of finding anything that could tell us more about the murder were slim to non-existent, but it was my job to search for them regardless.

"Mrs. Turner," David began.

"Betty, please," she interrupted, correcting him as politely as possible. Her voice wavered a bit, but the last few days hadn't been easy, and she likely didn't even realize it.

Been there. Done that.

"Betty," he amended. "Sorry." A brief pause. "I know our colleague, Detective O'Malley, came out to see you the other day, but we just wanted to double check a few things with you, if you don't mind. Maybe take a look inside Samantha's apartment."

"I thought the police had free access to her apartment during the investigation?"

I turned around and offered Mrs. Turner a warm smile. "We do, but I'd prefer to have your permission. Keep you informed."

Her eyes glistened with gratitude, her smile widening as she placed a hand over her heart. "Thank you. And I don't mind at all, as long as you think it'll help find the man who...who..." Her strangled sob filled the room, and my heart clenched. I empathized with her completely, because not too long ago, I had been where she was now.

Out of respect, we waited for Mrs. Turner's ability to answer our questions. I crossed the room and sat next to David on the couch, waiting for her to gather her composure. She apologized — which wasn't necessary — and asked what it was that we wanted to know. We started by asking about the day Samantha died. Apparently, she had been out celebrating a big win for the law firm she interned for. Her mother and sisters had joined her and a few of her colleagues for dinner and drinks before they went home for the night while Samantha and her friends went to a new club they'd heard about. That was the last she'd heard from her.

After learning that, the usual questions were asked: What was the name of this club? Did Samantha have any enemies? A scorned lover? Coworkers who were jealous of her promotion? Turned out, her life was damned near perfect and everyone loved her. As for the club, the mother had no idea, so we'd have to make sure to ask anyone she associated with, if O'Malley hadn't already done so. I'd have to be sure to ask about his progress back at the precinct.

My heart went out to this woman, because I knew what it was like to lose someone close to you. When I thought back to just after Bobby died, I regretted showing up here like this. Having been through repeated police interviews regarding Bobby's lifestyle choices, I knew how counter-productive this was to Mrs. Turner's need to move past this event. She was grieving, and the last thing she needed was to be reminded about her daughter's death. And worse, that we were no closer to solving her case.

Even though the thought of putting her through this made me a little queasy, what she didn't realize was that unless we found the person responsible for her daughter's death, she'd likely never find closure. Based on my own personal experience, that is.

After speaking with Mrs. Turner for just over an hour, I realized there was nothing more to learn that O'Malley didn't already report. I felt bad for taking up even more of Mrs. Turner's time and being no further ahead, and while any information she was able to give us was appreciated, it wasn't what I was hoping for. Honestly, I couldn't really be sure what I was looking for other than a flashing neon sign pointing us in the right direction.

"Thank you for your time, Mrs. Turner," I said as she walked us to the door.

"Any time, dear," she replied, her voice soft and uneven. "If there's anything else I can do, please, just let me know."

"We'll be sure to do that," I promised, reaching out and giving her hand a reassuring squeeze.

Once we were back in the car, David and I talked about what little we learned, and how it was all information that O'Malley already had. I really hoped we found something at the victim's apartment, otherwise I feared this case would never be solved.

When we arrived, we found a written notice from the police department was stuck on Miss Turner's third-floor apartment door, and the superintendent had to let us in. The minute the door opened, I was met with the most unpleasant smell I'd ever experienced. It was so pungent that I gagged slightly before tucking my nose into the crook of my elbow.

"What's wrong?" David asked, stepping into the room behind me.

Trying not to inhale too deeply, I turned to find him unfazed by whatever the cause of the god-awful stench was. "Are you kidding? You don't smell that?"

David sniffed the air, and then shook his head. "It's a little musty, I guess."

Shocked, my mouth fell open slightly, and my arm dropped to my side. I instantly regretted the reflexive action, because not only could I smell it now, but it infiltrated my mouth. I could *taste* the foulness on my tongue. It coated it like oil, and I couldn't shake it as it worked its way into every part of me, making my skin crawl and prickle all over. It was unsettling.

"It's not just musty," I informed him, inhaling just a little this time to see if I could further identify what it might be. A wave of nausea rolled in my stomach, but I fought it down. Along with the overpowering smell, I picked up subtle hints of jasmine — the victim's fragrance of choice, perhaps? — and something almost...chemical. I sniffed again, recognizing that the air still held trace amounts of luminol. This made sense given that, while I was holed up in the hospital, O'Malley conducted a thorough check of the apartment, spraying it on every surface imaginable. I looked around the main living space and took another step in, the smell only slightly more potent.

David saw how repulsed I was, because he watched me, concern written all over his face. "Are you sure, sweetheart? I don't smell anything."

Even though the smell was almost too much to bear, I knew I had to find a way to put up with it because I had a job to do. "It must just be me," I mumbled, moving toward the coffee table to look at the scattered mail there. There was nothing out of the ordinary—bills, flyers, various business cards to several companies and one black one with a Phoenix address—so I moved on to the kitchen after bagging it all. Just in case.

David remained two steps behind me, and the instant we were in the kitchen, he groaned. "Well, I guess we found the source of the smell," he said, pointing toward the fruit bowl on the counter. In it were a couple of bananas, three apples, and an orange—all of which were more than a little overripe. Sure enough, they smelled horrible, but they only added to the increasingly foul combination of aromas in the apartment. They weren't the source.

As I continued to make my way through the apartment, I found everything in pristine order—living room clean, dishes done, fridge and cupboards stocked, bed made—there was no sign of any struggle, which usually meant the murder never happened here. The lack of any of her missing blood suggested this also.

In her bedroom, I was overwhelmed by the potency of the smell again, and I fought the urge to wretch. My entire body broke out in a sweat, and I trembled when, out of nowhere, I made the connection: death. The apartment smelled like death.

When David entered the room behind me, I turned to him with watering eyes. "You still don't smell that?" He shook his head. "Seriously? David, it smells like somebody died in here."

"O'Malley and the CSU went over this place with a fine-toothed comb, Brooke. There's nothing here that suggests this is our primary," he reminded me. His expression changed from confusion to sympathy, and he placed a hand on my cheek, his brow furrowing with worry. "Sweetheart, you're burning up again. Maybe you're overworked and tired and it's throwing your senses off?"

He was probably right. It seemed a little odd, but, then again, nothing about this past week really screamed "normal" for me. Instead of leaving right away, I was able to convince David that we should finish looking around, but it wound up to be a wasted effort. There was nothing here that hadn't already been documented, and I only grew more and more frustrated.

It wasn't like I expected O'Malley's work to only be sub-par—my father wouldn't allow for any of that in his precinct—but I was hoping that I'd be able to find...I don't know, *something*. Why was there no evidence that would give us an idea about what happened to her? Honestly, the more I thought about it, the more I realized that if it hadn't been for finding her body, it might appear like this was all some kind of sick joke. That Samantha Turner could very well just be on vacation.

But she wasn't. We *did* find her body, and the only thing I'd been able to dig up on this investigation were more questions.

What exactly were we dealing with?

CHAPTER 10 | CRAVINGS

After conducting my own search of each victims' home — or in the case of our tourist, his hotel — David and I headed back to the precinct. It had been a couple days since the last attack, and it seemed like everyone was just waiting with baited breath for it to happen. It bothered me, because that meant we were basically waiting for another body to drop in our laps since we had nothing to help us predict his next move. Another body that would probably leave us with as much information as we had now. None.

Our behavioral analysts had been called in, but they were unable to tell us anything conclusive. They said the suspect could just be lying low, waiting to make his next move, calculating. Their other theory was that he'd moved onto another town.

Wouldn't that be just fantastic? The Scottsdale PD letting a lunatic slip through their fingers so he could move onto the next unsuspecting city. Yeah, that was just what we needed.

In all of our searching, we were unable to find anything that could tie the four murders together, aside from the C.O.D. I was beyond frustrated at this point and unable to think of anything else this whole time. The way this case consumed me was borderline obsessive-compulsive.

Every single one of the autopsy reports came back inconclusive. We knew each one of them died of exsanguination, and Dr. Hobbes seemed to think that the blood was drained from their bodies through the wounds on their necks since there were no other points of entry. Going with this theory — because it was the only one we had — she checked the wounds to figure out what the murder weapon could have been. When she found DNA, it was the most excited I'd been in as long as I could remember. Unfortunately, the DNA results showed nothing useful. It was neither human nor any animal we could identify, and they were all from different sources. My first thought was that maybe they were attacked by the same wolf I was that night, but that didn't explain the lack of blood in their bodies.

Truthfully, every second that passed and disproved one of our current theories frustrated us more and more. Some of the guys tried to lighten the mood by joking about how the victims were probably closet fetishists. Even though they were just goofing around, the suggestion intrigued me, and I didn't treat it as a joke. I treated it as a possible lead. They tried to laugh me off, but I pressed on, wondering what kind of fetishes could get these people killed.

One word out of Keaton's mouth, and I was sorry I even asked: Vampires.

I tried to let it go, but something about it niggled at me for the rest of the afternoon. In fact, the more I obsessed about it, the more I started to think it kind of made sense. Not so much that they were killed by a real vampire — because that would be ridiculous — but there was something deep in the pit of my stomach that told me to go with it. Call it instinct, but I realized that the only real evidence we had to go by suggested this could be a possibility. They were missing most of their blood, after all.

Going with the flow, I decided to do a little Internet search at home that night, and it turned out that this was an actual thing. Apparently blood-sharing was something these people practiced. *Gross.* People even had dental work done to give themselves fangs, and they called their groups "covens." The more I dug into this secret lifestyle, the more information I uprooted, and the more disturbed I grew. David was the only one I told about my unconventional investigation, and while he thought I was crazy at first, he started to see that this was a very real possibility with every article I read aloud. True, we never found anything that would tie our victims to this lifestyle, but it was possible that they kept it hidden from their families, friends, and colleagues for fear of being ridiculed and shunned.

When I thought about how they all could have kept this secret from their families, my mind wandered to Bobby. If it turned out to be some illicit underground activity involving a bunch of wannabe-vampires, was I going to be able to accept that maybe my brother had been delving into the same waters? And, if he was, how did I miss the signs?

I decided to deal with that when I got to it, because I couldn't have that clouding my judgment—not until I knew for sure that this was what actually happened.

My research told me that there were a few underground night clubs (literally) that catered to this *lifestyle* in Scottsdale alone, and while we couldn't find any ties to them in any of our victims' financial records, my gut told me we had to follow this lead. The feeling I had about this potential lead was unsettling. While used to having moments of clarity that lead me in the right direction, this felt almost...I don't know...angry? No...it was more than that. It was *vengeful*. The only explanation I came up with for the unexpected emotion was that Bobby's own murder was clouding my thoughts, and I wanted vengeance for him — I had for so long — and the thought that I could get it after all this time made me deliriously happy.

After gathering all of my information, I needed to take it to my team and, more importantly, the captain so we could plot our next course of action. I was unsure how he would react to this, and quite frankly, I was a little afraid he would tell me I wasted my time. I mean, his new detective's first case, and she goes off on a tangent, spewing nonsense about vampires? It was certifiable, and if anyone was going to tell me that, it would be him.

"You ready?" David asked as we entered the precinct the next morning.

"No," I quipped. "He's going to think I'm crazy."

David laughed. "He's not." Pausing, he considered his response. "Well, maybe a little," he teased.

His laughter was contagious, and I elbowed his side. "You're not funny."

"Then stop laughing." Stopping just outside the briefing room, David took my hand. "Look, I'll admit that it sounded a little out there at first, but I think it fits. In some weird way, your theory fits... Plus, it's the only one we've got right now."

"Still," I argued, "I don't think he'll accept it right away."

Releasing my hand, David reached out and turned the doorknob. "Only one way to find out."

My heart hammered in my chest as we entered the briefing room, not only because I was nervous to present my plan of action to our team and my father, but because a surge of adrenaline was rushing through me. That part of me that so desperately wanted to pursue this lead in the first place was excited to be following through.

My nerves took over as I stood at the front of the room. All eyes were on me, and my mouth dried out. I swallowed thickly, looking from David, to Dad, to the rest of the detectives here to listen to me. After taking a deep breath, I decided to bite the bullet and just begin.

"So, I know it's been tough this past week, and we appreciate everything you all have done to try and solve this case," I said, my voice shaking in the beginning, but steadying as I carried on. "While we haven't been able to find much of anything that can tell us what happened to any of the victims, I think I've stumbled onto a potential lead, thanks to Detective Keaton."

Keaton's head shot up, and he looked somewhat surprised. "Really?"

Smiling, I nodded, my confidence rising. "Now, I have to admit, that when I first heard it, I took it as the joke it was intended to be, but the more I looked into it, the more I realized he might be onto something." I opened the folder in my hand and grabbed a few of the pictures I pulled from my online research. "I know this is pretty outside the box, but I believe that we might be dealing with a coven of self-proclaimed vampires." Almost every detective looked at me like I just admitted to seeing Elvis flying on the back of a winged purple elephant, and I rushed to elaborate.

"I know how it sounds," I assured them, "but with no other leads, we really don't have anything to lose." A low rumble moved through the crowd as they spoke. They all talked below a whisper, and I was pretty sure I shouldn't have been able to hear them, but I heard things like "is she fucking serious?" and "she's lost her damn mind" floating around. Normally, hearing that sort of thing would shake my confidence, but it didn't. Somewhere deep down, it was like I *knew* this was the right path to follow.

Before I could say anything to force their eyes back to me, my father did. "Everybody, listen up." His loud voice bounced off every wall in the room, and everybody listened without objection. Satisfied, he looked to me and nodded. "Detective."

"Thank you, sir."

Someone in the back of the room muttered "daddy's girl" under their breath, and I saw red, my eyes zeroing in on Detective Clarke. He'd always been a pain in my ass and was a little sore that I'd been promoted so early in my career. He'd cited preferential treatment, when that couldn't be further from the truth. I was quite aware how unprofessional a father promoting his daughter probably looked to those who claimed this as a classic case of nepotism, but I worked my ass off to get this promotion. I deserved it, and I was determined to prove it.

Rage bubbled inside me as I stared at Clarke in his seat. His eyes locked with mine, widening with the realization that I'd heard him, and I started to imagine how wildly his heart must be thumping in his chest. I focused on the thought so intensely, in fact, that I swore I heard it. I inhaled another deep breath, this time feeling a little smug, and my mouth salivated when I sensed something even more satisfying than the look on his face. I wasn't sure how, but I recognized the smell for exactly what it was.

Fear. *His* fear.

I realized that he likely wasn't scared of *me* so much as the fact that I overheard his backhanded comment, and it was barely enough to infuse the air, but there it was…and it shocked me just how much I liked it. How much I thrived off it.

"Got something you wish to share with the class, Detective Clarke?" I snarled in his direction. "Something you need to contribute to the case?"

His head moved back and forth rapidly, his eyes locked on mine and his fear spiking. "N-no, Detective Leighton."

The right side of my mouth curled up into a cocky smirk. "Then if you could save any snide comments you have about me until we can discuss them at length — *privately* — I'd like to continue."

A deafening silence filled the room, satisfying me completely, and I continued to go through my findings in hopes it would help convince them that this was a viable option. It surprised me to find my father wasn't against my theory, nor did he think I'd lost my mind. Bonus.

There were skeptics in the room when I announced wanting to investigate these clubs, but no one contested me, probably afraid to be called out like Clarke was. By the end of the briefing, I decided that we'd split into four groups and hit each club armed with questions and a photo of each vic. If they were involved, someone was sure to have seen one of them.

At least, that's what I hoped.

CHAPTER 11 | URGES

Loud music poured from the subterranean club entrance, and bright lights flashed wildly through the heavily-tinted windows. Based on its underground location in Old Scottsdale, *The Dungeon* was actually an apt choice for this place's name, and it made me feel more on edge than I'd ever felt before. Something I didn't even realize was possible.

It wasn't like I'd never found myself in similar situations, but there was something about this that had my entire body on high-alert. Ever since this vampire theory was mentioned, my muscles had been tense, and my heart pumped harder and slightly faster as if preparing my body for a surge of adrenaline at a moment's notice. Acutely aware, I took in everything about my surroundings, my eyes darting around, looking in every direction and searching the shadows for danger. I focused my hearing on the sounds of passing pedestrians and vehicles while trying to block out the loud music.

David placed his hand on my back, and I jumped away, defensively swatting his arm in the process. His eyes widened in alarm, and I exhaled. "I'm sorry," I whispered.

"You okay? You seem tense."

I nodded as we made our way for the stairway that led to the club. "Yeah. I'm not sure why, but I feel like I'm poised to...I don't know...attack?" David listened intently as I explained what I've been going through these last few days. "It's weird, actually. Ever since Keaton joked around about vampires, I've been feeling anxious. Excited, even. Maybe it's because this is the first real — albeit strange — lead we've had on this case, but it's like some dormant part of me has been awakened and has been driving me forward this entire time."

"Sounds reasonable," David replied. "You're a detective now, and this is your first real case. You're thirst for justice is just stronger than you realized."

Thirst. Is that what this was? Something about the word definitely fit with how I had been chasing this lead. It was stronger than desire, though — much stronger — and I wasn't entirely convinced that justice was what I sought. Maybe a part of me did, but it didn't feel like it most of the time. At first, I thought it was vengeance — and I still believed this — but now it felt like something I had to do. Something I was *made* to do.

At the bottom of the stairs, David grabbed the door handle and tried to open it, but it didn't budge. He looked at me, confused, and then tried again. When the door remained closed, I shook my head, annoyed with this minor setback, and I pounded on the metal door loudly.

The small rectangular peephole in the door opened, and a pair of blood-red eyes appeared. I stared at them a moment, undeterred and unthreatened when I saw a ring of blue around the man's pupils where the contacts didn't cover. "Password," he boomed through the door, and I rolled my eyes.

David and I unclipped our badges from our belts

and held them up to the door. "Scottsdale PD. Sound about right?" I demanded firmly.

He cursed loudly before pulling the metal slide back over the peephole. I was about to knock again when the door suddenly flew open and he held an arm out, bowing with mock-chivalry and giving us a prime look at the top of his shiny, bald head. "Après vous," he said.

David and I entered the club together, and every hair on my body prickled as my eyes adjusted to the strobe lights. It took a minute, but eventually I could see enough to get me through without running into one of the many people crowding the place. There were wall-to-wall bodies, and the combination of smells overwhelmed and disoriented me. I stumbled as the unusual aroma of cologne, perfume, deodor-ant—and lack thereof—fogged my head even further. David reached out and placed his hand flat on my back, guiding me through the rest of the way. In an effort to help lessen the effect the smell of this place had on me, I pressed my nose into the back of my hand.

We made it to the bar, and I looked around. Even with the lights flashing, I could make out the hun-dreds of bodies crowded in here. Black seemed to be the shade of choice, but splashes of crimson and deep purple were thrown in. Countless individuals sported dark hair and heavy makeup—something the victims didn't seem to have in common. It was all very cliché.

I continued to scan the club, taking notice of the half-naked women writhing on several podiums around the room. There wasn't a lot of dancing by the rest of the patrons as they stood around and watched the dancers. The look in their eyes was dangerous, almost predatory, and I observed as one man held his hand out to one of them and helped her off her podium. He pulled her to him, and they shared a deep kiss that suggested they knew each other. I couldn't take my eyes off them, and not because it was titillating — quite the opposite, really. The strong reaction I was experiencing surprised me. It wasn't that I found exhibitionism and voyeurism particularly repulsive — nor did I find it arousing — but this visceral reaction to these people seemed to stem from how I saw *them* as abominations to the human race.

Yes. That was exactly it, I realized.

Of course, this revelation only upset me, because behind this phony vampire exterior, they were still human. A man and a woman, pretending to be something that excited them so they could get off. Why was I reading more into this than necessary?

"I'm going to take a look around," David said, leaning in so I could hear him over the music. The strange truth was, though, I could hear the couple across the room as the woman leaned in and suggested they step into the back room for some privacy. "You okay out here?"

I nodded, watching the couple disappear behind a set of red velvet curtains. "Uh huh. Do me a favor, though? See if you can find out what goes on behind those curtains."

"Will do. I'll be back in a few." David disappeared through the crowd before I turned toward the bar.

"You're new," the bartender said, leaning on the sticky-looking countertop. He was tall — just under six feet — his dark hair was spiked, and heavy eyeliner surrounded his blue-gray eyes. He was dressed in a tight black shirt and leather vest, and his arms were covered in tattoos. Basically, he appeared to be the stereotypical poster boy for the Goth scene.

I stepped toward the bar, and he stood up

straight. "What can I get you, Red?"

"You work here often?" I asked with an annoyed smile brought on by the use of a nickname I'd been plagued with given my fiery red hair.

The man shrugged. "Five nights a week. We're closed the other two. Why?"

I leaned on the bar. "I was just wondering if you could answer a couple of questions I had."

The bartender laughed, flashing me his sharp, elongated canines. My hands tensed, and my body trembled at the sight of them. I wasn't sure what to make of this reaction. It definitely wasn't fear, but I felt surges of adrenaline coursing through my arms and legs as my survival instincts kicked in and weighed all of my options.

Options? What options? I asked myself. *He's not a threat. He's just some guy caught up in the idea that vampires are glamorous and mysterious.* Telling myself this helped a little, calming my heart minutely, but not altogether. I reached for my badge and reminded myself why I was really here.

"What are you, a cop?" The question left his mouth at the exact moment I placed my badge on the counter. "Holy shit," he muttered under his breath, looking around. "What is it you wanna know, officer?"

"Detective," I corrected, pulling the pictures of our victims from the inside pocket of my leather jacket and holding them out one at a time. "Have you seen any of these people before? Like, in the last few weeks?"

He looked a little taken aback at first, but he pushed his shock aside and wiped his hands on his bar towel before reaching out and taking the pictures for a closer look. After a minute, he shook his head regretfully. "Sorry, they don't look familiar."

"You're sure?"

Nodding, he gave the photos back. "Well, they don't exactly look the type, you know? But that's not to say they didn't maybe alter their appearance before coming in once or twice."

"So it's possible they kept this part of their lives hidden during the day?"

"Definitely," he conceded, leaning forward again, almost as though he was trying to keep this conversation private. "But I will tell you that most of the people we cater to live and breathe this shit."

Somewhat bewildered by his choice of words, I questioned his statement. "You make it sound like you don't share their interest in all of this."

"Because I don't," he replied, sounding somewhat offended that I would even suggest it.

Really? Has he looked in a mirror?

He sighed heavily. "I'm here because it pays the bills and leaves me with quite a bit of money left over. Most of these people are regulars, and not just anyone can get in. It's a very exclusive club, and you get in by invite only...or if you flash your badge at the front door." So I'd be willing to bet none of them" — he pointed at the photos — "are regulars here."

Invite only. Something about that triggered a memory, but I couldn't quite recall it, and I didn't have the luxury of time to worry about it now. I would have to come back to the thought later and try to figure it out.

"Anything else?" he asked, growing more annoyed and impatient as he looked beyond me and at his growing line of patrons.

I didn't like the tone he took with me, and I fought back the sudden urge to reach across the bar and slam his head onto the countertop. This impulse opened up a floodgate of images, and I visualized the stream of blood pouring from his mouth and nose. It was so vivid, I could almost smell the coppery under-tones to it—feel the warmth of it on the tips of my fingers—and the sound of him pleading for me to stop was like music to my ears...

Shocked and horrified at myself for this unexpected and extremely violent train of thought, I inhaled deeply, drawing in another lungful of the pungent air, and swallowed thickly. That was when I realized that the smell of blood wasn't just a figment of my overactive—and disturbing—imagination. It was in the air. It was faint, but was there.

"Is there anything else I can help you with, Detective? Or can I get back to work? There's a line forming."

Distracted by the smell of blood, my eyes wandered from him, but I was wholly aware of his question. "That's fine. I'll need your name and number in case I have any more follow-up questions."

"Of course. I'm Adam, and I'll grab you a card with my information." His attitude shifted back to helpful, and I briefly questioned his mental stability before a new trace of copper invaded my nose, making my mouth water...

What the hell is wrong with me? I find that smell appealing? No. It wasn't actually the smell that made me react this way. It was something else that appealed to me. Something I still couldn't put my finger on.

The bartender—Adam—handed me his card, and I slipped the gray rectangle into my pocket along with the pictures. "Thanks," I said listlessly, following the coppery notes in the air. I made it to the velvet curtains, where the scent was overwhelmingly intense, and I was preparing to step through them when a thin man, about my height and dressed all in black, slipped into my view.

"Hey, baby," he said, his voice scratchy and his breath smelling of booze. "You wanna head back there and party?"

When he flashed his teeth and I saw the two pointy canines, something inside of me snapped like a rubberband that had been pulled too taut. Every muscle in my body tensed again, and a low rumble formed in my belly...

Wait. Am I growling?

"Come on, babe." He reached out and grabbed me around my wrist, leading me forward and pulling the curtain back slightly. "I promise you an unforgettable experience."

The minute he touched me, alarm bells blared in my head, screaming at me that this guy was a threat to my existence. The rush of adrenaline building outside earlier exploded, flooding my veins, and the tension in my muscles released like tightly wound springs as I yanked my arm from his hold. Everything happened so fast after that. I spun around, my elbow connecting with his nose, and before I could process what happened, my hand was around his neck, and I had him pressed against the wall.

Blood poured from his nose, and one of his pointy "fangs" was missing as he wept. I breathed heavily, a scratchy noise escaping my throat with each exhale, and I was only vaguely aware of the shocked bar patrons that surrounded us to take in the show. Using only my eyes, I glanced around to see their wide-eyed stares, and I heard the low murmurs as they wondered who the nut-job holding their brother off the ground was.

Off...the...ground?

Slowly, my eyes fell to the floor, and sure enough, the guy's feet were more than a foot from the ground, jerking wildly. *How did I...? When did I...?* Confusion filled my head, pushing out the previous urge to teach this guy a lesson, but before I could figure out what was going on with me, David stepped out from behind the thick curtains.

"Hey. What did you find out?" he asked before noticing the man pinned to the wall at my mercy.

Horrified, I dropped the thin creep and stepped back, looking at my hands as if I didn't even recognize them as my own. "I-I'm fine."

Clearly worried, David grabbed my upper arms and forced our gazes to lock. "Brooke? What the hell happened out here?"

The haze cleared the minute I stared into his wide blue eyes, and I looked at the man on the ground, holding his neck and surrounded by his alarmed friends. "I was coming to find you, and that guy grabbed my wrist. I don't know what happened, but I snapped. I-I wasn't thinking."

A fire erupted in David's eyes, and he shot a menacing glare down at the guy I attacked. Instead of beating this guy senseless, though, David pulled me off to the side, cradling my face protectively. It was sweet. "Are you okay?"

My head bobbed slowly. "Yeah. I think it was probably just a normal fight-or-flight instinct. And I don't think he was really going to hurt me. He probably thought I was one of...them, I guess." Pausing, I replayed the last couple of minutes since David showed up and registered his original question. "Oh, I talked to the bartender. He's never seen the victims before. Says the club is exclusive and all the people are regulars. I got his name and number in case I think of anything else. How about you? What's behind the curtain? The wizard?"

The tension left his body, and David chuckled.

"Not quite. It's a private room where the dancers go with patrons and they engage in..." he trailed off, pausing to try to find a way to explain. "Illicit activities."

"Illicit?"

He nodded once. "There's dancing, stripping—"

The lingering essence of blood in the air was the furthest thing from my mind, and David sure as hell found a way to get my full, undivided attention now. "Stripping?" I interrupted, jealousy haloing my tone as an inexplicable surge of anger washed through me. "So, I sent you into a room where women were taking their clothes off?"

"Among other things," he said, piquing my curiosity and ignoring my unnecessary attitude. "Let's just say, they take this vampire thing seriously."

"Meaning?"

David hesitated, but only briefly. "I caught a couple back there. The woman was on her knees, sucking his—"

Not quite ready for *that* visual, I held up my hand. "Whoa! Whoa! Whoa!" I cried, clenching my eyes and shaking my head. "I'm sorry I asked."

"—wrist," he concluded with a bit of a laugh, completely bypassing my assumption and making me feel like a total ass.

"Oh." Then what he said actually clicked. "Wait, his *wrist*? Why?"

I knew the answer before he replied, because the smell still hung in the air like smog, but he said it anyway. "Blood."

And I was right back to being repulsed...and angry. I was so angry, I acted without thinking—again—moving to push past David so I could go back there and...and...Quite honestly, what I visualized doing once back there was even more extreme than what happened with the man out here, and it frightened me a little. But I still had to do something.

"Where are you going?"

I stared at him like he'd lost his mind. "What do you mean *'where are you going?'* I'm going back there to stop it!"

"It's handled," David assured me calmly. "I've spoken to the club owner. He's shutting it down for the night and has agreed to come in for questioning."

"Sure he is." Yes. I was skeptical. "And what about the couple you found? You just left them?"

"Brooke, calm down. Really think about that." I searched his eyes and immediately realized I was overreacting. "Of course I put a stop to it. I asked them about our vics, and they told me they'd never seen them here before, either..."

I was about to vent my frustrations over hitting another dead end when David continued. "But then they told me that they were both new to the, um *coven*, and that I should talk to the owner. Donovan. I spoke with him for a bit, explained what we were doing here, and asked if he'd mind coming down for questioning. He was more than willing to comply."

Satisfied, I smiled. "Well then, I guess we'd better not keep him waiting."

Back at the station, David and I sat in the interrogation room across from the nightclub owner, Donovan Miller. Like the other club-goers, he was dressed in mostly black, from his shoulder-length hair right down to the nail polish on his fingernails, and he really had that smoky-eye technique down. If I wore more eye makeup, I'd probably ask him for some pointers.

"So, Mr. Miller—"

"Donovan," he interrupted, looking up at me with a sly smile that showed off his pointed teeth. "Mr. Miller is my father."

"Donovan," I repeated, trying not to be repulsed by his abundantly obvious attempt at flirtation. "Tell me about your club. From what we've seen and heard, it sounds like it has the potential to breed dangerous situations."

"On the contrary," he responded calmly. "I lead the only *coven*"—he spoke the word as though insulted that I called it a 'club'—"in this whole damn city that's exclusive. I don't let just anybody in, and any blood-sharing that goes on is one hundred percent safe. And consensual."

"Blood-sharing?" I repeated, disgusted. "Care to elaborate?"

He chuckled. It sounded dark and menacing and put me on edge. "You see, Detective Leighton, when male and female vampires are attracted to one another, it can lead to sexual encounters. Oftentimes, the sharing of each other's blood can heighten the experience."

Though difficult, I managed to keep myself from gagging in front of Donovan. "So they drink each other's blood? And you think this is *safe*?"

Flopping back in his chair, he dropped his hands to his lap. "You people would never understand." I looked at David, who appeared just as confounded as I was, and then back at Donovan. "Blood screening is mandatory before I welcome anyone into my coven, and there's regular testing that goes on quarterly. I understand the risks of the lifestyle we choose to lead, and I want to promise a safe place for us to exist as we were meant to. I'll give you copies of anything you need, but I assure you, everything that goes on within my coven is one hundred percent consensual."

"Thank you, we'd appreciate that, actually," I informed him before moving onto my next question. "Has anyone ever died during this...blood-sharing ritual?"

"Never. We never take more than we need," he responded honestly. "And I've never heard of it happening anywhere else, either."

"You're certain?" David spoke up.

Donovan sighed, sitting forward again. "Look, I heard about those victims and how they died. Exsanguination? Draining someone entirely isn't possible. Not during blood-sharing, at least." He released a single, mocking laugh. "Was that what made you think it was vampires?"

"There was a mark on her neck. Two puncture wounds," I replied. "Seemed like a good theory."

He laughed again, only this one, to me, sounded slightly more confident — cocky, even — and he started rolling the sleeves of his shirt up. "Normally, I'd agree, but I'm confident that you're probably not looking for any of my coven members," he told us, laying his arms on the table.

I glanced down at them, not sure what to think. Donovan was quick to explain. "Not every member of my coven has the dental implants since they all hold day jobs. Even those of us who do have them, they don't puncture deep enough to cause continuous blood flow — if you know what I'm saying." He took his right index finger and dragged it along a wound that was so fresh I thought I could still smell traces of his blood. A tremor moved through me, and my stomach rolled as I visualized how this happened. I didn't understand why this affected me in such a visceral way, but I couldn't help but feel like it went against the very core of my existence.

The wound wasn't very large—a straight, quarter-inch line with one small hole on either side of it. "There's usually a small incision made, and sometimes, depending on just how zealous our partner gets, we'll get lucky with the additional puncture wounds, but they're never deep enough to cause someone to bleed out."

David and I looked at each other again as Donovan pulled his sleeves back down, and when we returned our gaze to him, he raised his eyebrows and shrugged. "Plus, we never—ever—feed from the neck. It's always done in a place that can be easily concealed, and always away from any major arteries like the carotid and the femoral. That's just asking for trouble, if you ask me. And I'm not looking for trouble."

What he told us made sense—in a way—and we no longer had a reason to keep questioning him. We gathered his alibi information and gave him the standard "don't leave town" spiel. His business still worried me, but as far as I could tell, he wasn't breaking any laws. Due to his being nothing but completely open and forthright, we thanked him for his time, apologized for the trouble, and sent him on his way. On his way out, he assured us that he would cooperate with anything we might need to aide the investigation, including sending over any and all information regarding his club.

After he left, I turned to David and threw my hands up in defeat. "Well, that was a bust."

"Maybe so," he agreed, sitting on the edge of his desk and taking my hands, pulling me toward him. "There are still three other clubs. The odds are still in our favor."

I released an aggravated sigh. "I know. I guess I'm just frustrated. What if we don't find anything? We'll be right back at square one."

"Or, we could break this case wide open," he said confidently, trying to lift my spirits and reminding me why I fell in love with him.

When he fell silent, dropping his eyes from mine, I sensed his turmoil. I pulled one of my hands from his and looked to make sure no one was looking before I placed my hand on his shoulder and teased the soft hairs at the nape of his neck. "Hey," I whispered. "What's wrong?"

Raising his face, he hesitated briefly. "I'm worried."

"About?"

He exhaled heavily, and I started to fear his response. "About how you'll cope should we find out that your brother was messed up in all of this."

"I worry about that, too," I admitted quietly.

"Can you recall anything from back then that might have indicated something like this?" David inquired, treading carefully.

"I don't. But Bobby hung out with his friends more than he did with me once we hit college. The night of our birthday was the first time we'd gone out together in weeks." The minute the words left my mouth, I realized that, while I might not have known about Bobby's extracurricular activities, there was one person who probably did: his best friend...and my ex.

Nick.

Looked like he was going to get that phone call he seemed so desperate for after all.

CHAPTER 12 | CONTACT

I tapped the eraser of my pencil against my desk over and over again, staring at the creased piece of paper in front of me. I'd been trying to find the courage to pick up the phone and dial, but the truth of the matter was, the thought of making this call terrified me. Not only was I worried about Nick getting the wrong impression about *why* I was calling him, but a large part of me was terrified of finding out the truth about whether or not Bobby had been involved in this bizarre "vampire" lifestyle.

So far, two of the other three groups had returned from their investigation, reporting the same thing we'd already found out at Donovan's club. Just like David and me, they shut the clubs down and were currently interviewing the club owners. From what David and I were able to glean before they went into the interrogation rooms, our victims went unrecognized at both of these clubs, too. There was a possibility that someone was lying, and if that happened to be the case, then we'd have our work cut out for us.

Which was another reason I needed to bite the bullet and call Nick. If Bobby's death had anything to do with this, and Nick knew anything about it, this could be all we needed to finally bring this crazy son of a bitch to justice.

Resolute in my decision, I dropped my pencil to my desk and picked up my phone, dialing the number before I lost my nerve. When I first told David that if anyone knew whether or not Bobby was involved in this life, it would be Nick, he seemed skeptical. I understood his reluctance when I told him I could call to find out, but he agreed that it might be in the case's best interest.

There was no answer after the fourth ring, so I pulled the phone from my ear to hang it up. Before it hit the base, though, I heard a rushed and panicked "Hello?" almost as clear as if the phone were still against my ear.

"Oh, hey," I replied, bringing the phone back to my ear.

"Brooke?" he asked, sounding out of breath and slightly panicked. "What's going on? Are you okay?"

I dismissed the feeling that his concern meant anything more than it should to me. "Yeah. I just…I wanted to ask you about something."

Nick fell silent on the other end of the phone before sighing. "Look, it wasn't planned," he said. "Honestly, I didn't mean to, Brooke."

My brows pulled together with confusion. "Didn't mean to what, Nick?"

More silence. "Uh…what is it you're talking about?"

"Well, I was calling to ask about Bobby, but now I'm slightly more interested in what you didn't mean to do," I told him, sitting back in my chair and wondering if this was the part where he apologized for walking out on me. Not that it would matter at this point. I'd moved on and was finally at a place in my life where I was happy.

Completely out of character, Nick stumbled over

his words before reasserting his confidence. "It's nothing we can't talk about soon — in person, preferably." He paused, waiting for my answer that never came, and then continued. "What is it you wanted to know?"

I contemplated pursuing whatever he was talking about, but the open file in front of me reminded me of more important things to clear up first. "Back in college," I began, "you and Bobby were close."

"Yeah…"

"I know that you and he did things together without me sometimes, and I was just wondering what sort of…um, *stuff* that was."

Nick exhaled loudly, and he sounded almost annoyed. "Brooke, if you're suggesting I was seeing someone else behind your back—"

"What?" I asked, incredulous. "That's not what I was saying at all—not that any of that would even matter now." I pinched the bridge of my nose in frustration. "What I want to know is what kind of stuff Bobby was into."

"What do you mean? Like drugs?"

I bounced back and forth on just how much I could tell him without compromising the case before deciding to just figure out what he already knew regarding Bobby's murder. I sat forward and leaned on my desk, my hair curtaining one side of my face as I turned away from the few detectives milling around. "Remember when we found him in that alley?"

"Yeah," Nick replied with a sigh, and I imagined him running his hand through his hair.

"Well, remember the mark on his neck? And how he was drained of blood?"

"Y-yeah…" He dragged out this one word, seemingly curious about where I was headed.

"Did you…" I stopped, afraid that, while I was

able to win over my colleagues, I might seem crazy to Nick. "What I mean is...was Bobby a part of one of those underground clubs that claim all their patrons are vampires?"

Dead silence. It was so silent, I feared he'd hung up on me. "Nick?"

"Yeah," he responded quietly. "I'm here. What made you ask?"

I shrugged, looking out the window and up at the almost-full moon hanging in a star-filled sky. "A case I'm working on, actually," I confessed without thinking about it.

"The woman from the park?" Nick interjected, surprising me.

"Uh, yeah, actually. How did you know about that?"

"I read about it in the paper. So, what about it made you think about Bobby?"

"She had a similar mark on her neck," I informed him. "One of my colleagues joked about vampires, and it was the only lead we had. We found a few clubs where people gallivant around pretending to be vampires, and so far, we've come up with nothing. So I thought that maybe—"

"Vampires," Nick repeated, and I swore I heard him snarl the word.

Groaning, I pressed my forehead into my hand. "I know. It sounds so stupid, right?" Before he could answer, I kept going. "I just thought that maybe the two cases were connected somehow."

"They are," Nick said so quietly I wondered if he meant for me to hear it at all.

Just to be sure I wasn't hearing things, I said, "What?"

Nick cleared his throat. "Can you meet somewhere to talk? Tonight?"

Part of me wanted to say yes — needed to — and I didn't know why. It seemed to be a deeply rooted feeling. Almost instinctual. My brain, however, had the final say this time. "Nick, that's not a good idea."

"Why?"

"I'm working," I reminded him.

"Is that the only reason?"

"So, did you and Bobby hang out at any new clubs back then before the night of our birthday?" I asked, ignoring his question and changing the topic.

Seeming irritated, Nick exhaled heavily. "There were a couple we thought about going to because they didn't card, but only one like the ones you're describing... Brooke, I really think we should discuss this in person. It's...more complicated than you realize."

"What was the name of this club?" I continued, hoping it was one of the four we were investigating.

Nick hesitated before conceding. "*Gianna's*. But, Brooke, I'm serious. You can't go there alone."

"*Gianna's*." I leafed through the papers on my desk until I found my list of nightclubs. "That one's not on my list. Doesn't really sound like the type of club I'm looking for, either."

Nick chuckled. "It's not like the owners want to advertise what kind of club they're running, babe. Not to mention, it's not exactly a club that everyone is privy to," he told me.

My fingers moved across my keyboard at lightning speed as I tried to pull up any and all information about this club as possible. I found nothing except for a couple of Italian restaurants across the country and a hair salon in New York.

Nick continued speaking. "We only heard about it from some woman at a party who'd claimed she was a regular blood doll."

I froze, a shiver rolling down my spine, and my stomach rolled. "Blood doll?"

"Someone who offers themselves up to be fed from," he clarified hesitantly, like he regretted telling me in the first place, and I resumed my typing. "You won't find anything online," Nick informed me, somehow knowing what I was up to. "The club moves often, and it's very secretive. People get in by invitation only."

There it was again...*invitation only*. Why did that try to register every time I heard it? It had to mean something, but what?

"And you and Bobby went? To what? Be *blood dolls*?"

"Brooke, I really don't think we should talk about this over the phone. There's so much you don't understand."

Frustrated, I sighed. "Then help me."

"I'm trying. But I need to see you. I need to make sure you're okay." Concern laced his voice, and I wasn't entirely sure why.

I ignored his plea to see me again and repeated my question. "Did you and Bobby go to this club?"

Silence.

"Nick," I breathed, feeling slightly betrayed.

"It wasn't like that, I promise. We thought it would be different. It's not like we sought the place out initially. She approached us at that party, we only decided to use the invitations to see what all the hype was about."

That's when it hit me.

"The club we went to on our birthday," I mumbled. "Bobby said he got the tickets from some girl at a party." My anger flared, and I started to growl. "You took me to a secret wannabe-vampire club?"

"We didn't think she was serious," he tried to

justify. "We were curious."

Taking a beat, I attempted to get back to my line of questions. I couldn't change the past, but I should be able to use it to help me find this place. "So, are you sure it's involved in the vampire subculture? What exactly did this woman you met say?"

"Brooke—"

"How do I find out where it is?" I inquired further.

I should have known he wouldn't tolerate my ignoring him much longer. "Brooke!"

Just then, David returned from watching one of the interrogations, and sat at his desk, watching me. "Thanks for all your help, Nick. I'll find it on my own."

Just before I replaced the phone on its base, I heard an irate *"God damn it, Brooke!"*

David must have heard it too, because his eyes widened, but before he could ask about it, I smiled. "Apparently, we were looking for clubs that were too obvious in the subculture," I explained.

"What do you mean?"

"Nick told me that he and Bobby were approached about a club called *'Gianna's'* back in college." I told him. "Said some woman claiming she let them use her like some sort of donor bag invited them." He was shocked when I told him I'd actually been there, not knowing what kind of club I was actually in, but he refocused quickly.

"Did you get the address?" David asked. "Let's head over there now."

Shaking my head, I sighed. "Can't. Nick said the location moves around a lot." As I explained this to him, I wondered how Nick knew this. He didn't say it *moved* around, but that it *moves* around. How would he know that unless he was in some way a part of it now?

"Brooke?"

I didn't even realize I'd zoned out until David spoke up. "Sorry."

"No worries, you just went kind of blank there. You feeling all right?"

Nodding, I stood. "Yeah. Fine." Forcing my head back into the game, I grabbed my jacket from the back of my chair and pulled it on. "I say we head back to these clubs and start asking the patrons if they've heard of *Gianna's*. We'll go undercover if we have to."

For the next two days, we searched for this mysterious club. We asked around, but no one had heard of it. Donovan, the owner of *The Dungeon*, admitted to knowing of clubs like it, and even that his own had been modeled after them, but the name *Gianna's* didn't ring any bells.

None of the other three clubs had heard of it either, which only served to upset me further. It was frustrating as hell, but I refused to give up.

We worked all afternoon, trying to find the location of this place. I wasn't sure how much time had passed at first, but eventually, the captain came out of his office, making his way over to my desk where David and I were still brainstorming. We'd just gotten off the phone with Donovan, who agreed to contact a few people in his inner circle, when my dad interrupted.

"You two should head out. You've been working this case around the clock. Go out to dinner," he suggested. "You've got your phones. Someone will call if they find anything."

"Sir," I started, but he cut me off by raising his hand.

"No, Detective. Go." His tone was stern, and not one that I was ready to go up against.

David looked from my father to me and shrugged. "Maybe he's right."

Pleased with David's compliance, Dad scurried off back to his office, and I turned to David. "He already likes you. You don't need to keep kissing his ass."

Laughing, David grabbed our coats. "Come on, Detective. Let me take you out somewhere nice. What are you in the mood for?"

I thought about it for a second, weighing all my options before I decided. "Steak. Definitely steak." Then I noted the hour. It was almost well after eight. "But it's getting late."

David sloughed off my concern of the time as no big deal. "I'm sure we can find some place."

When we stepped out of the precinct, I had the distinct feeling like someone was watching me. My first impulse was to inhale deeply, and it surprised me when I picked up traces of something. It was woodsy and surprisingly comforting—but also concerning. I couldn't negate that fact. My eyes scanned the darkness on the way to the car, but I found nothing. That didn't mean I imagined things, though. While I could feel someone out there, I didn't sense an imminent threat, so David pulled the car out of the lot.

We decided on J&G Steakhouse—my favorite—and while David navigated the streets, I called ahead and asked if we could get a table, even if it was a little late. The manager said that there were still several tables that were still ordering, so he didn't have a problem getting us in.

After parking the car, David and I walked arm in arm into the restaurant and were seated quickly by the manager personally. We placed our drink orders and were given a minute more with our menus. When our server made his way over with our drinks, David took the liberty and ordered for the both of us to save a bit of time. "Can I get two of your prime rib dinners, please?"

"Definitely," our server replied, jotting our order down. "And how would you like them cooked?"

"Medium-well," David said, closing his menu. "And I'll have the baked potato and — "

"Rare," I interrupted. I don't know why I had the sudden desire for my steak to be cooked any other way than medium-well, because the truth was, bloody steaks grossed me out. Or…at least, they used to. Now it sounded strangely appealing, and my mouth watered at the thought. The server acknowledged me with a nod and marked my change down on the paper while David eyed me suspiciously from across the table.

We both put in our side orders for our meals, and then the server read everything back to us. With everything settled, he left to put our order in, and David turned to me. "You feeling okay?"

"Yeah. Why?" I shrugged.

"Brooke, you just ordered your steak *rare*. Even the slightest shade of pink usually has you sending your food back to the kitchen. What's up?"

He was right, but I couldn't explain the sudden change. "I don't know. I guess I'm just in the mood for something different." It seemed like David understood, and he let it go without pressing any further.

I picked up my wine and took a sip, looking across the table at a suddenly nervous-looking David. I'd never known him to be so fidgety, but seeing him focused so intently on his hands as he cracked his knuckles over and over again concerned me. Reaching across the table, I placed my hand over his, and he stilled.

"What's up?" I asked. "You're freaking me out here."

David chuckled; it wasn't a jovial sound, but hesitant instead. "Well, I've been waiting for the right time to bring this up, and I thought maybe now was perfect."

I inhaled a sharp breath at the seriousness of his tone, remembering the last *two* times a man said almost those exact words. Just like then, it could only mean one of two things: he was ready to end things between us or he was about to propose. Considering we'd spent almost every waking moment together — except for the few times he had to go back to his apartment for a few things — indicated that it was likely the latter. Were we ready for that? After everything with Nick, was *I* ready for that?

"David — "

David swapped the positioning of our hands so his encased mine, and his blue eyes glimmered with nervous excitement. "These last couple years have been unbelievable," he began his thumbs moving back and forth over my hands. "And this last week, with us finally being able to open up to those close to us about our relationship and spending so much time together has only brought us closer, I think. So, I was thinking that maybe it's time we took the next step and — "

"David, I don't think I'm ready for that."

" — move in together." The excitement in his eyes extinguished, and his hands fell slack around mine, releasing them. "You're not ready? But — "

I shook my head quickly, mentally chastising

myself for misreading the situation as a marriage proposal, and I took his hands back in mine. "No. Wait. That wasn't what I thought you were going to say." He didn't seem reassured.

"So, had this been a proposal, you'd have said no?" he asked.

I pinched the bridge of my nose, feeling a headache come on. "But it wasn't, so that doesn't even matter."

"But if it was?"

"Yeah, I guess I would have," I answered honestly. "But it doesn't matter, because clearly you're not ready either if you didn't ask. So this whole thing is a non-issue."

David contemplated what I was saying before his rigid posture relaxed. "You're right. I'm sorry."

Relieved, I smiled. I could tell he was still a little hurt by my answer to what I assumed was happening, so I decided to give him this one. Not that it was a hard decision to come to. "And in answer to your question, yeah, I think us living together is a great idea."

"Really?" Positively beaming, David stood and pulled me into his arms, kissing me and hugging me and drawing the attention of the other patrons. When they started clapping and congratulating us, I blushed. "This is going to be so great."

Wrapping my arms around his neck, I agreed. Admittedly, living together never really crossed my mind over the last few months, but being with David made me happier than I'd been in a long time. Besides, we'd already been practically living together since the night of my attack last week, so it sort of felt like it was the next logical step.

David held me tighter, and I looked out the window behind him and up at the sight of the almost-full moon in the clear sky. The way I was suddenly drawn to it confounded me, but, at the same time, something about it felt almost essential to a part of me that stirred just below the surface. While I couldn't quite explain what this new sensation was, I knew that I was both anxious and eager for whatever was coming next.

CHAPTER 13 | LEAD

When I woke up the next morning, I felt a little queasy and jittery. The only thing I could link it to was the steak at dinner. While it had tasted absolutely amazing, maybe in hindsight, ordering out of my comfort zone wasn't such a bright idea. David had tried to tell me—even asked if I was sure I didn't want to send it back to be cooked a little more. At the time, I was glad I didn't, because the minute I cut into that steak, its savory scent practically hypnotized me, and I devoured it.

During dinner, David suggested that we stop by his house after work the next day and pick up a few of his things to bring over to *our* house—it was still a little strange to call it that, but equally as thrilling. We then talked about what he should do with his apartment—rent it out or sell it—and I really had no idea. While I didn't foresee anything going wrong between us, would it be bad luck to sell it...you know, just in case? We eventually decided to think it over for a few days before revisiting the topic. It wasn't like we had to decide right that second.

I didn't know if it was the romantic setting, our new living arrangement, the wine going straight to my head, or the intense need to release the stress of the last few days, but as the minutes ticked by, I found it hard to focus on anything but how badly I wanted to get David home and into *our* bed. While he ate, I had focused a little too intently on his soft lips, imagining how satisfying it would be to have them on mine or anywhere else on my body. Every time he picked up his wine glass, my gaze would drift to his hands, fantasizing about the warmth of them setting my skin ablaze as they roamed over my skin. When he spoke, I imagined him whispering in my ear as we made love.

My eyes were instantly drawn to his bright blue eyes, and the desire that was reflected back at me made me realize just how long it had been since we'd made love. Not for lack of either of us trying; it just seemed like every time things started to heat up between us, something important happened like our new case and the attack, or my hospitalization and concurrent recovery. Naturally, David was the kind of guy who would never push—which of course only made me want to remedy this immediately and show him my appreciation.

The feeling only grew with every minute that passed, and we'd barely made it through the front door before I accosted him against it, crushing my lips to his and unbuttoning his shirt as quickly as I could. Kissing ravenously, lust clouding the air we struggled to take in, we moved down the hall toward the bedroom, stumbling and leaving a trail of clothes in our wake like breadcrumbs. When we were within inches of the bed, David eased me down onto it and hovered over me dominantly.

Something in me shifted unexpectedly when his eyes locked with mine. I wrapped my legs around his waist, rolling him onto his back and pinning him to the mattress, my hands around his wrists while I kissed his jaw and neck. My nose brushed against his throat, and I inhaled deeply, taking in his unique fragrance until it fogged my brain. He smelled so amazing—so tantalizing—and I couldn't seem to get enough of him.

I wanted to devour him.

He never once complained while we made love, but he did try to reposition us a few times, only to be thwarted by my newfound strength and unwillingness to be in any kind of submissive position. At one point, I did allow him to sit up, and he pushed my hair back off my face, threading his fingers into it and holding it in place as we neared the precipice of our release.

I smiled at the memory of last night, my body tingling all over as my desire ignited again before vanishing just as suddenly, giving way to a much less pleasurable feeling. Suddenly, every muscle in my body tensed, leaving me on-edge and jittery. My skin tightened over my body, my heart raced, and my head pounded. This was the first time in days that I'd felt this out of sorts, and I wasn't sure if I should be concerned. While it was an unusual sensation taking over my entire body, it didn't seem particularly life-threatening, so I decided to wait it out and see if it passed on its own. I'd hate to go to the doctor just to find out it was mild anxiety or something.

The tension in my body increased, forcing me from bed before dawn, while David was still sound asleep. I figured I could at least get an early start on the day, so I quietly padded down the hall toward the kitchen and started brewing the coffee. I really hoped that whatever I was feeling went away once I'd eaten.

The smell of coffee infused the air, and I heard David stirring in the bedroom. It was still a little strange to hear every little thing, but over the last few days, I'd grown accustomed to it, and had even learned to use it to my advantage. I tried doing the same with my other senses, but the ability to smell every little thing had yet to grow on me as much as the others.

I listened to see if David was awake, but when I heard his soft snores, I knew he wasn't. Not surprising considering it was only five in the morning, and it was rare if he woke before six.

Without any warning, my stomach cramped painfully, forcing me to grip the countertop as I doubled over. It was hard to distinguish whether it was due to nausea or hunger, and it only strengthened the more I focused on it. Thankfully, it passed as quickly as it had come on, and when my hands shook afterward, I determined the cause to be hunger. I yanked the refrigerator door open so hard, I almost tore it off its hinges — literally — and I dug through it until I found the bacon and eggs. Once I located them, I grabbed my frying pan and turned the stove on so I could cook breakfast before David woke up. My mouth salivated as I eyed the raw bacon, but I mentally chastised myself for even entertaining the idea of it being edible like that.

No sooner had I started cooking, when I heard David's soft footfalls in the hall. He was trying to be sneaky. I could tell, because, instead of the usual heal-toe footstep, I heard a slower, tiptoe-like shuffling over the hardwood floors. He was so adorable sometimes, and I just didn't have the heart to ruin his fun, so I carried on with breakfast, humming to let him think I was none the wiser. When his hands grabbed my waist, I pretended to be startled, jumping slightly and gasping.

"Good morning," he said, pressing his lips to my shoulder as he wrapped his arms all the way around my waist and rocked us both side to side. "Sorry if I startled you. You been up long?" His hands continued to travel south, toying with the waist of my skimpy sleep shorts.

"Mmm," I hummed, looking toward the digital clock on the coffee maker. "Not really. Less than an hour." Abandoning breakfast for a brief second, I turned in his arms to greet him properly, and he gripped my ass, pulling me against him. "Why are you awake so early? I figured you'd sleep in after last night."

Smirking, David leaned forward and kissed me softly. "So did I," he replied quietly. "I thought you'd sleep in a bit today, too."

"That would've been nice," I agreed, stretching my neck when it felt tight again. "I guess my body figures it needs to be up before the sun now. It's normally not so bad, but today I think I could have used the extra sleep."

Worry quickly filled David's eyes as they darted between mine, and he forgot all about his not-so-subtle seduction. "Are you feeling okay?"

"Um, kind of," I replied honestly. "I'm a little jittery…almost like I'm anxious about something, and I was a little nauseous this morning before I got out of bed."

David placed the back of his hand to my forehead, and his eyebrows pulled together. "You do feel a little warmer."

"Weird." I turned back to plate breakfast. "I don't feel like I have a fever."

I started eating right away, the heavenly smell making my stomach growl. I was suddenly ravenous, unable to get enough. It was a stark contrast to the nausea I experienced earlier, and while this should probably concern me, something about it definitely didn't feel off. In fact, it felt as natural as breathing — like it was my body's way of preparing for something. Something big. What, though? I had no idea, but I felt like I was just supposed to go with it, so I did.

While David and I sat at the table, his cell phone rang. After a couple rings, he picked it up. It was O'Malley. Apparently a young woman had come into the station after an odd exchange the night before, and as soon as the word *"Gianna's"* left her mouth, O'Malley put her in an interrogation room with a cup of coffee and called us.

My hands trembled for an entirely new reason after that.

David and I rushed to get ready, agreeing to worry about the dishes when we got home that evening. By the time we were headed to the station, I was still feeling a little off, but the strange cramps and rolling in my stomach had subsided. I was still pretty anxious about something, but I couldn't seem to pinpoint what it was. All I knew was that I felt the deep need to be outside.

Sitting in the car brought on an unusual bout of claustrophobia as David drove. It wasn't something that plagued me in the past, but for some reason, I felt like a caged animal. I couldn't sit still, my skin broke out in a cold sweat, and my heartbeat quickened with panic. David noticed my fidgeting, but he didn't ask and I said nothing, mainly because I wasn't sure anything was wrong. Just like earlier, I chalked it up to my meal last night since it was the only "unusual" thing I could attribute it to. With slight reservations, he accepted it as plausible.

When we arrived, I was relieved to get out of the car, instantly stretching my entire body until my shoulders, neck, and lower back cracked satisfactorily. I reveled in the relief and tranquility that passed over me, a delightful quiver moving beneath the surface of my skin which forced goosebumps to prickle all over my body.

David led me into the precinct, and when we arrived on our floor, we found our team already gathered around O'Malley's desk. When he lifted his head and saw us, his eyes widened with excitement, and he waved us over frantically.

"What's up?" David asked, shrugging out of his jacket and silently offering to take mine, as well.

I took him up on his offer and then perched myself against the edge of O'Malley's desk while he hung them up on the coat rack. While waiting for O'Malley to speak, I picked up on something in the room. It wasn't just the excitement that I saw gleaming in O'Malley's eyes when we first arrived, but the air was infused with celebration.

It electrified the surface of my skin, and not only could I feel it rolling off of everyone in waves, but I swear I could smell it. It confused me, because how did one *smell* something like that? Even that day we were organizing our investigation and I called Clarke out; while it was odd, his fear was more than just satisfying. It was mouthwatering.

"I think we found that club," O'Malley announced, and my heart beat faster with elation.

"What?" I asked, stunned, but also to make sure I heard him correctly.

His smile widened, flashing his teeth, and he nodded. "We won't be sure until we check it out, but we've got a couple of leads from that club-goer we've got waiting for you. She said she was approached by someone looking to recruit new members."

"So you've got an address?" I asked excitedly. His smile was answer enough, and I flew to my feet in an instant. "Then what are we waiting for? Let's go check it out."

David chuckled next to me. "You realize that it's likely not going to be open to the public at ten in the morning, right?"

"No, but we can go take a look around. Maybe the cleaning crews will be there," I countered, itching to check this place out and talking a mile a minute.

O'Malley held out a folder. "It's possible, but why don't you wait until you've talked to the girl they tried to recruit first? She's been waiting for the two of you."

We walked into the room together, and our witness looked up. She looked a little worse for wear, a key indicator that she'd been up half the night partying. This deduction wasn't solely based on her appearance—though her choppy black bob was standing up every which way, and her black eye makeup was smudged down her cheeks—but also because I could smell the alcohol seeping from her pores.

The harsh light above the table glinted off of her eyebrow, nose, and lip piercings when she looked around the room. She seemed nervous, ringing her hands on the tabletop in front of her and tugging on her lip piercing with her teeth as her eyes darted about like a frightened animal, and when the sleeve of her shirt rose up her right arm, I saw a small, familiar mark on her wrist.

She was from Donovan's club.

"So," I started, glancing down at the file in front of me, "Sarah—"

She released an annoyed breath and rolled her eyes. "It's *Raven*, actually," she corrected me.

"Raven," I repeated, suppressing an eye roll of my very own. "Cute."

Huffing again, her golden brown eyes narrowed

in my direction. I offended her, and I sensed her annoyance like a gentle vibration that moved between us. Before she had a chance to snap, David interjected gently. "Raven." Even though he was being as charming as possible, his voice indicated that he was working really hard to not snicker at the cliché Goth name this girl had chosen for herself. "Our colleague, Detective O'Malley, said you called the precinct this morning regarding an invite to an even more exclusive club than the one you're a part of. Is this correct?"

She turned her attention to him and nodded. "Yeah. I was at *The Dungeon*, partying with Lucia and Astrophel"—I bit my tongue, because there was no way to keep a straight face otherwise—"and this couple walked in. It was hard not to notice them, actually." Raven's eyes glazed over as she lost herself in the memory, and I sensed her mood shifting. I no longer felt the flare of annoyance, but instead picked up a trace of ... *lust*. It was bizarre, and it made me uncomfortable.

"She was blonde and thin, with legs that went on for days, and she had her arm looped through her companion's." She sighed, her body relaxing even further into the chair, and her voice took on a tone of longing as she described the man. "He was something else, you know. His brownish hair was a stark contrast to his flawless, bone-white skin, and the club lights would pick up hints of red scattered throughout—dude's got a wicked-good hair stylist. He was unbelievably handsome, the strong cut of his jaw made even more so when he would lean down and whisper into the ear of the stunning woman on his arm.

"They strolled through the place like they owned it—I don't even know how they got in, actually. Donovan noticed them from his spot near the stage and approached them immediately." Raven shrugged. "I don't know what they talked about, but the woman smiled at him, said something, and he nodded before heading back to his office in the back."

I turned to David and lowered my voice. "We should call Donovan down." David agreed with a nod and looked toward the two-way mirror along the wall to his right. Behind it, O'Malley and some of our other colleagues were watching, so one of them would make the call.

"What happened next?" I asked. "Did they approach you right away?"

Raven shook her head emphatically. "Not even. They continued to look around, and then they split up. The woman worked her way across the dance floor, drawing almost everyone's eyes to her as she stopped to dance with a few people."

"And the man?" I inquired.

Raven raised her big brown eyes to mine. "He stood by the bar, ordered a drink, and scanned the room. Then his eyes honed in on me." She swallowed thickly, her eyebrows pulling together somewhat nervously as her apprehension poured over me.

"And that's when he approached you," I deduced, but Raven shook her head again. "Then…?"

She shivered, pulling her hands from the table and into her lap, her eyes following them. "I don't know how to describe what happened. It's kind of…foggy."

"*Try*," I encouraged, leaning forward on the table. "Just, try."

Her head bobbed slightly, but she kept her eyes from mine. "I didn't even realize I was walking toward him at first—in fact, it didn't feel like I was walking at all. I felt like I was floating, being pulled toward him by some unseen force."

"Tell us more about this man," David spoke up. "What about him stood out to you?"

"His eyes," Raven replied without missing a beat, and her head snapped up, locking her gaze on me. "They were green—kind of like yours, actually, but darker...almost sinister."

"And what did he say to you?" I probed gently.

"Not much, really. He told me about his club, and how I was exactly the type they were looking for. I wasn't sure what that even meant, but his voice was so hypnotic that I'd have believed anything he tried to tell me."

Taking in everything she told me, I nodded. "What happened next?"

"The woman came back. She seemed on edge about something—pissed off, actually—and her eyes were searching the room frantically as she took her boyfriend's hand again. I don't think she intended for me to hear anything, but she muttered something about *The Dungeon* being compromised by mongrels. That their scent polluted the air."

The information that Raven gave us so far confounded me. What did they mean by mongrels? She couldn't possibly have meant the police, could she? We hadn't been there in days—mainly because Donovan had been so cooperative and was sure to give us any information we needed whenever we asked for it—so how could she have known?

I didn't get a chance to formulate a theory before an even more relevant question came to mind: if she did know that the police had already infiltrated *The Dungeon*, why was it such a big deal? Perhaps she had something to hide, after all. Maybe she did have a hand in these murders—and Bobby's.

"Did you get the address?" I blurted out, desperate to follow this lead as far as I could.

Raven's head bobbed unsteadily as she reached into her pocket and pulled out a business card. "Y-yeah. He didn't say anything else after she came back. He only handed me this card and told me to stop by later last night."

"And did you?" David asked, glancing down at the glossy black card as I took it, careful to hold it by the edges so we could dust it for prints in hopes of getting an ID on these two.

I stared at the card, struggling to make a connection that felt so obvious. There was something familiar about it, and yet I struggled to place it... *Why?*

"No. I mean, I was going to, but Lucia and Astrophel didn't think it was a good idea. They suggested I call you. They'd heard Donovan talking with one of your officers about some pretty hairy activity going down and figured this was worth reporting."

I turned the card over in my hand, where I found only an address in the Warehouse District of Phoenix printed in a basic white font in the lower right corner. The memory slammed into me, shining bright like a lightbulb in a dark room. I'd seen this card before...

At Samantha Turner's apartment, right there on her coffee table amongst several others. I remembered bagging it myself before we left that day, but didn't think it really meant anything.

A smile played at the corners of my lips upon realizing that this could very well be the beginning of the end for this case, and a strange feeling swelled within me. It was a strange combination of relief and elation at having gotten what was probably a vital piece of information after chasing our tails, but there something else crouched just below the surface.

Something *hungry*.

CHAPTER 14 | RUN

After thanking Raven for the information, we had her prints taken. She was confused at first, until we explained that it was to eliminate hers on the card from any others we might find. Once processed, we took her to the elevator and watched her leave before heading back to our desks to fill in our team.

O'Malley was just hanging up his phone when we approached, and he informed us that Donovan agreed to come down to talk to us. There was one problem, though; he apparently didn't remember much from the night in question and wasn't sure he'd be much help. O'Malley requested copies of any surveillance footage *The Dungeon* had, though. Hopefully it was useful.

Even though I was unsure what to make of Donovan's sudden bout of amnesia, we needed to get as much information as possible. While we waited for Donovan to arrive, David called the Phoenix precinct to see if he could get jurisdiction to investigate the address on the card. It turned out they were investigating a couple of murders that sounded very much like ours. When I told them about the card, they sounded as ecstatic as I was about it. Once we had the approval we needed, I hung up the phone and saw

Donovan approaching my desk.

"We really need to stop meeting like this, Detective Leighton," he greeted.

Laughing, I gestured toward the chair across from me, and Donovan took a seat, handing me the disc. "You really do spoil me."

"Flowers are so cliché," Donovan quipped, relaxing back into the chair. "So, I'm told you wanted to talk about my visitors last night?"

David joined our conversation, standing next to me. "We do."

"Well," Donovan replied, "as I told the detective on the phone, I'm not sure how much help I'll be. It's all kind of a blur."

"Had a little too much to drink last night?" I inquired, equal parts teasing and seriousness.

Donovan quickly shook his head. "Not at all."

"How can you be sure? You did say you can't remember anything," I reminded him, and he shrugged.

"I realize how sketchy it sounds to say I don't remember what happened—believe me, I do—but my bartender, Adam, assures me I hadn't had anything to drink the entire night." I recognized the name of the bartender as the one I spoke to when we were last here. Would he remember anything from last night? I'd have to remember to give him a call to find out. In fact, it might not be a bad idea to pay another visit to *The Dungeon* just to be sure.

"So you don't even remember what happened *before* they came into your club?" I asked. "How is that possible?"

Donovan looked frustrated, but I was confident my line of questioning wasn't the cause. He hated that he couldn't remember. "I don't know."

"Well, one of your club-goers said she saw you

approach them," I told him. "Did you?"

Donovan fell silent, his eyebrows pulling together as he thought back. "I vaguely remember sitting near the stage in my usual seat, and then seeing them." He clenched his eyes shut, possibly in an attempt to jog his memory. "At first, I had no idea how they even got in—I'd never seen them before, and I hadn't approved any new members or potentials for last night."

"So you approached them?"

Eyes still shut, Donovan nodded. "That's what the surveillance video shows. Honestly, I vaguely remember speaking with the woman, but, for the life of me, I don't recall what it was about." Frustrated or weary, he rubbed his hands over his face. "It feels like it was a dream, to be honest. One that's quickly fading away."

Things just kept getting weirder by the second. Either he was lying about not remembering, or he had the worst memory in the world, because how could he not remember a conversation with an uninvited guest in his *exclusive* club? What did she do? Hypnotize him? And his doorman? A ridiculous theory. The only way I would know for sure was if I located this woman and her companion and figured out exactly what went on at this club they were advertising.

After watching the surveillance video that Donovan brought over, we were no closer to identifying this couple. One camera showed them entering the club, but they seemed aware of it, keeping their faces hidden. The woman was dressed in a tight black dress, showing off as much skin as possible, even with the cooler evening temperatures, and the man wore jeans, a basic black shirt, and a leather jacket. Nothing about either of them really stood out to me, except when I saw what Raven was talking about:

they moved with confidence and purpose, and all eyes were on them.

While I continued to study this couple, trying to see anything that could help me figure out who they were, Donovan approached the couple. The woman talked to him, leaning in as though whispering to him, and then he disappeared, presumably back to his office since we didn't see him again. Even watching the recording with us frustrated him. The other cameras showed the mystery couple walk the floor — still being sure to avoid the cameras — and then they split up. The woman made her rounds, and, just as Raven said he did, the male parked himself at the bar until she approached him. She was right, too; the way she walked toward him seemed off. Having met her and walked her out, her gait was completely different in this video. It looked as though she was locked in some kind of trance, like she was being pulled to him by some unseen force, and it made no *logical* sense.

Sure, I could keep going with my hypnosis theory, but what were the chances that was actually valid?

I was starting to lose hope when the woman reentered the frame. Her posture seemed less fluid than before — rigid and panicked...*afraid* — as she leaned in to speak with her partner. His own posture stiffened, and while he glanced around their surroundings, still sure to keep his identity hidden, her eyes flashed up at the camera and she bared her teeth for the briefest of seconds. It all happened so fast that I actually questioned whether or not it happened at all. While my brain tried to figure out whether or not I imagined it, my body reacted as though it was real. The hairs on the back of my neck bristled, my entire body quivered, and I found myself pulling my own lips back in a silent snarl. It felt instinctive.

David's hand touching down on my shoulder

grounded me, and I pushed the defensive feeling aside. "Did you see that?" I asked him quietly, my voice noticeably lower and trembling slightly.

"What?"

I rewound the recording to where she looked at the camera, and we watched it again, but he still missed it. I didn't, though, and it brought about the same reaction in me. Time and time again, I witnessed the absolute look of disgust on this woman's face when she made eye contact with the camera. It was as though she knew we were watching her, and it only further cemented my theory that she had something to do with these deaths.

We watched this part of the tape at least a dozen times, and David continued to look at me like he was questioning whether or not to have me committed. When I finally froze the feed on the exact millisecond that this woman glared at the camera, I excitedly pointed at the monitor.

"Aha! See! Right there!" My excitement faded as I examined the look in her eyes and determined it as challenging. But who was she challenging? The club's security guards? The police? No, the more I let her eyes burn into mine through the monitor, I felt like she was challenging *me*.

That couldn't be right. The only reason I felt that way was because I was on the other side of the video feed. She meant the look for whoever was watching and no one in particular. She knew on some level that we'd come into possession of the security feed eventually, so maybe this was her way of daring the cops to come find her.

If that was the case, though, why was every one of my instincts telling me to watch my back?

The thirty-minute drive from the precinct to the Warehouse District in Phoenix had my stomach in knots and my heart pounding so hard and fast that it became uncomfortable. In order to assuage the feeling, I chose to focus on how the color of the blue sky was streaked with the gold and orange hues of the setting sun.

When David and I rolled the car to a stop outside the address on the card, the sun was dipping even lower on the horizon. My skin hummed, a dull throb beginning in my shoulder at the point of my almost two-week-old injury. The pulse was hot in my veins, moving down my arm and throughout the rest of my body, and I swallowed the warm saliva that gathered in my mouth. I don't know why I felt this way, but I tried to push it aside, because now was clearly not the time.

A Phoenix PD car was here waiting already, the two male detectives on the sidewalk, having a smoke. We waited a few more minutes for O'Malley and Keaton to arrive, and when they pulled up behind us, we stepped out of the car and onto the sidewalk. The first thing I did — only because it seemed to be my first impulse now — was sniff the air, picking up faint traces of something familiar and unpleasant.

I sniffed again in an effort to place the smells, drawing strange glances from the three men around me, before I shrugged. "Thought I smelled a hot dog vendor." A horrible lie, because my nose told me the nearest vendor was ten blocks away…

Weird.

Pushing through the mental detour, I turned and nodded toward the waiting Phoenix detectives.

"Come on."

The taller of the two men tossed his cigarette butt to the curb and stomped it out. Dressed in a brown suit, he looked to be about fifty, his eyes brown and his head bald, and he was no taller than David. His frame was heavier, though, most of his weight resting in his slightly distended belly. He reached out his hand toward me. "You must be Detective Leighton," he said as I gripped his hand. "I'm Detective Burns."

"Pleasure," I said, eyeing his approaching partner.

"Adams," his partner said, his dirty-blond hair slicked back and his hazel eyes soft and inquisitive. He was new. I could smell the inexperience on him. His apprehension, too.

They told us about the three homicides they'd been investigating, all of the details sounding eerily similar to our own investigation. Naturally, they scoffed when I told them about my underground vampire club theory. It annoyed me. My nostrils flared, and my vision was clouded with red.

"Got me this far," I snarled through gritted teeth. "So, if you wanna continue to ride on my coattail, I suggest we get moving."

That shut them up. Satisfied, I turned abruptly on my heel and led the way toward the entrance. The closer we got, the stronger the scent was. My stomach rolled, and I fought to suppress the urge to retch. I tried to focus on the scent of the trash that wafted from the alley, but even the smell of rotting food wasn't enough to relieve the assault on my nose. I inhaled deeply, thinking I could hold it until we got inside and away from the stench, and just like that, my sensory memory kicked in. I was instantly transported to when I smelled it last: in Samantha Turner's apartment, just the other day. It was death I smelled in the air, only this time, it held the coppery notes of blood…and a lot of it.

But where was it coming from?

The combination of smells attacked each of my senses, burning my throat like acid, and my skin prickled as tiny beads of sweat formed all over my body. Blood pounded through my veins, my heart increased in tempo and strength while my arms trembled, and every muscle in my back tensed almost painfully. I didn't know what to make of what was happening to me, but it worried me. A lot.

Even though I found it repulsive, I followed the scent to the door, reaching out and grabbing the doorknob. It didn't turn all the way. Locked. I considered knocking to announce our presence, but something pushed me to try the door again. This time, the muscles in my arm tensed as I turned the knob one more time. Something metallic snapped within the door, and the knob turned effortlessly in my hand before the door swung open. The guys didn't notice, which was fortunate, because I wouldn't have known how to explain it if they did.

What happened next caught me completely off guard. The smell that plagued me in the alley hit me like a freight train, knocking all the clean air from my lungs until my entire body felt polluted. We'd found the source of the smell, and my skin crawled as I took the first hesitant step into the building with David, Keaton, O'Malley, and the two Phoenix detectives on my heels. Waves of nausea crashed in my stomach the farther inside I walked, and my eyes adjusted to the dark quickly. Much quicker than normal.

The stench filled the air like a heavy smog. It was hard to keep moving forward, my movements slow and staggered, almost debilitated. My eyes scanned the dark for anything out of the ordinary as my fingers curled like talons. It didn't take long for me to realize that my reaction to this smell wasn't just disgust, but that my body seemed to be readying itself to attack.

David noticed this, coming up beside me and looking at me with concern etched into his forehead. "You feeling all right?" he asked.

The warehouse was suddenly bathed in light. David and I to whipped around to see Keaton over by the wall, pointing at the light switch with his thumb. "Not all of us have natural night vision," he joked, and I realized that it hadn't even occurred to me how dark it was.

The six of us looked around the open space together. It looked like any night club would look after a wild night: chairs knocked over, bottles and glasses littering the floor and tabletops. There was nothing special or particularly memorable about this place; it looked like an abandoned building that had been turned into a night club with little to no renovations.

David, O'Malley, and Keaton had their hands on their guns while I didn't. It took a minute before finding it weird that my first instinct *wasn't* to reach for my weapon in the off chance we might be ambushed. Normally, having my gun ready to grab would give me a sense of security, but I didn't feel like I needed it. I felt like if something were to jump out at me, I could deal with it without the use of a firearm.

It was a very strange feeling...but at the same time, a very powerful one.

"I'm okay. It just smells in here," I confessed to him, only to be met with a quizzical stare. "Doesn't it?" I inhaled another big whiff and instantly regretted it when the smell hit the back of my throat, making me gag.

I expected David to look at me as if I'd lost my

mind, but instead he urged me to continue. "I don't smell anything other than stale beer and alcohol that's been spilled and left to dry, but that doesn't mean you don't. You seem to have picked up an uncanny sense of smell, so if you say you smell something, I believe you." My lips curled up into a relieved smile, and he continued. "What do you smell?"

I glanced over to where O'Malley and Keaton were currently looking around the building, then over at Burns and Adams behind the abandoned bar. "Well, in addition to the alcohol, the most dominant smell is…decay. It smells like something rotten has been in here for days—maybe even weeks."

"Anything else?"

"Blood," was all I said. "And a lot of it. This could be where the murders were committed."

I don't think it was intended for me to see, but David's entire frame shuddered. "Okay, we'll get CSU down here to check the place out."

David talked to Burns and Adams, who made the call while I continued to look around the building. Glass bottles littered the floor, and we walked carefully to keep from kicking them as we navigated the room so we didn't disturb anything. Our shoes stuck to the alcohol that had been spilled, and we weaved around upturned tables and bar stools as we looked for something useful. Really, I'd been hoping to find actual people to question, but this place looked abandoned. And recently.

It was beginning to look like we were too late. Maybe they decided to move onto another location when they found out the police had been to Donovan's club back home. My frustration mounted quickly, the rage at being too damn late making my entire body shake. By the time CSU arrived, I was too anxious and unable to take it anymore; there were too many people in one space, and I couldn't focus on anything other than how trapped I felt. Always underfoot.

I started for the door when David stopped me, catching my hand. "Where are you going?"

I looked through the open door and caught sight of the full moon in the darkening blue sky. *Freedom,* a soft voice — mine — whispered in the back of my mind. I was...*drawn* to it in a way that I couldn't even begin to describe, and, suddenly, being outside was all I thought about. All I wanted. "I need some fresh air to clear my head. It's crowded in here, and I can't think straight. I'm going to take a walk around the area, see if there's something there."

David nodded, understanding. "Okay. Hurry back, though, okay?"

"I will. I've got my phone. Call me if they find anything," I told him before squeezing his hand and heading outside.

The minute the cool air hit my face, I closed my eyes. It felt amazing against my skin, and I inhaled deeply, the air out here seeming so much cleaner than it did inside. It was still tainted, though, and I wandered a little farther down the sidewalk, rounding the corner in search of a less polluted source of air.

When I found it, my entire body felt rejuvenated, and my feet picked up their pace. I was speed walking, and I didn't know where I was heading; I was just happy to be outside and moving. All of my frustration and anxiety slowly faded as my legs moved a little faster than before.

Cars passed on the street, and I noticed all the people milling by me, sidestepping. The city never bothered me before, but for some reason, now it was too busy — suffocating, actually — and claustrophobia threatened to grab hold of me again. My palms were sweaty, my heart still racing. Every pair of eyes seemed to turn to me, like I was on display, so I ran.

I didn't know where I was going, but the feel of the wind through my hair and on my face as I ran faster and faster was exhilarating. For a moment, all I heard was my pulse pounding in my ears, my adrenaline spiking as I rounded another corner and followed a path away from the bustling activity of the city. My body temperature rose, which wasn't uncommon when I ran, but my skin itched, crawling and rippling, and every muscle in my body burned like it was on fire. Instead of making me want to stop, though, it pushed me forward. It struck me as weird. It was unlike anything I'd ever felt before, but I accepted it because it felt oddly natural.

The sensation of running with wild abandon wrapped around me, allowing me to get so lost that I didn't hear my phone ringing at first. Even when the sound did register, I ignored it. I was no longer in control of my own body. Something else was. It should've worried me, but I felt strong—stronger than ever before—and I welcomed the feeling.

When my phone rang again, my hand, feeling dislocated from my body, pulled it from my pocket and tossed it to the ground. Shocked by this, I considered going back for it, but was quickly overruled by whatever force controlled me, and I kept on my path toward the outskirts of the city. Soon I forgot all about the phone and civilization as the bright full moon pulled my focus again, and I darted into the night.

Chapter 15 | Confused

Warmth surrounded me as my mind breached the barrier between sleep and reality, and I groaned as my eyes fluttered open. The instant the sunlight streaming in from the window above the bed caught my eyes, pain pierced my brain and forced me to slam them shut again. A painful jackhammer-like pounding lingered even as I pressed the heels of my hands against my eyes, plunging me back into darkness. Sadly, this did little to cease the relentless throb, so I pressed harder until bright white spots formed, eventually merging into *one* bright white spot.

The moon.

I knew that wasn't what it really was, but for some reason, it invited a flashflood of images that felt both dream-like and real at the same time. While I had trouble sorting through them, one thing remained constant, and that was the silver orb that hung in the darkness like a full moon on a starless night.

The threat of rain was thick in the air as the wind rustled through the leaves of the trees overhead. The rich smell of the cool soil was almost intoxicating, but that feeling soon dissipated when a sharp growl cut through the blackness. Yellow eyes and a threatening flash of white directly below them gleamed as the animal — a large wolf — stalked out from its hiding place amongst the bushes that appeared out of nowhere, but that wasn't where the growling came from.

Its light brown fur gleamed in the silver light of the moon, and it looked oddly familiar as it stepped closer. I passed the thought off as ridiculous because all wolves looked alike, didn't they? A deep pulse — a heartbeat, I realized in my conscious state *— filled the silent night air as it stalked forward, one deliberate step at a time. Its amber eyes shined bright, never blinking as its hot breath mixed with the cool desert air, forming a thick cloud of fog that spiraled up around its head.*

Then, with a threatening bark, it leapt, its jaws open wide and ready to strike.

With a jolt, my eyes snapped open, my pulse thundering in my ears as I stared at the white wall in front of me. In addition to my headache, my memory of last night was somewhat muddled, mixing with the strange recurring dream I'd been having of the wolf attack. My mouth was dry, feeling like it was full of cotton balls. If I didn't know any better, I'd swear I was suffering the world's worst hangover. The problem with that theory, though, was that I didn't have a single drop of alcohol. This didn't negate the very real fact that something was seriously wrong with me.

Slowly, I pushed myself off the bed, focusing my attention on anything other than how my arms trembled under the physical exertion this one simple act used. Every muscle in my back tensed and ached as I struggled. When my eyes fell to my hands, I gasped upon finding them filthy, dirt and bits of grass wedged beneath my fingernails.

Confused, I tried to jog my memory, but came up empty time and time again. As I continued to rise, the cool bed sheet fell from my body — my apparently very naked body. My eyes wandered over my arms, noticing thin, pink scratches running the length of them beneath the dirt and grime that covered my skin. They also covered my chest, upraised, and they tingled slightly like newly healing skin when I touched them. I should have been able to remember how I got them, but I didn't.

White teeth and amber eyes flashed against black again and again, but I continued to shake it off as another bad dream brought on by the memory of the wolf attack. For some reason, it wasn't so easy. I let my head fall back, staring at the roof, as the flashes continued and the faint taste of copper formed on my tongue. Each of these little revelations made my head hurt more, and I sat up tall, stretching my arms up over my head in an effort to release the tension in my spine as my eyes wandered around my room...

...or, what I *thought* was my room up until I really took in my surroundings. The haze of sleep snapped back like a recoiled spring, slapping me in the face. Honestly, I wasn't sure how I made this mistake to begin with. The white walls were the only thing in common with my bedroom. Gone was all of the artwork that adorned my walls, and my furniture was missing, having been replaced with contemporary black pieces I didn't recognize at all. Plus the windows weren't in the same place as the ones in my room, and the bed was on the opposite wall.

Frantic, my heart raced when I failed to recognize where I was. Last I knew, I was in Phoenix... Was I still? I took several deep breaths, running my trembling fingers partially through my tangled hair as I tried to figure things out, but my fear and anxiety continued to rise, making my stomach churn. Where was I? What the hell happened last night?

Unable to answer my own silent questions, my

eyes tingled and burned, but I couldn't afford to break down right now, not while I could be in very real danger… Though, the more I considered that possibility, the more I realized I didn't actually *feel* threatened in the least. If anything, I felt like I was in a safe place.

The bed dipped behind me, and a low groan filled the room. At first, I was relieved, until I realized it *wasn't* David behind me. Startled from my feelings of security, I stood up and rushed across the room in a flash. I pressed my back to the cold wall and stared at the uncovered and equally naked body of a blond man. But not just *any* blond man. No, this was a man I knew all too well.

Nick rolled over on the bed, which I noted was covered in dirt transferred from my body—and, as it would seem, his as well. I was so incredibly lost and confused, unable to even begin to piece together the events of last night. All I knew was that guilt quickly built inside me, and my head pounded as I tried to make sense of everything.

Propping his head in his hand, Nick's dark eyes found me pressed against his bedroom wall, and a goofy smile played at his lips. "Good morning, beautiful," he said, his voice still low and gravelly with sleep. "Sleep well?"

The way his eyes devoured me made me suddenly aware of how very naked I was in front of a man who *wasn't* David, and I leaned forward, snatched the corner of the sheet that hung from the corner of the bed, and held it against my body as a shield. Admittedly, I didn't really think far enough in advance to realize that this would leave Nick completely exposed, and I quickly forced my eyes to his so as not to stare. He seemed unfazed by his own nudity, but he'd always been pretty confident in his own skin.

And rightfully so, I mused inwardly, my eyes betraying their orders and glancing south.

"Wh-what happened last night?" I stammered, looking around the room as though it would somehow hold the answers. "How did I get here? Where are my clothes?"

"That's a lot of questions for a guy who just woke up after a long, exhausting night," he replied cockily, and I had the extremely violent urge to rush across the room and attack him. "Your clothes are probably still in the woods, but you'd better forget about finding them in one piece." With a wink, he scratched his stubble-ridden jawline, and an image of my tongue running along it surfaced in my mind. A memory? Fantasy? I couldn't tell, but I swear the sensation of the act, as well as subtle notes of copper, still lingered on my tongue.

The underlying implication to his answer caused my heart to strain despite the ferocity of its unusual rhythm, and my lips curled up into an angry snarl. Nick sat up, possibly sensing my escalating anger. "Easy, Brooke," he said, his voice no longer holding a smug note, but one of concern. "You need to harness that before you do something you'll regret. Deep breaths, baby."

"Don't," I snarled through gritted teeth, my self-control starting to slip away inch by fragile inch, "call me that." Warmth traveled under my skin, which prickled and crawled as I grew more agitated, and my hands trembled as rage consumed me. It was a feeling I recognized, and it didn't take long to make the connection to last night...right before everything went blank.

Nick's eyes grew even more serious, and he pushed himself up off the bed, slowly rounding the end of it. "Okay, I'm sorry. You're right. I was out of line." His voice remained steady — calm — and he took a few steps toward me.

My eyes betrayed my loyalty to David again, and I glanced down at Nick's naked lower half. Surprised and horrified with myself, I found my desire for him awakened, burning through my veins like wildfire. It pushed my anger aside for the moment, and I reveled in the feeling. Something drew me to him against my better judgment, and I knew he sensed it from his position several feet away, because I saw the same yearning in his darkening eyes. I shouldn't have felt this way, but this went beyond simple want. This felt deeper. It felt familiar. *Primal.*

"What" — I took a deep, unsteady breath through my nose — "happened?" The prickling sensation continued as Nick stepped even closer, stopping once he reached his dresser to grab a pair of long pants to pull on. As he covered himself up, I noticed his upper body was covered in pink scratches similar to mine, and bile churned in my stomach when I realized that we must have gotten carried away. Knowing that we woke up naked in bed together only pushed me toward this conclusion, and I couldn't help but feel even guiltier about what we likely did.

"Did we…?" I couldn't bring myself to finish the question that scorched the tip of my tongue.

That cocky, one-sided smirk returned to Nick's face as he perched himself on the edge of his messy bed. "Have fun?" he quipped with an arched brow. "Well, I know I haven't had that much fun in years. You've got quite the bite."

My heart dropped like a lead weight into my roiling stomach, and my legs threatened to give out beneath me. I clutched the sheet tighter to my chest and looked away from him, noticing with tunnel-visioned clarity the two sets of muddy footprints that covered his pale laminate floors. *Ours. They're ours.* I knew this because I saw a brief flash of the two of us stumbling naked down the hall in the darkness, seemingly intoxicated and laughing with blood trickling from the corners of our mouths. The image slipped away into the dark recesses of my mind.

Holding the sheet against me with my left hand, I pinched the bridge of my nose with the thumb and forefinger of the other and clenched my eyes shut. "I don't...I don't remember what happened. How is that possible?" The question wasn't directed toward him. I was merely thinking out loud, but he answered anyway.

"Memory loss is common the first time."

Confused and concerned, my gaze snapped back to his, only to find his forehead furrowed with remorse. "What do you mean, 'the first time'? Did you... Did you *drug* me?" I seethed, glaring accusingly at him.

Looking more than a little offended, he held his hands in front of him in some sort of surrender. "Whoa. Back the hell up, Brooke. Did I *drug* you? Are you serious? I love you..." His confession left me breathless, and he quickly backpedaled, running his dirt-covered fingers through his hair. "*Loved.*"

The pounding in my head returned, but it traveled down my neck and into my left shoulder where it settled and burned. "Nick," I whispered, my tone taking on an air of pleading. Before I could ask him about last night again, the tremble in my knees turned a little more severe, and I slid down the wall as they eventually buckled beneath me.

Nick crossed the room in a hurry, wrapping his arms around my shoulders. He grabbed a corner of the sheet and draped it around my shoulders to cover me completely as he led me toward the bed to sit

...own. Without thinking, I rested my head on his shoulder and tried with everything I had to recall *anything* from the missing hours in my brain. His hand moved up and down my back, comforting me, and I shivered as the tips of his fingers occasionally grazed the skin above the drape of the sheet.

It was easy to get lost in the familiar sensation of being wrapped in Nick's arms. The way my body fit against his, the musky way he smelled — like warmth and nature and man — and the way his lips felt pressed against the top of my head took me back to a time when things were simple. When Bobby was alive. I held onto this feeling in the wake of my confused state, because it helped keep me grounded.

I inhaled deeply, smelling the nutrient-rich soil that coated our bodies as well as the subtle notes of rain and clipped grass, and it forced the same images as before: the moon in a pitch black sky, the amber eyes and white teeth of the wolf as it lunged for my throat...no, wait. Upon digging into my dream a little deeper, I saw that it wasn't *my* throat, but that of another wolf. One with a red-brown coat and yellow-green eyes.

That was as far as the image seemed to go, though, and it both frustrated and unnerved me, because something in the depths of my mind told me — screamed at me — that this wasn't just the lingering remnants of a dream, but a memory. I closed my eyes again, trying to force my thoughts back to the two wolves. Deep down I knew this was important, but it didn't happen no matter how hard I tried.

Nick sighed, and I snapped back to reality, pushing myself away from him until my back was pressed against the simple wooden headboard of his bed. I clutched the sheet to my body, pulling my knees to my chest and noticing the dirt and grass stains all over my feet.

"Please," I pleaded quietly, the confusion weighing heavily on me. "Nick, what did we do?"

Heaving a deep sigh, Nick leaned forward and rested his forearms on his thighs. "Over the next few hours—maybe even days—your memory will return."

I shook my head slowly and thrust my fingers through my hair. I clutched it tightly at the top, the sting travelling down my spine. "I don't have the next few days, Nick. I have a life...a *boyfriend*. I need to know. I *deserve* to know."

He sighed again, dropping his eyes to the bed between us, but not before I caught what looked like disappointment flashing in them. "We didn't have sex," he assured me. I believed him. While all the evidence could prove that we must have slept together, the tenor of his voice was all the proof I needed to know he was telling me the truth.

Of course, the fact that our clothes were nowhere to be found and the bedroom was covered in bits of mud and grass still left a lot of unanswered questions.

"But we..." I paused, still confused and trying to wrap my head around this piece of information. "If we didn't sleep together," I said quietly, my eyes slowly meeting his again, "then what happened?"

His eyebrows pulled together, and a heavy silence filled the air between us. Seconds passed by, but the weight of the situation made time feel like it stretched on infinitely. He looked exactly how I felt—minus the confusion, because something told me he knew more than I did about last night. His distress was evident in the heavy creases of his forehead and the darkening of his eyes, though, and as I watched him carefully, waiting for his reply, it was the first time since he re-inserted himself back into my life that

I *really* saw him.

Not only had his body filled out and his hair gotten a little longer, but there was a sadness in his eyes — one that I recognized all too well — and it made me wonder if he was still as deeply affected by what happened to Bobby as I was. We continued to stare at each other, and I lost myself in the depth of his blue-green eyes, admiring how they faded to a bright amber color around his pupil. I don't think I'd ever noticed this before.

He blinked, breaking the trance I'd fallen into, and I held my breath when he opened his mouth to speak. I don't know what I expected him to say, but what came out of his mouth wasn't it.

"You changed."

CHAPTER 16 | DENIAL

"Changed?"

Nick stared at me like he expected me to understand immediately, and I waited in silence for him to elaborate. I didn't know what took him so long, but I grew tired of waiting. "You need to give me a little more than that," I snapped. "You can't just come back into my life after seven years and tell me I've 'changed.'"

Frustrated—which was a feeling I wholeheartedly related to—Nick rubbed his hand over his face and turned toward me, bringing one of his legs up onto the mattress. "No," he started, bringing his intense gaze to mine. "That's not what I mean."

"Then what?" I impatiently prodded. "I don't understand, Nick." My chin quivered and warm tears stung my eyes.

His expression softened, and he scooted toward me on the bed. My first instinct was to go to him and seek comfort, but my second was to move away from him. I did neither. "What can you remember from last night?" he asked gently.

Everything played out in my head again before I replied. "I was with my team at that club—"

"*Gianna's*?" I nodded, and Nick growled in frustration. "Damn it, Brooke, I told you not to go there!" he boomed.

"It's my job, Nick," I argued, getting off point. "*Anyway*, I remember feeling overwhelmed and a little sick, so I went outside for some fresh air. I...I ran, and I kept running, and that's it. Everything else is kind of fuzzy."

I could see he was still upset about my going against his demand — not that he was in any position to tell me where I could and could not go — but he dropped it. For now. I had this strong feeling he'd bring it up again before we were done.

"Did you dream?" he asked.

I found the question odd, but I placated him with a simple, "Yes."

"What about?"

"I'm not sure what my dreams have to do with how I wound up naked *in your bed*, Nick," I fired back, annoyed that he seemed more interested in my dreams than helping me figure out what the hell happened to me.

"Just answer the question, Brooke. I promise it's relevant."

"Wolves," I supplied, annoyance haloing the word. "I dreamt about wolves. I've dreamt about the damned things for almost two weeks. Ever since my attack."

Nick shrugged, dropping his face, but keeping his eyes locked on mine. "And you never once asked yourself why you've been having these dreams?"

I dropped my knees in front of me, crisscrossing my legs and leaning away from the headboard to get in his face without getting too close. "I was *traumatized*. I was attacked in the park one night, remember?"

"That's not why you're dreaming about them,

Brooke," he informed me. I laughed humorlessly, shaking my head and leaning back again as I clutched the sheet to my chest. "And what you *think* was a dream last night... well, it wasn't."

Confused, my eyebrows pulled together and my face screwed up. "What the hell are you talking about?"

Nick looked nervous as he continued to stall his explanation, and it pissed me off. With an aggravated growl, I threw my legs over the edge of the bed, but the sheet tangled and I stumbled. Nick was quick to grab my arm and keep me from falling. I tried to yank it away from him, but his grip was strong, and he held me tight, locking his eyes with mine.

Breathing heavily, I was pulled into the depth of his stare, admiring the amber rings around the inner edge of his aqua-colored irises until they seemed overtaken. Something clicked into place just then, the amber color sparking a memory of eyes the same color against sandy-brown fur and a night sky. My eyes widened as I stepped back, forcing him to release my arm.

"No," I whispered, shaking my head in disbelief. "That's impossible."

"Is it, Brooke? Think about it."

"Are you high?" I demanded, ignoring the beginning niggle in the back of my mind that ordered me to hear him out. "What exactly are you trying to say? That I'm — what? — a *werewolf*?"

Nick's silence told me that he believed this, and I laughed hysterically. "You've lost your damn mind," I told him through my fit of laughter, but he remained serious, and this sobered me. "Oh, god. You actually *believe* this is possible, don't you?"

"You wanted me to tell you what happened, and I am. That night in the woods...it was no ordinary wolf that attacked you. Deep down, you *know* this. You just refuse to admit it to yourself."

I tried to tell myself that he was wrong—that he had absolutely no idea what he was talking about—but that little feeling kept pushing through my denial. It clawed its way to the surface, until my dreams from last night resurfaced.

At first, the colors seemed wavy and warped, and my vision looked tunneled again. It was disorienting at first, but I quickly adjusted. Trees snapped by at an alarming rate, and when I looked down, I didn't see human feet, but paws covered in red fur disrupting the dirt, leaves, and grass…

I gasped, backing up until I slammed into Nick's dresser, and I looked up at him to see him waiting patiently for me to piece it all together and believe it.

"Tell me what you remember," he urged gently.

"I…I'm not sure." I dove back into the vision, finding this wolf in the middle of the desert.

A bush to the right rustled and a low growl filled the air. It was confusing and the red wolf seemed taken by surprise. A darker, almost brown wolf stepped out, its yellow eyes wide and curious, and its pink tongue hanging out the side of its mouth in a way that seemed non-threatening. This didn't stop the red wolf from leaping anyway, its instinct to survive taking over. I didn't understand how I was able to feel what this wolf did or why I saw things from its point of view, but, like a runaway train, there was no stopping the images from playing out in my mind.

With a loud growl from the red wolf, they collided before rolling through the dirt as both wolves fought for dominance. Teeth snapped and feral growls filled the forest, causing birds and other critters to flee. Fur flew every which way and finally the red wolf's teeth sunk in at the apex of the darker wolf's neck and shoulders. It wasn't deep enough to be fatal, and for some odd reason, I felt the memory of warm blood wash over my tongue. Before the red wolf could bite down harder, the brown one fought back, its teeth piercing its attacker's right shoulder and causing it to yelp...

The sting breached the barrier to reality, bringing me back to the here and now, and I looked down at my now-throbbing right shoulder. There were already-healing teeth marks amongst the myriad of other pink wounds that had almost fully healed. They were sensitive to the touch, and just as the first of several tears fell, Nick took my hand, pulling it toward him and pressing it over the wounds at the apex of his neck and shoulder. They were warm to the touch, my palm tingling, and a bizarre twinge of guilt paralyzed me.

If what he's saying is true, I *did that.*

No. It was impossible.

He was feeding me a bullshit story. He *had* to be. I didn't care how vivid and real the dreams over the last couple weeks had felt, none of this could be real.

Can't it? a voice from deep in my head inquired, trying to make itself known as I continued to pass off Nick's ramblings as those of a crazy person. Denial flooded my entire body again, muting any progress I might have made toward accepting what I'd just learned, and my labored breathing filled the room. My fingers traced the upraised pink marks along his strong neck and shoulders, following them down his chest, and I clenched my eyes shut as hot tears streamed silently down my cheeks.

"Brooke," Nick whispered, bringing his large hand up to cup my face. His thumb brushed the wetness from my cheek while his fingers reached around the back of my neck and tangled in my hair.

Even though I shouldn't have, I leaned into his touch and allowed him to pull me forward. His eyes remained locked on mine, and I could tell that he understood exactly what I was going through.

Whatever that was. I still wasn't even sure *I* understood it.

Confusion clouded my judgment as he pulled me even closer. We stood so close, I could feel the heat from of his body, smell the lingering sweat on his skin. Every breath I took filled my lungs with a heavenly scent. It wasn't just the scent that was uniquely Nick, but something else I couldn't quite place.

It wasn't until I looked deep into his eyes and felt the way one of his hands gripped my hip that I figured it out. Apparently, along with fear and excitement, I was capable of picking up the scent of his lust and desire.

The fog of Nick's desire blanketed me in an instant, and it was beyond inappropriate, but I couldn't help but fantasize about kissing him. I was still angry and hurt about our past, not to mention whatever happened last night, but the urges were strong. It all felt beyond my control.

As Nick moved closer, my skin warmed and goosebumps rippled up my arms and down over the rest of my body. It was all so intense, but the minute his soft lips brushed against mine, reality slapped me, forcing me to stumble away from him.

David.

Sniffling, I held the sheet around me while harshly tugging at the roots of my hair. "I-I have to go," I murmured, my voice hoarse and cracking with every confusing emotion that still coursed through my body.

Denial. Possibility. Desire. But most prominently, *guilt.*

"Brooke, we should talk about this," Nick said, taking a step back and giving me some much-needed space. "You don't understand how serious this is."

"How serious what is?" I demanded, letting denial win this round. "Do you realize how crazy all of this sounds? Do you really expect me to believe all of this?"

Nick looked surprised — like he actually expected me to just accept everything he tried to tell me. "How can you not believe it?" he asked.

"How *can* I?" I shouted. "You're asking me to believe in werewolves, Nick. It's ridiculous."

"Is it?"

"Yes!"

Nick's eyes narrowed in challenge as they met and held my gaze. "How have you been feeling?"

I balked at the question, my mouth opening and closing as I struggled to reply. This seemed to amuse him, and he arched an eyebrow triumphantly. "Craving red meat? Increased sense of smell? Taste? How's your eyesight and hearing?"

Staring at him, slack-jawed, my heart pounded furiously as I tried to speak, but no sound came out. How could he possibly know about any of that? Once again ignoring the possibility that he might be telling the truth, and suppressing that inner voice that really worked to make itself known, I tossed my head back and forth defiantly. "That doesn't mean anything. Low iron can make you crave red meats, and as for my senses — "

Nick chuckled. "You tell yourself whatever you have to if it helps you sleep at night."

Anger coursed through my veins, and I glared at him. "You know what? Screw you, Nick. I never asked for any of this, and I sure as hell don't need to sit here and listen to you feed me some bullshit story about werewolves."

To my surprise, Nick's amused expression disappeared, replaced by one of sadness. "I know you didn't ask for this, and I'm *sorry*," he replied gently, "but now that—"

I couldn't listen to him tell me everything again, because if I did, I was afraid I'd start to believe him. And I was already going back and forth on that front. "N-no," I said, covering my ears like a crazy person trying to block out the voices in her head to no avail. "I can't hear this again. I have to get home." I glanced up at him to see he looked...rejected, and the urge to take him by the hand and console him consumed me, but I refrained.

"Is this about him?" The question came out of left field, and the tone of Nick's voice was like a punch to the gut. I found it weird that it had this affect on me; we'd been broken up for seven years. I shouldn't feel bad about moving on after all this time.

So why did I?

"Along with my mother and father," I replied carefully, hoping to ease that blow. "I've been missing all night. I left a potential crime scene...in *Phoenix*. They're bound to be worried, Nick."

Nick nodded his agreement, his expression turning cold as steel. "You're right. You should go."

I turned to leave the room when I remembered I only wore his bedsheet. "Um..."

Sighing, he opened his top dresser drawer. "Right." He reached in and produced a few things. "I know they're not yours, but they're better than that sheet."

I accepted the clothes and gasped when I recognized the old concert T-shirt as one I used to wear all the time. Fond memories of those early years together washed over me, forcing a smile to my face. "You still have this," I whispered, placing it to my chest sentimentally.

"Of course."

"But it doesn't even fit you — it hasn't for some time," I reminded him, recalling the time I dared him to try it on and he looked ridiculous with it plastered to his upper body while his lower abdomen showed.

His eyes appeared sad as he laughed nervously, scratching at the back of his head. "It's always held a bit of sentimental value," he confessed before turning away from me. "The, uh, bathroom's down the hall and to the left. I'll give you a ride home when you're done."

"Uh...I think it might be best if I didn't get a ride home from my ex. I'm still not sure what I'm going to tell David, but I do know that if he sees you, he'll jump to all the wrong conclusions, and I'm not ready to deal with that right now. I can call a cab."

"Did you happen to swallow your wallet before you changed last night?" Nick asked, once again reminding me of the one thing I tried to deny.

"Um..."

He shook his head. "Don't worry about it. I'll pay for your cab...on one condition." I met his eyes once more and saw how serious he was. "You'll meet with me again. Don't ignore me, Brooke, because you don't understand just how dangerous this part of you is. I can help you learn how to control it."

The entire situation was still pretty unbelievable, but hearing the conviction in his voice every time he talked about it made me waver. There was a very large part of me — the rational part — that continued to refuse to believe that another world existed within our own.

Or that I was somehow a part of it.

I wanted to continue to deny that any of this was

happening to me, but the memories kept coming, each one more vivid than the last. That definitely made it more difficult for me to do. If I had to be entirely honest, I wanted to tell him I still didn't believe him, all in an effort to ignore it in hopes that it would all go away and things would return to normal.

I didn't, though. I nodded instead, hoping to placate him long enough to get him to let me leave.

When he seemed content with my response, I headed to the washroom to clean myself up before pulling on the clothes he gave me. I looked in the mirror for a minute after dropping the sheet around my feet, and I couldn't believe my eyes. The pink marks were slowly disappearing, looking more like light scratches, and my skin was marred with streaks of dirt and grass. I would need to shower when I got home.

I dressed and found his shirt still fit the same as it did back then—a little loose, but comforting and it smelled like him—and the shorts he'd given me were a few sizes too big in the waist and really long in the leg. I remedied that by rolling the waistband of them a few times until they sat on my hips and fell to about mid-thigh. I looked ridiculous, but it was definitely better than finding my way home in a filthy dirt and grass-stained bedsheet. How horrible would *that* have looked?

It took a while for me to remove most of the twigs, grass, and bits of dead leaves from my tangled hair, but I managed to make myself look at least partway presentable. The entire time I groomed myself, I tried to come up with so many other—and much more realistic—scenarios that could have happened to me last night. I hoped this might help kickstart my memory and prove Nick to be as crazy as he sounded, but all I remembered were the wolves.

When my cab arrived, Nick walked me out to it. There was a slight chill in the air, but I could smell and feel the arid warmth that would greet us come noon. Something I would have learned from the weather channel on a normal day.

"You have my number, Brooke. Call me if you need to talk about *anything*. We should meet up in a few days, though. Once everything settles down with your folks...and David."

Still not sure what to say, I nodded once more. I probably looked like a bobble-head.

A sad smile played at his lips, and before he closed the door, he sighed. "I really am sorry about what happened," he said. "You didn't ask for any of this."

The question left my lips before I really thought it through. "Did you?"

Laughing dryly, he tucked a strand of hair behind my ear. The gesture was so gentle and familiar that it invited those same feelings from before that I shouldn't have been entertaining. "How about we save that story for next time?" he suggested, his thumb moving softly over my cheek. More tremors rippled beneath my skin, and I smiled for the first time this morning when I recognized the playful glint in his eyes. "You know, leave you salivating for answers so you keep your word to come back to me."

I inhaled sharply, my breath shuddering, at his choice of words. He likely didn't mean it the way I'd interpreted it, so I let it go without questioning or correcting him. "Deal."

"One last thing," he added, this time stopping me from pulling the door closed. The playfulness disappeared from his face, with no sign of it even existing lingering in his expression. His eyes suggested that what he was about to say was to be taken seri-

ously. "You can't tell them *what* you are. It's dangerous, and they won't be able to handle it...and that's *if*
they even take you seriously."

I looked at him, so many questions still begging
to be asked, and before he shut the door, I stopped it
with my hand. "Nick, I don't even know if *I* believe
you." With that, I pulled the door shut, and Nick
slapped the roof a couple times to tell the driver that
it was safe to go.

As the cab pulled away from the curb and onto
the street, a nervous roll swelled in my belly, and my
palms grew sweaty with increasing anxiety. Nick's
last words repeated over and over in my mind, and
while I wasn't sure what really happened last night, I
did know that I was worried about how I would try
and explain any of this to my family — to David.

How did one even begin to explain a twelve-hour
disappearance, a body covered with unexplainable
wounds, and clothes that weren't theirs?

I was willing to bet that nothing about this would
be easy...

CHAPTER 17 | INTERROGATION

Even though we were still five houses away, I asked the driver to pull over. I still wasn't quite ready to face whatever awaited me. If anything even did. For all I knew, David was still in Phoenix, looking for me. If I had my cell phone, I'd have tried to get a hold of him before now.

When I did see him, I knew David was going to ask a hundred questions, and I wouldn't blame him; I'd been missing for well over twelve hours. Honestly, I would be worried if he wasn't freaking out.

After what had to be a half hour, the driver turned around and looked at me expectantly. "Hey, lady, I've got a living to make, and your boyfriend only gave me thirty bucks. Your time's up."

"He's not my boyfriend," I muttered, opening the door and stepping, barefoot, onto the sidewalk. The cold fall air attacked every inch of my exposed flesh as another bout of unease swept over me. I wrapped my arms around my middle as my body quivered. I tried to ignore the feeling as I refocused on how to explain myself, and I headed for home.

Much slower than one normally would.

The short walk to the house offered me a few more minutes to figure out what to say. Not that it helped in the least. I hated the idea of lying to David, but I was still so confused about what may or may not have happened that I didn't have much of a choice. Even if Nick was telling the truth—big *if*—it wasn't like I could just open the conversation with "So, when I took off last night it was actually because I was turning into some kind of werewolf, even though I didn't know it at the time." Nick made that perfectly clear, and I was pretty sure that would get me locked up and fitted for a straightjacket anyway. Even if he did believe Nick's bullshit story, I still couldn't tell David that I was with him. He'd lose his mind.

Remember when I once thought that a club for vampire wannabes sounded ridiculous? I missed that. Somehow in the course of these last couple weeks, my life turned into some kind of horror movie, and I had no clue how I was supposed to process it all.

Two houses from my own, and no closer to piecing together an explanation, I heard a door open and my name being shouted. While I'd kind of hoped to make it to my front door undetected, I should have known this wasn't going to happen. I closed my eyes when the voice registered as David's, and I braced myself for the impact of his body against mine, my anxiety spiking and the tremble in my hands increasing.

"Thank God you're all right," he breathed into my ear, holding me tightly in his arms. I tried to be strong, to not fall apart on David, but when his hands moved over my body, probably checking for injuries, I cracked. I pulled my arms from between us and wound them around his neck and inhaled deeply, noticing how David's natural scent was laced with fear and desperation.

"Where the hell have you been?" he whispered softly, and I nuzzled my face into his chest as best I could, unable to answer. His warmth—while a noticeable few degrees cooler than my own—was comforting, and I sensed his fear beginning to ebb the longer we held each other.

"David, I—"

There was no chance to respond before I heard my parents cry out their own relief, and David released me from his hold to allow them to embrace me next. It was hard for me to make sense of everything happening as they assailed me with questions, but I tried to sort through it all as best as possible so I could maybe try to answer some things without looking crazy.

"We had everyone in Phoenix out searching for you," my dad said.

"We checked all the hospitals from here to the city," my mom sobbed at the same time, running her fingers through my still-matted hair.

"Everyone was so scared," David informed me, holding my hand so tight, I was certain he'd never let go of it again.

They ushered me inside the house and David closed the door behind us. "I found your phone on the side of the road," he said, reminding me of the exact moment I threw it to the ground. "I kept calling you and calling you, and when you didn't answer, I went off looking. I heard it ringing, and…" The pain in his voice cut me deep, and I tried to offer him a silent apology with just a look because I still didn't know what to say…

…what I *could* say.

Tears streamed down Mom's face, and the guilt of my disappearing on her weighed down on me, making my knees buckle slightly. Her fear thickened the air I breathed, and I suddenly heard Nick's voice in my head: *"Craving red meat? Increased sense of smell?*

Taste? How's your eyesight and hearing?" Swallowing thickly, I tried to slough it off. It proved to be more difficult than it should have been, and it all started to fall into place and make sense: why I'd been so sensitive to people's emotions...my heightened hearing...impressive vision...

In the living room, I sat down in the middle of my couch, pushing down my revelation for the time being and mentally filing it in a box I decided to call *"Questions for Nick."*

"I'm sorry. I didn't mean to alarm you all."

"You just *took off* from an active investigation," my dad spoke up, anger and fear obvious in his tone. I wasn't sure if he was more pissed about his daughter going missing, or his detective leaving a crime scene. Logically, I knew it was probably the first one, but I felt fairly confident it was a little from column B as well. He wasn't finished laying into me, yet, and I let him. What else could I do? "David finds your phone, discarded and shattered, on the side of the road and your clothes..."

Inhaling sharply, I covered my mouth, remembering how Nick told me that my clothes were shredded and in the woods. It didn't take a genius to know how this looked; I'd worked with the department long enough to understand what they must have thought given the evidence they'd found.

Before I could rush to explain in whatever way possible, my mom's eyes scanned me from head to toe. Panic gnawed at my insides when she held her breath, her eyes widening as they fell on the familiar-looking T-shirt, and I shook my head once, hoping more than anything that she wouldn't say anything about who it belonged to.

Thankfully, she remained quiet, and I relaxed minutely. Unfortunately, this was the only reprieve to be granted, because there was still so much tension between the three of them. I took it, though, because, no matter how small the victory, I figured I'd dodged at least one silver bullet.

This is no time for jokes, I inwardly chastised myself before slowly raising my eyes to David. He was still watching me with a combination of relief and expectance. "So?" he asked. "What happened?"

"I—" I started, taking a deep breath and trying again. "I walked around, trying to get some fresh air like I said I was going to…and then I guess I blacked out."

"Brooke, I found *pieces* of your clothes near the outskirts of the city…in the desert—*miles* from the club we were searching!" David's voice rose, and I looked to my dad, afraid—and maybe hoping?—that he might step in and tell David to calm down.

He didn't; he also watched me and waited for my explanation.

"Not to mention your badge and your gun," David tacked on.

"I don't know what to say," I whispered, suddenly feeling trapped; I never liked being on the receiving end of an interrogation, and this was no exception.

Mom still looked upset and confused, but she seemed a little less concerned than Dad and David as she sat beside me and held my hand. Maybe the fact that she knew I was with Nick assuaged her fear? It was a question I couldn't find in myself to ever ask her, because I was still pretty ashamed of how I felt when I was with him this morning.

I still worried she might say something to allude to where I was, but she surprised me by staying quiet and offering me her silent support while David and Dad continued to overwhelm me with questions.

"I'm just glad you're okay," she said, her voice

cracking with emotion, and she wrapped her arms around me again. "We all thought…"

"I know," I told her softly. "I'm sorry for putting you all through this."

"Your clothes are being tested," David interrupted, drawing my focus back to him.

"What?" I demanded. "Why?"

He thrust his hands through his disheveled hair, frustrated, and I grimaced when I noticed the same lines of worry etched into his face and the dark circles under his eyes that had been missing for several days. "They looked like they were *ripped* from your body, Brooke. You *blacked out*. Don't tell me that doesn't scream 'sex crime' to you."

"David," I said, pulling free of Mom and crossing the room to where he paced. "I wasn't attacked. Don't you think I'd know if I had been?"

He was skeptical, and I didn't blame him. I'd think the same thing given the circumstances. I placed my hands on his cheeks, coaxing his eyes to mine. I hoped he'd see the truth in my eyes, but I wouldn't hold my breath. "I'm fine," I whispered. "Just…a little confused."

"We should get you to a hospital. Run a tox screen," Dad suggested.

"Keith," Mom interrupted from behind me.

"What, Laura?" he countered. "She was probably drugged!"

Suddenly, my head pounded. It was all too much, and I started to feel faint. "I think I need to lie down," I whimpered, my hands slipping from David's face and down his chest where he captured them in his and turned them over.

When I followed his gaze, I realized that I hadn't gotten all the dirt and grass stains off of them, and he was freaking out all over again. I yanked them from his grasp and clenched them into fists in front of me as I stepped back.

"Brooke..." he started. "Maybe your dad's right..."

With a sigh, I conceded defeat. "Fine. I'll go. Can I use the washroom and change, though?"

David looked to my father, who nodded his assent, and then tilted his head toward the bathroom. "Yeah. Go ahead."

The minute I closed the bathroom door, I pressed my back against it and slid to the floor as I listened to them talk about me. "Maybe I should take her alone," David suggested in a voice just above a whisper. I probably shouldn't have been able to hear him, but with my newly heightened senses, I could hear the couple three doors down discussing what to have for lunch. This only forced me to question everything Nick told me again, but I continued to convince myself that it wasn't possible.

"Do you really think this is necessary," my mother argued. It was a wasted effort, though, because they were bound to use cop-logic on her.

And they did. Dad mentioned that the date-rape drug, Rohypnol, often showcased the same symptoms of memory loss that I seemed to be exhibiting, and David was quick to remind her about the shreds of clothing they found. Again, I worried she might say something to try and set their minds at ease, and I knew that if she did, David would be the furthest thing from calm. He'd be irate.

Without mentioning any of her suspicions, she finally admitted defeat, and my father agreed to let David take me alone. I wasn't sure if this was a good thing or a bad thing, because David seemed much more apt to prod me for information without them around.

The front door closed, and I pushed myself to my feet, deciding to wash the stains from my hands and the dirt from beneath my nails. I tried to work the tangles in my hair free with my fingers before giving up and grabbing my brush. I could feel the dirt and grime that coated every strand, and I craved a shower.

With my parents gone, I figured I had time for one. I started to strip, dropping Nick's clothes to the ground. I was just about to step beneath the water when the door opened and I heard David gasp.

"What the hell happened to you?" he asked, his eyes trained on my body. I didn't need to look to know he was talking about the scratches that covered my flesh.

"David—" I started to say as he crossed the room to get a closer look. "It's not what you think. They're just scratches. I must have fallen on the trails."

His fingers passed over a few of the fading marks, and when I looked down at them, I noticed they were almost completely healed already. This baffled me, but it also made me extremely happy, because I could actually just play them off as minor scratches now. They didn't even hurt anymore.

"I was so worried," he whispered, letting his fingers trail down my arm until he captured my hand and lifted it to his lips. His trembling hands explored the length of my arm, like he was trying to memorize the way my skin felt, and I noticed his blue eyes glistening with tears. I'd never known him to cry, and it made me physically ill to think I caused this.

"Hey," I replied softly, pushing a smile to my face. "I'm fine. I promise."

His breath shuddered as he exhaled, clenching his eyes shut and forcing the tears from them. Then, before I even registered the act, he pulled me into his arms, his hands splayed over my naked back as he pressed me against his chest. Sighing, I returned the embrace, closing my eyes and winding my fingers into the short hairs at the nape of his neck.

His warm scent filled my nostrils, the notes of fear still quite strong, but there, hidden somewhere far beneath the surface, was relief and something else I glommed onto in the fraction of a second it presented itself: desire. It was probably wrong to want to forget my morning by getting lost in a moment of passion with him, but I refused to find it in myself to stop as I pressed my lips to his neck. He groaned, and when he tried to pull away, I held him firm, refusing to deprive us both of what we so desperately craved.

After everything that happened last night and this morning, I *needed* him like never before. I also realized that Nick was a part of my past that I was able to give up once, and I was pretty sure I could do it again. Why? Because David was my present—my future—and he was always there for me. Even when I couldn't admit to myself how much he truly meant to me. He was everything I needed when I needed it, and I knew he'd never abandon me the way Nick did.

This was the kind of man I wanted in my life…the kind of man I *needed*.

Fog filled the bathroom as the hot water streamed from the showerhead, and I drew David's lips to mine, kissing him deeply. He hesitated, but only for a moment before his mouth moved against mine, both desperate and eager, his need for solace thick and undeniable. Caught in the haze of our passion, I pulled him toward the shower, both of us stumbling as we stepped inside and closed the glass door.

The kiss started out as a perfect combination of hard yet tender, delightful and frantic. It was everything I expected from David. It was enough to leave me breathless, and when I pressed my naked body against him, something crept into our embrace: an insistency that I, *maybe*, hadn't entirely seen coming.

David was still fully dressed, and the water soaked his clothes through, making them stick to his body as he tried to break us apart long enough to remove them. So blinded by the lust that consumed us, I pushed him against the tile wall and placed my hands on his chest, curling my fingers slightly and gathering the fabric between them. My finger nails cut through the wet cotton with ease, and before I knew it, I tore his shirt in half, pulling it down his arms and dropping it to the shower floor with a heavy *splat!*

He looked at me, eyes wide with surprise without seeming bothered by it. I just smiled up at him wickedly while I undid his belt and jeans, discarding them as well. Now that I had him naked, I placed my hand on the side of his neck and pulled him toward me, turning us both until he sandwiched my body between his and the cool tile wall.

Despite the heat of the water raining down on us, goosebumps erupted all over my body as his lips moved over my neck, and his hands grasped at me with such urgency that it rendered me incapable of rational thought. Desire surged beneath my skin, my entire body tingling and humming with anticipation.

Nothing else mattered in this one perfect moment. Not whatever happened last night. Not whatever happened this morning. All that mattered was that we were here together. Yes, our problems were far from solved, but this time together was essential right now.

The air was thick with shower steam and the mutual need for our bodies to unite. When David's hands gripped my thighs and lifted me off the ground, I gasped with surprise, reveling in the way he felt as he slid inside me with ease. With my legs around his waist, we moved together. I coaxed his face to mine, kissing him so zealously that our teeth hit before we found our rhythm.

Because I was so sensitive to other people's emotions as well as my own, I was easily overwhelmed by pleasure—his and mine. The heady combination of his fear combined with his desire and relief only intensified everything, and I struggled to keep myself from shattering in his arms. My hands flattened on his water-slickened back, my fingers curling and slipping against his skin, and I trailed my lips along his jaw and then his neck, where his natural musk was strongest and most tempting.

Intoxicated, my lips curled back as the first wave of my climax threatened to overwhelm me, and I grazed my teeth over his skin. It was the barest of touches, but it made him groan, his hips moving with a little more ferocity. It seemed odd, but I felt the strong urge to bite down.

I barely heard it, but somewhere in the deepest parts of my mind, that inner voice from earlier told me that doing this would only have dire consequences, and I managed to resist it. It was too strong to ignore completely, though.

Instincts drove me, and I prepared to do it, regardless of the warning signs that blared in my head.

Just before I was able to succeed, David cried out, throwing his head back and his hips forward as he pushed me over the precipice. Distracted by the waves of pleasure that rolled through me, my head fell back, hitting the tile wall with a dull *thud*, and my legs tightened around him. As the sensation ebbed, my curled fingers dragged up his back until they were in his hair again, and I brought his mouth to mine for a soft kiss. The impulse to bite him disappeared completely as my arms and legs trembled around him, and David chuckled, lowering my feet to the floor and pushing me under the water to wash my hair and body.

He took his time, lathering the shampoo and working as many of the tangles in my hair as free as he could with his fingers. Everything was so wonderful that I momentarily forgot about the drama that led us here…

…until we stepped out of the shower and David gathered our clothes.

As he stared at the two articles of clothing I wore moments earlier, I realized that his relief to see me alive this morning overpowered his attention to minor details. Yes, he mentioned that *my* clothes had been shredded, but he never once noticed or questioned the clothes I had on. The only one who'd noticed was my mother.

So, now, as he stared at them, his eyebrows pulled together and he raised his questioning gaze to mine. Nervous, I bit my lower lip and pulled my towel tighter around my body, waiting for the inquiry to begin.

And begin, it did.

"These are men's clothes," he pointed out, his voice eerily calm and collected. It was unnerving, given the circumstances. Unsure what to say, I remained silent as he continued. "Where did you get these?"

While I knew the truth would upset him, I knew that lying to him would be even worse when the truth finally did surface. So, after taking a deep breath, I said, "They're Nick's."

His eyes widened, and I picked up on his growing anger, seeing the subtle tremor in his hands as they clenched the clothes so tightly his knuckles whitened. When he didn't say anything, instead tossing the clothes back onto the floor and exiting the bathroom, I went after him.

"Nothing happened!" I tried to explain, grabbing his wrist.

He wrenched it away from me, wheeling around and staring down at me, hurt and anger fighting for first in his expression. "If nothing happened, then why did you wait until just now to say something?" His voice was no longer calm; it was laced with so much rage, I barely recognized it.

"Because I knew you'd assume the worst and wouldn't listen to reason," I tried to tell him, hoping that my honesty would get him to stop and allow me to explain. When he fell silent, I saw my window and jumped through it. "He…he said he found me after I blacked out and took me back to his place."

David let this information sink in, and I sensed his anger fade a little. But only a little.

"So, let me get this straight," he started, crossing his arms in front of him. "Nick knew where you were all night, and he never once thought to call someone? Not even your parents?"

"I—" Honestly, I had no explanation for this, because David was absolutely right; Nick should have, at the very least, called my parents to let them know where I was. "I don't know why he didn't," I replied honestly, taking a step toward him and grabbing his hand again. "But I do know that *nothing* happened. Please, you have to trust me," I pleaded.

"It's not you I don't trust," he muttered through gritted teeth, his tone indicating that he might not be telling the truth.

Anger thrummed through my veins, making my hands shake violently, and I crossed my arms over my towel-covered body, feeling a bit defensive. "Funny, because that's not how it looks from here."

"I don't trust *him*," he clarified, venom lacing every syllable.

"Nick didn't *do* anything," I argued, deciding to omit the part where I woke up naked in his bed. That wouldn't end well — not that this showed much promise, either.

"Are you really that dense, Brooke?"

I stared at him, my eyes widening as I struggled to keep a leash on my increasing anger, but I was slowly losing my grip. He had *never* spoken to me like this before, and the condescension in his tone pissed me off. "Excuse me?"

"You're a detective, and you can't seem to see what's really going on because you have a past with *him*." There was so much disdain in his tone, and guilt consumed me, suddenly snuffing out my burning anger.

Before I could try to tell him — *again* — that nothing happened, David laid into me some more. "It seems a little coincidental that Nick would find you passed out in a city that isn't even where we live."

"Do you think I'm lying?"

"Not at all," David responded, his tone settling slightly. I sensed he was telling the truth, but his eyes showed just how upset he still was as he continued. "I think Nick is the reason you went missing. If I had to hazard a guess, based on how little you remember, I'd say he's been following you since he got back into town."

"David —" I tried to interject, but he bulldozed me.

"He followed us from the precinct and to that shithole club in Phoenix last night. When you left, he saw his opportunity and sedated you."

"Sedated me?" I tried to stifle a laugh. Nick might be crazy with his cock-and-bull story of werewolves, but I knew him well enough — even after seven years apart — to know he'd never do that. Even if I accused him of the exact same thing at first. Deep down, I knew he wasn't capable of something like that.

David looked irritated. "He sedated you and then did god knows what before dragging you off to his house."

I shook my head, smiling faintly in hopes of lightening the mood. "You make him sound like some kind of animal, David."

"Isn't he? Tell me I'm wrong."

I looked him dead in the eye and reinforced what I'd been saying all along. "You're wrong. I may not remember what happened, David, but I know Nick well enough to know he'd never do that. Besides, if he really did what you're suggesting, do you really think he'd just let me go?"

David's mouth opened and then closed just as quickly. I had him.

"I'm a cop," I reminded him. "So are you, and so is my father. Do you really think he'd drug me, kidnap me, *assault* me, and then just let me go the next day?"

With a sigh that signaled David's defeat, he sat on the end of the bed, pressing his face into his hands as he rested his elbows on his knees. "No, I suppose not."

I knelt on the floor in front of him, coaxing his face from his hands and forcing his eyes to mine. "I get that you were scared, and I'm truly sorry for having put you and my parents through that, but I'm fine. Really."

Reaching out, he cradled my face in his right

hand, and I leaned into his touch. "I'm sorry," he said, and I quickly cut him off.

"You have nothing to be sorry about. I never should have left the scene last night. It was stupid."

David didn't argue with me, instead pulling me to my feet and onto his lap. His hand rested just above my knee, his thumb moving over the exposed skin there and causing goosebumps to ripple up my legs.

"You say nothing happened," he whispered, his lips brushing my bare shoulder lightly, "and I believe you. But, Brooke, if I see him hanging around..." His sentence hung, threat unfinished, and I nodded slowly.

"I know. I don't...*plan* on seeing him again." I couldn't promise that Nick wouldn't pop up unannounced again, and David knew that, but my response satisfied him for the time being. Remnants of our argument still lingered between us, but he seemed just as willing as me to put it all behind us. Maybe even more so.

This conversation was far from over, and I knew Nick wasn't just going to walk away from whatever this was — not any time soon, anyway — but I accepted this one small victory.

CHAPTER 18 | RECALL

Going to the lab for a tox screen wasn't exactly my idea of a good time. I hated needles. The thought of sharp metal piercing my skin made me unbearably nauseous. Add to that the fact they wanted to draw blood from my body? We were lucky I didn't pass the hell out. David was great, though. He sat with me and kept me as distracted as possible. Too bad the woman drawing my blood was incompetent and missed the vein several times before she succeeded. It took everything in my power to keep my newly acquired violent streak from showing, and she was lucky I didn't attempt to toss her across the room.

Something told me I would have accomplished this with a mere flick of my wrist.

Afterward, David and I headed to the station. I worried about showing up, knowing that I likely scared my coworkers as well. Relief definitely thickened the air as we stepped onto our floor, but no one mentioned my disappearing act. It seemed as though O'Malley wanted to, but one look from David and he clammed right up, looking through a case file instead. Anything he might have said would probably have been harmless fun, but I sensed David wasn't ready to make light of any of this just yet.

Which was completely understandable.

Back at my desk, David handed me my phone. The screen was shattered, the cracks spider-webbing from the upper right corner and down the length of the phone. Served me right for tossing it to the ground as I ran from the abandoned club. I remembered how strong the conflict was before I dropped it, and how I'd tried to fight it. But something in me won out over rationality. I still didn't understand it. I had never been as impulsive as these past two weeks. My ability to keep a level head and fully assess a situation were some of my finer attributes, but somewhere along the way, impatience and irrationality had pushed them aside.

Because I went unexplainably MIA last night, I tried to catch up on what was uncovered at the club. I could feel the watchful eye of my father from his corner office, which was actually even more distracting than my own inability to focus. It got so bad that I had to ask Keaton and O'Malley to repeat themselves a couple of times each before I just decided to read their findings. Even this wasn't an easy task, though, and I wound up reading and rereading everything several times in an attempt to absorb the information. I probably shouldn't have been here, to be honest. Clearly I wasn't going to be any help to the case like this.

Having been watching me like a hawk, David picked up on this and suggested we go grab a bite to eat, maybe stop by the abandoned club, and he'd give me a walk-through and briefing. I jumped at the opportunity, hoping that escaping the concerned stares of my peers might help.

Of course, my dad took a little convincing.

He was worried that something might happen again, but I assured him that I wouldn't leave David's side. The fact that it was early afternoon helped ease his worry a little as well, and he reached into his bottom desk drawer, pulling out my gun and badge. A pang of guilt paralyzed me momentarily, and as he placed the cool metal Glock in my hand, an image shot forward from the dark depths of my memory.

The edges of this vision — like every other one I had since waking up this morning — were somewhat hazy and dreamlike, and I saw my gun and badge on the ground, the dirt around them disturbed. Then a dark nose appeared, and the sound of sniffing filled my head. Sensory recall kicked in, and the smell of dirt and dead leaves caught me off guard. I had this happen before, but it was never so intense as to render me momentarily disoriented. Perhaps it was due to my increased sense of smell, but I took a confused step back, hitting the doorframe of my dad's office, and I shook my head in an effort to clear it.

What the hell was that?

There was no time to question what I just saw any further, noticing the concerned looks both my father and David gave me. Apologizing, I fastened my gun and badge to my belt with repeated assurances that everything would be fine, and then David and I were off.

Within an hour, David and I were rolling into the Warehouse District of Phoenix. There was no need for the entire team to come along; this was just for me to better understand what was found last night — which, as David explained it, didn't sound like a whole hell of a lot. The rest of our coworkers stayed behind to keep investigating the information they had.

The familiar stench of death and rot hung in the cool autumn air as I stepped out of the car, and I forced myself to push past it as we advanced on the yellow tape that blocked off the entrance. Inside, not much changed aside from the smell of Luminol now mingling with the blood I'd smelled the night before.

As we looked around, David explained the findings. Blood sources from several victims were found, and the lab was currently running the results through the system to find out exactly how many and if they could get any hits. The problem with that was, unless these people were previously in our system, we wouldn't have any luck. I didn't need David or the CSU to tell me that some of these people might not be around for questioning anymore; I could smell that there was a lot of blood. In an even more bizarre twist, I didn't need David to tell me that the blood came from several different people. I could smell it. I sniffed again, trying hard to ignore the smell of rot and focusing on the unique copper notes of each blood type.

Yup. Four…maybe five different sources were dominant, and there were even more underlying the more potent smells. Now to see what the lab had to say.

At first, the fact that I used my sense of smell like this didn't faze me. Why? I suppose I'd grown used to it as it heightened over the weeks. But, the more I thought about it, the more I started to question everything Nick told me only a few hours ago.

No. It's ridiculous. Werewolves? I couldn't believe I even entertained the thought for a second.

I forced my head back in the game, but it didn't stay there as we stepped back outside. We exited the alley, David's protective hand on the small of my back as he led me to the car. Ever the gentleman — or maybe because he was afraid I might bolt — he opened my door for me and waited for me to get in. I was about to, stepping one leg into the car, but before I slid into the seat, I froze, looking off to the left as the breeze brought with it a familiar scent.

Mine.

"Brooke?"

Something deep down—that unexplainable feeling I had lately—pulled my attention in that direction. It only took a second for me to realize that it was where I ran the night before.

"Brooke?" David repeated, placing his hand over mine on the top of the car door.

Jarred from the instinct to follow my own invisible trail, I turned to him. "Sorry." I made another move to get into the car, but every fiber of my being rebelled against what logic told me I had to do. "Hey," I said, nervous that David would refuse what I knew was a ridiculous request. "Do we have to head back right this second?" David's right brow arched in question, prodding me silently to continue. "It's just...I'd like to see."

The second he sighed, I knew he understood my vague request. I feared his refusal, but he surprised me, stepping back and allowing me the chance to walk the path he did last night. We walked together side by side, and after a block, David grabbed my hand. Everything looked a little different with the sun out, but when I looked around, I recognized it as the area I discarded my phone. This was where he realized something was wrong.

We walked further, following my fading scent— at least, I was. It definitely wasn't a strong trail, but I recognized it. I followed it, my eyes searching, nose sniffing, ears straining to hear... Once again, I was forced back to Nick's explanation for all of this, and once again, I brushed it off as impossible. Ridiculous.

In just over an hour, we're at the edge of the city. Nothing but desert for miles. David seemed nervous beside me, his worry written all over his face and emanating off his body, infusing the air I breathed. When he looked down at me, it was like he was reliving my disappearance. I gently squeezed his hand, and he relaxed slightly. Another breeze picked up as we stepped through the light brush, and it frustrated me when my scent disappeared...I inhaled again—deeper—and my eyes fluttered slightly.

No. Not disappeared. It just...changed. Not only had it changed, but as I inhaled another breath, I picked up something else. Something more than familiar. In fact, the other smell I registered was one that surrounded me all morning. A smell that lingered on my skin even now, despite my shower.

Nick.

Not wanting to revisit our argument from earlier, I failed to mention this revelation to David. Instead, I continued forward, eyes scanning every square inch as I walked. The only way to describe what flew through my head was a vivid slideshow of images flashing between patches of extreme darkness, almost like a strobe light effect. It was unsettling, and a cold sweat traveled across my entire body, prickling.

There'd been a lot of foot traffic on these trails, but what stood out to me most were the spaced out, *bare* footprints amongst all the shoe treads. They were spaced far enough apart to indicate the person—me, I suspected based on the recent flashes in my mind—was running. I didn't recall being chased, but the adrenaline that coursed through my body—that *currently* coursed through my body as I relived all of this—would prove otherwise. I dug deeper into the memory, feeling the cold earth on my feet, the low, thin branches whipping at my face and arms, and I knew without a doubt that I wasn't running *from* anything. I was running *toward* it.

I stopped, forcing David to do the same, and I

glanced toward the ground, confused at first.

"We suspect this is where you disappeared," David whispered, his voice soft and broken.

The detective in me needed a closer look at the tracks, and I knelt down. It was the last of my bare footprints. Beyond that, it looked like something — me — collapsed, disturbing the dirt, grass, and dried up desert plants on the ground. Another step forward, and I saw fresh tracks…fresh *wolf* tracks.

No, I told myself, imagining a wolf ripping its way out of my body. I felt the tension of my skin before it gave way, heard the snarl… *It's impossible. This is just a coincidence. Wild animals prowl these areas all the time.* I looked to the right and saw rabbit footprints, forcing the logic to overrule what I refused to believe. *See. Wild animals are everywhere.*

My stomach growled, and I started salivating. I made the connection to the fact that I only had a small, extremely unsatisfying breakfast bagel. It wasn't until I started thinking about the rabbit that I even realized I was hungry. This disturbed me, but I continued to chalk it up as mere coincidence.

Still kneeling, my gaze drifted over the desert floor. Another wolf's tracks joined the ones I was following with my eyes a moment ago, and it was hard to deny what Nick told me this morning as his scent surrounded me. As *our* scents surrounded me.

"We saw the wolf tracks amongst your torn clothing and assumed the worst," David continued as I stood up and moved toward a big rock. Another scent was present, and it took me a moment to place it…

Leather. I distinctly smelled leather.

There, at the base of this rock was a scrap of it. I picked up the brown, supple material, recognizing it as a piece of my jacket. I grew instantly annoyed. This was the second jacket in as many weeks that I'd ruined. What were the odds?

Even though I would have loved nothing more than to dwell on this particular detail and forget about all of the weird shit that was becoming harder and harder to ignore, I couldn't. I clenched the fabric in my hand and continued to look around, wanting to make *logical* sense of everything that happened last night.

Shards of rock littered the ground, having broken off a larger one embedded in dirt. I felt a strange jolt of pain in my back as another flash of a brown wolf pinning me against it assaulted me. Instinctively, I reached around and placed a hand on my lower back, trying to pass this off as another coincidence. Maybe even some kind of post-dream empathy.

Though, it was getting much harder to deny.

David's hand rested on my back, and I recoiled, still trapped in these strange flashes or hallucinations, and swatted his arm away as I breathed heavily. Reality continued to slip away until the blackness between visions disappeared completely and all I saw .was this darker wolf on top of me, then under me, then over me again. His breath was hot and his teeth were sharp as they bit down on the side of my neck. His bite was tentative, non-fatal, and his eyes were anything but threatening. They were playful...and *so* familiar.

I must have recognized this, because I rolled from beneath him, tail wagging...

Wait. That can't be right.

Before I could even look into that particular thought, David pulled my focus back to him. "What is it?" he prodded, his bright blue eyes searching mine for some kind of clue. "Do you remember something?"

A headache formed at the base of my neck, everything throbbing even more profusely as I tossed my head back and forth. Just like that, the strange wolf fight disappeared from my head, but the sensations that told me it was all too real lingered: my sore back from being thrown against the rock, my neck where the other wolf — *Nick?* — bit down...

It was all too much. I couldn't... It wasn't possible... Was it?

Worried, David ushered me to the oversized rock and sat us down on it. He asked me over and over again what I remembered, but I avoided the question. What was I supposed to say? There was no way he'd ever believe me even if I did tell him the truth. At best, he'd have me committed to the mental health unit at the hospital and they'd have me evaluated before locking me up in a padded room.

Besides, I still wasn't sure I believed it. I mean, I think I was starting to, but there were so many questions...

...and only one person who seemed to hold all the answers.

CHAPTER 19 | DISCOVERY

Two days passed since my disappearing act, and I was still trying to make sense of everything. The scenes with the wolves played over and over inside my head. I wanted to keep telling myself that none of it was true, but I couldn't. The things I saw seemed too real; if it were all just a dream, I wouldn't be feeling the things I felt or smelling the things I smelled when I thought of them.

I arrived at the park a few blocks from my house just before four in the morning. David was still at home sleeping, none the wiser that I'd slipped out of bed to come here. If he did happen to wake up, I'd taken the liberty of dressing in clothes fit for an early morning run and left him a note on his bedside table telling him that was exactly what I was doing.

He continued to be pretty over-protective, so if he did wake up in an empty bed, I was positive he'd still flip the hell out.

But I needed answers, and this was the only way I could think to get them.

The park was empty when I arrived, each and every piece of equipment uninhabited by children—which only made sense at this hour. A thick, early morning fog hovered in the air, making the playground look somewhat frightening. While it was un-common this time of year, it definitely set the stage for the impending conversation.

I grabbed one of the swings and had a seat, grip-ping the cold metal chains as I swayed back and forth. The sky was still dark, the stars bright, and the round moon shining, but I could see dawn starting to warm the horizon. While I sat there, waiting, I took in the sights, smells, and sounds of the empty park. I never would have thought that sunrise had a specific scent, but it did. I could smell the damp soil, the moisture as it lingered on the grass, and the condensation in the fog as the climate slowly changed.

I was so lost to the miniscule changes every mi-nute that I didn't sense my company until he stood right behind me. He startled me when he grabbed my sides and a defensive snarl surprised me even more as it ripped from my throat. It died in the relief and realization that it was just Nick being Nick.

He looked at me apologetically, smiling nervous-ly as he moved around to face me. "Sorry. I didn't think I'd scare you. Figured you'd know I was there."

"I guess I was lost in thought," I replied.

Nick claimed the swing next to me, and I bit back a girlish giggle at the sight of his hulkish frame on a swing meant for children. He swayed back and forth and side to side, his eyes on me the entire time.

"I'm glad you called," he said, eyeing me some-what nervously. "Does that mean…you believe me?"

Hesitant to reply right away, I shrugged. "I don't want to," I admitted quietly, looking down as I toed the dirt with my running shoe. "But, as much as I hate to admit it, nothing else makes sense."

"It usually doesn't at first," Nick replied softly, drawing my eyes to his. "Honestly, I'm surprised you came around as quickly as you did, given your reaction the other morning."

"It was…" I paused. "A lot to take in. I couldn't allow myself to believe something so…"

"Ridiculous?" I nodded once in response to his inquiry, and he chuckled lightly. "I get that."

I watched him carefully, picking up on the subtle shifts in his expression, body language, and even his scent. He was nervous about something, and it didn't take me long to figure him out: he was here once. I didn't know how long ago, but he got it, and it comforted me to know I wasn't alone.

Every question I'd come up with over the last couple of days sped through my head, each one of them colliding with another at some point in the race to be the first one asked. But I honestly wouldn't know where to start. How was a person just supposed to ask these sorts of questions like it was no different than asking about the weather?

Thankfully, Nick broke the ice.

"So, what do you want to know?"

I sat there, stunned for just a moment before I decided to say, "You claim that I'm a…"

"A werewolf," Nick added after I trailed off, a cocky smirk spreading across his face.

The word still struck me as ridiculous, but I agreed to hear him out. I fought the denial from sneaking back in. Hoping to finally get some answers to all the weird stuff that happened to me, I agreed with a slight nod. "Yeah. That. But what does it even mean? Howling at the full moon? Silver bullets? Chasing my tail?"

A loud peal of laughter filled the night air, and my cheeks heated. Suddenly, I felt stupid that these were the first questions I asked. Though, I suppose there weren't many questions I could ask that wouldn't sound like I'd seen one too many horror movies.

When his laughter died down to a low chuckle, Nick acknowledged my questions. "Silver burns like hell if we come into contact with it, but any old bullet will do the trick if the shooter hits his mark."

I let this information sink in, remembering the irritation I felt when I wore my silver necklace. I just passed it off as some kind of allergic reaction, but with everything else that happened, I suppose this could have been a better explanation. Especially since I'd never had a problem wearing it for the last few years...

"The full moon will force a shift in the beginning," Nick continued, pulling me out of my silent reverie. "But as you become familiar with this side of you, you'll be able to change whenever."

Hope swelled in my chest. "So, I'd be able to avoid this altogether?"

Nick's face twisted with remorse. "No. You still need to shift. If you go too long between, you'll become volatile—unpredictable—and the wolf could take over at any time. It..." He sighed, and I thought I saw something in his eyes that told me he knew this firsthand. "You'll feel agitated, and the slightest upset could trigger the transformation. People could get hurt."

The optimism I felt just a moment ago deflated, and I absorbed this new information. "Okay, so how long until I can control it?"

He stared at me, his eyes dark and intense, and I swore that amber inner ring of his irises appeared brighter for a second. "The minute you accept it as a part of who you are."

"I-I do. I believe you."

Shaking his head, Nick laughed humorlessly. "No. You don't. Not entirely, anyway." Silence. I was about to argue when he continued. "You're coming around, but you haven't accepted it yet. Belief and acceptance are two totally different things, Brooke. Once you accept that this is as much a part of you as being human, you'll be in control of it."

"How long…" I cleared my throat, swallowing the lump that formed. "What I mean to say is…you're a…" I had trouble forming the end of my sentence, so I was grateful when Nick stepped in.

"You want to know how long until I could control it? Or how long I've been this way?" He lowered his face but kept his eyes locked on mine. "A werewolf."

"Yeah," I agreed, tucking a piece of hair that had fallen free of my ponytail behind my ear, still unable to take the word seriously. "That. Have you always been…? I mean, can it work that way? Can people be born…?"

"Werewolves," he repeated, this time a little more firmly. I could tell he wasn't upset, but he was trying to get me used to the idea. It wasn't working as quickly as he probably hoped. When I nodded, the right side of his mouth curled up into a half-smirk. "It is possible for someone to be born with the gene." Pausing, he seemed to be gauging my reaction. "But I wasn't. I was bitten." He nodded to my shoulder, covered beneath my light pullover sweater. "Like you."

A tingle moved beneath my skin, originating where I was bitten, but it was probably just due to the memory of that night. "When?"

Nick sighed, running his fingers through his unruly hair. "Brooke, do you really want to know all of this?"

I answered with a hesitant nod, not sure I trusted myself to speak aloud. I did want to know, but I was afraid. Why? Because if I really thought back to the changes in my own behavior since the attack, I could pinpoint similar changes in Nick right before…

"Shortly after Bobby's death."

…he left me.

Even though I'd already come to this conclusion a second ago, his confession hit me hard, leaving me winded. My hands gripped the metal chains of the swing tightly, and I stared at Nick, unblinking. I wondered if I heard him right, but the remorse in his eyes didn't leave me wondering for long. "Seven years?"

Nick's head bobbed up and down. "It's why I left."

"No." The chains rattled as I stood abruptly and walked away from him. Then I turned and walked toward him. I was pacing now, thinking about the night he left over and over before repeating the reasons he gave me that night out loud. "You told me you needed space."

"I did."

"That you were going through some changes."

"I was."

"You wanted me to understand." I was slowly losing grip on my calm demeanor, my heart thudding against my ribs, and my stomach twisting into knots. "But I didn't understand. All I knew was that within the span of a few weeks—"

"Just over a month," Nick interrupted, garnering himself an evil glare from me.

"Does it really matter?" I demanded coldly. "I lost Bobby, and then you left. I needed you, and you just left."

"I know." He dropped his gaze, and a pang of guilt stung me when I recognized his own self-hatred all over his face. "I think about how we left things every day," he confessed, eyes slowly rising again. "But it was something that needed to be done. I was dangerous. Out of control."

My hands trembled, the vibration increasing until it moved through my entire body. I instantly recognized it as residual anger from Nick leaving me. I shouldn't have felt this way. It had been seven years, and I'd moved on with a wonderful man. Unfortunately, ever since Nick returned I felt like I'd been on an emotional rollercoaster.

And now this.

Nick stood from his swing and stepped toward me hesitantly, his eyes continually locked with mine. "That tremble in your hand..." he started. "Your elevated heart rate... The anger... The hurt... You're starting to lose control. You need to harness it. Close your eyes and take a deep breath."

I don't know why, but I did as he said.

Inhale. The smell of the grass and dirt filled my head, the cool early morning air revitalizing my body and mind.

Exhale. I could practically feel my breath form the cloud against the cool morning air.

Inhale. Along with the familiar scents of the nature that surrounded me, I picked up notes of the woods and a musk that was uniquely Nick. For some reason, this caused the feeling to dissipate, and as I exhaled, I opened my eyes to see Nick standing right in front of me. His smile was wide—proud—and he lifted his right hand to brush his fingers over my cheek.

"Good," he praised, his warm breath fanning over my face and numbing my senses momentarily. It was intoxicating, even.

My body betrayed me, awakening my desire for the man who abandoned me in my time of need so many years ago, and I let him tilt my face toward his as he leaned down. I was so hurt and confused. Everything I thought I knew had been ripped away, and all I wanted was to get lost in something familiar... Some*one* familiar.

His lips brushed against mine, but before I could give in to this temptation completely, a twig snapped to my left. Thrust back into reality, I shoved Nick away and scanned the perimeter, inhaling deeply and picking up the scent of...a wolf? Was that what it was? The second the deep amber eyes appeared in the darkness, and its canines gleamed in the light cast off by one of the streetlamps, my suspicion was confirmed.

Nick noticed our visitor and didn't even try to hide his annoyance. I was still on high alert, not recognizing the scent. When the wolf stepped out of the darkness, I took in its appearance and ice-cold fear raced down my spine. His brown coat, amber eyes, and size were unsettlingly familiar, and I stepped back, ready to run.

"Jackson, what the hell are you doing here?" The wolf regarded Nick with a tilt of its head, and I momentarily wondered if they were able to communicate telepathically.

Nick turned to me, his annoyance quickly shifting to concern when he saw me staring wide-eyed at the wolf that joined us. "Brooke?" His gaze moved between me and this wolf — this *Jackson* — and he tried to comfort me. "This is Jackson. He's one of my Packmates."

It didn't matter to me what he was to Nick. To me, he looked an awful lot like the wolf that bit me and condemned me to this...this nightmare. I continued to back away, never taking my eyes off the wolf, afraid that if I did, he'd attack me. Again.

"Jackson, you've gotta go. Tell the others to keep looking for what we came here for. We're close—I can feel it."

Jackson released a low snarl, communicating in some way, before eyeing me. I swore he winked at me before darting back into what remained of the darkness as the sun continued to creep higher in the sky. The second he was gone, his scent fading on the breeze, my entire body relaxed and I fell to my knees, breathing heavily.

Concerned, Nick knelt next to me, his hand running over the length of my back in an attempt to soothe me. "I'm sorry," he said. "I didn't think he'd show up here. He was supposed to be out with the others…searching."

My fear ebbed and I started to register what Nick had said. "Searching?" My detective instincts kicked into overdrive, and I turned to face him. "There are more of you?" Nick nodded, waiting for this tidbit of knowledge to freak me out. It didn't. Instead, I decided to focus on something else. "What exactly are you looking for?"

When Nick laughed, I detected a nervous lilt to it. "That's a very long story." He looked to the east and noticed daylight was fast approaching. "And I don't think we have time for that today."

As the sunlight stretched over the ground, I realized he was right, and I pushed myself to my feet. Nick followed suit, walking with me to the edge of the park. "I'll walk part of the way with you."

I agreed, partly because I was still a little rattled about the wolf and partly because I didn't think I was ready to be apart from Nick just yet. I hated feeling this way, especially while David slept soundly back at the house. It wasn't like I planned to leave David for Nick. That would never happen. Nick had his chance, and he blew it. Besides, it sounded like he was only here temporarily anyway, and my life was here. My family, career, David... Nick was just passing through.

"I promise to tell you more about what brought me back here," Nick said as we wandered down the sidewalk. "But I want to make sure you're ready and able to control your urges."

Despite the warmth of the morning sun, a chill moved through me, and I wrapped my arms around myself. "How am I supposed to do that?" I asked, glancing at him through my periphery.

"One day at a time," was his reply as he shoved his hands into his jean pockets. "Can you meet me later tonight?"

I didn't hesitate, even though I probably should have. My need to know what was coming next heavily outweighed any common sense I might have had left. "Yes. Where?"

"Come by my place."

This sounded like a recipe for disaster, but I couldn't seem to resist, because, the truth of it was, I believed him now.

And, even though he broke my heart so many years ago, I felt like I could trust him with my life.

CHAPTER 20 | DECEIT

Did I feel bad about deceiving David to go and see Nick? Of course. I wasn't heartless. But I needed to know how to control this if I was going to have any kind of life. After learning what I did, acknowledging that what Nick said was the truth, I could feel that part of me fighting for dominance. Perhaps I was just more aware of everything I was feeling, or maybe I just wasn't strong enough to maintain control.

Whatever it was, I needed to figure out what to do.

David and I had been at work all day, still trying to track down this club that mysteriously vanished on us. We were no closer to figuring out what the hell went down there, and the entire team was starting to feel the pressure. By eleven that night—after having worked fifteen straight hours—Dad sent David and me home. David wanted to stay, and a part of me did as well, because I wanted to nail the son of a bitch responsible for these murders, but I also wanted to see Nick again. There was still so much he needed to tell me.

When I sided with Dad, David agreed, and we headed for home. Once there, I feigned a yawn and suggested we head to bed in order to rest up and start fresh on the case in the morning. Truthfully, I wasn't tired in the slightest, but I needed to be able to sneak out without being detected. It was low and deceitful, and if David did it to me, I'd be crushed.

But I had my reasons, and right now, I believed they were pretty sound. Nick suggested that I was dangerous as long as I couldn't control my urges. What if he was right?

In bed, David curled up behind me, draping his arm over my waist and pulling me against his body. He kissed my neck and shoulder, sending a shiver of contentment down my spine that made my toes curl. I momentarily reconsidered my plan, but when that telltale sign of anxiety and agitation settled in like clockwork, seeping into my bones and causing me to become restless, I knew I couldn't.

Behind me, David's breathing evened out, becoming deeper, and I felt his steady heartbeat against my back. It was soothing and kept me from bolting out of the bed, grounding me in some way. It wasn't enough to settle me completely, but it helped a little.

"David?" I whispered, turning my head slightly. His brow furrowed as his subconscious registered the sound of my voice, but he didn't respond. Slowly, I wiggled out from beneath his hold, waiting and watching as he rolled over onto his stomach and buried his hands beneath his pillow. I remained still for a few more minutes to be sure he stayed asleep, and then I crept around the room silently, pulling on a pair of yoga pants and a blue long-sleeved T-shirt. After putting my hair up into a ponytail, I exited my room, pulled my shoes on at the front door, and silently slipped outside. I thought about taking the car, but my increased energy screamed for release.

So I walked. And then I ran.

Feeling the wind on my face before it slipped

through my hair was exhilarating, and it revitalized me. I inhaled deeply, taking in the combination of smells. I tried to bypass any of the more unpleasant smells — exhaust, oil, sewage, day-old trash — in favor of the leaves on the trees, the freshly clipped grass from earlier in the day, and an impending rain that hung heavy in the air. It would be the first, and one of few, this season.

There weren't very many people out, given it was near one in the morning now, but the few that were, looked my way only briefly before going about their business. Cars passed me on the street, one of them honking their horn before someone hung out the window and started whistling and catcalling.

I supposed this was normal for one in the morning; people would be heading home after a night out drinking with their friends.

"Hey, baby," the man called out, his words slurred. I picked up traces of beer and whiskey on his breath as it left his mouth and traveled on the breeze. Normally, this would be impossible, but given what I now knew about myself...

When I ignored him, he tried again, the driver slowing the beat-up old Chevy down to a crawl. "Where you off to? Little late to be out runnin', don't ya think?"

Again, I ignored him and continued on my way, focusing on my breathing.

"Aw, don't be like that."

Up ahead, I spotted Nick's house. Only four houses away. The front light was on, as were a couple of the upstairs lights. I never did call ahead to let him know I was coming, but he would be home...at least, I hoped he was, because I'd hate to have to deal with these guys any longer than necessary.

The guy kept trying to get my attention and finally asked the driver to stop the car. I wasn't too concerned with my own well-being; I was a cop and had taken more than my fair share of self-defense training courses. Not to mention, I was much stronger than I'd ever been in my entire life.

This didn't mean I wanted to have to use any of this knowledge. I'd honestly prefer he just left me alone.

His clumsy footsteps were loud and unsteady as he tried to catch up. I was only one house away now, and just as I was about to use the neighbor's front yard as a short cut, the guy grabbed for my wrist as he caught up. He missed — probably because his depth perception was a little skewed given his current intoxication — and I stopped in my tracks, suddenly angry that he'd even *think* about laying a hand on me.

I whipped around to face him, and his drunken smile disappeared from his face, his unfocused eyes widening as he realized his error. I clenched my hands at my sides, my heart still racing from my run. My blood boiled beneath my skin, which started itching and crawling. My breath came hot and heavy, turning to fog in the cool night air between us. His mouth opened and closed a few times, likely trying to find a way to explain his brazen attempt to physically stop me, but I refused to hear what he had to say. Several violent outcomes flickered through my mind, ranging from tearing his throat out with my bare hands to ripping his arm from his body and beating him with it. These thoughts should have concerned me, but I apparently shot right past rational thought and directly into extreme measures.

Before I could act on any of these scenarios, I inhaled deeply, stopping the minute I picked up the unique woodsy musk I'd come to recognize. As usual, it calmed me in a way that nothing else had been able to since this all began. It was then that I realized the drunk boy's eyes seemed unfocused not because of how much he'd had to drink, but because he wasn't looking at *me*. He was looking *past* me…

…at Nick.

Slowly, I turned around to find Nick sauntering down the sidewalk toward us. He didn't have a shirt on, and I admit to staring just a little too long and hard at his broad shoulders, chiseled chest, and well-defined abs. I swallowed thickly when I noticed that V-shaped muscle as it dipped below his low-slung jeans, and I had to remind myself to take a breath before I passed out. I didn't remember him being this in shape when the two of us were together. Sure, he'd always been fit, but never like this.

"You lost, boy?" Nick demanded, his voice deep and gruff. I even picked up a hint of a growl, but forgot all about it when I felt the heat of his body so close to mine. He rested his hand on the small of my back, assuring me of my safety—not that I ever questioned it, remember—and I turned my focus back to the guy who tried to stop me.

While I doubted this guy had any idea what he'd gotten himself into, it was obvious he wasn't stupid enough to challenge it further. Instead, he stammered, his eyes never leaving Nick. He looked so terrified, and I worried he might lose bladder control. But then that worry turned to hope.

It would serve him right.

When he still failed to say anything—which was weird considering just how chatty he'd seemed before Nick showed up—Nick took my hand. What surprised me was I let him without pause. "Come on, babe," he said, pulling me toward the house. "Let's go inside."

I let him tug me along, but I kept my narrowed

eyes on the stunned boy. I was still pretty angry, and while I knew I couldn't hurt him, something deep inside me still *wanted* to. This alarmed me more than anything. This must have been what Nick was talking about. My urges needed to be harnessed, and I needed to learn how to do it.

Before I turned my eyes toward the house, I watched as the guy ran, stumbling a few times before reaching his friend's vehicle. The tires squealed against the pavement as they took off, and I felt the need to go after them — no, not because I was a werewolf and chasing cars was something dogs enjoyed doing, but because I was a cop and they were speeding.

At least, I was pretty sure it was the latter...

Finally, I shifted my focus to the house, noticing the three motorcycles and one car — a newer red Camaro — in the driveway for the first time. This meant that Nick wasn't the only one staying here. Did these vehicles belong to his — what did he call them? — his *Packmates*?

Once inside, Nick closed the door. He didn't lock it, but I supposed he probably felt he and his buddies were a good enough security system, being supernatural creatures and all.

Yes, it was still weird to even consider what he'd said to be true, but it also felt oddly natural. Like I'd been repressing the knowledge, but deep down knew it to be true all along. It only took Nick explaining it to me to stimulate the information.

"You know, I had that under control," I told Nick very matter-of-factly.

He only laughed. "Brooke, you were two seconds from tearing out his throat."

My jaw dropped. Not because he was wrong — because the thought had crossed my mind quite vividly — but also because, in hindsight of the actual incident, it was such a violent resolution. I was ashamed I'd even entertained the idea. I wanted to believe I would never have actually followed through with it, but I wasn't so sure. It did seem to be the more dominant "solution" I could come up with. Dismemberment coming in a close second.

"I was not," I denied weakly.

"No?" Nick challenged. "Dismemberment then?"

Silent, I pressed my lips firmly together, looking up at Nick sheepishly through my lashes, and he smirked. The cocky son of a bitch *smirked*.

"That's what I thought."

We wandered farther into the house, my eyes moving about and taking it all in for the first time. My head was in such a foggy state when I had been in a mad rush to leave the other morning, I never really noticed all of the little details. Not that this surprised me; a lot had happened, and I wasn't ready to accept any of it as the truth.

"Can I get you anything?" Nick offered. "Coffee? Tea?"

"Um, tea? I probably shouldn't have caffeine if I plan to sleep any time soon," I replied, wrapping my arms around myself as I continued to look around.

It wasn't an overly large house, and the floor plan was pretty basic. The living room was off to the right of the front door, furnished as only a bachelor pad would be — leather furniture with glass and chrome coffee and end tables — and the kitchen was next to it. There was a dining nook that adjoined the kitchen and living room, and a second entry to the kitchen off the hall we were currently in. There was also another hall that exited off this one. What was down it, I didn't know. I guessed a bathroom and maybe a bedroom. Upstairs, as I already knew, housed Nick's bedroom, a bathroom, and another two rooms.

In addition to the visual details, I also picked up on the various scents that surrounded me. Obviously, this place was filled with Nick's scent, even mine lingered from the other day — weird — but in addition to ours, I also picked up on a few others. One of them I immediately recognized as Jackson's, and it forced a deep, guttural reaction from me. I may not have DNA evidence that he was the one who did this to me, but I remembered with perfect clarity what the wolf that bit me looked like, and I saw something in his amber eyes earlier that shook me to my core.

Three other scents I didn't recognize joined the others, swirling around me and forcing me into some kind of sensory overload. I just assumed they belonged to the other guys that were staying here with Nick.

Nick disappeared into the kitchen, telling me to make myself at home. This was much easier than it probably should have been, and I couldn't quite figure out if that was because I was in Nick's space, or if I felt like I belonged here.

No. I don't belong here, I told myself, the feeling that filled me reminding me an awful lot like the denial I was working to overcome. *It's all just familiar because it's Nick.*

I took a seat on the couch, sitting in the center of it, and soon, I heard the shrill whistle of the teakettle. Nick emerged from the kitchen a moment later with two steaming mugs in his hands and joined me on the sofa. Still shirtless. Still distracting.

Knowing it was rude to ogle — not to mention inappropriate since my boyfriend was at home sleeping while I sat here with my ex — I avoided looking at him, instead focusing on the rising steam and swirling golden liquid in my cup.

Nick set his mug on the table in front of us before shifting toward me. He reached out hesitantly, resting his hand on my forearm. "You okay?"

"Yeah," I croaked, glancing at him. My eyes wandered south, and I noticed the scars on his torso for the first time. Some looked like bites, some like cuts and gashes. Then I realized they were battle wounds from seven years as a werewolf. "You're just...well, shirtless."

This made him laugh. Loudly. My cheeks warmed, and I avoided his gaze once more. I knew I shouldn't have been this uncomfortable around him; it wasn't like I'd never seen him without a shirt—or pants, for that matter—before. But this was different for so many reasons.

"I just woke up, and then I caught your scent," he explained, standing up. "I was getting dressed when I smelled that guy, too. It worried me, especially when I picked up on your anger, so I rushed outside. I'm sorry."

Nick disappeared, his heavy footsteps clomping up the stairs, and when he returned moments later he was in a black T-shirt that did little to hide the chiseled planes of his body. So, really, it was no better than being shirtless. I actually stared even more at his biceps, wondering how the sleeves of his shirt weren't ripping under the strain of his muscles.

"I'm glad you came tonight," he said, pulling me from the inappropriate thoughts that swirled in my imagination. "There's still so much we need to talk about."

After taking a sip, I set my tea down next to his and nodded. "I think it's important for me to get a handle on this sooner rather than later. I'm still so confused."

"That's normal."

"How long before you could control it?"

Nick paused a minute, running his hands through his hair. "About two years."

Hearing this sent my heart plummeting into my stomach. Two years? While I didn't expect this to happen overnight, I definitely didn't want to have to suffer through this transition for two years.

"But I was angry and hated that my life had been uprooted."

This was something I could relate to.

"I'd just lost my best friend, and then I was bitten — in the same damn alley — forcing me to — "

What he said registered quickly, and my eyes snapped to his. "What?" He looked at me, blinking. "You were attacked in the..." I swallowed thickly, trying to keep my voice even and calm. "In the same alley that Bobby died in?"

Nick nodded solemnly. "I returned to that alley almost every night after the cops released the scene from their investigation. Your dad didn't seem to be making much progress, and I was so sure that they had to be missing something. Every time I showed up, I felt like I was being watched, but no one ever appeared...until the night I came face to face with a wolf. It wasn't your average wolf though. This one was almost twice as big and built like a brick house. At first, I didn't know why it attacked me without hesitation, but now I do."

"It wanted to change you," I deduced, but Nick shook his head.

"He thought I was the thing he was looking for."

Nick's extremely vague explanation prompted me further. "He?"

"Jackson."

I scoffed, even more resolute in my suspicion of

Jackson's involvement in my own attack. He seemed a little too quick to bite.

"I didn't think much of it at first, until the changes started. I didn't know what to make of it in the beginning. The heightened senses, my increased strength..." I nodded along, understanding wholeheartedly what he was saying. "Then Marcus approached me before the next full moon—my first transformation."

"Marcus?" I inquired, unfamiliar with this new name.

"Our Pack leader." Nick laughed as if remembering something. "I thought the man was bat-shit crazy—much like you thought I was, I suppose. Though, I was a little more violent about it. Perhaps because, deep down, I knew the truth, and I was beyond pissed off about it.

"I told him to fuck off and leave me alone, that I didn't need him or his bullshit theories..." Nick sighed, and I saw something familiar in his eyes—something I'd been dealing with these last few days. I reached out to take his hand. It was only meant to be a comforting gesture, but Nick threaded his fingers through mine, smiling as he continued. I knew I should correct the act, but I couldn't bring myself to do it. "And when I woke up the next morning, naked, alone, and in the woods, he was there. Sitting, fully-clothed, against a tree with his arms resting on his bent knees. He had this smug look on his face, and I just lost it.

"I started beating the shit out of him, accusing him of drugging me—like you'd accused me. I couldn't remember anything. I didn't come around nearly as quickly as you," he told me. "I stuck around town for a few more days, and by then, little fragments of that night started to come back."

"So you left." My voice was quiet, barely audible.

Nick shook his head. "It wasn't my change that prompted me to leave," he admitted sadly. "I thought for sure I could manage it. I mean, changing once a month? Sounds easy enough, right?" Something dark flashed in his eyes before he dropped them to our still-joined hands. "In the wake of my mounting frustration, I almost hurt my mom."

"Wh-what?"

"I don't even know how it happened. I'd been going out a lot at night—the need to be outside overpowering the need to sleep." Yet another thing I empathized with. "I came home at dawn one day. Mom had been up, sick with worry. I couldn't blame her for being scared something happened, especially after Bobby, but when she started in on me…" A visible shudder rocked through Nick, and he seemed hesitant to continue. "I recognized what was happening before anything bad could transpire. But the things I imagined doing… I was so unbelievably angry—not necessarily at her, but at everything that had happened—and I just snapped. I got outside and away from the house before I shifted."

"During the day?"

Nick nodded. "It can happen if your emotions get too intense. Fear, confusion, stress, anger. They can all escalate and trigger the change.

"Marcus found me hiding in a shrub three blocks from home. He coaxed me out and led me here." He looked around the living room, indicating the house. "He owns houses in several towns and cities since the Pack tends to travel around quite a bit. After I was calm enough to change back, he gave me clothes and something to eat and then explained everything to me. Again, it took a bit for the memory of such a violent shift to come back to me, but it did, and it was then that I decided to go with him."

"Where?"

"To his main residence. He owns a large plot of land near the mountains in Canada where he built an above average house that we all stay in. He likes to keep the Pack close together. A unified front."

Canada. Nick's been in Canada this whole time.

"So, Marcus taught you to control it," I said, trying to steer the conversation toward something that I hoped would be a little less stressful on Nick. It was clear that, even seven years later, this still bothered him.

"He did." Nick paused, smiling. "It wasn't easy, and as you know, I'm easily frustrated if I don't catch onto something right away." I laughed, because he was absolutely right. He'd always been a pain in the ass in that regard.

"But two years later, you had it figured out." While I knew this was going to be a process, I had hoped for it to take less time. Especially based on what he told me earlier this morning. "I thought you said that once you accepted it, it was easier."

"And it is, but you're never really out of the woods until you've got absolute control."

"Meaning?"

Nick grinned, his smile reaching the outer corners of his eyes and brightening them. He pulled his hand from mine, and I looked down in shock; I'd been so completely content that I'd forgotten all about the connection. And now I missed it. It was confusing, so I tamped it down with every other unsettling thought I'd had regarding Nick and tried to ignore it.

The key word being *tried*.

"When you have absolute control, it's possible to focus the change on one particular part of your body." I eyed him, at a complete loss for words. Nick still seemed pretty amped about it though, turning to face me and pulling his right leg up onto the couch between us. "You want to see?"

CHAPTER 21 | SURRENDER

I sat for a moment, looking at Nick like he'd lost his ever-loving mind — something I realized I'd been doing a lot of the last couple days.

Did he just ask if I wanted to watch him transform part of his body? Was this some kind of perverted euphemism? Nick always had a strange sense of humor, so I honestly wouldn't doubt it.

But, no. Something in Nick's eyes told me he wasn't kidding around. He seemed excited about sharing this strange ability. I know I said I believed all of this — because I was pretty sure I did — but now that I was being offered the opportunity to witness an actual transformation firsthand, I wasn't sure I was ready to fully let go of that last thread of denial.

Naturally, that curious — and fast-becoming dominant — part of me that I kept trying to repress answered for me, forcing my head to move up and down. I don't know what exactly I expected, but I watched with complete awe and shock as Nick held his right arm out and stared at it.

Nothing happened at first, and I started to doubt everything he'd told me. A strange combination of relief and disappointment filled me. Relief because I started to believe I could go back to my normal life, and disappointment because...actually, I didn't quite know why. I think it was that part of me that I'd been repressing that was disappointed.

Yup. That was exactly where the disappointment originated, but at the same time, it seemed to be cheering Nick on. It was bizarre and very disorienting to have my brain so split on what to believe.

The warring emotions were suddenly yanked back the second I heard the telltale sound of bone cracking. No, *bones*. Plural. It wasn't an overly loud sound, meaning it wasn't a large bone that splintered, and the minute I saw his fingers begin to bend, his knuckles contorting at impossible angles, I realized *that* was what I heard, and I panicked, thinking something had gone terribly wrong.

This can't be normal, I tried to tell myself, unable to take in enough oxygen as alarm set in completely. My first thought was that I needed to call an ambulance or get him to a hospital, but I couldn't even move. I remained seated next to him, completely transfixed by what was happening to him. My eyes momentarily left his hands, expecting to find pain and agony all over Nick's face, but all I found was focus and determination in the furrow of his brow. His skin slowly turned red and beads of sweat started to form on his forehead. It wasn't until a smile of satisfaction slowly formed on his face that I glanced back to his hand and gasped audibly.

It was...well, it was unlike anything I'd ever seen. What I witnessed was nothing like what you saw in the movies or even the milder television shows where it was an instantaneous and magical change with absolutely no trauma to the body. This looked excruciating, not to mention grotesque and absolutely horrifying. Forget trauma to the body...what happened to a person's mental stability during this process? Concerned, I tried to speak up, but I was para-lyzed. A light sheen of sweat covered his arms now, and I watched in abject horror as his wrist snapped back, the sound of his bones continuing to crack burning into my memory. Nothing could cleanse this from my memory. His fingers curled in toward the palm of his hand, and I watched in absolute terror as new skin formed over his hand somehow.

Believe it or not, that wasn't even the worst of it. While it definitely wasn't the most appealing sight in the world, a pretty violent bout of nausea presented itself as five sharp claws started tearing through his skin, right below his knuckles. It trumped everything I'd seen so far. I could smell the small amount of blood that mixed with the sweat on his skin, and then I watched as his skin darkened... No, it wasn't the actual skin that darkened; new hair was sprouting, coming in quickly, thicker, coarser, and a shade darker than the light hair that currently covered his forearms and head.

My breathing increased, my heart hammering almost painfully against my ribs. I tried to tell myself that this had to be normal, but it looked bad. Really, *really* bad.

Then it was all over. The scent of sweat and blood still lingered in the air, but nowhere near as potent. I stared, unable to process what I was looking at. One minute, it was his hand — a hand I'd held — and now there was a much larger version of a dog's paw attached to Nick's arm where said hand *used* to be. I couldn't stop myself from reaching out and touching it, feeling the coarse fur against the pads of my fingers.

Is this really happening?

It never occurred to me that Nick might not have been a fan of being petted like a domesticated dog, but when I looked up and found him smiling proudly, I realized I was wrong. He loved this far more than I'd thought possible.

Suddenly, the front door slammed, startling me and making me jump. Nick pulled back his arm, almost like he was trying to hide it from our unannounced company. One sniff of the air was all it took for me to recognize who it was...even though I'd only met him once before. His scent was vaguely different—a little more human and a little less dirty dog—but I'd know it anywhere.

Jackson.

The second he entered the room, the hairs on the back of my neck stood on end, and a rumble formed in my throat. I realized this was something I did when I felt defensive or territorial.

Weird.

The fact that I experienced such a visceral reaction to his scent had to mean something. Yes, I suspected he was the one who bit me—and by suspected, I mean I was pretty damn sure of it—but there was something else about the way he carried himself that was off-putting.

This was the first time I'd met him in his human state, but I could recognize him by his eyes alone. Not only were the color of his eyes the same as that wolf, with an added bit of dark brown around the edge of his irises, but the way he leered at me unnerved me.

"Showing off again?" he quipped, leaning against the wall and tilting his head toward Nick's hand.

Nick released a warning growl, shooting a glare at our unwelcome interruption. Within seconds, and with far less effort than the initial transformation took moments ago, Nick's hand was back to normal. It raised the question of increased difficulty when maintaining control over a partial shift when you lost focus. I guess that was something I'd have to ask about.

"Why are you back here already, Jax?" Nick demanded, an edge of authority in his voice. "I'm pretty sure you haven't accomplished what I've asked of you."

I looked between the two of them to find Nick's eyes on Jackson, but the gesture was not returned. Instead, Jackson's brown eyes were fixed on me. Partially shielded with Nick's body between us, I took the opportunity to look the man over. He was tall, but not as tall as Nick, falling two—maybe three—inches shorter, and he wasn't as broad-shouldered either. It was obvious that he kept himself in pretty decent shape. I noted the cocky smirk and how his brown hair, long and wild like he'd been caught in a windstorm, framed his slim, hard-angled face, and when his smile broadened, I realized how perfect and white his teeth were. If his presence wasn't so upsetting to me, I might have found him attractive.

Big "might."

His eyes scanned down the length of my body appraisingly before Nick shifted two inches to the right, blocking me further. "Lost the scent. The guys are still out looking, but thought we could use you and your superior sense of smell to help us out."

Notes of jealousy and sarcasm haloed his words, and the way Nick's arms and neck tensed indicated that I was right. There was definitely animosity between these two. Did Nick blame Jackson for forcing this life on him too? I would understand that and jump right on the bandwagon.

"L-lost the scent of what?" I asked, stepping forward slightly and placing a hand on Nick's arm. I hadn't even realized I'd been thinking it until I heard it out loud.

Jackson chuckled darkly, dropping his eyes to his dirt-covered fingers as if inspecting them. "The bastards we're here to kill, kid."

Kill? He wasn't serious. No. Clearly, I didn't hear him correctly, because that was a pretty brazen admission to be making in front of a cop. I had to ask, though, but just as I prepared to prod him for a little more info, Nick cut in.

"Jax..." The rumble returned to Nick's deep voice. "Leave her out of this. She's not ready for that shit."

I pulled back on Nick's bicep to get him to look at me — his big, strong bicep...

I gave my head a quick shake and chastised myself inwardly. *Now is* not *the time.* "What are you talking about?" I asked.

With an aggravated sigh, Nick turned around. "There's still so much you don't know," he explained, looking increasingly nervous as he shot an angry glare over his shoulder at Jackson. "And until we know more about what we're up against, I think it's best I keep you as uninformed as possible. I'm afraid that if I tell you too much too soon it could put you and..." cue awkward pause "...your loved ones at unnecessary risk."

Frustrated, I crossed my arms and narrowed my eyes at Nick. "And you think that by keeping me in the dark, I'll be safer?"

"Yes."

"I'll be waiting outside," Jackson interrupted, and I heard the satisfaction in his voice at having ruffled our feathers. Bastard. "Nice seeing you again, kid."

"Go to hell," I muttered under my breath, the hairs on the back of my neck prickling again.

"Oooh," he replied with a smug laugh, his voice

fading as he made his way back to the front door. "She bites."

Anger pulsed through my veins, and I took a threatening step forward. I tried to move around Nick, but he gripped my upper arm firmly, holding me in place. "Brooke," he warned softly, "let it go. I don't need you going head to head with my second in command." When I continued to scowl, Nick smirked. "I don't think he'd appreciate you kicking his ass and taking his place. He doesn't take too kindly to those who do that to him."

There was a mischievous glimmer in his eyes, leading me to believe that Nick knew this from personal experience. "Did you…?"

His shrug mirrored his expression, which was equal parts smug and confident. "He pissed me off about a year after I'd joined the Pack. Marcus had us all out on a mission, and one night Jax put Marcus in jeopardy — not intentionally, he says — but I was having none of it. We fought. I won. Marcus promoted me to Jax's position. It's a dog-eat-dog world out there."

It was obvious that he used this ridiculous pun as a ploy to take the edge off my existing anger…and damn him, it worked. My lips curled up into a smile, and I rolled my eyes. "Funny."

"I've always tried to keep you entertained," he quipped before reaching forward and taking my hand in his. A look of shame flashed in his eyes, but this didn't stop his thumb from moving back and forth over my skin. And I let him, breath shuddering and heart beating faster as I glanced down between us.

"So, honestly, how are you with everything?" he inquired nervously. "Did I freak you out?"

"Surprisingly, no. Even though the idea should sound preposterous — I mean, werewolves? Come on.

There's a part of me that, I think, always knew the truth. I just wouldn't let myself make sense of it," I confessed. "But I think I'm ready to learn, and I have to admit, the added strength and heightened senses kind of kick ass."

Nick laughed heartily. "Yeah, I didn't think you'd have a problem with that part."

He continued to hold my hand, slowly bringing it up between us, and when his eyes caught mine, looking at me with a longing that mirrored my own, I grew flustered. I tried to tamp it down, to extinguish it before it burned out of control, but it was a wasted effort. Every time I pushed him from my thoughts, he forced his way back in, regardless of whom my heart might belong to at the moment. Maybe it had something to do with our past, or maybe it was just hard-wired into my new self — some kind of primal need to be close to others like me. Whatever the reason, I wanted to deny the pull he had over me, but I just…couldn't.

Then my guilt crept back in, because I remembered how David was back at home, sleeping. Completely unaware of where I was or who I was with.

Tugging my hand away from Nick, severing our physical connection — though it did nothing to break the emotional one that was reforming day by day — I wrapped my arms around my middle and turned toward the living room window. "I should head home," I whispered, focusing on the yellow-orange glow of the streetlight on the asphalt. "In case David wakes."

The air in the room shifted from pleasant to hostile in less than a second. "Yeah," Nick agreed, his voice clipped. "I suppose you should. I've got shit to do anyway."

"Right." Leaving it at that, I walked around Nick and headed for the door. I couldn't help but feel rejected and like he was pushing me away—even if I was the one to push first. It was completely unfounded for me to even feel this way, but I did.

I pulled the front door open and was about to leave when Nick appeared beside me, his hand gripping the side of it and holding firm so I couldn't slip through. "Let me walk you home," he offered, his apology unspoken but visible in his warm eyes. "While I'm sure you can handle yourself, I'd hate if you encountered any more assholes... Really, I'd be protecting them."

Unable to contain a light laugh, I accepted. "Sure. Thanks."

The instant we walked out onto the front stoop, Jackson turned to us expectantly, his eyes wide. Then he spotted me and rolled his eyes. "So now she's tagging along?"

"I'm taking her home," Nick barked. "Go on without me. Gather the others and I'll catch up."

It looked like Jackson might try to argue, but one sharp look from Nick and he kept his mouth shut. But not happily. Turning on his heel with far more hostility than a grown man should be able to muster, he stalked off into the night, picking up the pace as he crossed the street and disappeared into the darkness. Nick and I walked side by side down the sidewalk, and a few seconds later we heard a wolf howl in the night. Shortly after that, and from a little further in the distance, more joined in.

"How many of you are there?"

"Total?" Nick asked. "Or in town?"

"In town." Though, now I was curious and wanted to know the answer to the former, too.

"Just the five of us," Nick informed me as coolly as if he was talking about the weather. "From the Pack at least. There are others of our kind out there, but they just stick to the shadows when any of us are around since they don't really abide by Pack Law."

"Pack Law?" It amazed me that there was this whole other world existing within our own, and I'd never even realized it. Ignorance apparently was bliss, after all. "So, these others...they're the seedy underbelly of your organization?"

Nick chuckled, shaking his head and pushing his shaggy hair off his forehead. "I suppose that's one way of looking at it."

"And there are certain rules you all follow?"

He nodded once. "Yeah. But we don't have to worry about that too much right now. They're really just a basic set of principles we live by. Don't tell anyone about our existence. Listen to your Alpha. Don't kill humans. That sort of thing."

I stopped dead in my tracks when I heard that last "principle," forcing Nick to do the same. "Have you ever..." I swallowed thickly, unable to form the rest of my question.

Nick read me, though. As always. "Killed someone?" My head bobbed, nervous. "Not a human."

Not a human, I mentally repeated. That wasn't exactly the "no" I had been hoping for. "Wh-who?"

With a sigh, Nick urged me back on our way. "It was a while ago, and believe me when I say they all had it coming. But they weren't human."

"Were they your — *our* kind?" I asked, my curiosity still not satiated.

Another headshake, and I was even more confused than before. If they weren't human, and they weren't werewolves, then...what?

"Look," he spoke up, interrupting the cacophony in my head. "As I said before, there's still so much I have to tell you, but this is one of those things I need to keep from you until you're ready. Can you trust in that…trust in me?"

If I was being totally honest with myself, I could trust him. Even though he betrayed that trust the day he walked out on me, something deep down told me he would be here for me through this. So I agreed without pause. "Yeah. I can. Just…promise you'll tell me sooner rather than later."

"Deal."

With three blocks between us and my house left, Nick asked me about work. At first, I missed any and all undertones, thinking he was only trying to fill the silence between us with casual conversation. But then his attention focused solely on that club we'd been unable to locate.

Gianna's.

"It's still nowhere to be found," I informed him. "We found the location it was believed to be, based on a witness's encounter with one of the clients—"

"Encounter?"

"She was approached in another creepy-ass 'vampire'"—yes, I even used air quotes—"club, and was given a business card. Unfortunately, we were unable to lift any prints, DNA, or any useful information from it. Other than the address, of course."

"And when you got there?"

"That was the night I blacked out," I reminded him, blushing as the memory of us stumbling naked down his hallway and falling into his bed rushed back. "The place was abandoned. Almost like they knew we were onto them… We just don't understand how they found out."

Nick fell silent for a minute, his eyebrows pulling together contemplatively. "It's possible they knew," he agreed, "but I told you it moves around a lot. It could be that they just switched locations. Got bored of Arizona."

I shook my head, disagreeing wholeheartedly. "No way. That place was trashed—as in midnight-move trashed. They panicked. Unfortunately, they're not sloppy under pressure like every other criminal out there."

"That they're not," Nick muttered under his breath. There was a good possibility he never meant for me to hear him, but I did.

One question that kept me going this entire time rested on the tip of my tongue, and before I could weigh the pros and cons of asking it, it just slipped out. "Is Bobby's death related to all of this?"

It was Nick's turn to stop walking suddenly, and I followed suit, turning and standing directly in front of him. "Brooke…"

"I know you want to keep things from me—out of safety or whatever—so I'm not going to ask for specifics if you have them…yet. But I think I deserve to know if I'm even going after the bastard who killed my brother." A pause. "Your best friend."

After a moment's hesitation, Nick conceded. "Yes. But trust me when I say that's all I can tell you right now."

While I wanted to know more—*needed* to know more—I was content enough with his answer. I believed he would tell me when the time was right. Until then, I would just keep using my super-sleuth prowess as a detective and hopefully uncover a few clues of my own.

When we arrived at my house, Nick walked me to the door. Normally, this would be pretty risky, but we both heard David's gentle snoring from the upstairs window. That same unreceptive look returned to his face, like he was building a wall around any emotion he might have toward me, and before he turned to leave, I reached out and grabbed his wrist.

"Thank you," I told him. "For being there earlier and keeping me from doing anything stupid."

His resolve slipped, but only for a second. "I promised I'd look out for you, and that's what I intend to do, Brooke." His tone held firm, but I heard the subtle notes of affection underneath.

I slipped my key into the lock, and just as I pushed the door open, Nick stopped me. I turned to acknowledge him. His eyes were hard—steely—and it made me shiver. "You know it can't work, right?" Confused, I looked at him. Even though I was happy and in a relationship with David, it still cut me deep to hear him just come right out and tell me he and I would never work.

It was stupid to think this way—I knew that. I loved David, but I couldn't deny the growing emotions I had for Nick either. I was a terrible person.

"You and him," he clarified. "He's human. You're not. It's dangerous for you to be with him."

And just like that, any warm and fuzzy feelings I had for Nick evaporated, and my defensiveness reared its ugly head. The emotional whiplash I'd been put through lately finally took its toll. I stalked toward him, menace and fury blazing in my eyes. "Excuse me?" I demanded, keeping my voice low so as not to alert David to my absence. "Who the hell do you think you are to think you can just prance back into my life and tell me who I can and can't have a relationship with? I'm pretty sure you gave up that right the day you walked out on me."

"And I told you why I did that," he argued. "Having almost hurt my own mother, I knew I couldn't put you at risk. Just like, if you love him as much as you say you do, you won't put him at risk either. What we are..." He sighed, his resolve finally slipping away completely. "We're unpredictable.

Dangerous. Just…think about it, okay? If not for him, then for your own peace of mind. You wouldn't be able to live with yourself if something happened."

Speechless, I stood there and watched him disappear into the darkness. Once again, moments later, I heard a wolf howl, but this time it wasn't to locate the rest of his pack. This sounded almost broken.

While I knew I should, I couldn't seem to find it in myself to care that he was hurt; telling me that my relationship wouldn't work pissed me off. If I could survive losing my brother and who I thought was the love of my life within weeks of each other, I could figure out how to make my relationship with David work. I was resilient. I was strong. But, more importantly, I wasn't Nick.

He'd proven himself to me time and time again, and it was time I did the same.

CHAPTER 22 | AFFIRMATION

David was none the wiser as I slipped into the bedroom and removed my yoga pants and shirt, leaving me in the same skimpy tank and sleep short set I was in when we crawled into bed. I placed them in my top drawer before settling into the cool sheets next to him, and his body barely shifted as I pulled the blankets over myself.

I should have been tired considering it was just past three in the morning, but I was wide awake, and it was all Nick's fault. I was still raging over what he said about my future with David. Hurt him? Did he really think I could do something like that?

I understood that he left because he lost control, but how could he compare the two of us like that?

The bed dipped beside me, and it startled me when David draped his arm over my waist, pulling me toward his body. His body was warm as he pressed it along the length of mine, and he groaned as he pressed a kiss to the spot just below my ear. "You cold?" he asked, his voice still thick and heavy with sleep. "You feel cold."

"Hmm?" I hummed softly, trying to make it sound as though I just woke up. "Oh, a little, maybe."

Yes. I hated myself for lying. I was a terrible person. I know I should've just told him, but what would that accomplish besides a fight of epic proportions?

Ever so thoughtfully, David tugged the duvet up over my shoulders before getting up and closing the bedroom window. Because the chill lingered in the room, he grabbed the throw blanket I kept at the end of the bed and pulled it over us as well. I really wasn't uncomfortable with the temperature, but he was probably feeling the chill of the night air on my skin.

"Better?" he asked, slipping back in behind me and sounding a little more awake.

Looking over my shoulder as he pressed against me, I smiled and nodded. "Toasty. Thanks."

"I'm nothing if not considerate," he murmured, resting his head on my pillow. His breath fanned across my neck, blowing a few strands of hair over it that tickled. I expected him to fall right back asleep, but when his hand roamed over my belly and down between my thighs, I knew he had other plans.

Goosebumps rippled up in the wake of his lips as they brushed across my shoulder, and my breath shuddered when his teeth scraped my skin, using them to pull the strap of my tank top down. I knew we needed sleep, especially given the hour, but my body immediately warmed to David's intentions when I felt him grow aroused behind me. I rolled over to face him, my desire sparking to life and flaring rapidly.

His arm remained around my waist, holding me tight against him as we kissed. David's lips were firm and insistent against my own, and there was an eager yearning that burned between us as he slipped his hand under my shirt and palmed my breast with urgency. Moaning, I arched my body into his touch, reveling in the way his hands played my body like a well-tuned instrument and greedy for more. He knew me like no one else. Not even Nick…at least, not anymore.

Nick used to know me better than anyone. His ability to know what I needed or what I was thinking far surpassed anyone's. I used to think it was because we were meant to be, but since David seemed to be capable of it also, perhaps it was as simple as my willingness to let someone in. Let someone love me.

The mere thought of Nick forced a fresh surge of rage through my body. How could I even think of him at a time like this? Who did that?

Angry at myself and desperate to push my ex from my mind, I made short work of the few articles of clothing we had on and straddled David's hips, slowly lowering myself onto him. When he brought his hands to my waist in an effort to set our pace, I grabbed and raised them up over his head. Holding them there as our bodies writhed against each other, I leaned forward and kissed him hungrily.

It didn't take long for my climax to build, my skin buzzing and alight with desire as I released his arms and dragged my nails lightly down them. His biceps quivered beneath my touch, registering the ticklish sensation for what it was on his increasingly sensitive flesh, and I deepened our already voracious kiss…

"You know it can't work, right?"

I bit back a snarl and continued to try to focus solely on David.

Sadly, Nick kept worming his way into my thoughts, and it made me increasingly more forceful and dominant with David.

Lost in my thoughts about Nick, David caught me off guard, flipping us over on the bed and pinning me beneath him. While I usually welcomed a change of pace and position, I needed to be in control. If I wasn't in control, my thoughts might slip at any moment.

Like they're not slipping already, Brooke.

I used my body weight and rolled us over once again, but I misjudged just how much bed was left, and we toppled to the floor, a mess of tangled limbs and joined body parts. I banged my elbow, the pain rocketing up my arm, but I forgot about it when David laughed and pulled my face back to his. He kissed me softly, picking up where we left off, and I sighed as a wave of contentedness washed over me. He didn't really seem to care that we were on the cold hardwood floor as opposed to our warm, soft bed, and to be honest, neither did I. This moment was perfect because we were together, so I lost myself in him completely, moving my hands over his sweat-slickened skin and feeling his heartbeat quicken beneath my hands as I dragged them over his chest...

"He's human. You're not. It's dangerous for you to be with him."

No! Just because Nick was too scared to even try to make our relationship work didn't mean he could scare me away from the one man who'd made me happy after he left. Yes, I'd changed, but I wasn't *dangerous*. I cared for David...loved him. So much. How could I possibly hurt him?

"I love you," I breathed against his lips, hoping that declaring it aloud would keep Nick from intruding with his unwelcome opinions. The first wave of pleasure passed through me, my skin tingling as it radiated from every pore. My fingers and toes curled when David returned the sentiment, his words coming out somewhat broken as his hips stilled beneath mine.

Out of breath, I collapsed onto David's chest, and when my gaze traveled along the dark wooden floors,

I giggled, having momentarily forgotten falling out of bed. I lifted my head, resting my chin on David's sternum, and met his eyes. He still looked tired—satisfied, but tired, nonetheless—so I moved to slip away from him, but he held me in place for a moment longer, lifting his head to kiss me lightly.

We remained like this for a few minutes, enjoying the closeness after such intensity, and David's hand stroked the length of my hair, tickling my back until I shivered. All traces of Nick disappeared, much to my relief. The last thing I needed was for my thoughts to be clouded with him right before falling asleep.

I shivered again as David's fingers moved down my spine, and with a soft, exhausted chuckle, he took this as his cue to usher me back into bed and beneath the thick blanket. The second my head hit my pillow, the exhaustion that avoided me all night hit me like a bus. I yawned as David pulled me closer, and I rested my head in the crook of his neck, letting sleep finally take over.

Coffee was the first thing I smelled, and it pulled me from sleep. Inhaling deeply, I rubbed my eyes and sat up. That's when I smelled the bacon...and the eggs. I already knew what I would find when I looked to my left, but I did it out of habit; the bed was empty, save for me. I reached over to find David's side of the bed chilly, and I smiled fondly as I reminisced about the night we shared.

I could practically feel his hands on every inch of my skin, and it warmed me entirely, the heat moving down my body as my toes curled again. There was nothing about last night that wasn't amazing. In fact, the intensity still hung in the air, stimulating my longing for him all over again. Seemed last night made me more than a little insatiable.

The combined smells of my breakfast pulled me further from my slightly dazed and sleepy state, and I placed my feet on the chilly floor, reaching my arms up over my head and stretching. There was a satisfying pop in my spine, and my skin tingled from the release of tension.

Before exiting the room, I grabbed the yoga pants I'd stuffed in my top drawer the night before and pulled them on, padding down the hall barefoot. In the kitchen, David stood at the stove, dressed in nothing more than his plaid sleep pants, as he cooked breakfast like a pro. There weren't many people who would risk cooking a food like bacon in next to nothing, and I crossed my arms, leaning against the entryway wall and watched raptly.

Turning his head, he caught me watching him and grinned. "You're awake," he said. "I didn't hear you come down the hall."

Laughing lightly, I stepped toward him and wrapped my arms around his waist and watched him cook. "I'm pretty stealthy." As he flipped the bacon over in the frying pan, I glanced up at the clock on the stove and gasped. "It's almost ten in the morning."

"Yup."

I was stunned. It'd been over two weeks since I'd slept this late. Lately, I'd been waking up before dawn with an insane burst of energy. The energy was still very much there, so I was willing to bet that this change was simply due to the fact that I went to bed later than usual, altering my internal clock slightly.

Or maybe you just expelled all that extra energy into the amazing sex last night, I told myself.

Whatever the cause, it was a bit surprising.

While David finished up with breakfast, I set the table. By the time everything was in place, David brought the food over, and we sat down to dish up. Everything smelled amazing, and looked even better. Having gotten used to my increased appetite, David prepared more than double what the two of us would normally eat—which meant I ate almost three times what I used to. It concerned me in the first few days, but because I'd never felt better, I didn't worry for long.

After David had a chance to dish up, I loaded my own plate with bacon, eggs, and even a huge heap of hashbrowns since I was no longer repulsed by anything that wasn't meat. David seemed pleased by this turn in my appetite as he brought his fork to his mouth. I was just about to do the same when my attention shifted from the food on my fork in front of me to the dark rings around his wrist.

My stomach turned violently, and I gasped, dropping my own food-filled fork as I reached for his hand. Eggs splattered across the table and onto the floor, but I didn't care. "What the hell?" I asked, inspecting the faint bruises circling his wrist. I glanced over at the other one—the one I'd watched flip the bacon in the pan—and noticed that it, too, had some bruising, but it wasn't nearly as noticeable.

David chuckled, flipping his hand over to show me the rest of the injury. It was then I realized they were a perfect outline for my fingers. "You were pretty aggressive last night. All of your early morning workouts must be paying off." I ghosted the angry-looking marks with my fingertips, being careful not to press too hard. "It's okay, they don't hurt."

Bile churned in my stomach.

"He's human. You're not. It's dangerous for you to be

with him."

I hated to let Nick invade my thoughts again, but given the evidence in front of me, it was a little difficult to not take stock in his previous warnings: *It's dangerous for me to be with him...I'm dangerous.*

"I-I'm sorry," I stammered, still unable to believe I was — *am* — capable of something like this.

"I'm not. Shit happens, Brooke. Besides, I didn't complain last night, and you're sure as hell not going to hear me start now." He laughed again, withdrawing his hand from my grip. "If you're worried that you hurt me, you didn't."

I had trouble believing him, thinking that maybe he was just trying to placate me, because the proof was right there around his wrists in a deepening purple hue. Regardless of how many times he told me not to worry about it, guilt consumed me, and I replayed what happened in the bedroom over and over again. Unlike earlier when I fondly reminisced about it, now I analyzed it, trying to figure out when I lost my self-restraint.

And it all pointed to one conclusion: Nick.

It was Nick telling me that David and I couldn't work due to what happened to me. His stupid warning got to me on a much deeper level, and in the heat of the moment, I felt the best way to eliminate his taunting from my mind was to push past it forcefully. What I hadn't expected was that I would be as physically forceful toward David while mentally willing Nick from my thoughts. I'd done what I wanted to prove I would never do: I hurt him because I lost control.

I hurt him. I'm dangerous.

I tried to shake the thoughts from my head, but it wasn't easy. The more I tried, the more I wondered if Nick was right, and I hated myself for that.

I thought about everything I'd learned over the past few days in regard to what had been happening to me — my strange surges of strength and energy, my heightened senses, my cravings. Yes, I hadn't been acting like myself in the beginning, and while I initially questioned it, I admit that I grew accustomed to everything — liked it even — and as time went on, it was as if something deep inside told me that this was how it was supposed to be. That it was okay for me to be experiencing all of this, and that it was natural.

Then Nick came barreling back into my life with information that would change my life as I knew it, and now all I could think about was how I hurt someone I loved.

My guilt continued to mount, tightening like a knot in my churning stomach, and my appetite disappeared. David noticed this, and repeated again and again that I shouldn't dwell on it, but how could I not? How could I know for certain that this wouldn't happen again next time?

Next time? I surprised myself when I inwardly voiced the question, and I immediately resolved that there wouldn't *be* a next time. There couldn't be. At least, not until I knew how to control my strength completely — which, according to Nick, could take quite some time.

When I looked up again, I could see in David's eyes that he was worried about my reaction to all of this, and I realized that I might not have the luxury of time. If I pulled away again — even to fix this — I risked losing him.

CHAPTER 23 | DETACHED

It wasn't easy, pretending everything was fine, and I knew David saw through each and every reassurance. And he was right to be skeptical. Any idiot could see that, never mind my police detective boyfriend. I wasn't intentionally pushing him away, but I was terrified of hurting him again.

The reality of harming him still weighed heavily on my mind. It was no longer just a possibility, and I realized I was lucky to have only harmed him minutely. But it was only a matter of time before I lost control completely. The full moon was coming in just over three weeks, and until I learned to shift of my own volition, it would be forced upon me again and again and again.

Nick promised to help me with this, but I was afraid to contact him. This, of course, didn't mean *he* hadn't contacted me. He had. Several times a day. It was a real chore keeping it from David.

Why hadn't I pick up or call him back? Because I was a coward. I feared he might see what I'd done, the shame I felt, and tell me that he told me so. I wouldn't be able to handle that. I didn't need him to add to my guilt.

That didn't mean I *wouldn't* contact him. I just

needed another day or two. I needed...time. Not that it helped me in any way.

But I had to. With every day that passed, I knew I did. If not for me, then for David. He was the best thing to ever happen to me—I knew that now—and I wouldn't leave him. I knew what that felt like, and I refused to run away. No, I would learn to control this so we could be together.

And what about those reemerging feelings for Nick? I hadn't forgotten about them. How could I? I was reminded of what we used to share every time we were in the same room together. I could feel the heat of his gaze, feel the pull he had over the desires I thought long gone, but I kept telling myself that what I felt was just residual emotions from the past. That it was all just familiar, and that they'd be forgotten the second he left town.

But deep down, I knew better. I knew it was more. I could feel it.

And it terrified me.

"You okay?" David's voice startled me from my thoughts, and I looked across the car at him. Letting his eyes wander from the road for a second, he grinned at me. "You seem scared."

See. He was rather astute as of late.

"You have no reason to be nervous," he told me with a genuine snicker. "It's not like I haven't already met your parents."

I *wished* it was just my mother's dinner invitation that had me so preoccupied.

Probably in hopes of drawing me from my tumultuous thoughts, David laid a hand over mine as they sat clenched in my lap. Glancing down, I watched the sleeve of his leather jacket creep up, exposing his wrist. The bruises had faded, but they were still there; a faint yellow-tinted reminder of what I did to him. I still couldn't bear the sight, and with a shaky breath, I gently pulled my hands from his grasp and pretended to fix my hair. I hoped he wouldn't see the gesture for what it was, but he did.

He exhaled heavily, placing both hands back on the wheel and tightening his grip around it. He didn't bring up the issue; he knew what it was, and it frustrated him to no end that he had no idea how to fix it.

Truthfully, neither did I. But I was working on it, and I hoped to figure it out before it was too late.

Even though he already knew the source of my unease, I offered him a gentle smile. "Yes. I realize you've already met them both," I said. "But this is entirely different. We're together now. *Openly* together and living under the same roof. I don't think you fully understand what this means to my mother."

The tension in the car lifted slightly, and I was thankful for it.

My mother's invitation to dinner wasn't too big a shock. It was bound to happen eventually, and the only thing that surprised me was that it had taken her this long to organize something. Mind you, David and I had been pretty tied up with work lately, and with my father being in charge of our department, I suppose she was privy to our availability through him. Add to that my recent wolf attack and hospitalization, and we were almost impossible to plan around.

While we still had yet to break ground on our case, my dad suggested we needed a break from everything. He felt like we were running around in circles, chasing our tails — an analogy that wasn't nearly as humorous as it was now, given my circumstances when the full moon came around every month.

When we arrived at my parents' house, David rushed around and opened my door for me before I got the chance. It was sweet, and I smiled apprecia- tively as he reached into the backseat and grabbed the bouquet of flowers and bottle of wine he'd picked up earlier. As we made our way up the walk, I grew in- creasingly more nervous because I didn't know what to expect.

My mom opened the door only moments after we knocked, and she pulled me into her arms. "Brooke, honey," she said. "I'm so glad you two could make it." After releasing me, she looked over at David, wearing the biggest smile I'd ever seen, and then she hugged him too.

It caught him slightly off guard, but he recovered quickly. "Mrs. Leighton," David responded. "Thanks for having us." He held out the wine and flowers. "These are for you."

"How sweet," was her response as she accepted them from him and ushered us inside. "And it's Laura. Now come on, you two. Dinner's ready."

I took David's jacket and hung it with mine in the coat closet before we followed my mother into the dining room. The rich smell of her cooking infused the air, making my mouth water as I inhaled deeply and pinpointed what we were having. *Roast beef...* I inhaled again, licking my bottom lip. *Mashed pota- toes...* Swallowing the saliva that continued to pool in my mouth, I took one more deep breath. *Steamed broc- coli in Mom's homemade cheese sauce.*

If I thought I was hungry before, it was nothing compared to what I felt now.

"Is there anything I can help with, Mrs..." David paused for a minute before amending himself. "Laura."

Laughing, my mom graciously declined his offer before heading to the kitchen, where I heard my dad moving around. Dishes clanked together, platters hit the countertops, and a cork was pulled from a bottle of wine while my parents were gone, and soon they rejoined us, bringing a couple of items each to the table. David took the wine from my mother and filled our glasses while Mom and Dad finished setting the table.

"Everything looks and smells amazing, Mom," I told her, taking the seat David so gallantly pulled out for me.

As we all dished up our food, passing it to the right before taking the next item, my dad tried to initiate the conversation. "How did things at the office go after I left? Any progress?"

I shook my head, my frustration returning. Ever since finding the abandoned nightclub, we'd hit a brick wall. Donovan had been as much help as he could be, and we still checked in often in case the suspects resurfaced there. I wasn't so optimistic given their reaction according to our witness. If they truly did sense our involvement with the club, it was unlikely they'd go back there looking for future victims.

"Nothing," I replied, scooping some broccoli onto my plate. While I still didn't crave vegetables, they weren't as unappealing as they were a couple weeks ago. Plus, I didn't want to hear my mother complaining about the lack of green on my plate. I might be twenty-eight years old, but that didn't mean she'd stopped mothering me. "Keaton and O'Malley are still digging around, but—"

"Uh uh," Mom interrupted in an admonishing tone. "No shop-talk tonight. You know the rules, Keith."

The rules.

Mom had always been proud of what my dad did for a living—what I now do for a living—and even more so since Bobby died. She knew what it felt like to be on the receiving end of bad news, and while we never got closure after his death, she appreciated that we worked hard to give others in similar situations the chance to heal and move on.

But she didn't like to hear details over dinner. Ever, actually.

We never went into specifics, though, because it actually wasn't allowed. Having always been more of a sensitive soul, Mom liked to look at the world through rose-colored glasses. Especially after Bobby's unexplained death. She knew what happened in the real world, but she was so empathetic that it affected her deeply. Occasionally she'd ask, but we kept details to a bare minimum, glossing over everything enough that she wouldn't have nightmares or relive what we'd already been through.

Some days I struggled with the same thing, but my need to stop it from happening again kept me going.

"Sorry, dear." Dad was quick to apologize, reaching over and taking my mom's hand, giving it a gentle squeeze.

It always warmed my heart to see those little looks of affection they shared, and I looked across the table with a smirk out of habit, only to find the chair there empty. One would think I'd get used to that empty chair staring back at me after this many years, but I didn't. Bobby and I always used to exchange a look during one of these moments between our parents. Growing up with so many people whose parents split when we were all younger made us appreciate the strong connection our parents shared. It gave us something to look up to.

I shook off the twinge of sadness that gnawed at me and picked up my fork, spearing a piece of broccoli. It wasn't easy to forget, and I didn't really want to. Even though Bobby had been gone for the last seven years, I still sensed his presence in everything I did. Sometimes more than others. It used to comfort me to think he might be watching over me in some way.

My last thought gave me pause. *Used* to? Before I could slough it off as one of those things you said or did without much forethought, my mother's voice filled the room.

"So, how are things going, you two?"

Next to me, David shifted in his seat, turning his head and smiling at me. "Really well." A pause. "Right?"

Offering him a smile that felt as genuine as I was capable given what happened the other day, I nodded. "Yeah. I mean, there's definitely been an adjustment period, but things are good."

I saw something in my mom's eyes—the very thing that had me worried about accepting this dinner invitation in the first place, and I tried to give her that look that told her not to go there. She must have missed it.

"I'm so happy to hear that." She pushed her roast beef around her plate before picking up some potatoes. "It's been so wonderful to see Brooke ready to settle down again."

And there it was. That one little word that would open the flood gates of this conversation: "Again." Prefaced with the words "settle down."

I didn't need to look at David to know his curiosity had been piqued; I felt it billowing off of him. I gripped my fork so tightly, the metal bit into my palms, and I stared nervously at my dinner plate, my heart beating unevenly. When he didn't say anything right away, I relaxed, thinking that maybe he'd let it go since it was in my past and I'd proven my efforts to move on. With him.

"Laura, sweetheart," my dad began, his voice low and uneasy as he poured another glass of wine, polishing off the bottle. "Maybe we shouldn't—"

Mom finally realized the potential for how uncomfortable this conversation could turn out, because she nodded. "You're right," she agreed. "I didn't mean to suggest they're ready to get engaged…"

Beside me, David choked on a sip of his wine, and my face heated as I clenched my eyes shut. And there it was. David would finally know just how serious Nick and I were, which would only add fuel to the fire of his hatred and jealousy. He'd been pushing for us to come out as a couple for so long, and I knew that he saw marriage in our future. But, after a failed engagement to a man I honestly thought I would spend the rest of my life with, I'd grown quite content with the idea of just living happily ever after with the man I now loved. No piece of paper binding us together. No gathering of friends and family at an overly expensive celebration.

Just us. Living together. In love.

That was enough for me, and I figured I could get David to be okay with that as well…until now, that is. Now that he was on the verge of learning the one piece of my past I deliberately shielded him from, all bets were off. He'd want more. Or at the very least, he'd wonder why I didn't if I'd been able to commit myself to someone else before.

And he'd have a point. Why shouldn't I commit to another if it was something I'd done before with someone else? Well, it all stemmed back to how my engagement ended, and the one simple truth remained: I was afraid. I let Nick into my heart completely and he stomped on it when he walked away from us. Yes, he had his reasons, but that didn't excuse the fact that I was left behind, broken and destroyed. It wasn't exactly something I wanted to ever relive, so I vowed to never take that step. Why would I set myself up for something like that to happen again?

Now, deep down, I truly believed that David wouldn't do that to me — he wasn't Nick — but the fear still lingered, keeping me from opening that small part of my heart back up. Did I imagine what it would be like to marry David? Sure. More so lately than the first year we were together — or up until a couple weeks ago when my life irrevocably changed — but then those musings shifted into my worst nightmare: David left me with no explanation. He just took off. So I dropped it, burying it as deep as possible.

And now, there I was, sitting at the table, awkward silence hovering in the air, my heart thundering and my stomach clenching as I struggled to find the words to explain why I hadn't told him about my failed engagement.

I couldn't, though. My cowardice reared its ugly head, and I set my fork down gingerly before pushing my chair back. The legs scraped against the tile floor, the sound obnoxiously echoing off the walls. David stood beside me, and when I met his eyes briefly, I found worry. Hoping to reassure him that I was okay, I smiled. Like before, it didn't work. But he let me go without a fight. "I'll be right back," I said, my tone soft but loud enough that they all heard me. "I'm just going to grab another bottle of wine."

My eyes met my mother's on my way out of the dining room, and I recognized her remorse. She tried to follow me, but I shook my head, telling her silently that I needed a moment alone.

From the kitchen, I heard nothing. The awkward

silence continued to suffocate them all, and I placed my hands on the countertop, holding myself up as I dropped my head and closed my eyes. I took a deep breath, and the crisp scent of autumn traveled in on a breeze through the open window above the sink, filling my head. It wasn't the only scent swirling around me, though; with it, I picked up the one scent that still called to me even though I kept trying to ignore its pull.

"You've *got* to be kidding me," I grumbled under my breath, pushing off the counter and silently making my way for the patio doors.

I opened them as quietly as possible and slipped out into the night. It was completely black out, the moon hiding behind a cover of cloud, but I left the light off to keep from alerting my parents and David that I slipped outside for a moment. Plus, I picked up the ability to see better in the dark, rendering the light unnecessary anyway.

The back deck was empty, but Nick's scent hung in the dry desert air. I descended the few stairs and walked past the pool, and the minute my feet hit the grass, Nick stepped out from the shadows, hair unruly, jaw more unshaven than usual, black T-shirt fitted to his upper body, and his hands thrust into the pockets of his purposefully ragged-looking jeans.

"Hey," he greeted, eyes locked on mine, hard yet concerned at the same time.

"What are you doing here?" I demanded through clenched teeth, annoyed that he continued to pop up unannounced like this. Sure, there was that small part of me that was happy to see him, but I kept a tight leash on it. I refused to give him the satisfaction. "You realize that stalking a cop probably isn't the best idea, don't you?"

"I've been calling. When you didn't return any of

my messages..." He sighed, and I didn't need to be a mind reader to know what he was thinking. He wasn't just worried about me, but about what I could have done. To David. "I was concerned."

"We're both fine," I informed him, my voice cracking at the end, giving me away.

Nick definitely picked up on it, his eyebrows rising. "Did you...?"

Unable to meet his gaze, I crossed my arms in front of me defensively and averted my eyes to the left. "He's fine."

Naturally, he didn't buy it. "What happened?"

Embarrassed to be having this conversation with my ex about the man I was currently involved with, I buried my reddening face in my hands. "It's nothing," I mumbled. "Everything turned out fine." I was starting to sound like a broken record.

The warmth of Nick's touch on my upper arms pulled me from my mortification, his hands moving up and down them in a soothing manner. "What happened?" he repeated in a soft and soothing tone, drawing my confession from me with ease. "Did you lose control and hurt him?"

Peeking up at him above the tips of my fingers, I shook my head. "Not the way you think," I mumbled into my hands before dropping them. "We..." I thought back to what happened that night, and the skin all over my body warmed with a blush that I hoped the dark would conceal. What it couldn't hide was the unexpected shift in my hormones, its heady scent alerting even me, so I didn't finish explaining everything.

Understanding and sorrow filled Nick's expressive eyes, and he took two large steps back. "Oh."

"He's fine, though," I repeated, sighing and rubbing my hands up and down my arms in an act of self-comfort. "But I'm…struggling with the memory of it. I didn't even realize I was being that rough."

A rumble escaped Nick, and he was quick to quell it. But not before I recognized it for envy. It was obvious that he wanted to tell me how he told me so, but instead, he expressed it with the silent intensity of his stare. Then his eyes turned angry without warning. "As much as I want to hear about how kinky things are in the bedroom now, that's not why I'm here."

My annoyance flared when his concern melted away completely. "Then what the hell do you want?" I don't know why, but he seemed taken aback by my reaction. "I mean, if you didn't come here to check up on me, which is kind of the impression that you initially gave off, then what is it? What is so important that you'd interrupt a *family* dinner?"

Flustered, Nick stumbled over his words for a second before releasing an aggravated sigh and thrusting his fingers through his hair. I mentally patted myself on the back for even momentarily throwing him off for once. "Look, I didn't come here to argue with you," he informed me. "I was concerned about you — still am, if that means anything to you — but I also came to talk to you about that case you're working."

Shocked, I tightened my grip around myself. "Wh-what about it?"

Back in the house, I heard footsteps, and I looked up to see movement in the kitchen window. It would only be a couple of minutes before whoever was in there found me out here with Nick, so I prodded him again.

"We need you to back off a bit," he said, his expression clearly telling me he knew it was a stupid request, and one I obviously couldn't grant.

"You can't be serious."

Nick sighed, his eyes moving about as if scanning the darkness for something. He didn't seem at all threatened. One sniff of the air, and I picked up Jackson's scent as well as his other pack mates. They weren't close, keeping their distance, but they were there somewhere. Probably waiting for Nick to return.

"I realize what it is I'm asking—"

"Do you?" I interrupted, confused and angry. "We're trying to solve several murders. Murders, Nick. Murders, I might add, that you told me are tied to my brother's own unsolved case. And now you want me to just walk away?"

"No," he said, shaking his head emphatically. "Not walk away, just...back off a bit. Maybe lead them in another direction."

"You want me to impede my own investigation?"

"Believe me when I tell you that you and your team aren't properly equipped to deal with this. Your investigation is only scaring them off."

"Them?" I questioned. "So, you know who *they* are?" Nick's silence was all the confirmation I needed. "And why, exactly, do you think we can't handle this?"

"Because," Nick explained, conflict growing in his eyes. "It's nothing you've ever dealt with before, Brooke. It's...not of this world."

"Werewolves," I offered without a questioning lilt in my tone.

"In order to keep you safe from them, I can't tell you just yet," Nick supplied. "But it's not other wolves. It's something else entirely." Another brief pause before Nick looked up, and when I heard the screen door open slightly, he quickly concluded. "They're moving on—most of them—so it's making them harder to track. Your involvement is only complicating matters further, forcing them to lie low."

"So, you're upset that they're not killing anymore?" His logic didn't resemble mine.

"Of course not, but with you guys constantly sniffing around, they're packing up shop. We are so close to stopping them, but the more interference from the police, the harder it's becoming."

Before I could defend the actions of the department and point out his demands for how ridiculous they were, Nick stepped back into the cover of darkness. Just as he disappeared, warm hands appeared on my shoulders, causing me to jump in surprise. Turning, I found David behind me, and I offered him a smile. Had I not been so wrapped up in my conversation with Nick, I might have sensed him before his arrival startled me.

"You okay?" he asked, kissing my cheek lightly. I sensed the hesitation behind the gesture, but he didn't falter, trying to make things better between us.

It was comforting, and I leaned into it, humming contentedly as the distance between us was momentarily forgotten. "Yeah. I thought I saw something out here when I was in the kitchen. Figured I should check it out." It wasn't a total lie, so I didn't feel overly guilty keeping the real reason I was out here from him.

Then I remembered the reason I went into the kitchen, and I turned around to face David, ready to apologize for my total lack of regard when it came to disclosing my past with Nick. "Are *you* okay? I'm sorry I didn't tell you. I guess I—"

David stopped me. "You don't need to apologize. That entire conversation was equally as awkward for me."

"Somehow, I doubt that."

Chuckling, David pushed a length of my hair back over my shoulder, his hand trailing down my arm and making me shiver. When it reached my elbow, he flattened it on my back and pulled me toward him abruptly, exciting me. "Come back inside. Your mom feels terrible and promises to be on her best behavior. No more talk of marriage until we're ready."

My lips fought the smile I forced as David led me back toward the house. Before leading me through the doorway, I stopped him. "David…"

Seeing the look in my eyes for what it was, he sighed. "Brooke, I know you're not ready, but I'm willing to wait until you are." Leaning in, he kissed my forehead. "That's how much I love you and believe in us."

I let him take me back inside. When we returned to the dining room, my mom didn't allude to my future with David at all—just as promised—and I was grateful for it. Instead, our conversation revolved around the upcoming holiday season. Thanksgiving was only two weeks away, and David was all too eager to talk about his hopes for that day.

"Well, Brooke and I haven't really discussed it yet," he began, reaching over and taking my hand, "but I was thinking we'd host this year. Have you two join us and invite my parents down."

I choked slightly on the bite I'd just taken, and pulled my hand from his to grab my wine. David rested his hand on my back, moving it up and down in a soothing manner as I dislodged the piece of roast beef and finally swallowed it. "Sorry," I said, glancing over at David.

He smiled sheepishly and shrugged. "They want to meet you."

"You've talked about me?" I was both flattered

and worried — the latter because I hadn't quite been myself, and I'd hate if he painted me in a bad light. I loved him, and I really wanted his parents to like me.

Almost as though he'd forgotten we were in the presence of my parents, he reached over and cupped my face. I leaned into the touch and smiled. "Of course I have."

Mom cleared her throat, and we turned back to them. "I, for one, think that's a wonderful idea." She looked at us both pointedly. "But I expect to help out with something. Whether it's bringing dessert or helping in the kitchen."

Laughing, I regarded her demand. "It wouldn't feel like Thanksgiving if you didn't."

After dinner, I helped Mom clear the table and do the dishes while the guys enjoyed a glass of cognac. I dried the dishes while Mom washed, and we were about halfway through them when she broke the silence. "I am sorry about earlier," she whispered. "I didn't mean to imply or pressure the two of you."

"I know, Mom," I assured her, taking a plate and drying it before putting it away with the rest.

"I got the impression David didn't know just how serious you and Nick were."

"He didn't." Mom looked over at me, shocked. "He knew we were together, but I didn't think that a broken engagement was worth mentioning. It's not like I'm divorced or a widow or anything," I explained, trying to justify my omission of facts.

She drained the sink and rinsed the suds from it before turning to me and resting her hip against the counter. "Do you think it's something you want?"

I regarded her curiously before she elaborated.

"Marriage. Kids."

Kids. Was that even possible now? Would they be human, or would my recently altered DNA affect them, too?

"I-I don't know," I stammered softly, my voice cracking. "I've seen things since joining the force, Mom. I'm so aware of the kinds of things that happen in the world today... Not to mention what happened to Bobby. How could I bring a child into this world, knowing what I know now?"

I didn't expect my mom to understand my stance on this. She was the most maternal woman I'd ever known, and she was unable to have the large family she so badly wanted. Bobby and I were her "little miracles" after several years of trying to get pregnant with no success. This didn't mean she wasn't happy; she was definitely a very attentive mother, always there to listen or help you with a problem.

I could tell she had questions, or maybe she wanted to try and tell me that I was still young and could change my mind — which I was, and I could. Before she could, a throat cleared behind us, startling me and forcing the blood in my veins to run cold. Dread fell like a lead weight into the pit of my stomach when I identified the familiar scent of our unexpected company. I mentally kicked myself for being too wrapped up in my tumultuous thoughts about marriage and the children I may never have — not to mention who they'll most resemble when the full moon comes around — to sense him.

I slowly turned around, ready to explain everything in a way I hoped he would understand, but the look in David's eyes as he stood in the doorway indicated it wouldn't be that easy.

CHAPTER 24 | BLAME

As we all stood in uneasy silence, I wondered how much he had heard. Everything? Nothing at all? We hadn't ever talked about kids, but something told me David wanted a family some day...even if we never married.

Nervous and unable to hold his stare, I folded the towel and hung it on the oven handle. "Hey," I said softly, tucking my hair behind my ears and slowly lifting my head. I saw in his expression that he was uncertain of something — agitated, even.

His eyebrows knit together, and he clenched his eyes shut as if snapping himself out of some kind of stupor. "You ready?"

I looked over at Mom, whose own expression seemed anxious for me; I think she could sense as well as I could that he overheard everything. "Y-yeah, we just finished up here," I replied before pulling my mom into my arms. "Thanks for dinner, Mom. It was delicious."

"It was my pleasure, sweetie." She kissed my cheek, apologizing with her eyes. "Be sure to say goodbye to your father on your way out, or you'll never hear the end of it."

"I will."

I walked past David, and I could feel the cold blast of tension rolling off of him. I tried to offer him a smile, but the one he responded with was forced and weak.

"Dinner was wonderful, Mrs. Leighton," David said.

"Laura," she corrected one last time. "And you keep us informed about that Thanksgiving dinner."

I studied David's face again, but he had his game face on now, his eyes belying nothing. "Yeah. We'll let you know whatever it is we decide." Something about the way he worded that sent a chill down my spine, but I chose not to question it in the wake of what he most likely overheard a moment ago.

On our way to the front door, we found my dad in the living room and said goodnight, even though we'd see him at work in the morning. He incited the usual warning to drive safe as he walked us outside, and I gave him a hug before climbing into the car.

If I thought the ride to my parents' house was awkward, the one home was worse. David's hands remained at ten and two on the wheel, his eyes locked on the road, only occasionally peering in his mirrors before changing lanes. He did everything but look at me, and that wasn't normal for him. I went over how I was going to try and explain what he overheard in my head, but I was unable to figure out a way that wouldn't upset him further… Okay, so truthfully, this was just an excuse. I realized that no matter how I brought it up, it would upset him. I was just acting like a chicken-shit.

When we arrived home and let ourselves inside, David shrugged out of his jacket and put it away. I continued to sense the building anxiety in the space between us, and I knew it was just a matter of minutes before he exploded, so I decided to apologize.

Again. I actually seemed to be doing a lot of that lately.

"David, I—"

"Don't, Brooke," he interrupted, his tone clipped and on edge. "Just...don't."

Frustrated, I reached for his arm and turned him to face me. "How can you be this upset?" I demanded. "It's not like we've ever talked about this stuff before!"

"We've been together two years, Brooke. You had to think that this was a possibility."

Apologetic, I shrugged my shoulders. "Not really," I replied honestly.

"So, you don't want to get married or have children?"

I crossed my arms in front of me defensively, my hands starting to shake. "I never said that." I paused and considered my next words before blurting out, "But I have reservations, yes."

"Like...?"

Other than the reasons I gave my mom in the kitchen, there was nothing more I could say that he would believe or even begin to understand. "You already know why," I reminded him. "How can you act like bringing a child into this world is no big deal? We've seen some pretty scary shit, David."

And I could be something far more dangerous to any potential family we could have, I mentally tacked on. *Or they could be dangerous to* you.

"That's bullshit, and you know it," he retaliated, his words stinging as though I'd been struck. Before I could respond, David pushed his fingers through his dark hair and groaned in frustration. "I want to marry you, Brooke."

Feeling short of breath, my knees threatened to

give out on me at any second.

"You know it can't work, right?" Nick's voice haunted me again, and it brought back the memory of the other night when I was so forceful with him. How I'd bruised him...

Shit. Maybe Nick was right.

"I know you're not ready, and I'm not going to push, but you should know it's what I want."

Breathing heavily now, my heart hammering in my chest, I took a wobbly step back toward the door. The room appeared to be closing in around me, and Nick's voice was unrelenting. *"He's human. You're not. It's dangerous for you to be with him."* The bruises on David's wrists flashed in the darkness of my mind, and I shuddered before panic gripped me firmly in its grasp, suffocating me further.

"I love you," David continued, keeping in step with me as I continued on with my nervous breakdown. "I want a life with you."

I was scared. Scared because of everything Nick told me about how I might never make it work with David. Scared because I feared that David and I would never agree on what we each expected out of our relationship. And, mostly, scared because of what I'd become.

My back hit the solid wood door, the knob pressing into the small of my back, and I reached behind me and turned it. "I... David, I..."

"Brooke, just hear me out."

"I can't do this right now," I mumbled, tears stinging my eyes and threatening to spill over onto my cheeks. I loved him, but I couldn't forget Nick's warnings; he'd gotten into my head and muddled everything up. I thought I could do this—have a life with David—but what if I couldn't? What if everything Nick said was true? "I'm sorry."

And, with that, I pulled open the door and walked briskly down the sidewalk, the cool air whipping across my face as I picked up my pace. David called after me, but I kept going, needing time to sort through the crap in my head. It upset me that I started to question my feelings when I was so ready to make things work with David, despite Nick's warnings. I loved him more than I ever thought I would be capable of again, and now I was pushing him away. Why? All because I let my stupid ex get into my head.

The panic I felt back at the house continued to mount, making me feel anxious and uneasy. And what did I do lately when that happened? I ran. I ran with everything I had. I ran until my thighs ached and my lungs burned. I ran until the cold air hitting my eyes formed tears that obscured my vision. I lost all sense of direction as I turned corner after corner, letting my instincts take me wherever I was headed, and I didn't question it.

When I finally stopped running, I took a deep breath, letting the cold fall air fill my lungs. It was invigorating as it flowed through my body, so I took another as I turned around and absorbed my surroundings. It surprised me when I realized I was on Nick's front step, and then that surprise turned to irritation, because the last person I needed to see right now was the one who started this whole mess in the first place.

Grunting in frustration, I dropped onto the front step, refusing to knock on the front door, but not ready to head back home yet, and I pushed my face into my arms as they rested on my knees. I tried to block out everything—the cars that drove by, the couple fighting three doors down over who drank the last of the milk and would run to the store, the rustle of the trees and bushes moving in the wind—and I tried to focus on David and how I was going to fix this. It worried me that I might not be able to. Maybe he would decide he'd finally had enough of my bullshit.

The sound of an engine pulled my attention, bringing me out of my little pity-party, and I raised my head to find Nick pulling into the driveway on a red Harley. Something about seeing him on that bike made my libido spike, but I pushed it down and remembered how upset I was with him.

Nick seemed confused to see me on his front step as he cut the engine and dismounted his bike, but he also looked somewhat pleased. "Brooke." His expression turned grim upon seeing the pain and confusion in my eyes as he stepped closer, and he sighed, pushing open his door and coaxing me to my feet and inside. The second the door closed, he turned to me and offered me a sad smile. "What happened?"

What happened? What *didn't* happen?

The events of the past week ran through my head on loop: David's bruises, how I pulled away in hopes of trying to control my urges before I did any more damage, dinner where my mom spilled the beans about the true extent of my relationship with Nick, Nick showing up at their place, David overhearing my conversation with my mom—a conversation I tried to tell myself I would have had with him eventually—and finally how I left him.

I...left...*him*.

Not forever, I tried to tell myself, but it did no good. I had done to David what Nick did to me. I pulled away without warning or an explanation or even really understanding what was happening or why I was doing it, and I walked away when things started to get heavy.

I. Am. An. *Asshole*.

Even though I was angry with myself more than anything, I wheeled around on Nick, thrusting an extended finger in his face. "This is all *your* fault."

In all the years I'd known him, Nick had never looked this terrified, and I was suddenly conflicted. On one hand, I was still really upset that I let him get into my head like this and ruin my chance to be truly happy, but on the other, I didn't relish hurting him.

Damn these warring emotions.

"What the hell are you talking about?" His tone was surprisingly firm, contradicting the fear in his eyes only a second ago. "I thought everything was fine?"

"It was!" I shouted unexpectedly. "And then I let *you*"—I jabbed my finger into his chest—*hard*—"get into my head and poison everything I've worked so hard for."

Still confused, Nick's eyebrows pulled together, and he grabbed my hand, pulling me into the living room. I flopped down on his couch and he sat on the coffee table in front of me. It must have been made of pretty durable materials, because it didn't even bow beneath his solid frame as he leaned forward, resting his arms on his thighs.

"You told me my relationship was doomed." Nick nodded, but didn't say anything. "You said I was dangerous." Another nod. "Well, it's all I can seem to think about lately, and it's driving me crazy—so crazy that I'm unintentionally sabotaging my relationship with David."

"Are you sure it's unintentional?"

Angry, I inhaled deeply, trying to keep myself from punching him in the face—though, I wasn't entirely ruling that out as a possibility. "Of course it is. You think I meant to get rough with him the other night or walk away from him when he wanted to talk about our future together?" Nick grimaced, but his eyes continued to hold mine, waiting for me to finish. Even if he might not necessarily want to hear it. "I keep hearing *your* voice. Every time I start to think things really can work between David and me, *you* creep in and tell me otherwise." My voice dropped to just above a whisper. "You're making me doubt that my feelings for him are anything but true."

Nick sighed. "Look, all I did was tell you how it was for me, Brooke. Do I think you can make it work with a human? No. Truthfully, I don't. Especially not until you fully understand what it is you're capable of. Do I feel good about how I left things with you? Of course not. I loved you, Brooke—Jesus, I still do."

His confession surprised me, but not nearly as much as my reaction to hearing it: my heart skipped a beat, my skin warmed with a blush, and a flurry of butterflies flourished deep in my belly. I felt the need to return the sentiment out of habit, but I resisted, because my love for David should mean more to me than the love of the man who left me without an explanation.

Should?

Nick took my hands in his again, the warmth intense but not unnatural for our kind, apparently. "I love you, Brooke, and on some level, I think you still love me."

I yanked my hands from his, wiping them on my jeans as though that would help get rid of the warm tingle that covered my skin. "I love David," I reminded him, my voice shaking, uncertain, and he heard it. "You and I are over. You decided that the day you left. Did I go to sleep every night hoping you'd come back? Of course I did. But you didn't. It took me a long time to accept that you'd moved on...and then I met David. He's everything you're not." Even though

I knew it would hurt Nick, it needed to be said. "I can depend on him."

As I expected it would, my confession seemed to cut through Nick like a sword through the heart. He flinched briefly, but he shrugged it off, sitting up a little straighter and pretending like I didn't just kick him in the balls.

"I'm sorry, Nick," I whispered softly. "I'm sure you don't want to hear it, but he's the one thing in my life that makes sense right now."

"You only feel that way because you're trying to hold onto your humanity."

"Is that such a bad thing?" I demanded.

"Not necessarily, but it does keep you from fully accepting who you are now." He must have sensed my bewilderment, because he elaborated. "You've said you accept what you are now—a wolf—yet you choose to cling to everything that reminds you of your human life: your job, your boyfriend, your family. You cling to these things because they're *normal*, and that tiny part of you that still refuses to accept what you've become craves the normalcy."

"Again, I ask, is that so bad?"

Nick exhaled heavily and stood up so he could pace the room. "The longer you take to fully accept who you are, the more volatile you become. If you fight your true nature, your human side will fight with the wolf. It won't want to leave. That's when you'll black out. And, like last time, you won't remember."

"So, you want me to just walk away from it all?"

He stopped pacing and faced me. "Brooke, I learned a long time ago that I can't tell you what to do. Only you know what your heart wants." His expression fell, despair reflected in his eyes. "You know what you are, and only you can choose to embrace it.

If you think you can do that and hold onto your human life, then do it." His sorrow was palpable, filling the room like a dark cloud as his gloomy eyes held mine. "Living with regret isn't so easy. Trust me."

Having said his piece, Nick exited the living room, leaving me alone to digest everything he just said. He gave me his blessing to try to keep my life intact through all of this. Was it really possible? He seemed hesitant, but I experienced a renewed surge of conviction regarding my relationship.

Without wasting another minute, I ran from the house and all the way home. I *could* make this work. I was determined to. David and I could be together and figure out the next step toward our future. No regrets.

The front door was still unlocked when I arrived home, and I expected to find him waiting for me behind it. But he wasn't. I didn't hear him — could barely smell him — but I did sense something else.

Recoiling slightly, I took another tiny whiff, choking on the smell and fighting back the bile that started to rise in my throat. My mind registered it as familiar in an instant, the hairs on the back of my neck standing as awareness raced up my spine...

Death.

CHAPTER 25 | CASUALTY

Ice ran through my veins and panic hit me like a brick wall when I remembered I left David here. Alone. Even though he was fully capable of taking care of himself, I couldn't help but fear the worst; that something might have happened to him. As I quickly stepped forward to go find him—*help* him—the smell enveloped me, shrouding my thoughts and triggering that feeling of familiarity again. There were definitely subtle hints of David's warm scent in the air, but they were merely traces, which meant he wasn't here. I silently rejoiced, knowing that wherever he was, he was safer than he would be here.

How did I know this? While I couldn't quite pinpoint it right now, I sensed on a visceral level that whatever was in my house was dangerous, and it unleashed something defensive...something wild.

The repulsive odor was thick in the air, slowly suffocating me, even with every stunted breath I took in an effort to keep it from filling my lungs completely. Like any other unpleasant smell, I cringed at the thought that it would seep into everything it touched. The walls, the carpet, my furniture, my clothes... My skin crawled as if repelling the stench from infiltrating my body as well, and I fought back the urge to wretch.

As I took another step into my house, my disgust gave way to something else. While the smell still made it difficult for me to keep my dinner down, something deep down recognized whatever this was as a threat to my existence. Then it hit me, taking me a couple weeks back to when we stumbled onto *The Dungeon*. A growl slowly formed in my belly, my hands clenching at my sides as I instinctively crouched down into a defensive stance, readying myself to pounce on whatever lurked around the corner. I felt this way after seeing the club-goers and knowing what kind of lifestyle they engaged in, and while this feeling was similar, it was also quite a bit stronger. The beast within snarled and clawed its way to the surface, but I kept it at bay to the best of my ability. It had been a couple of weeks since I had felt this way — not since the last full moon. It was too soon for me to give into this feeling. I wasn't ready.

From my living room, I heard books being pulled from my shelves and tossed carelessly to the floor before papers fluttered through the air and joined them. Who was it? Didn't know. Why were they doing this? No idea. All I could gather was that someone — no, some*thing*, my instincts screamed — was conducting a thorough search of my home, invading my personal space, and just generally pissing me off.

I had nothing to go on other than my instincts telling me that whatever was in my house went against the very laws of nature. It was evil, pure and simple.

Pressing my body against the wall, I listened a little more carefully, trying to pick up some of my visitor's unique traits. It confused me when I failed to hear much of anything. There was no pulse when I expected to hear something elevated by the adrenaline of committing a crime. There was no excited breathing pattern. The only thing I was able to pick up was that smell. The smell of death combined with a sickly-sweet smell I couldn't quite describe.

Then I heard nothing at all. The books stopped being tossed around, papers stopped fluttering. I honed my hearing a little more as I crept along the wall, stopping when I caught a glimpse of my intruder in the mirror on the wall across from me. Silent, I stood as still as possible, waiting for my opportunity to strike before it noticed me.

While it appeared to be human, based on its reflection in the mirror, the smell that continued to pollute my home told me otherwise. Even with her back to me, I saw her frame was slender, her long brown hair hanging midway down her back. She was dressed in jeans and a strapless black top, and her four-inch gold heels were covered in glitter. It looked like something one would wear to a nightclub, not on a B and E.

I continued to watch in the mirror while this woman tossed my belongings to the floor like she was looking for something, but then she froze unexpectedly. Slowly, she turned her head, and I saw a whisper of a smile play at the outer corner of her lips through her refection.

"You ever going to show yourself?" Her voice was soft and airy — almost melodic — but it made my skin crawl and my stomach cramp as another wave of nausea tugged at me. Such a visceral reaction to someone's voice had to stem from something deeper, but I didn't have time to figure that all out right now. She knew I was here, and she turned around fully, crossing her arms in front of her. "I've been making an awful mess in here in hopes you'd come play."

Since I never really held the element of surprise

over my intruder, I stepped out from around the corner to face her. Even though she was slight of frame, something about her was still off-putting to me. I felt like I should be afraid of her, but I also felt like I could handle anything she might try to throw at me. Which feeling was most prominent, though? I was still trying to figure that out.

She stared at me with a smug look on her face. She was confident about whatever she had planned, but I refused to let her rattle me. I returned her icy stare, finally getting a good look at my uninvited guest...and then I momentarily faltered. Her eyes... The unique shape of her nose... Her long brown hair... Why did she look so damn familiar? I couldn't shake the feeling, and was having difficulty placing where exactly I knew her from.

Then she turned her head to the side, the stream of silver moonlight bouncing off the side of her neck...her smooth, pale neck. Unmarked...

But it wasn't always, a voice reminded me.

Over a month ago, I came across this woman in a park, her neck cut open and her blood drained from her body. Exsanguination was her C.O.D. And now, here she was, standing in front of me, seemingly the picture of health.

"Samantha Turner?" I questioned, unsure.

Her smile widened; she looked positively giddy with excitement as she clapped her hands triumphantly. "Oh, goodie! You do remember me."

Fear swelled in my stomach, tying into painful knots as my knees threatened to give out. I held strong, though, still not wanting to show her any weakness. Something told me she wouldn't hesitate upon sensing even a smidge of it. I knew I wouldn't.

"What...? How...?" None of this made any sense, and my head started to spin. If she was here—alive, if that's what she was — then what about the other victims we'd come across these past few weeks? Were they out there somewhere? Not dead?

"What are you?" I demanded.

Samantha looked disappointed, jutting out her bottom lip in a false pout. "Oh, come on, Brooke...can I call you Brooke? Or would you prefer Detective Leighton?"

She knew my name. How the hell did she know my name?

Panic raced up my spine, and everything about this woman screamed "threat" to some baser instinct within me, but her tone and the way she looked at me belied this. Thankfully my common sense kicked in the second she stepped toward me, and I realized she was likely trying to lull me into a false sense of security. She toyed with me like a cat with a mouse.

She took another step, and my defenses flew back up, my posture rigid, my teeth curled back, and an unexpected snarl rising from deep in my belly. "Detective, it is then," she replied, her eyes narrowing sinisterly as she sidestepped around me, circling me; probably calculating her next move.

I turned with every step she took, never letting her out of my sight, and with every second that passed, the storm inside me continued to build. The pressure pushed out anything remotely human and replaced it with something primal and feral. I didn't even know her, but her mere presence seemed to drive me to the brink of pure, unbridled rage.

"What do you want? Why are you here?" I finally demanded through clenched teeth.

"You really don't know?" she purred. "I thought for sure that brute you've been sneaking around with would have told you by now. Especially given the history."

The history? What the hell was she talking about? How would she even know Nick and I *had* a history?

She laughed, a light tinkling sound that sent a shiver down my spine like nails on a chalkboard might. "He thought he had them," she said cryptically. "Setting that fire up in Alaska was brave...stupid, but brave. He destroyed everything she's been working for these last seven years. Filthy mutt." Her voice held an immeasurable level of disdain as she lowered her eyes, and then it dropped off to a mumbled whisper when she resumed eye contact. "I was told to keep you alive, but I honestly can't stomach the idea of another one of your kind existing. If you're still breathing by the time that animal stumbles over your dying body, make sure you tell him this is his fault."

Before I was even given the chance to fully process everything she was saying, her façade slipped away like a veil, and I was privy to a glimpse of her true self—the monster that had me feeling on edge. The wolf lapped thirstily at the chance to destroy her. In a fraction of a second, her blue eyes darkened dangerously until they were black as pitch—demonic—and she opened her mouth in a threatening shriek as she lunged for me. Her elongated canines gleamed in the moonlight that streamed through my window.

Even though my brain needed a second to catch up, still trying to put the pieces together, my reflexes didn't let me down, and I bobbed when she weaved...the first time, anyway. Sadly, I wasn't expecting the speed at which she moved. It wasn't human—and it definitely wasn't wolf. Not from what I'd seen anyway. I had noticed an increase in my speed among everything else, but it was nothing like how Samantha moved. She was graceful and swift as she moved across the room in the blink of an eye and slammed me up against the wall, sending the mirror crashing to the floor. It shattered, and the wall crumbled behind me. She wasn't only fast, but strong, using only one hand to keep me subdued.

She held her hand around my neck, slowly squeezing and crushing my windpipe as my legs flailed and kick several inches off the ground, unable to connect with her. I attempted to pry her hand from around my neck, but it was no use. As I was denied oxygen, my strength started to wane and I panicked. My anxiety spiked, but then the beast was back, ripping its way through me, threatening to bury my human side in an effort to survive. It didn't seem to matter that we were still weeks away from the next full moon. Nick had warned me that this was possible, but I didn't fully believe him until now.

Even though it was difficult to ignore, I refused to give it complete control. This was my first mistake, because my vision darkened as a feral growl filled the room, and I knew it came from me. It reminded me of how I felt right before I woke up naked in Nick's bed and learned the truth about what had happened.

I'm slipping. I should just let it happen. Don't deny who you are anymore, I ordered myself.

All of a sudden, there was a loud bang that pulled me from the darkness, and I gasped for air when Samantha very briefly loosened her grip. She righted this slip-up, but not before I had a moment to regain my bearings. Of course, any plan I might have been able to come up with in a fraction of a second was shot to hell when I heard loud footsteps racing down the hall, followed by a very familiar and extremely angry voice.

"Hey!" David yelled, and I craned my neck toward him. His blue eyes did nothing to hide his fear, but he held his gun steady, aiming it at my attacker.

"Let her go!"

I feared for his life when Samantha turned her murderous gaze on him, and I kicked her swiftly in the shin to draw her focus back to me. It didn't even faze her, and instead she smiled at David.

"Well, hello, handsome," she purred, her voice returning to that soft, melodic tone from earlier. It suddenly occurred to me that this was what she did to draw people in. I could see how it might be hypnotic, even though, to me, it was reminiscent of a banshee.

"I said, let her *go*." He put heavy emphasis on each word, taking a wary step forward and placing his finger on the trigger, preparing to fire. It relieved me that he seemed unaffected by her, but it worried me that he didn't sense the very real danger that he was in. While I wasn't sure what she was exactly, I knew she wasn't human, and I knew she wouldn't hesitate to hurt him…

Or worse.

Samantha turned to me. Her smile was positively wicked as she brought her face closer, her cheek resting against mine as she whispered in my ear. "This'll only take a sec," she said, her confident tone sounding like a promise. As she pulled her face from mine, I felt the point of her canines scrape along my jaw before her tongue trailed along my skin.

My vision darkened again as my humanity slipped away. Every muscle in my body tensed, my skin tightening, and I felt the overwhelming urge to let go. To accept what was happening, but when I looked at David again, I repressed it.

He can't know. It's dangerous for him to know.

These were warnings I couldn't ignore. If I lost control and shifted, he could get hurt. *I* could hurt him. There was no way I could live with that… But I had to do something. I needed to find a way to st—

Suddenly, two shots were fired, and I fell to the ground, dazed. I gasped desperately for air, my lungs burning like I'd just swallowed a red-hot branding iron. I momentarily forgot about what was going on around me as I tried desperately to replenish my oxygen supply. When I looked up, I saw Samantha advancing on David. She moved much slower than she was with me, and her arm was bleeding. David's aim didn't quite hit home—or maybe it did. Maybe he was just trying to incapacitate her.

David warned her to stay put and stop moving toward him, but she ignored him. I tried to stand up, but my legs were weak, so it was a bit of a struggle. Usually, when someone was staring down the barrel of a gun, there was a certain level of fear involved. Sometimes this fear manifested itself differently. Some people's hormones went crazy, some people's hearts beat furiously, and some people pissed themselves. Samantha Turner did none of the above. Instead of fear, all I could smell on her—besides the undeniable sickly odor of death—was excitement. Whatever she had planned turned her on.

I finally made it to my feet, but I didn't reach them in time. I was an arm's length away when she reached out—her movements once again quick and inhuman—and tossed David aside like he was nothing more than a rag doll. He flew across the living room before crashing into the large front window, and it shattered upon impact. I screamed when I watched his limp body fall to the ground and a pool of red start to form around him.

Blood. The coppery scent was overwhelming, quickly filling the air. At the speed it invaded my senses, I knew without a doubt that David's injuries were severe. If I didn't get to him fast, I could lose—

I choked on the thought, my anger and need for vengeance overpowering even my fear. The tight muscles and quivering skin returned, that growl from earlier once again building in the pit of my stomach and working its way free. I continued to fight what was happening to my body, but it was too difficult. Pain tore through my body, the sound of bone cracking and cloth ripping echoing in my ears. It felt like my entire body had been lit on fire as I cried out in pain.

Then everything went black. I couldn't hear anything. See anything. *Feel* anything. I was numb to everything around me. Lost in a sea of black, I relaxed, and that was when things started to slip through.

There was growling — wild, animalistic growling — not to be outdone by the hissing and shrieking of whatever the hell Samantha was. My vision was blurred along the outer edges, tunneling inward until my main line of view was crystal clear. I watched her barrel toward me until our bodies collided and slid across the floor. We hit the wall, pain exploded in my back and ribs, and then everything was black again. The numbness from before returned, and I reveled in it. It was safe here. There was no pain, no fear, no blood...

Remembering David lying in a growing pool of his own blood, my eyes snapped open, and I scrambled onto all fours. My feet skittered on the floor, my limbs foreign and gangly beneath me, before the pads of my feet found traction on the slick surface. Samantha was still quick, but I had the advantage of being slightly lower to the ground as I slipped away from her and bit down on her arm. My jaws were ridiculously strong, and I shook her from side to side, refusing to let go. She cried out in agony, and then I felt a *pop* as I dislocated her shoulder.

Before I could rip it from her body, she wound up and kicked me square in the throat. The act forced me to let go—but not without tearing a chunk of her disgustingly cold flesh from her arm—and I slammed into the couch. The cushions kept me from getting too winded this time, but the blackness still descended again.

I like it here, but I know I can't stay.

Breathing heavily and my heart racing, I pushed myself back up, shaking off the disorientation in my head, but by the time the fog cleared, Samantha was gone. I growled when I found a scrap of fabric from her shirt on a thick shard of glass that remained lodged in the window frame. I made a move to go after her when I heard the low, bubbling groan of David just below.

Panting breathlessly, I looked down and noticed the red-brown fur covering what used to be my hands. Now they were paws. The blackness threatened to take over as I refused to accept what just happened. My knees weakened, and I stumbled when I pushed myself forward, my vision clearing and then darkening once more.

Hold on, I mentally willed David as I approached him, nudging his hand with my nose. His eyes stared at me, wide and disbelieving as he struggled for each breath; he looked terrified, and that's when I mentally retreated. I disappeared back into the darkness, unwilling to acknowledge that he'd really just witnessed any of this. I spiraled deeper and deeper into denial, the pit bottomless as I continued to plummet.

"Brooke," The voice I heard was hoarse…strained and quiet. My name was repeated over and over again, and I felt something cool against my cheek. Slowly, the shadows slipped away once more, and when I opened my eyes, I was staring down at David

in my arms...my *human* arms. I was mostly naked, my clothes having torn when I shifted, only shreds of them remaining and hanging around my neck and waist. They did little to conceal me, but I couldn't be bothered to worry about that right now.

Pain radiated from my right wrist, left shoulder, and both of my hips, but I pushed all of that aside when I watched David struggle for another breath, blood bubbling out from a horrible neck wound. The glass had sliced through his carotid and he was bleeding out. I placed my hand over the wound, hoping to staunch the bleeding, but with every beat of his heart, blood oozed between my fingers.

His hand was on my cheek — that was what I felt when I was lost — and he stroked my cheek with his thumb. "I'm so sorry about earlier," I whispered, pressing my face into his touch while I continued to slow the bleeding. "I was scared."

He shook his head; it looked painful and like it took a lot of effort on his part. "N-no," he managed to say, blood filling his mouth due to the severity of the laceration.

Things looked grim. I choked back a cry, trying to remain strong for him. His breaths came fewer and shorter in between, and I leaned forward and pressed my forehead to his. The difference in our temperatures was a frightening contrast. "Don't leave me," I pleaded, holding him tighter. "You can't leave me. You promised we'd be together. You have to fight."

Not seeing any sign of him fighting, I decided to try my hand at bargaining. I needed to make him see that he had something to fight for. *Me.* "I'll marry you," I told him between my sobs. "We'll have babies — tons of them — just...*please* don't leave me. I-I love you."

"Love...you...too," he managed to gasp, his lips

turning up into a small smile.

I stroked his dark hair as I held him against my chest, trying to regulate his body temperature. Based on touch alone, I knew it was dangerously low and dropping by the second. The naturally pink color of his complexion was noticeably paler, and when his hand dropped limply from my face, tears fell from my eyes.

"David?" I whispered, my voice cracking with emotion. He inhaled in one more short breath and exhaled it before letting his eyes close. Afraid when he didn't take another breath, I shook him. "David!" While he didn't say anything or open his eyes, he took a shaky breath, and I sighed with relief. His heartbeat was still weak and uneven, but the sound of sirens in the distance told me that help was on the way. Someone must have called the cops when they heard the gunshots and all the noise. They'd make it here in time to save him. They had to.

I looked around the room. It was in shambles, the window broken, and I was sitting, practically bare-assed, my clothing shredded, in a pool of David's blood. I knew I should stay until the emergency response teams arrived, but my anger started to escalate until my skin blazed and my hands trembled. I had to find Samantha Turner and make her pay for what she did.

No, I told myself. *I have to stay here. It's the right thing to do.*

"G-go," David stammered weakly, opening his eyes as much as he could.

"No!" I cried. "I can't leave you."

"You n-need to find h-her. St-stop her."

Even though I knew I should stay until the paramedics got here and stabilized him, I knew he was right. Every fiber of my being told me as much. Shaking, I slowly lowered David's head back to the floor. "Hold on," I told him softly. "Fight, David. Help is on the way."

He nodded once, his eyes fluttering closed again as if to preserve his energy. Gauging how far away the sirens were, I told myself he'd be in good hands within less than a minute. I stood up and stared out my broken window. Samantha was out there. I didn't know where, but she was close. I could still smell her. Without another thought, I launched myself into the night to go after her.

CHAPTER 26 | EVASION

I let her scent guide me as I ran down the sidewalk. I kept to the shadows, hoping for the element of surprise should I find her. I followed her scent as it steadily grew, but then it faded into the night for no reason. I wasn't sure what happened, but I was about to double-back when Nick jumped out of the yard to my right, surprising me.

I took in his frazzled expression, his eyes wide, mouth open as he looked me up and down. "Jesus, Brooke," Nick exclaimed, horrified. "What happened?"

"I… David… He…" I stammered. He waited expectantly, and I immediately realized how this must have looked to him. What was worse, he wasn't entirely wrong: this was my fault.

"It wasn't me," I rasped. He remained silent, and I grew defensive, like maybe he didn't believe me. "I swear I didn't do what you must be thinking!"

Eyes widening in surprise at my outburst, Nick held his hands up in surrender. "I know," he assured me softly. "I was at the house already. The place was crawling with cops. I got as close as the broken window and caught a brief glimpse before I was almost spotted. I followed your scent here."

A cold breeze picked up, reminding me that my clothes weren't doing what they were intended to, and I shivered.

"Come on, we should find you some clothes," Nick offered, but I stopped him.

"We can't. I have to find her. She'll get away."

"I've got her scent. I'll help you track her, but first, we need to get you into something that's not going to get you noticed," Nick explained, leading me to a neighboring house.

All of the lights were out as we walked through the yard and toward the back door. I had my suspicions about what he might do, so when he reached for the knob, I stopped him. "This is illegal," I hissed.

"You need clothes, and we don't have time to go shopping," he shot back.

There was a metallic snap as he turned his wrist and broke the doorknob. "Wait here. I don't need you tracking anything inside."

Looking down at my legs, I noticed the blood and dirt that covered them, and I understood. He wasn't gone long, returning a few minutes later with a damp towel, long-sleeved shirt, jeans, and a pair of sneakers. "These should fit." I was about to start stripping when Nick shook his head. "Not here. The alley."

Once we were shrouded in darkness, I wiped the blood from my body as best I could before stripping out of my torn clothes and putting on the others. The clothes he'd stolen covered any dried patches of blood that remained on my body, and for that I was grateful. But I could still smell it, and it only invited flashes of David's barely breathing body.

I replaced that image with one of the paramedics helping him. In that vision, he was still weak, but he was awake and the bleeding had stopped. By the time

I got back there, he'd be okay. Maybe even in the hospital, but he'd be okay. He had to be.

Once I was changed, Nick took the towel and my clothes, tossed them in a near-empty trash bin, and lit them on fire. I really had to fight to ignore the fact that he was destroying evidence, but I understood why. As I watched the flames brighten the alley, its warmth spreading toward me, I reflected back on what the hell just happened.

Out of the corner of my eye, I saw Nick draw something to his nose, and I recognized it as the scrap of fabric from the window.

"Hey," I whispered, approaching him. "That's evidence."

Nick turned around, eyebrows raised. "You really want your entire department—your father—chasing that thing? Trust me when I say it won't end well. She's headed back to her nest. There are more of them."

The thought of more of those—whatever she was—running around stressed me out, and I could feel the beginning stages of the change happening again. My bones shifted, muscles realigned. What the hell was going on in this world?

The dancing flames were almost hypnotic, making it easy for me to get lost in thought as I replayed everything that happened and tried to make sense of it all. This woman—Samantha Turner—was *dead*. We found her body in the park, completely drained of blood, and yet, she stood in my living room, looking and acting stronger than any other corpse I'd ever come across. How was that even possible?

You know how it's possible, Brooke, a voice told me. *You just refused to believe it was possible before now.*

I remembered how her eyes had darkened, how her strength rivaled my own, how sharp her teeth were as they grazed along my skin... I gasped, but before I was able to dispose of the idea, Nick came up behind me and placed his hands on my shoulders, anchoring me in my new reality.

"She's a vampire, isn't she?" I deduced, feeling the tension in Nick's hands. He turned me around slowly. His brows were raised and his eyes were wide as he regarded me. "And not the warm and fuzzy wanna-be type." Nick still didn't reply, possibly out of shock that I figured it out. "I'm right, aren't I?"

Offering me one solitary nod, Nick beckoned me closer. "Yes," he replied hoarsely. "Vampires do exist...and the woman who attacked you is one of them."

The tempo of my heart increased until all I could hear was my blood pounding through my veins and in my ears. His confirmation shouldn't have made me uneasy, but it did. I no longer lived in a world where the only monsters out there could be handcuffed and put behind bars. Vampires and werewolves were in a league all their own. How could I fight that?

"For decades—centuries, even," Nick continued, "we've hunted vampires. It's just what we do."

Every word he said affected me in the exact opposite way I thought it would. I figured I'd have been less receptive to his explanation, ready to slough it all off as the ramblings of a crazy person. So it surprised me to find I actually felt better knowing all of this. It was like everything made sense now.

"So, yes," Nick said. "She is a vampire..." Another pause, this one lending an extremely dramatic air to our conversation. "But she's not the one you need to worry about."

My blood turned to ice in my veins, and my body prickled with sweat. "Sh-she's not?"

Nick shook his head solemnly. "The one you

need to worry about is the one who sent her."

"Wh-what do you mean 'the one who sent her?'" I asked, my voice trembling slightly.

Nick took a moment, probably trying to find the best way to explain himself—he'd always been cautious, especially as of late. "We—the Pack and I—are almost certain that she was turned as a message...to you. We've been tailing her for a week now."

Confused, I stepped back, the backs of my legs hitting a pile of trash. I fought the tremble in my knees, using someone's fence to hold myself up as this new information swirled in my head like an early morning fog. "A message? From whom?"

"From the one we're hunting," he replied, staring down at his hands. My eyes followed his gaze, watching as he fidgeted and cracked his knuckles nervously. "Gianna."

That was the name of the club we had been searching for. Clearly not a coincidence, I realized. This information made me dizzy, almost as though I'd been on a carousel that was moving much too fast, and my head buzzed. Who was Gianna? Why was she sending someone after me?

Before I could verbalize any of these thoughts, however, something shoved its way to the front of my mind. It was muddled, but eventually the image cleared, and I remembered something I saw recently. Something I never thought to tell Nick about until just now because I didn't believe it to be true at the time.

"She was there," I mumbled.

"What?"

My vision blurred as the image in my head sharpened. "At the club..." Still confused, Nick turned to me, and I brought my eyes to his. "A couple weeks ago, David and I took the statement of a girl at that creepy nightclub, and the owner brought us surveillance footage of a man and a woman making their way through the bar."

Nick cleared his throat, his eyebrows pulling together as something strange flickered through his eyes. It disappeared before I could figure out what it meant, but it bothered him. That much was obvious. "A man? You're sure?"

"Yeah," I confirmed, recalling more and more of the tape. "The way they moved was eerie, and the girl we questioned described her interaction with them as almost hypnotic."

"Compulsion," Nick interjected, shaking off whatever haunted him moments ago. "Their very presence can be intoxicating for humans." Pausing briefly, he looked at me as though afraid to say whatever was on his mind. But he found the courage necessary. "Do you have it? The disc?"

"It's at the precinct." I wondered why he asked at first, and it didn't take long for me to pick up the reason behind his question. "Locked away in an evidence locker. Why?" I only asked because I could be assuming wrong...at least, I hoped I was, because he couldn't possibly be asking me to—

"I'd like to see it," he replied. "Can you get it?"

I stared at him a moment, uncertain if I heard him correctly. Of course I did; I just couldn't believe he would even suggest it. "You want me to just waltz right in there and take the disc?" Nick stared at me, his expression blank yet expectant. "You know that's obstruction, right? I could get into a lot of trouble."

Looking apologetic, he shrugged. "I do realize that, I just thought maybe..." He sighed, running his hands over his face. "Maybe I'd be able to see something that might have been missed."

"I've watched it repeatedly," I explained gently. "Other than the way she looked at the camera—"

"You saw her face?" I nodded and saw that same haunted flicker in Nick's eyes again. "What about the man?"

Shaking my head, I said, "No. He seemed to be a little more reserved…guarded."

"So you didn't see his face? You couldn't identify him?"

Confused, I furrowed my eyebrows. Why did it feel like there was something he wasn't telling me? "No." The relief on his face after hearing my reply was even more perplexing than the troubled expression he wore moments earlier, and it brought back my earlier question. "Nick? Why me? Why did she send Samantha after *me*?" He didn't answer at first, so I kept going. "Is it because I'm a cop? Because we were closing in on her?"

His dry laugh echoed around us. "Cops are of little concern to Gianna," he said very matter-of-factly. "She could obliterate your entire team within seconds." When I didn't understand him right away, he exhaled loudly. "Just like we can smell them, they can smell us. I'm assuming your scent was all over that club."

Something stirred inside me, telling me that it was more than that, and I was suddenly thrust back to when Samantha was in my house. I wracked my memory until I remembered it was something she said that made me feel like this wasn't about *what* I am, but *who*.

"She said that if you found me alive to tell you this was your fault," I whispered, drawing Nick's full attention as he swallowed thickly. He definitely knew something. "She also mentioned a fire up in Alaska." Nick's face blanched as he held his breath. I could smell the light sheen of perspiration that covered his body, and his heart picked up speed. I was like a human lie detector now. "Did she send someone after me because of that?" While he didn't vocally confirm this, I could see in his tense expression that I was right. "Why?"

"I-I can't say for sure," he stammered slightly. I sensed he wasn't being entirely honest, but before I could call him out on it, a breeze picked up, bringing with it Samantha Turner's scent.

We both turned our heads to the mouth of the alley, and there, standing confidently with her arms crossed, was Samantha Turner. Her mouth spread into a wicked grin, canines gleaming against her ruby-red lips. "Tag," she said. "You're it."

CHAPTER 27 | REGRET

Nick and I wasted no time running toward her. She moved so quickly that I thought maybe my eyes were playing tricks on me. Her lingering scent on the air made me realize I wasn't. My endurance was incredible, surge after surge of adrenaline pumping as I pushed myself faster and faster. I was gaining on her, and she knew it. It caught her off guard and frightened her. I lapped up her fear like it was my oasis in the middle of the Sahara.

Maybe trying to throw us off, she hopped a fence and then led us down another alley, farther away from my house. I jumped the fence with ease, Nick followed, and we kept pursuit. When I saw the flashing red and blue lights in the distance, I got distracted and faltered slightly. My instincts to destroy her kept me going, but my heart wanted me to go back home and check on David.

I was torn, and I didn't know what to do.

Samantha jumped at my momentary lapse and sprang for me. Nick and I didn't see it coming, because one minute she was leading us in one direction, and the next she was flying at me, teeth and claws engaged as she dove for my face.

She got me to the ground, straddling me while

her hands wrapped around my neck for a second time that day, and she started to squeeze the life out of me. "They wanted you alive, you know," she sneered. "But I think you're more trouble than you're worth. I'm sure they'd believe me if I cited self-defense."

My vision started to darken as I tried to wrench my body from beneath her, but before I could succumb to it, her body was ripped from mine, and I gasped for air, each glorious breath feeling like a red-hot poker was being shoved down my throat.

I pushed myself into a sitting position, rubbing my neck as my eyes focused on what was happening. Nick was holding Samantha more than a foot off the ground by her neck. She didn't seem fazed by his hold on her. Her body remained still and she smiled down at him evilly.

"Where's Gianna?" Nick demanded, his voice deep-throated and rumbling.

Samantha grinned wickedly at him, her eyes glimmering but narrow. "Gone."

"Gone?" Nick queried. "Somehow I doubt that. She's sadistic, but she's not stupid enough to leave a loose cannon like you in charge of something like this. Tell me where she is."

"Who says I'm in charge of anything?"

Desperate for answers, I peered around Nick's hulking frame. "Why me?" I bellowed, my throat raw from being strangled. For the second time that night.

Seemingly bored — or maybe annoyed — she looked at me pointedly. "Funny, I've asked myself the same thing." Glancing at Nick, she rolled her eyes. "Especially given the company you choose to keep."

"Where is she?" he demanded again, his voice so loud and rough I no longer recognized it.

Samantha just laughed. She wasn't afraid, and

her lack of self-preservation baffled me.

"You think if you kill me they won't come for her eventually?" she goaded him. She flashed her elongated canines with a smile and leaned forward, not affected by his hold on her neck whatsoever as she whispered. She must have figured I couldn't hear her, but my enhanced hearing allowed me the advantage. "You already know this, though, don't you? It's why you jumped at the opportunity to come out here, right? Did you really think you could save her? You are aware that they don't care *what* she is, right? So what you did—"

Nothing she said made any sense, but questions arose and I craved the answers. Before I could even get them, Nick reacted.

With a flick of his wrist, he snapped her neck, and I screamed, slapping my hands over my mouth. I watched, somewhat horrified as he let her body drop to the ground, pulled out his matches and lit her body on fire. There was an ear-piercing shriek as the flame ignited, then nothing but the crackle of flames as her body turned to ash.

Nick walked toward me, but I was too stunned to move, watching the fire as it quickly engulfed her and then dwindled to smoldering ash within a couple minutes.

"We have to go," Nick said. "You should get back to the house."

"You… You just…"

Nick exhaled heavily. "She wasn't human. It's what we do." There was no remorse in his voice. It frightened me.

My hands trembled in a combination of fear, irritation, and shock over what I'd just witnessed. I was numb. From my head to my feet, I was frozen, but Nick grabbed my arm and pulled me to the mouth of the alley. "We have to go," he repeated urgently.

As he pulled me farther and farther away, my anger lessened, making room for my concern regarding David's condition again. I picked up the pace, following Nick through the darkness, always looking over my shoulder as if Samantha could pop out again. Then I remembered she was nothing more than a pile of dust in a filthy alley.

The flashing lights of the ambulance and police cruisers in front of my house came into view, and I stopped abruptly, unable to find the courage to go on. What would I find when I got there? Would David be conscious? What would my dad have to say? What was *I* going to say?

"Tell them you guys fought and you went for a walk to clear your head," Nick said, turning my body toward his. It was as if he could read my thoughts. "You don't know anything beyond that. Do you understand?"

I was looking at him, but I wasn't really; my mind was so overwhelmed that I looked more through him than anything.

"Nod if you understand." Slowly, my head bobbed up and down. "Good. I'm going to try and pinpoint Gianna's whereabouts, but I'll check in soon, okay?"

"O-okay," I rasped, pulling out of his hold on me and turning for my house without another word.

I'd made it to the end of the block before I heard my dad's relieved voice. "Brooke?" He was standing in my driveway as I started to cross the street.

I looked up and increased my pace to a jog. The flashing lights were messing with my perception of everything because he looked off somehow. Worried? Scared? Sad? For some reason, I just couldn't pinpoint it. Then my eyes drifted past him and I noticed the gurney being brought out of my house…

The gurney with the zippered black bag.

My knees buckled, but I pushed through it and ran forward. "No," I whispered, head shaking, heart racing, pulse pounding in my ears. Tears burned my eyes and obscured my vision. I was seeing things. This wasn't happening. It couldn't be happening. "No!"

Before I could get close to the ambulance, my dad grabbed me around the waist and held me back. He was saying something I couldn't comprehend in my frazzled state. I picked up bits and pieces — "thank god you're okay…so worried" — but all I could focus on was the black bag that looked like there was a body in it.

"He was fine when I left!" I sobbed, tears flowing down my cheeks as I tried to wrench myself out of my father's unrelenting grasp. I punched his arm and pushed against his chest, trying to force him to let me go. He held firm. "He's fine!"

My dad used all his strength to drop to his knees on the pavement, taking me with him, and I gave up trying to escape. I was far too overcome by emotion. "He was fine," I repeated quietly, crying into his shoulder while he stroked my hair and tried to calm me down.

"Someone broke in. It looks like there was a struggle as David tried to stop it. Sweetheart, I'm so sorry. They did everything they could, but his heart stopped shortly after they got here. They couldn't bring him back."

My cries became louder until even I couldn't recognize them.

David was gone.

CHAPTER 28 | GRIEF

Everybody works through their grief differently. Some people barricade themselves in their house and cry for days on end, while others try to distract themselves with whatever they can to try and forget. Drugs, alcohol, sex, or whatever other vice they might have. They shut down, the loss they feel so overwhelming it makes them numb to everything and nothing makes sense. None of what happens is right, every bit of it still hazy and surreal in the wake of emotional trauma.

I know this, because I lived it once before.

There was a light knock on the bathroom door before it slowly opened. I sat on the porcelain floor of the tub while warm water beat down on me, and I rested my chin on my knees and sighed. There was only one person it could be.

"Brooke, honey?" my mom inquired softly, carefully. She'd been tiptoeing around me these last couple days — everyone had — and for good reason. "You doing okay?" She pulled the steam-covered glass door open a little to find me on the floor, and her forehead furrowed with concern.

"I'm fine," I lied, tucking my legs closer to my body and turning my face away from hers before she could see the quiver in my lip. "Just tired." I sensed she was about to add something, so I cut her off. "I'll be right out."

She exhaled softly, defeated. "All right. Well, just remember, the funeral starts at two."

There was a soft click as she closed the door behind her, and I stood up, pushing my face beneath the warm spray of water, washing away a fresh onslaught of tears that started to fall. I was so sick of crying, but I couldn't seem to stop. I knew exhaustion had something to do with it, but it wasn't the main source.

David was gone. He died in my living room—without me there, because I'd been so hell-bent on tracking down the monster that did this—and there was nothing I could do to bring him back. I should have stayed with him.

Nick warned me that *I* was dangerous, and now I believed him. How could I not? I was so careful around David, and yet he died anyway. Was it because of what I had become? I was starting to think so, but I was having difficulty sorting it all out in my head. Everything was pretty jumbled in there due to my lack of sleep. I didn't get much the night before—if any, to be honest. My eyes were swollen and heavy from a combination of crying and exhaustion, but every time I closed them, all I saw was David being thrown across the room before bleeding out on our living room floor.

The memory made me shudder violently, but I let it play out, feeling far too weak to fight it this time.

It had been five days since David's death. Five days, and it still wasn't any easier. How was I supposed to go on knowing that Samantha Turner was there for *me* and David just got in her way? He was nothing to her...and everything to me.

I hadn't done much since it happened. I was put on bereavement leave, and I didn't argue the strong recommendation from my father. There was no way I could be expected to put my all into a case, given the circumstances. So, I did nothing. I didn't go to work. I didn't watch TV. My parents offered me my old room since my house was still an active crime scene. I was okay with this new living arrangement, though, because I didn't think I could walk by my living room every day and not relive every detail of that night.

I already felt the emptiness that his absence brought. My anxiety heightened exponentially by the second and refused to relent, and I didn't like it one bit. The reality of David's absence in my life suffocated me until it felt like all the air had been sucked from the room.

Taking several deep, cleansing breaths, I pressed my head against the cool tile wall, closing my eyes as the water rolled down my back. Soon, my thoughts were thrust right back to that night.

My anxiety spiked, rage consuming me wholly, and I pulled my arm back and punched the tile wall of my parents' shower, over and over and over again. I screamed as tears flowed freely down my face. Blood covered my knuckles as shards of tile fell at my feet. The bathroom door flew open so forcefully that the knob cracked the wall behind it, and my mom rushed to my side, draping a towel over me before leading me out of the tub and to my old bedroom.

As she sat me on the end of my bed, my hands shaking and oozing blood, I looked up to find my father watching from the hall, horrified and looking helpless. It was a look I hadn't seen in his eyes in years.

"I'm sorry," I whispered, not really sure what I was apologizing for. The cuts? The mess in their bathroom? Being an absolute train wreck? What happened to David? Everything?

"Oh, honey," Mom soothed. "You have no reason to apologize. Not after everything you've been through." She assessed my wounds as best she could before turning to my father, who made his way to the doorway of my bedroom. "Keith, grab me the first aid kit from the bathroom, please," she requested, taking my hands in hers as gingerly as possible and trying to gauge the severity of my injuries.

When Dad returned with the first aid kit, Mom took everything from him and soaked some of the gauze in rubbing alcohol to clean my cuts. It didn't matter how lightly she touched; each pass over my skin set my nerves on fire. I welcomed the pain though, because I deserved it. It should have been me, not David.

Sadly, the pain lessened with every second that ticked by, and as the blood was cleared away, I saw that my skin was already knitting itself back together—a wolfy perk I had forgotten about. I chanced a quick glance her way to see her eyebrows pull together, confused.

"I, uh, guess it looked worse than it really is," I said, trying to draw her focus from this oddity.

She looked doubtful at first, but since she didn't really have an explanation for it, she accepted it at face value and continued to clean and bandage my hand. Meanwhile, I heard my dad down the hall, cleaning up the shattered tile and tossing it in the wastebasket.

After she left, I took a few minutes before getting dressed. I pulled on a black knee-length shift dress and a pair of black heels and walked out of my closet. I paused at the foot of the bed. Even though it wasn't the bed from my house, I stared at it for much longer than any sane person would, focusing on how the blankets on my side were rumpled while David's side looked untouched.

Because it is, I reminded myself. He'd never lie next to me again.

The phone rang from the kitchen, jarring me from the morbid turn in my thoughts. This wasn't new or unusual as of late. The phone had been ringing off the hook since the day after the incident. My mom offered to unplug it since I had no intention of talking to anyone yet, but I told her not to worry about it. It was the only thing that kept pulling me back from reliving that awful night over and over again.

In addition to all the calls, people also kept sending flowers. The house was starting to resemble a florist's shop, and while the gesture was intended to be sweet, I was baffled as to why someone would send something as delicate as flowers to someone whose loved one just died. To remind them that something beautiful only lasted so long before it wilted, died, and then began to rot? Nice sentiment.

Assholes.

All right, so I was a little bitter. Could I really be faulted? I'd finally made peace with what I had become and was ready to tell David that I wanted more from our relationship. This news would have made him happy, but before I could deliver it, his life was taken from him by something even I didn't fully understand yet.

But I was going to figure it out. As a cop, that was what I did.

When the phone stopped ringing, I deduced that either the machine or my mother picked up. With a sigh, I headed back toward the bathroom so I could get ready to face the day...even if it was the last thing

I wanted to do. Every day since losing David had been rough, but I feared today would be the most difficult of all. Today, we buried him. This made it final. This made it *real*.

After my hair was done, parted in the middle and pulled back into a sleek chignon, I met my parents out in the living room. Dad helped me into my black knee-length jacket before doing the same for my mother, and then we left the house. I slid into the back seat of his car, clasping my hands in my lap and staring a little too intently at them as we drove across the city.

All of this took me back to the day of Bobby's funeral. It was all too familiar and unsettling, and I knew my parents felt it too. I sensed it rolling off them in waves of despair and fear. Mom might not have known David as well as Dad and I, but she knew how I felt about him, and she approved. He was the first guy she approved of since Nick.

Nick.

I still hadn't heard from him since that night. He said he'd check in when he knew something, and the fact that I hadn't heard from him meant one of two things: he'd come up empty-handed, or he'd suffered the same fate as David.

Or maybe he bailed. Wouldn't be the first time he left you to deal with tragedy alone…

I refused to believe the uninvited suggestion, because something deep inside told me he'd changed. And he couldn't be dead, because I felt certain I'd have sensed it. I had to believe that, because I didn't know that I could handle the alternative.

We arrived at the church, and I wasn't surprised to see so many officers in their uniforms. O'Malley, Keaton, Clarke, and the rest of the department donned their uniforms as a sign of respect for their fallen comrade. I debated doing the same, but ultimately decided against it. I just wasn't feeling worthy of the badge these days.

Dad led Mom and me to the front of the church where we sat in the second row behind several people. The woman directly in front of me was crying, while the man next to her — her husband, presumably — had his arm around her, holding her against him while she sobbed onto his shoulder.

David's parents. Not only would it explain why they felt the way I did — like their hearts had been ripped from their chests — but I could tell by their smell. They shared a similar and unique scent with their son.

Before I could even think about what I was doing, I reached forward and laid a supportive hand on the woman's shoulder. Startled, she lifted her head from her husband's shoulder and turned to face me. She was shocked and confused at first, but then a look of recognition flashed in her eyes, and she offered me a small smile.

"Brooke?" she asked, and I responded with a nod, not trusting my voice enough to speak. "I can finally put a face to the name."

"Mr. and Mrs. Samuels," I managed to say, my voice breaking as guilt consumed me again. "I'm...I'm so sorry for your loss."

"*Our* loss, sweetheart," she corrected, tilting her head to one side as she reached out and tucked a wayward strand of my hair behind my ear. "He cared so deeply for you."

Tears formed in my eyes, blurring my vision, but before they had a chance to fall, the pastor started the service. Everything about it was beautiful, and David's cousin, Darryl, delivered an emotional eulogy filled with only the best memories. It made me wish that I'd known David back then, or at least gotten more time with him to hear those stories in his words.

After the service ended, O'Malley, Keaton, Clarke, and a few others from the precinct joined a couple of David's cousins, and they carried David's coffin, draped with the American flag, out to the hearse that would transport him to the cemetery. When everyone arrived, we gathered around the plot of land where David would be laid to rest, and I looked across the hole in the ground to find his parents.

Seeing David's name on the dark gray headstone made my stomach roll, the reality already starting to set in. The first of several tears fell as the pastor spoke again, and when the 21-gun salute started, I jumped with every shot, the sound of the shots drowning out every gut-wrenching sob I released.

Standing next to the grave with my arms crossed in front of me, I watched as the flag was removed from his coffin and folded into the standard triangle, and I empathized with how his mom and dad must have felt as they were presented with it. She couldn't stop crying, and this definitely wasn't helping. I'd barely composed myself as the coffin was lowered into the ground, and when the pastor spoke his final words, people started leaving for the celebration of life function being held at a nearby hall.

My well had run dry as the tears finally stopped. Not because I wasn't still sad, but because the shock had finally set in. O'Malley and the rest of the precinct—including Clarke—gave me their condolences after having done the same to David's parents, and then headed to the hall. I stayed for a minute, staring down into the grave as dirt slowly covered his coffin.

Even though I tried, I couldn't will myself to move, even as David's parents approached and we officially met for the first time. Just one more regret to add to my ever-growing list, I suppose.

God, I was a shitty girlfriend.

"Are you coming?" Dad prodded, nodding in the direction he parked the car.

"Uh..." I croaked, clenching my eyes and shaking my head. "Go on ahead. I need a minute."

He looked down at Mom, who nodded her assent. "Okay," he agreed. "Do you want to take my car?"

I shook my head again. "No. I'll walk or call a cab or something."

"You're sure?" Mom asked, seeming uncertain, but when I assured her I'd prefer to walk the few blocks, she acquiesced.

Time had no real value once I was alone. Seconds blurred into minutes, and minutes into hours. The only thing that alerted me to the passing time was the setting sun and darkening sky. The sky exploded in a brilliant burst of color before darkening, and soon, the wind picked up, bringing with it the late-autumn chill that traveled up my spine like an icy finger, paralyzing me in place.

Then Nick's familiar woodsy scent filled my head, and I felt a slight reprieve. "You're okay," I said aloud as he approached, the grass and leaves crunching under his feet. I kept my back to him, still staring down at the fresh grave before me, but my shoulders softened with relief.

"I am," Nick responded, coming up behind me and resting a hand on the small of my back. "How are you holding up?"

My lip quivered, and tears threatened to fall again. "It's touch and go," I replied honestly. "Where have you been? You were supposed to check in. I was worried."

Nick was silent for a moment. "I figured you had enough to deal with without me showing up."

"I killed him."

Nick grabbed my upper arm and turned me to face him. Holding me at arm's length, he gazed deep into my eyes with the deepest sympathy. "Brooke, no."

"M-maybe not directly, but she was there for me, wasn't she?" He didn't need to answer; I saw the truth in his eyes that I was right. "She was there for me, and he was just a fly in her ointment."

"Yes."

I processed this for a moment, my anger returning and turning into something else I hadn't felt in years. The emotion built and took on a life of its own. My body trembled. I recognized this from the other night: this was the first stage of the change. If I didn't keep it from overtaking me completely, I'd fall victim to it again, and I needed to maintain my focus and stay lucid now more than ever.

"Did you find her? Gianna?"

"No. The trail came up dry." He sighed. "Listen, Brooke, there's still so much you need to learn about our world."

I nodded. "Then teach me. I can't be in the dark any longer. You said I would be safe—that my loved ones would be safe—but you were wrong. I'm not safe, and I won't be safe until I know what I'm up against and how I can stop it." My hands shook as the fires of rage flared inside me. "I want to find this bitch and tear her apart for what she's done."

It didn't take him longer than a few seconds to concur, looking down at me with nothing but understanding. "You're absolutely right. It's time you knew the truth."

With that, I agreed to let Nick lead me through

the cemetery and off into the night. My need to
this terrible injustice was stronger than it had ever
been.

Denial.

Anger.

Bargaining.

Depression.

Acceptance.

These are the five stages of grief. Everyone expe-
riences them in their own time and at their own pace,
and I believed this to be true, based on personal experience. David had been dead almost a week now, and
I was slowly coming to terms with it. But as I stood
and watched fresh dirt cover his grave that afternoon,
I realized that the people who classified these five
emotions left off one more. One that I welcomed with
everything I had. One that would bring me closure.

Revenge.

CHAPTER 29 | LESSONS

Sleep wasn't easy. Every time I closed my eyes, my nightmares alternated between David's death and watching his coffin being lowered into the ground. Both of these were memories that would likely haunt me for the rest of my life. Exhaustion eventually overpowered me, and I slept in short bursts every couple hours.

When I finally woke in the morning, my throat was sore, and I felt the warmth of the sunlight as it streamed in from the window. I rolled over onto my right side, hoping that all of this was just a nightmare and that David was fine and lying next to me. Deep down, I knew this to be wishful thinking, but my brain was still muddled with sleep, and I held onto the possibility for a little longer.

When I found the bed empty, the extreme sadness returned, my chest aching as I fought another sob. I also remembered I wasn't in my own room...or my own house, for that matter.

After Nick found me at the cemetery, I asked him to take me back to his place. It wasn't because I wanted to lose myself in him; that would be an insult to David's memory. While I admitted to still having feelings for Nick, I wasn't about to act on those feelings.

Not even for a moment of solace.

Because I didn't want to worry my parents, I called them and let them know that I didn't think I was in any shape to join them at the celebration of life. I wasn't trying to be rude or disrespectful to David's memory, I just didn't think I was mentally stable enough to attend. Besides my undeniable grief, I was feeling an insurmountable level of rage and vengeance. It actually eclipsed my grief more and more as time passed, shielding me from everything else until it was all I focused on. Even now, as I slowly pushed myself up to sit on the edge of Nick's bed.

My back and shoulders ached from all the crying over the last few days, and I inhaled a shuddering breath, holding it until my lungs burned. When I released it, I looked over my shoulder at the unoccupied side of the bed, my heart straining as I willed David to appear.

But it was Nick's head that appeared as he sat up from his makeshift bed on the floor, startling me.

"Holy shit!" I exclaimed, slapping my hand over my chest, my heart hammering and my adrenaline pumping. It shouldn't have caught me off guard the way it did; it wasn't like I didn't remember where I was.

"Sorry," he apologized softly, standing up. He wore a pair of flannel sleep pants and nothing more, so I turned away. "How was your sleep?"

"Restless." I fixed the blankets on the bed while Nick folded his up and placed them in the red armchair in the corner of his room. "You don't have to pretend like you hadn't noticed."

Nick shrugged, grabbing a black T-shirt from his dresser and pulling it on. "I was trying to be polite. Are you...?" He hesitated briefly. "Are you all right?"

Why was it when people asked you that question, you felt like falling apart? It was like a chink in my armor, causing my need for vengeance to ebb. I hated it. I felt what little strength I had found begin to waver, and I tried to hold onto it as best I could. "I'm about as well as can be expected."

"Of course," Nick said. "It was stupid of me to even ask."

"No," I tried to assure him. "It was sweet to ask... It's just hard for me to talk about right now."

Nick looked at me and smiled. "You hungry?"

My stomach growled at the prospect of a meal, but it still felt like a roiling sea of nerves and nausea. I couldn't remember the last time I had a decent meal, though, so I figured I should at least try. "Sure," I replied before looking down at my rumpled dress.

"We can stop by your place afterward if you want to change."

I tried to smooth out some of the wrinkles that formed while I slept. "Yeah. That might be a good idea," I agreed, following him out to the hall where I was suddenly very aware of the movements and voices of Nick's Packmates in the kitchen. I froze, and Nick noticed, sensing what my problem was.

"It's fine," he whispered, taking my hand in his, and I clung to him like he was my lifeline. "They know enough to be respectful."

We entered the kitchen and all talking ceased as they turned to look at me. The only face I recognized was Jackson's, who looked surprisingly empathetic while eating his eggs and coffee. While I didn't know the other three, I recognized their scents from the few times I'd been here.

"Brooke," Nick started, placing his hand on the small of my back, "These are a few of the guys from my Pack. Zack..." He gestured toward the guy to Jackson's right with the dark skin, almost-black hair, and expressive brown eyes. He was just lifting the spoon out of his cereal bowl and nodded his greeting since his mouth was full. "Vincent..." To Jackson's left sat a slightly smaller, yet no less intimidating man with bright blond hair and sea-green eyes. "Corbin... And you already know Jackson." Corbin looked to be about the same size as Vincent, but his frame was a bit more slender. He regarded me with dark blue eyes as he pushed his fingers through his light brown hair, while Jackson continued to stare.

"Hi," I returned quietly. "It's...uh...nice to meet you all."

Zack smiled warmly, excitement flashing in his dark eyes. "We've heard a lot about you," he said.

"Zack..." Nick warned, his voice low and threatening as he walked to the fridge and perused its contents.

It was hard not to smile as Zack playfully challenged Nick, his youth more obvious as he ignored his superior. "All good things," he assured me with a wink. "It's nice to finally put a face to the s—"

The fridge door slammed, and Nick whipped around, chucking a loaf of bread at Zack's head. "If you want her to like you, I suggest you *don't* finish that sentence."

Confused, I looked toward Nick. He rolled his eyes and brushed his finger across his nose as if to itch it...and that's when I realized what it was Zach had meant, and my face heated up with embarrassment.

"Stories," Zach tacked on, throwing the bread back at Nick, who caught it in his huge hand, crushing it in the process. "How crass do you think I am?"

Nick shot a pointed glare at him. "Do you really want me to answer that?"

Smirking, Zack leaned back in his chair. "Yeah,

maybe not."

Listening to them react to one another, playing off what the other one said, reminded me of the kind of relationship Bobby and I used to have. How he and Nick used to do the same thing. It brought a smile to my face, even in the midst of all this sorrow and anger that flowed through me. It was nice to feel something other than grief.

The scrape of chair legs across the tile pulled my attention to Corbin, who pushed out one of the two available chairs around the table. "Why don't you join us, Brooke? Nick'll bring you a coffee, won't you, big guy?"

Nick nodded, his hand moving from the small of my back and over my hair as though smoothing it a little. "Yeah. Have a seat. They don't bite."

My eyes snapped to Jackson, who conveniently looked away from me and took a sip of his own coffee. My resentment toward him flared again as it occurred to me this might not have happened had he not bit me that night in the park. But I didn't say anything, because my time just wasn't worth the strife it might cause. I needed Nick right now, and I was sure at some point I'd need his Pack, too. Especially if I was going to get justice for David.

Nick handed me a cup of coffee, and I added cream and sugar from the containers on the table. Zack, Corbin, and Vincent all watched as I put teaspoon after teaspoon of sugar into it before stirring and taking my first sip. It wasn't the first time people had stared at me like I was crazy when making my coffee, and it likely wouldn't be the last.

I wasn't really in the mood for making conversation—which was only natural, given it was the day after my boyfriend and partner's funeral. None of the guys pressured me for any details on my life, and I appreciated it. Instead, they continued to carry on their conversation about their mission for the day, and how they were looking forward to getting the job done so they could head back home. Behind me, Nick cooked bacon and eggs, and when it was ready, he put a heaping plate down in front of me.

"Thanks," I whispered, placing a napkin in my lap before picking up my fork.

Nodding, he took the empty seat next to me, the outside of his leg brushing mine, and was about to dig in when Corbin spoke up. "How come you never cook like that for us?" he asked with a teasing lilt to his voice.

Smirking, Nick met his stare. "Because you don't appreciate me," he fired back.

My stomach was still in knots, but I knew I had to eat something. It had been far too long, and I was weak. Weaker than I had been in a long time. Thankfully my appetite flourished after my first bite instead of dwindling further, and I ate in silence while the guys talked about where they planned to patrol later.

I didn't understand most of what they were talking about, but one look at Nick told me he'd fill me in later. It was why I was here, after all: to learn about this way of life.

Well, that and to avenge David's death.

Out of nowhere, Jackson pushed his chair back loudly and stood up. "I'm heading out," he announced curtly. "I'll let you know what I find." With that, Jackson took his cup and plate to the sink and then left the kitchen, the front door slamming a minute later.

"He's a ray of sunshine, isn't he?" I quipped.

Zack laughed loudly. "I like her!" he declared. "She's way more fun than any of the other strays you've brought home."

Shocked, I inhaled sharply, dropping my fork onto my plate with a loud *clank*. "I'm sorry, what? Strays?"

Nick shook his head and wiped his mouth with his napkin. "Ignore him. He's young...a *pup*. He doesn't know when to keep his mouth shut." He stood up and grabbed his plate. "You done?"

Shoveling one more forkful of food into my mouth, I nodded once, and Nick took our dishes to the sink and quickly washed them while I finished my coffee. "You guys planning on heading out today? Marcus wants an update this afternoon. He's getting antsy and threatening to come out here himself. You know he's got enough shit to deal with back home, he doesn't need to think he can't trust us to get this done."

Zack, Corbin, and Vincent stood up, taking their dishes to the sink. Nick grumbled, but agreed to do them, and after they left, I grabbed a dishtowel, offering to pitch in.

"You really don't have to help," Nick said as I grabbed the first dish. "You should be relaxing. We've got a lot of work to do today."

"It's fine. You've done so much for me by letting me stay here. It's the least I can do."

Once the dishes were done and put away, Nick and I headed to my place. He offered to drive us on his motorcycle, but I refused, saying I'd prefer to walk. Within the better part of an hour, we were walking up my front steps, and I grabbed my hide-a-key from a fake rock in my garden.

There was still a police notice on the door that they posted when this was deemed an active crime scene. The house still hadn't been released, and wouldn't be until the case was solved, but I needed a few more things and Nick said he needed one more look around. I shouldn't have even been here, but if it was going to help us find Gianna, then I didn't give a shit what the rules were anymore. Everything worthwhile had already been filed, taken into account, and photographed, but they needed to keep everything "as-is" in case they had to come back and reevaluate something. Knowing this, I wouldn't disturb the crime scene. It'd be like I wasn't even here. No one would even have to know.

Carefully, we stepped inside the house, and I purposely avoided the living room, heading straight for my bedroom, while Nick lingered in the entryway, sniffing around for anything useful. Everything was still in shambles, so I carefully sidestepped any debris from the fight, telling Nick to do the same. He assured me he wouldn't touch a thing, so I headed to my room to grab a few more things and change out of my dress.

I paused at the end of my bed, staring down at the perfectly smooth blanket. My heart seized at the thought that I'd never share this bed with David again, and I walked over to his side of the bed, picking up his pillow. His scent still lingered on it, so I drew it to my face and inhaled deeply, committing his scent to my memory in hopes I'd never forget it. This awakened the memory of his fear that night when he came in to find me under attack, and the confusion he probably felt as he died…alone.

Even though I wasn't in the living room to see the exact spot where David drew his last breath, just being in this house caused anxiety to claw at my chest, curling its gnarled fingers so tightly around my lungs, I found it hard to breathe. I couldn't bear to stay here for any prolonged period of time, so I quickly stripped out of my rumpled dress, tossed it in my hamper, and found a pair of jeans and a gray long-sleeved cotton tee. I grabbed another duffle bag and threw more clothes inside of it before slinging it over my shoulder. When I exited my room, I was surprised to find Nick had wandered to the living room. He looked around, not touching anything, and I hesitantly stepped forward.

"Wh-what are you doing?" I asked, my eyes instantly finding the spot where David bled out. It had been cleaned up, but the hardwood was stained from his blood. It had seeped into the wood grain, and I could still smell it beneath the lingering scent of all the cleaning chemicals used. Amongst the stains were scratches from my claws as I'd fought Samantha. I briefly wondered what the police report might read regarding them. Perhaps the suspect had a dog with him.

"Just trying to see if there's anything else we can use to track down where their nest might be," Nick replied, scanning the room from his position. "Can you tell me a little more about what happened? Maybe the one that was here left behind some kind of clue about where they've been holing up?"

Again, I hesitated, but I told him. Everything. I told him how I came home from his place, ready to apologize and tell David I wanted more out of our relationship. I explained how David wasn't home, and I found this woman—a woman I thought to be dead given I was assigned her case and had been over her autopsy report multiple times—snooping around before she attacked me. It embarrassed me when I told him how I fought back poorly, and then my anger spiked when I got to the part where David walked in.

Nick continued to listen as I told him how she threw David through the air like he weighed no more than a pillow, and when I got to the part where I shifted, he seemed particularly intrigued. "And you remember? The shift, I mean?"

I nodded. "Most of it, yeah. It's still a little hazy, and I was definitely in and out of consciousness. Is it..." I cringed, remembering the way my bones shifted beneath my skin and the rippling and tearing sensation of my fevered skin. "...always that painful?"

"In the beginning," Nick replied, seeming to ponder the question for a moment. "The pain lessens over time." He shrugged, looking contemplative. "Or maybe we just grow used to it. I guess it's hard to really tell." Glancing down at my duffle bag, he added, "You ready?"

"Yeah. I think so."

"Okay." We walked toward the door, but before I could reach for the knob, he opened it for me. A small smile of appreciation formed on my lips as I whispered my thanks, and we were on our way.

My car had remained in my driveway since David parked it there after our dinner with my folks, and I balked before opening the driver's door, remembering that David was the last one to sit in this seat. And the last thing we did before he died was fight. That would eat at me forever.

It wasn't until I felt a hand on my back and heard Nick's soft voice that I snapped out of it.

"Brooke?"

Shaking my head, I tossed my bag in the backseat. "Sorry. I got lost in thought."

"You wanna talk about it?"

"Not really," I muttered, nodding toward the passenger side. "Get in."

Complying, Nick rounded the front of the car and opened the passenger door. Once we were both belted in, he turned his head to me. "So, did you want to drop your things at your parents' house?"

Shrugging, I put the car into gear and pulled out of the drive. "Nah. I'll give them a call and let them know I'll be over later tonight."

"You know," Nick said gently. "You could always just stay with me and the Pack." Glancing over, I found him staring at me hopefully. "Obviously, you'd take my bed and I could continue to camp on the floor...or I could even take the couch to offer you more privacy." There was a brief pause, and I sensed his slight discomfort. "I just think it might be easier if I'm going to teach you how to track and hunt...not to mention how to shift."

I contemplated his offer, knowing that it would probably be easier — for a number of reasons, not just the obvious werewolf-in-training parts. For one thing, Nick and the guys were less likely to bring David up at every turn, whereas my parents would want to talk about it as a way to overcome the grief. I didn't want to talk about it. Not right now, anyway. All I wanted to focus on was catching the bitch responsible for this whole mess and teaching her a lesson.

So, while it might have made sense to stay with Nick, I honestly didn't know what I would tell my parents. This meant I would have to resort to sneaking out or coming home late. It would be like being a teenager again. On the plus side, I should be able to pass off any strange behavior as grief.

"Thanks for the offer," I began. "Really. But I think it might be best if I stay with them a little longer. I'll probably find myself in a hotel in a few days if I find I need the privacy, but I'll keep you informed."

"Brooke," Nick interjected. "If you find yourself looking for privacy from your parents, don't waste money on a hotel. My door is always open to you."

I promised to consider his offer seriously before he instructed me to head just outside the city. In such a heavily populated area, it would be hard for us to find the privacy we needed to talk about everything that was going on while teaching me the tools I would need to master my new abilities.

We drove out to Apache Trail. It was late enough in the year that there wouldn't be too many people out hiking the trails, and we'd be sure to keep off them enough to stay out of sight. As we drove, Nick explained that he and his Pack frequently hunted here. It should have been weird to me that he didn't just shop at the grocery store to eat some of his meals, but I actually understood it—craved it, even. The thought of running carefree through the trails, weaving around cacti, bursting through a bush, or leaping over other obstacles or desert terrain sounded exhilarating. But when I added in the possibility of a rabbit or some other kind of prey, I found myself salivating and desperate for that release of adrenaline.

Two hours had gone by, and I wasn't growing any closer to figuring any of it out. The only thing that seemed to be increasing was my irritation level. I was in the middle of the desert, stark naked and barely hidden by a bougainvillea bush. My entire body trembled, beads of sweat covered every inch of my skin, and my breathing was deep and ragged after having failed again.

Initially, I worried about stripping down in front of Nick, but then acknowledged the upside: my clothes would remain in one piece so I could walk out of here after all of this and not look like I'd been mauled by a wild animal or physically assaulted. Besides, it wasn't like Nick had never seen me naked, and what did I have to be embarrassed about? It helped that he was a gentleman and turned around while I disrobed.

Never mind the fact that there was absolutely nothing sexy about this entire situation. Thankfully, Nick didn't ogle; his eyes always remained on mine to keep me from getting uncomfortable.

"This isn't working," I growled, frustrated.

Nick went over the steps once more: relax, clear your mind, and let your instincts take over.

Seemed simple enough, but the problem lay in the fact that trying to change your entire anatomy put a lot of stress on the body. It was all I could think about, and my instincts were to get dressed and call it a day. Nick informed me that I'd almost done it a couple of times, but I couldn't recall what I did differently, having given into the pain and blocked it out briefly.

"You need to focus," Nick reminded me over and over again, sounding slightly frustrated. "Stay alert and *accept* the wolf. Don't deny it access to your body and mind."

"I am," I barked angrily. "I'm not ready."

"Yes," he interjected. "You are. You shifted days ago — without the full moon. You can do it again. You just have to *believe* you can."

Closing my eyes, I took a deep breath and tried again. I visualized the changes my body would go through, and while they weren't particularly pleasant, I forced my way through it. But imagining it didn't make it real. Everything stayed the same, with the exception of the monstrous headache I now sported.

"I *can't*," I repeated, my emotions quickly morphing from frustration to anger and disappointment.

"You can."

I know he was trying to be supportive, but I

wanted to punch him in the face. Really fucking hard.

Seeing my growing ire for his irritating positivity, he smirked. "Okay, maybe we should try this another way. Instead of trying to bring the wolf out unnecessarily, what if we tried to trigger it?"

"Trigger it?" I asked. "How, exactly?"

"By recreating how you feel when you're around one of *them*," he explained.

My stomach clenched and turned, and my blood burned through my veins. I knew this feeling. I recognized it, and like Nick recommended, I embraced it instead of ignoring it.

Unfortunately, that was as far as it went.

Before I could admit defeat again, though, Nick reached into his pocket and threw something at me. It startled me at first when it hit me in the face, and as I pulled it away, I inhaled deeply. Flames ignited, licking the walls of my veins and setting my lungs on fire as the memory of the smell slammed into me.

The smell of death and rot burned my insides, the subtle hint of jasmine doing very little to mask it. My skin itched and tingled as heat emanated from my pores, and my body trembled. I identified the feeling, and I knew I was supposed to accept what was happening, but my previous inclination to push it down took over.

"Don't fight it," Nick said, taking a satisfied step back, folding his arms across his chest.

I shook my head, though I wasn't sure if it was to push away my acceptance or my denial. My vision darkened, and the beast clawed its way to the surface, unrelenting and unwilling to let me suppress it.

My muscles tensed, my flesh burned and tightened like it was two sizes too small for my body. The urge to let go arose—just like it did last time. I prepared to refuse it again, but I looked up, meeting

Nick's gaze, and I focused.

"It's amazing, isn't it?" he asked, his voice low and gravelly. "Feeling your body become stronger."

His words affected me physically as well as mentally, and I reveled in how powerful I felt. In an effort to help the process along, I thought about how my bone structure would change, forcing me onto all fours instead of my more natural upright posture. I imagined the way my organs would have to shift in my new body, how my teeth would elongate, and the hair that would sprout all over my body — that last one was the most disturbing to me considering how much time and energy went into hair removal. Then the imagery recoiled like a spring, snapping back almost painfully.

Instead of going back to feeling...*normal*...I was dizzy and out of sorts, unable to concentrate on anything. My eyes failed to see much of anything, and I fell to my knees. The pain didn't stop, though, and my mind started to retreat.

"Don't fight it, Brooke," Nick encouraged, dropping to his knees right in front of me, having rushed over to help me through this. He was blurry at first, but soon he came into focus, and my breathing increased along with my heart rate. "It's incredible — unlike anything you've ever experienced before." I glanced down at his hands as he leaned forward and curled his fingers into the dirt. "Feel the dirt beneath your feet. Revel in the way the air runs through your hair as you dash through the woods, hunting with your pack at your side."

The tightness in my muscles intensified, and my skin quivered and crawled. A rumble built in my chest, the sound increasing with every passing second. Then the pain took over. My body experienced the equivalent of being engulfed in flames and then ripped apart as my bones shifted and cracked beneath my fevered skin. I clenched my eyes shut tightly, digging my fingers so far into the earth that the cool, moist clay embedded itself under my nails. The low growl that had been building in my chest escaped in the form of a painful scream that echoed through the desert, forcing the birds from their homes and the smaller animals to scurry from their hiding places among us.

I felt his finger beneath my chin, coaxing my eyes back to his. They were brighter around the pupils now, the amber rings growing and taking over the blue, and his voice was comforting as his thumb stroked my cheek. "You're fighting this — and that's only natural. Your mind doesn't want to leave. It thinks something dangerous is trying to take over." My arms and legs trembled beneath my weight, and I tried to retreat back into the darkness — to escape the pain and confusion. But Nick wouldn't let me. His intense stare held me captive. It grounded me.

"If you allow yourself to believe you're in danger — even for a second — you'll lose control. You'll black out like the first time."

Everything calmed down around me, but my heart continued to race. Darkness crept in around the outer edges of my eyes, slowly overtaking my entire line of vision. There was a ringing in my ears before I heard nothing at all, and I quickly succumbed to the anesthetized state I found myself in, sinking deeper and deeper into the abyss. When I finally allowed myself to rest, something clicked, and Nick's voice broke through the darkness like a beacon guiding me home.

"But if you just acknowledge the wolf — accept everything she has to offer — you'll realize you *are* the wolf, and that's the most powerful lesson."

My eyes fluttered open slowly, the smell of soil and grass filling my head. Nothing was clear at first, that weird tunnel vision taking over before clearing up, and I pushed myself to my feet. My legs were unsteady, barely holding me up, but I finally found my bearings...on all fours.

I've done it.

While it wasn't the first time I'd shifted — nor was it the first time I'd remembered parts of it — it was the first time I did it of my own volition. I made this happen, and I remembered every excruciating detail.

"Brooke?" Nick inquired, searching my eyes for some kind of sign that it was me in control and not the wolf.

Because I wasn't used to being like this, I tried to tell him. Obviously my human vocal chords didn't quite work the same, and all I could manage was a bark. The sound startled me at first until I realized it came from me, and my skin warmed beneath my fur with a blush.

Chuckling, Nick pulled his shirt off, and I turned away out of respect. "You want to go for a run?" he asked. Beside me, the bush rustled, and I looked over to find his shirt and jeans hit the ground, then his socks and shoes. Forgetting my manners for a brief moment, I glanced back to find him on all fours, going through the beginning stages of the change. Curious, I turned around fully and sat down to watch, hoping to maybe catch a few pointers.

His change was much swifter than mine was, but this likely had something to do with his seven years of experience. He didn't appear to be in pain as his bones cracked and hair replaced his slightly tanned skin, and soon, there was a light sandy-brown wolf before me. He approached me warily, his eyes bright and tail wagging behind him. My own tail swished back and forth as his nose touched the hair at my neck, pressing deeper and inhaling. I did the same, standing up and running my head and neck along his affectionately, memorizing his scent as I brushed against him.

This is weird, I thought to myself as he licked my left shoulder, his wolfy brow furrowing sadly. Before I could overanalyze everything, Nick turned his head and nipped my flank before running off, his tongue hanging out of the side of his mouth and a playful glimmer in his eyes. With a yelp of surprise and then a bark of challenge, I bolted after him. I raced through the desert, kicking up dirt and dead grass with my feet as I darted around and beneath the bushes in hopes of closing the gap between Nick and me.

Feeling the wind through my fur was exhilarating, and my adrenaline surged. I picked up speed until I was neck and neck with Nick, playfully nudging him. All my worries were temporarily forgotten, and I reveled in the reprieve...until my attention was suddenly diverted when the wind picked up, bringing with it a strong odor that pulled me inexplicably from my carefree jaunt through the woods.

It didn't take me very long to recognize the foul smell, stopping me dead in my tracks so abruptly that I left grooves in the dry trail. Nick stopped almost as suddenly when he realized I was no longer beside him, and when his eyes met mine, he made the same connection that I did: there was a vampires somewhere nearby. Another sniff. It was distinctly female. And confident.

Without another thought or any indication as to what I was going to do, I took off in the direction the smell came from, not once stopping or slowing down. My desire for vengeance drove me again, and nothing was going to stop me from destroying this bitch.

CHAPTER 30 | VENGEANCE

The world around me ceased to exist as I raced toward the edge of the desert and straight toward civilization. I knew I should have been more aware, but the only thing I could think about was how amazing it would feel to rip Gianna limb from limb. The violent thoughts were unbridled, and I should have been more concerned, but I actually took comfort in them. I imagined what it might feel like to wrap my powerful jaws around her throat, biting down until I felt her neck snap.

The second I was clear of the trails, something slammed into my side, distracting me from the hunt as I rolled over a few times before finding my footing again. My skin trembled, releasing the dirt and grass from my coat as I looked in the direction the hit came from, and I saw a large sand-colored wolf standing in my path.

Nick.

My ears flattened against my head, and my lips curled back in an angry snarl. Nick took on a defensive stance, readying himself for whatever attack might be coming his way, but he didn't match my aggression. Instead, he looked at me calmly, almost pleadingly. I couldn't read the expression on his face, but I desperately wished there was a way to communicate with him. Did he not smell it? Why was he stopping me? He should be *helping* me.

Slowly, he stalked toward me, and when I defied him with a growl, he flattened his ears and challenged right back, nipping at me until I stepped backward. Every time I tried to dart around him, he jumped in my way, snapping at my feet like he...like he was shepherding me.

Yes! That was exactly what he was doing! He was pushing me back, and it only served to infuriate me further. I continued to try and dodge him, but he was quicker than me, anticipating my every move, and soon we were back on the trails. Angry at being driven away from what I so desperately craved—Gianna's life and retribution for David's death—I lunged for Nick, and we tumbled to the ground. My teeth snapped wildly, finally sinking deep into the scruff of his neck, but he twisted beneath me, gaining the upper hand until he had me pinned to the ground, his mouth around my throat. His teeth didn't puncture my skin, but I felt them pressed against my jugular menacingly, and I submitted, much to my chagrin.

Hesitant, Nick released me, taking a step back but never taking his eyes off me. I was still upset about being interrupted, but I slowly came to my senses, rolling onto my stomach. Breathing heavily, I watched as Nick's body quivered before he reverted to his human form.

Completely naked, he stood up, and my eyes remained locked on his, waves of defiance still coursing through my veins. He held his hands up in front of him and stepped toward me. "Brooke," he said softly, his deep voice having an odd calming effect on me. "I need you to shift back. Concentrate—just like you did when you changed before."

With an unintentional whimper, I stood and looked away, trying to visualize my body changing back. I tried to will my fur to shed — or whatever the hell it was supposed to do — and I focused on my bones, hoping it didn't hurt as much this time around.

But nothing happened after a few minutes, and I collapsed onto the dirt floor of the desert, exhausted and defeated, closing my eyes tightly. Soon, Nick's warm hand rested on my back, and I jolted upright, frightened and a little irritated that he thought it okay to *pet* me...

Then I realized I was standing. On two legs. Completely naked.

Averting his gaze, Nick held out his hand. In it were my clothes. That was when I noticed he was already fully dressed. Clearly I'd blocked out a bit of time, because in the seconds that I thought I was down, there was no way he'd have found the time to run back to where we left our clothes and return.

I accepted his offering and quickly dressed, my anger at being denied my hunt still festering and slowly rebuilding. He must have sensed this, because he approached me and grabbed my upper arms.

"You know I had to stop you," he said tentatively. "Right?"

Silent, I raised my eyebrows, waiting for him to elaborate.

With an exasperated sigh, he thrust his right hand through his hair, tugging harshly at the ends. "I couldn't just let you run in there blind," he continued. "You are absolutely in no way ready to take her on right now."

"Excuse me?" I replied, more than a little offended. "She created that thing that killed David...that tried to kill me! Why does it feel like you're protecting her?" My voice carried through the vast desert, but I didn't care. I wanted Gianna dead for everything she'd done, and Nick was keeping me from making that a reality.

"I'm not *protecting* her." He said this like it was physically painful for him to even contemplate—a werewolf protecting a vampire—and as soon as I made that connection, I, too, was repulsed by it…and also a little repentant for having suggested such a thing.

"Then give me one good reason why I shouldn't track her down and make her pay for what she's done?" I demanded, a growl teetering on the edge of my voice.

"Because she could destroy you. I can't lose you… I just…" He hesitated, seeming unsure, but then finished his thought. "I just got you back." His voice dropped to a low whisper at the end, almost sounding ashamed for saying it. The confession reawakened those warring emotions I had between him and David lately, and this upset me. It upset me because David was barely laid to rest and Nick was saying shit like this…and worse, part of me liked hearing it. Needed to hear it.

I ignored the feeling, resolving to deal with it later—if at all—and stared up at Nick. "She needs to pay," I snarled. "If we don't go after her now, she could get away."

"You think I don't know that?" Nick demanded. "I hate the idea that Gianna sent some psycho disciple after you, and all because of what I…" He cut himself off, piquing my curiosity, but before I could ask him to continue, he changed course. "It was a trap."

I stared blankly, unsure how to respond to this.

"She must have followed us." Frustrated, he paced back and forth, wearing a groove in the unbeaten desert ground. "I don't know how I didn't re-

alize it, but she came out here to entice you, hoping you'd take the bait and run off after her. And you almost did."

"You can't know that."

"Gianna's not stupid," he challenged. "This is *exactly* the kind of thing she would do to get to you. She's taunting you. Dangling your chance for vengeance in front of you like a worm on a hook."

This fascination she had with me was confusing. I'd never even met this woman before, and she had this personal vendetta against me. Even though Nick wouldn't talk about why she might be interested in me for who I am and not what, I knew it to be true.

Call it woman's intuition with a heaping side of werewolf instincts.

"Okay... Let's say this was a trap," I began to say, "now that we know that, maybe we stand a better chance against her."

Nick still seemed unsure. "Brooke—"

"It doesn't make sense to just sit around. What if this is our only opportunity?"

"It won't be."

"You don't know that." Before I could argue my case further, Nick shut me down.

"We can't just rush this, going in half-cocked and ill-prepared. Why don't we wait just a few days? I'll talk to the guys and we can formulate a plan of attack. She won't go anywhere until she's accomplished what she came here to do."

If I thought about it rationally—like a *cop*—what Nick suggested really was the best plan. I still wasn't happy about it as we headed back to my car, but I promised to wait for his instructions. Her scent was so potent...so close I could taste the foulness of it on my tongue, and I fought to pull myself away from it.

I dropped Nick off at his place before heading

back to my parents'. He invited me to stay for dinner, but I politely declined, half-joking when I told him I should give my parents proof of life. By the time I arrived, Mom was just putting dinner on the table. They both seemed surprised to see me, but I kissed them on the cheek before taking my seat at the table. Having had a big brunch at Nick's place earlier, my appetite had returned, and I dished up heaps of the roasted chicken and vegetables they prepared.

"So," Dad said, taking the bowl of vegetables from me, "where did you stay last night?"

I almost choked on the chicken in my mouth, not expecting the question. It was a fair one; it just caught me off guard. "I stayed with a friend. I just couldn't bring myself to face anyone else." And just like that, my grief came crashing back down around me, suffocating me.

My mom reached over and placed her hand on mine. "That's understandable, sweetheart." She went back to cutting a piece of chicken while segueing the conversation. "The service really was beautiful."

My stomach clenched, and my hand tightened around my fork, the cool metal biting into my palm. "Y-yeah. It was."

"David's parents were sorry to have missed you afterward." She carried on like this conversation wasn't painful as hell for me. And truthfully, it probably wouldn't have been if I hadn't been spending most of my day ignoring my grief while I plotted revenge against the monster responsible. Talking about it was supposed to be therapeutic. I knew this. But that was only if I acknowledged the grieving process. I didn't. I couldn't. There was far too much to accomplish before I could even *think* about it.

Sensing my discomfort, Dad cleared his throat. "What are your plans for tomorrow, Brooke?"

Thankful for the change in topic, I shrugged. "I'm not too sure. Hang around here. Maybe go for a drive or a walk. We'll see how I'm feeling."

Dad steered the conversation back to my mom, asking her about her workload this week. She seemed happy to be talking about something other than this week's events, because she launched into express detail about some of the design projects she would be doing this week. She did the same thing a couple of weeks after Bobby passed away. Buried herself in any distraction she could.

After dinner, I offered to clean up so my parents could enjoy a little down time, and I welcomed the silence that cleaning the kitchen brought with it. Once everything was put away and the kitchen was clean, I retired to my old room for the night. Being back in here, surrounded by my old track and cheerleading trophies took me back to happier times, so I relished it for a moment as I sat down on my bed.

My eyes scanned the room, letting the memories fill my head and distract me from everything that happened lately. As they roamed past the window, I saw a blur of movement that forced me to my feet. Everything in my body screamed at me to be on alert: ears straining to hear something, eyes narrowing to zero in on whatever lurked out there, nose twitching to pick up a scent, and skin prickling as all of the tiny hairs covering my body stood on end. I pressed my face so close to the windowpane, I could feel the chill of the glass. I didn't see anything, and I wondered if I was hallucinating from my lack of sleep. Just as I was about to give up, a face appeared in front of me from out of nowhere, making me jump in surprise.

Only the pane of glass separated us as she leaned forward, putting us practically nose to nose. A sadistic smile toyed at her blood-red lips, and the hairs on the back of my neck rose as the smell hit me even through the window.

I instantly recognized her from the grainy surveillance video. Her long blonde hair falling straight down her back and around her shoulders, her icy stare, and the malicious smile that spread across her face as she challenged me through my second-floor bedroom window. "Gianna," I snarled, making her smile even wider as she raised her hand and waggled her fingers at me in greeting.

She disappeared as quickly as she had appeared, and the only thought going through my mind was that I had to go after her. Not just because of what she had done to David and me, but also because she knew where my parents lived. And there was absolutely no way in hell I was going to stand idly by while Nick and his Pack came up with a plan when she could easily dispose of my parents and me in our sleep.

After locking my bedroom door, I opened my window carefully, trying to avoid the creak that had existed for as long as I could remember, and I slipped out onto the roof. Most people would sidle up to the side of the house and side step along until they reached the drainpipe, where they'd more than likely shimmy down it, but not me. Not anymore, anyway.

Once out onto the roof, I leapt to the ground, bending at the knee to absorb most of the shock, and immediately sprinted across the lawn and down the street, following the stench that she left behind.

I remembered what Nick said earlier about how she was leading me into a trap, and I knew I should heed that warning yet again, but I couldn't. Not when my parents' lives were now at risk.

Her trail ended several blocks away at an old foreclosed house. Breathing heavily and sweating from over-exertion, I stood at the end of the drive, staring at the beat-up front door as I tried to formulate a plan. She was in there. I felt it right down to the marrow in my bones and no longer cared about a plan. I just wanted this done. Desperate with the need to end this once and for all, I stepped forward, but was stopped by a strong hand around my wrist.

It would figure Nick would follow me here. Before I could get angry or question his sudden appearance, I heard rustling inside, and in a flash I was on the porch and opening the door.

"Brooke," Nick hissed as he caught up to me. "Wait a damn minute. Think about this!"

"What are you doing here?" I demanded, shocked to find him here.

Nick exhaled heavily. "I was vetting the place. Preparing a plan of attack. What are you doing here?"

"She showed up at my parents' house." Her smell floated on the breeze, making me shudder. It was impossible to think about what I was doing, my need to end this blinding me to anything else as we crossed the threshold. Her stench surrounded us both, and a maniacal laugh filled the room. That was all it took for the tremble in my hands to start, moving up my arms and through the rest of my body as the fever burned hotter by the second.

"I'm so glad you came," she purred as she descended the stairs fluidly, her fingers caressing the blood-red pendant that hang between her collarbones. Her gaze landed on Nick, who growled and stepped in front of me protectively. "And you brought company." She eyed him up and down and then wrinkled her nose distastefully. "I liked the last one much more. He smelled a lot more delicious. A shame his blood went to waste, really. I thought I trained my dear Samantha better than to waste a perfectly good meal."

That was all it took. I lunged forward, ready to rip her fucking head off, but Nick caught me by the arm, holding me back as I struggled against his brute strength.

She laughed again, coming off the last step and walking toward us with an almost regal grace in her step. It reminded me of how she moved in the tape I'd watched. Nick anticipated her every move, turning with her as she circled us like a shark did its prey. "You know," she continued in a wistful tone, "I really hoped you'd come to me earlier. You ruined my plans."

She reached out, and her cold finger touched my cheek, trailing down my neck, right along my pulsing carotid. Her eyes held mine, captivating me even though this was just one of her parlor tricks that only humans should be susceptible to. I tried to push the hazy feeling away, but I was unable to. She was powerful, and I just wasn't strong enough yet.

A deep growl behind me snapped me out of the hold she had on me, and I suddenly recoiled from her, slapping her hand away from me. Nick shot forward, pressing Gianna against a nearby wall by her neck. He was going to kill her; I recognized the murderous gleam in his eyes. His hands trembled as the transformation started, his claws emerging from the ends of his fingers, splitting the skin there.

"Don't be too hasty," she said, her tone cocky and confident. "Don't you think poor Brooke deserves to know what happened to her brother? About the night you—"

"*You* killed him! What happened after that was all on you." Nick shouted, interrupting her, and I gasped. I flashed back to the night of our birthday party and recalled Bobby sitting at the table with a blonde woman—a blonde woman who looked an awful lot like the woman on the surveillance recording...the woman who was in front of me right now. I'd only ever seen her from afar, but I was certain they were the same person.

Before she said anything else, his fury exploded, and his bones began shifting into their new positions to accept the change, his back rippling and straining beneath his shirt. Gianna cried out when he pulled her forward and slammed her back against the wall, another loud crack of bone echoing through the house, and I knew I had to act fast.

"Nick, no!" I cried out, not because I wanted her alive—I didn't. She deserved to die for what she did—planned to do. While I originally came here to kill her, I now realized that she might be the key to getting the answers I needed to move past Bobby's death.

The sounds of their collective growls filled the small, broken down house as I rushed toward them. Hesitant, based on the rage pouring off him, I reached out and grabbed Nick's arm, using more strength than I thought I had to try and pry him off of her. "Don't do this. We need her."

Struggling against Nick's hold on her, Gianna laughed weakly. "Can't let him kill me, honey? Perhaps I misjudged you. Maybe I should reevaluate your worth."

Nick glanced toward me, and she used the distraction to her advantage, forcing herself out of his grip. Quickly rushing toward me, she wrapped her hand around my neck, bending her arm until my back was against her chest. She used me as a human shield, leaving Nick at her mercy. I whimpered as her fingers dug into my skin, bringing my hands up to try and wrench her hand away. Nick moved quickly, rushing to my rescue, but when her nail pressed against my carotid, he stopped dead in his tracks, looking equal parts angry and terrified.

"Now, now, now," she warned. "You wouldn't want to be too hasty, would you?" Her fingernail pierced my neck, warm blood trickling down over my skin, and Nick continued to snarl at her as she held me. Her grip tightened further. After a very intense stare-down, she must have felt content that Nick was no longer an immediate threat, because she relaxed. This allowed me the opportunity to gasp for air, my lungs burning with each breath.

"Now," she said, her tone steady and authoritative, "we're going to walk out of here, mutt, and you're going to let us. You're not going to follow us, and you're going to tell your Pack to heel, got it?"

"If you're going to kill me, just do it," I ordered, my voice soft and strangled.

Gianna only laughed. "Why? So the minute you drop to the floor, he can attack me? How dumb do you think I am? Besides, I've got plans for you."

She took her first few steps back toward the door, dragging me with her and away from Nick. Alarm bells blared in my head, telling me I couldn't give up; it wasn't in my nature.

With a surge of adrenaline flowing through my veins, I threw my head back, hearing a satisfying crack as it connected with her nose. I was momentarily dazed from the impact as she stumbled back a few paces, and as she did, I turned and rushed forward, jumping on her back. I'd only intended to incapacitate her in hopes of binding her to a chair or something so I could interrogate her, but as she struggled, my anger intensified. The wolf ripped past my humanity, the signs of the change becoming apparent, clawing at the surface and begging to be freed.

I wasn't experienced enough to force the change

on a whim, though, because I remained lucid—and human—as I wrapped my arms around her and squeezed, causing her to cry out. Another crack sounded through the room, her ribs collapsing in my arms.

Gianna continued to struggle in my arms, even with her broken ribs, but this only made me squeeze her harder. I no longer cared about the questions I had, certain I could find the answers elsewhere, and I lost all sight of anything other than the blind rage that fueled my attack. And the wolf inside of me ate up every morsel of Gianna's fear and panic.

She sought me out…

…created that thing that broke into my home…

…that tried to kill me…

…that killed David.

What happened next—or more so, how it happened—was a little unclear, but Gianna managed to gain the upper hand. She broke free of my vice-like grip and attempted to make a run for it. Unfortunately for her, she didn't make it very far.

Without planning or even thinking about it, I leapt into the air and brought her down to the ground. I knew I wanted to keep her alive, but I was being driven purely by instinct at this point. There was just no room for rationality as I grabbed her by the hair and twisted her neck, severing her head in one fluid movement. Her necklace slipped off her headless body as it fell to the floor, and as her head rolled to the side, landing face up, her lifeless eyes gaped at me in disbelief.

I took a drunken step back as her body slowly crumbled into ash, the fury ebbing and making the quiver in my hands more noticeable. It wasn't the same as when shifting was inevitable, however. No, this was definitely different. This was borne out of fear and the physical sign of adrenaline being re-leased from my body. I was in shock.

What have I done?

"Brooke?" Nick's voice was quiet and nervous as it called out to me. He sounded far away, but I sensed his presence right next to me. It was disorienting. "Are you all right?"

"I killed her," I whispered in disbelief, staring down at my trembling hands, unable to come to grips with my actions. "I-I just...*killed* someone."

Nick pulled me into his arms, but my body was stiff and resistant as it collided with his. I was ap-palled in myself over having actually done something so horrifying and so...so *wrong*.

"Brooke, she wasn't human," Nick soothed, his hand moving over my head and down my back. He was trying to justify my actions, but I failed to take comfort in his words.

Pushing myself free of his arms, I looked at him. "I know...but—"

Nick was having none of it, grabbing my wrist and pulling me back into a strong hug. While I prob-ably shouldn't have felt anything but self-loathing, it was hard to focus on anything other than the way his arms felt around me. For the first time in weeks, I felt safe.

Then that blanket of safety slowly slipped away and I felt something else. With my need for revenge satiated, that hole left by David's death was slowly hollowed out again, and I let my grief slip back into place. I fell to my knees in Nick's arms and cried. Cried for my loss. Cried for the closure I finally felt.

I'd killed the monster responsible for his death, and in doing so, learned she was also responsible for my brother's. While this wasn't exactly the closure I'd been hoping for seven years ago, knowing what happened to him did give me a semblance of peace, and, given enough time, I felt pretty confident that I'd me able to move on from all of this and live a relatively normal life.

There would definitely be some adjustments, and I would need Nick's help to try and control my transformations. But, for the first time in a really long time, I would be allowed to grieve, knowing that the person responsible for all of this couldn't hurt anybody else.

EPILOGUE | FAREWELL

" What do you mean you're leaving?"

I didn't blame my father for being upset by my unexpected announcement. It wasn't like I gave him or my mother any warning about my decision. Not that I'd have been able to give them much anyway; I'd only just decided last night.

It had been almost a week since I killed Gianna. I never returned to my parents' house that night, too rattled to face them then or even the next morning. After leading me from the abandoned house, Nick took me back to his place where he made me tea and offered me his bed. I didn't sleep much, instead hearing everything he and his Pack discussed.

With Gianna disposed of, their mission here in Arizona was complete. So what next? They were ordered to return home to Canada, where they would take care of her existing army. It was suspected she had planned to start a war with the Pack for their interference, and Marcus wanted to put a stop to it before they gained power or appointed a new leader.

I think it was hearing that Nick was leaving again that stung the most. True, while I was still mourning the loss of the life I could have had with David, I knew that I wouldn't be able to handle Nick leaving me again. He'd been so great and done so much to help me through everything, so when he brought up the possibility that I could join him, I jumped at the opportunity.

He suggested we go before the next full moon, though, wanting us to be at the compound before it happened, just in case the shift was forced upon me again. It made sense, and as much as I hated the idea of leaving my parents before the holidays without much of an explanation, I knew Nick was right. This was best for everyone.

I shrugged, looking around my dad's office. I let my eyes linger on all of the framed commendations that decorated his walls, remembering each and every ceremony we'd attended to show our support. As they traveled more to the left, I avoided my mother's eyes as she stood beside me silently. "I know it's sudden, but I think it's for the best."

"For who?" he demanded, standing up and pushing his desk chair back so hard it hit the wall behind him. "Because I can guaran-damn-tee you that it's not *best* for your mother and me."

"Dad—"

"Where will you go?" he asked, cutting me off. He didn't let me answer before asking another question. "How long will you be gone?"

"Canada," I replied. "Up to the mountains." I paused, catching his eyes. "And I don't know how long. I just…need some time."

"Canada," he repeated, his eyebrows knitting together with doubt. "You hate the cold. Where will you stay?"

He wasn't wrong; I'd never been a fan of sub-zero temperatures, and I was fully aware of the climate difference from Arizona to the Canadian Rockies, but this was just something I had to do. Deep down, my dad knew this.

"I do," I replied carefully. "And I'll be staying with..." Unsure of just how much I should tell him, I paused. Then I realized it was best to be as forthright as possible, because he would just find out in his own way if I wasn't. "Nick. I'll be staying with Nick. He's got a place near the mountains. It's hidden and away from any major cities, so it's quiet and I'd be able to get the space I need right now."

He wasn't happy hearing this—I could see it in his eyes—but he kept quiet, looking to where my mother stood next to the closed door. "And you're okay with this, Laura?"

It hadn't escaped my notice that she'd been silent this entire time, and I worried because silence had never been a good thing when it came to Laura Leighton.

Her blue eyes held mine, instantly transporting me to a time where I was just six years old and being scolded for threatening to run away. I felt about three feet tall as her stare burned into me, and I dropped my head, unworthy.

With a quiver in her voice, she stepped forward and took my hand, showing me her support, even though I felt the conflict in the warmth of her skin and the tension in her eyes. "I don't think we have much of a choice, Keith. She needs this."

Relieved to have my mother—mostly—on my side, I pulled her into my arms, using a little more of my strength than necessary, which made her stumble slightly before slamming into me. "Thank you," I breathed as she stroked the length of my hair and cried onto my shoulder.

Dad walked up behind me and wrapped his arms around the both of us, and when we parted, I handed him my gun and badge, effectively ending my bereavement leave and extending it to a leave of absence. Even though I knew my first investigation would never really be solved, O'Malley had taken it over after David died. It was originally only supposed to be temporary until I returned from my leave, but now he'd take the lead until it inevitably ran cold. Clarke was still trying to find the person responsible for David's murder, too. He wouldn't, though, because she was nothing more than a pile of ash in an alley while her maker's ashes mingled with the dirt of an abandoned house.

"What about your place?" Mom asked, wiping the tears from her cheeks.

"As soon as it's released, I'll try to rent it out," I explained. "I'll still have my cell phone, and I'll call when we get there and give you the number there, too. This is just...something I have to do. It's all just too much."

With a few more hugs and promises to keep in touch, I exited the building. My colleagues all wished me well, and for the first time I realized just how much I would miss all of them, too.

It's not forever, I tried to tell myself, even though I wasn't sure if it was entirely true or not. I'd love to be able to come back, but would I ever be able to exist in this world, knowing what I am? The last time I tried that, someone I loved died. I wouldn't be able to live with myself if that happened again.

Which is why I have to go with Nick. I need to learn how to fully control what I am.

In my car, my hands trembled, making me grip the wheel tighter until my knuckles turned white. I was nervous about what I had to do next, but I couldn't leave without saying goodbye to two more people.

I stopped at David's grave first, kneeling before

his headstone and telling him again how sorry I was about what happened. Guilt needled at me as I danced around the subject of leaving town with Nick. If he were here, David wouldn't be happy about this, so I assured him that it was because he was gone that I had to go. I explained that I needed to learn how to control what I was, and that was all there was to my decision.

Could he hear me? Honestly, I didn't know. I liked to believe he was still with me in some way, and if things like werewolves and vampires could exist, why couldn't spirits?

Even in the crisp, late-November air, I felt warmth all around me. It seeped into every pore of my body, reminding me of the way I felt in David's arms. With one final goodbye, I stood and walked through the cemetery until I was at the foot of Bobby's grave.

I stood in silence for a minute, not quite sure what to say at first, but then the one-sided conversation just seemed to flow naturally. It usually did.

"I'm sorry I haven't been by in a while," I began. "There's a lot that's been going on lately." Everything that had happened this last month poured out of my mouth. I started with the attack in the park, the weird changes I went through, the cases I was working on, and finally the discovery that there was an unknown world within our own. I imagined the look that would be on his face when I told him that I was a werewolf, and I laughed, because I knew he'd find it ridiculous without some kind of proof.

"Who even knew any of this was real?" I continued before taking a long pause. "Anyway, I came to say goodbye. Now that I know the truth about what happened to you and took care of the thing responsible, I'm going up to Canada with Nick. I need to learn a little more about what I've become and how to control it." Another long pause, and I heard the wind whistle in my ears. I sighed. "I don't know when I'll be back—or if it'll even be for good when it happens—but know I love you, and that you're always with me."

As the sun continued to set, darkening the sky slightly, I turned away from his gravesite, ready to leave this life behind me and find a place in my new one.

The wind picked up again, this time a little stronger, and the smell that surrounded me seemed...off somehow. I couldn't explain it, and it might have been nothing at all, but I thought back to the smell of the early stages of decay that greeted me at David's grave, and I realized that the dirt above Bobby's grave smelled strangely clean.

I knew that after seven years, the smell wasn't going to be quite as potent—to animals and werewolves alike, I suppose—but there still should have been something. Even an unembalmed corpse could take upward of ten years to fully decompose. Add to the equation a solid oak coffin, and you'd be looking at double that. Maybe more. Even the grave next to Bobby's carried the subtle notes of rotting flesh, and its occupant had been dead over twelve years.

Curious, I knelt down and sniffed a little more deeply. I didn't pay much attention to the few people that walked by me on their way toward the parking lot, looking my way strangely or talking in hushed whispers about the strange red-head who was sniffing someone's grave.

I smelled the minerals in the dirt, heard the worms shifting through the earth beneath the thick, green sod, but that was it. There was absolutely no hint of decay from this spot, only the subtle notes that continued to carry on the breeze from neighboring graves.

Frustrated and confused by this, my fingers curled into the grass, the blades threading between my fingers, and before I realized what was happening, I started tearing it up. My heart thumped wildly as my fingers breached the top layer of soil and I tossed it aside. When I glanced down at what I was doing, shocked to find I was doing it without my brain having consented to it, I noticed that my nails had extended into claws, my fingers longer and in the first stage of transition. It was an unattractive sight, and something that happened before they retracted completely and turned into paws. It was also the first time I had directed the change to one specific body part before. Part of me was proud of this achievement.

I dug. And I dug. And I dug some more. I tried ordering myself to stop once I realized what it was I was doing, but it was a futile attempt. I was on a mission, and nothing could stop me.

Nothing, that is, except the feeling of my hand hitting the coffin buried six feet into the ground.

Hours must have passed. The sky was completely dark by the time this happened, and I was covered in sweat, my chest heaving with labored breaths. Dirt soiled my clothes and skin, and it was trapped painfully beneath my claws. I stared down at the mahogany coffin I stood upon, the full realization of what I'd just done finally hitting me. My stomach knotted; I couldn't believe I disrespected Bobby's memory by digging up his grave. Who does that?

Ashamed, I prepared to claw my way out of the grave when my heightened night-vision allowed me to spot a piece of wood. Kneeling down, I picked it up and noticed that it was the same mahogany color as the coffin. The wood surface creaked beneath me when I shifted my weight, and when I looked down, I noticed a small crack that led beneath the small mound of dirt still on half of the coffin. Frantic for answers, I shoveled the soil away until I fell back on my ass in shock at the sight that greeted me.

There, in the top half of Bobby's coffin, was a large hole, the inside empty. Its edges were jagged, like someone had broken out. So many scenarios ran through my mind from Bobby being buried alive and digging his way out to someone robbing his grave.

Before I could cook up more ridiculous theories, a voice from above startled me. "It was only a matter of time before you found out," Nick said, kneeling down and extending his hand out to me. "Come on. It's time I told you the truth about the night your brother died. You're ready."

Slowly, I stood and accepted his help, finding myself more desperate than ever before for answers.

Blood Moon

THE **BLOOD MOON** TRILOGY CONTINUES IN...

WOLF MOON

Nick and I continued walking, and he took me to the gazebo I'd sought refuge in earlier. He sniffed the air, and I did the same, knowing instantly what he smelled.

"You and Jackson talked?" He seemed uneasy, maybe worried about something.

"We did. He found me in here earlier and told me about his family," I confessed. "That's it."

Nick seemed surprised. "Wow. That's a big step for him. He's usually reluctant to open up like that to anyone."

"I think he wanted me to know that I wasn't alone," I whispered, sitting on the bench.

"Still... Definitely explains how he was quick to jump to your defense at the table. Makes me wonder what his ulterior motive is."

I looked up at him as he paced in front of me. "He can't just be cordial? He has to have some sinister plan for befriending me after what he did in the park that night?"

Nick exhaled heavily, his breath creating a dense fog as it mingled with the cold winter air. "Listen, Brooke... About that night—"

Suddenly, a scream pierced the night, forcing from my feet and the both of us across the yard and back toward the front of the house. There stood Colby and Zach, his arms around her protectively as she clung to his jacket, her face buried against his chest.

"What is it?" Nick demanded as we both came to a stop beside them.

I smelled the blood before I saw the steam rising up from the driveway. When I looked down, I gasped loudly, reaching out and grabbing Nick's arm. My nails dug into his bicep, even through his parka while my other hand covered my mouth.

There, on the ground, was a wolf. Not a werewolf from the smell of it. No, this was one hundred percent animal. I didn't know the different breeds of wolves that were out there, having been born and raised in Arizona where wolves were a rarity in and of themselves, but it was gray and white and about the size of a German Shepherd. It had been cut from pelvis to throat, all of its organs spilling out onto the snow-covered concrete, and its eyes were wide and unseeing. Frozen in shock and pain for all eternity.

Nick stepped forward, but I remained paralyzed in place, being forced to relinquish my hold on him. He knelt down next to the animal, cringing as the smell hit him harder than a second ago. "It's a gray wolf," he announced. "Not anyone we know." While I'd already suspected it wasn't one of our kind, I assumed he was saying this for Colby's benefit.

When I turned toward her, I found we'd been joined by the rest of the Pack, and Marcus did not look pleased as he stared off into the night. I knew in that instant who was responsible...

Gianna's slighted coven.

And they had just declared war on the Pack.

COMING JANUARY 2015

A.D. Ryan

ABOUT THE AUTHOR

A.D. Ryan resides in Edmonton, Alberta with her extremely supportive husband and children (two sons and a stepdaughter). Reading and writing have always been a big part of her life, and she hopes that her books will entertain countless others the way that other authors have done for her. Even as a small child, she enjoyed creating new and interesting characters and molding their worlds around them.

To learn more about the author and stay up-to-date on future publications, please look for her on Facebook and her blog.

https://www.facebook.com/pages/AD-Ryan-Author

http://adryanauthorblog.wordpress.com

38952768R10237

Made in the USA
Charleston, SC
20 February 2015